AXLE
BUST
CREEK

AXLE BUST CREEK

JOHN SHIRLEY

PINNACLE BOOKS
Kensington Publishing Corp.
www.kensingtonbooks.com

PINNACLE BOOKS are published by

Kensington Publishing Corp.
119 West 40th Street
New York, NY 10018

All Kensington titles, imprints, and distributed lines are available at special quantity discounts for bulk purchases for sales promotion, premiums, fund-raising, and educational or institutional use.

Special book excerpts or customized printings can also be created to fit specific needs. For details, write or phone the office of the Kensington Sales Manager: Kensington Publishing Corp., 119 West 40th Street, New York, NY 10018. Attn. Sales Department. Phone: 1-800-221-2647.

PINNACLE BOOKS and the Pinnacle logo Reg. U.S. Pat. and TM Off.

First Printing: October 2022

ISBN-13: 978-0-7860-4925-7
ISBN-13: 978-0-7860-4926-4 (eBook)

10 9 8 7 6 5 4 3 2 1

Printed in the United States of America

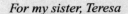

For my sister, Teresa

Chapter 1

Nevada. Spring of 1874.

Cleveland Terwilliger Trewe was trying to get to Axle Bust before sundown. He kept Ulysses at a canter whenever the rugged northward trail allowed, and a trot when it didn't. He'd been told the thin trail skirting the steep hillside was prone to collapse, and rain was coming. Steady rain was rare in northeast Nevada, but sudden gulley-washers came along in April, and he had no wish to dig his horse out of a mudslide. The late-afternoon sky was closed by gray clouds, and now and then they rumbled, growling low like sleeping bears.

"Step carefully, Ulysses," he told the sorrel stallion, patting his neck. "And we'll get you to grain and rest." They'd ridden for many hours with scarce a respite. Cleve and his mount were getting tired and thirsty.

Another mile, and he reined in and got a drink from his canteen. He climbed down off the horse, knuckled dust from his gray-blue eyes, and took off his dark gray Stetson. He used the hat to slap dust from his long charcoal coat, muttering, "Yesterday it was dust, tonight it'll be mud."

Cleve got a small tin cooking pan from his saddlebags, filled it with water from his canteen, and held it under the sorrel's mouth. Ulysses' drank it all. He patted the horse's neck. "We'd best get on. See if we can beat the rain."

Cleve ran his thumb along his jawline, feeling a thorny bristle. Better see a barber when he got to town, especially seeing as he just might have to stand before a judge.

He put the pan away, slapped his hat on his head, re-mounted, and nudged Ulysses into a trot. His gaze returned often to the stands of white bark pine and quaking aspen on the hills. He was alert for the long-riders said to sometimes lie in wait on the trail to Axle. They were known to pounce on travelers who might be carrying gold dust panned from a claim or cash money.

Cleve Trewe had been a Union Scout, before his time as a battlefield commander, and watchfulness was ingrained. Besides bandits, it was possible that Les Wissel had learned he was on his way; for Cleve had made inquiries at the claims recording office in Elko. Wissel might purpose to waylay Cleveland Trewe before he could testify as to his uncle's claim in Axle.

He cantered Ulysses 'round a sharp bend—and slowed to a trot when he heard men talking not far ahead. The voices came from a defile opening between hills, on the east side of the trail. Cleve reined in at the gap, and peered east in the dimming light. He made out three of them, about thirty paces from him, standing in a lantern's glow just within the mouth of an old mine burrowed into the hillside. Dusty tailings lay in humps to either side of the adit. The mine's age was attested by weeds growing within its entry, the vines dangling from above, and the half-buckled state of the timbers straining to hold it open. Two horses and a mule were picketed near the opening.

Cleve knew one of the trio instantly, for the fellow had a distinct profile and voice. It was Leon Studge. He was a stocky, sandy-haired, stub-nosed man with a high forehead and small unruly beard. He was gazing intently at something glittery in the palm of his hand.

Leon had been a friend to Cleveland Trewe, despite the hard truth of their relationship—Cleve had kept Leon Studge a prisoner for half of 1865. Leon had been a Confederate prisoner of war at Fort Slocum when Cleve was in command.

Cleve swung Ulysses down the side trail.

Riding closer, Cleve heard Leon's Texas drawl, "I could not be more satisfied, sir!" His voice came clearly from the tunnel entrance, as if from a speaking-trumpet. "Ya'll have done a kingly thing!"

The other two men were wearing suits of mismatched parts, which operators of their sort slapped together in a hasty effort to look respectable. They had fresh shaves, waxed mustaches, and their hair oiled back. One was a large, swag-bellied man in a frock coat a little too small for him; he rocked on the balls of his feet as he counted a stack of greenbacks. The third man, in a checked coat and copper-colored vest, was also familiar to Cleve. This was Salty Jones, a confidence man from Virginia City. Cleve instantly knew his darting, deep-set eyes, and the strikingly large mouth, which was forever in motion.

Salty slapped Leon on the shoulder and declared, "I am obliged to you for taking this weighty responsibility from my shoulders, Mr. Studge. To let such a bounty go unclaimed would be sinful; to remain here when calamity at home calls my brother and myself to the long journey would be shameful. All the way to Boston, sir! For a mother's pleas cannot be ignored."

"Mr. Culp, I'm obliged to you for the opportunity, I surely am," said Leon.

"His name isn't Culp," said Cleve, trotting Ulysses up close to the mine. He drew his Winchester rifle from its saddle scabbard. He had an Army Colt revolver and shell-belt in his saddlebags, but he rarely wore them. "Leastways, Culp wasn't the name he was using in Virginia City," Cleve went on. He dismounted, and said, "He called himself Tom Fairbanks, there. But he was known familiarly as "Salty," around the benzinery he was pleased to call a saloon."

Leon gaped wide-eyed at Cleve. "Why it's Major Trewe!"

"No more the Major, but Cleveland Trewe I am, Leon."

Carrying the rifle in both hands, thus far pointed away from the men, Cleve stepped up to block them from their mounts.

"I believe you have mistaken me, sir," Salty began. "I have that peculiar face, that mercuriality of feature, that seems sometimes one fellow and sometimes another. I recall one occasion in Boston—"

"I doubt you've ever been to Boston, Salty," Cleve interrupted, noticing that the other man was squeezing the sheaf of bills in his left hand, while his right was moving toward the interior of his frock coat.

Cleve swung the rifle to center on the man's substantial belly. "Do not reach into that coat, mister. Drop your hand."

"You think to rob me?" asked Salty's partner, in a low-pitched voice of outrage, as he dropped the hand to his side.

"No, sir. I am here to prevent a robbery."

"What! I am a Deputy U.S. Marshal—on leave!"

"A marshal?" said Cleve. "What is your name?"

"I am U.S. Marshal Washburn!" he sputtered.

"I doubt it." Cleve turned to Salty. "I take it that you boys have sold mining rights to Mr. Studge, here?"

"We have!" declared Salty. He was frowning, himself,

his eyes darting about, having recognized Cleve now. "All is honest and aboveboard!"

"I know gold when I see it, Cleve!" Leon said, coming over to show his glittery palm. "Just wiped it right off the rock in there!"

Cleve nodded. "That no doubt is gold dust—which is not often found in mines in its free form. Mines are worked for veins and gold-bearing quartz and the like. Gold dust, loose like that, is found in creek sand, or gravel bars. Let us have a look at that sparkling rock in the mine."

"Just as you say," grumbled Washburn. "I will not dispute with that rifle. Have your look. You will find us, when you are ready to render an apology, in the Gideon Hotel, in Axle. Goodbye, sir!" He made to go.

"No, I think we will all look at the mine together, boys," said Cleve, raising a hand. "That is to say—if Leon does not object. I do not intend to embarrass you, Leon. I ask only that you trust me for a minute or two."

"Major, you kept me alive, and you fed me when I needed it most badly," said Leon. "Come the time, you gave me ten Yankee dollars from your own purse for the road. So, I reckon I owe you at least my trust."

Cleve gestured with his rifle at the other two men. "Washburn, hand that money back to Mr. Studge. If he chooses, he'll give it back to you shortly."

"I will in no wise part with it!" Washburn declared, his piggish eyes narrowing. "We have a signed contract!"

"If it's not signed with your real name, it has no force," Cleve said. "I doubt your name is Washburn. Hand him the money."

Salty cleared his throat. "I expect you'd better give it over for now. I have seen this gentleman in action. He does not ask thrice."

The big man growled but slapped the money into Leon's outstretched hand.

"Now, Leon," said Cleve, "if you would pick up that lantern, we'll follow these two into the mine. And boys, do not try my patience."

As if deeply affronted, "Washburn" and Salty turned away, muttering bitterly.

They had not gone but fifty feet in, past cobwebs and rat-holes, when Leon pointed at the clay and stone wall to the left. "There, you see it, Cleve? Gold!"

Leon raised the lantern and it set the wall aglitter with points of gold. A distinct smell hung in the air, too.

Cleve nodded. "Do you notice the odor of a shotgun charge in here, Leon?"

"I do, now you mention it."

"Ah," said Salty. "As to that, when we inspected the mine this morning, we found a rattlesnake and had to shoot it."

Cleve smiled and pointed at the black marks about six feet above the wall. "The famous 'leaping rattlesnake' was it?"

Leon laughed.

Cleve said, "Leon—are you aware that one of the common ways to salt a claim is to take a little gold dust, put it in a shotgun shell, and fire on the ground you want to sell?"

Leon stared. "I was surely not aware of that!"

"It's one way to 'salt' a mine, as it's called—an expression that may cast some light on Salty's nickname. Now normally it's done 'round about a creek, for hawking a placer claim. But these two got this mine for next to nothing, I expect, since it was played out years ago, and so they fired their charge of gold dust in here. They then told you the usual sad tale of having to rush home on a mission of mercy. I'm afraid you've been honey-fogled, Leon."

"Why, I gave them a thousand dollars!"

"They calculated that a thousand dollars for twenty dollars' worth of gold dust is a prodigious good trade."

"Why, these aspersions . . ." Salty began.

Cleve pointed the rifle at him. "Shut your bazoo, Salty."

Salty clamped his mouth into a scowl.

Leon lifted the lantern again and peered closer at the rocky wall. "It does look some . . . unnatural. The way it's all in one spot there. And I believe I see some black marks . . ."

"Yes, they stood too close to the rock, and left gunpowder there along with the gold."

Cleve was alerted by the sudden motion of Washburn reaching for a pistol. His hands responded on their own, pointing the Winchester and squeezing the trigger.

The rifle barked, loud in the enclosed space, and the ball took Washburn in his right shoulder, as Cleve intended.

The bunko artist shouted in startlement and pain; he stumbled backward and fell with a grunt. Gun smoke swirled, and made the men blink.

"He was pulling his weapon," explained Cleve. "Leon, could I trouble you to take the gun from his coat, while I watch Salty? Be careful when you do it. He may have a knife." He turned the rifle to Salty—who looked set to hie from the mine. "Do not attempt to bolt, Salty. I'll shoot you too."

"I got his gun," said Leon, straightening up over the fallen man. "It's one of those little hideaway guns. Suppose he *is* a real Deputy Marshal?"

"Did he show you a badge?"

"He surely did not."

"Because there's none to show."

"I'm shot!" groaned Washburn. "I'm bleeding out! Salty why'd you get me into this?"

"Shut up, Digley!" Salty snapped.

"Digley—is that his real name?" Cleve said. "I have

heard that name, somewheres. I'd be obliged, Leon, if you'd come over and find Salty's gun. He's surely armed."

Salty suffered Leon to search him, and another small gun was found.

Leon stuck the two-shot into his pocket.

"Come along then, Salty," Cleve said. "You take Digley by the ankles and drag him out."

"That great oaf!" Salty protested. "I cannot manage him!"

"You do it, or you'll find yourself there beside him."

Growling to himself, Salty attempted to pull the big man toward the mine entrance. Digley set up a yelping. "That's hurting me, damn you! I shall walk out!"

Digley pulled away from Salty, then got awkwardly to his knees and struggled to his feet. "I believe a bone is cracked in my shoulder . . . I'm bleedin' like a stuck pig . . . Someone shall pay!"

"Leon, pass me that lantern and head on out, if you will please," said Cleve. He did not feel comfortable giving Leon orders, as he had at Fort Slocum. Leon Studge was a free man now, and Cleve had no authority over him.

Leon made his way out, and Cleve backed out after him, lantern in one hand and rifle in the other, keeping an eye on the scoundrels.

Cleve and Leon were soon out in the clean air. The rain had not yet commenced, but the sky was sullen and darkening as Salty came out. Digley came stumbling after, moaning and cursing.

"Cease that squalling, Digley," said Salty, gazing longingly toward the horses.

"I carry bandages and medical spirits with me," Cleve said. "You shall have the good of them, Digley, and we will take you into Axle Bust."

"There is a man named Hull in Axle Bust who says he's

a physician," said Leon. "Saw his signboard. I haven't had his ministrations, so I cain't say if he truly is. I've known men to say they were surgeons when they were but barbers."

Cleve nodded. Fort Slocum had given them both a considerable respect for real surgeons. "Sit down, Digley, and I'll see to your wound. Leon, I'll trouble you to hold the rifle on these men . . ."

Digley attended to, they were soon mounted, riding north on the main trail, all in a line: the scalawags on their aging nags, Cleve astride the sorrel, Leon on his mule Lily. On the west side was a steep valley, channeling the southern reach of Axle Bust Creek southward; on the east rose the increasingly sere, gray hills. The slopes here were flecked with scrub and stands of trees, and knobbed with boulders. The sun was dipping behind the hills beyond the narrow valley. It was dusk, and night would soon be upon them. The tang of impending rain was in the air.

"Leon," Cleve called, over his shoulder, "how far do you suppose it is to Axle Bust?"

"Not much above two miles," Leon replied. "Perhaps three."

"How's that mule for a mount?" Cleve asked.

"Lily? This mule has carried me all the way here from South Texas! She was intent on living up to her mulishness at first, but she came to like me, for I treated her well, and we had many a talk—with me doing the talking—and now we are the best of friends."

They clopped along a quarter-mile more, when they came to a narrow canyon between two hills on the right, where a rock-strewn trail branched up into the hills. The main trail continued north.

Of a sudden, Salty whooped and kicked his mount into a

turn, veering down the side trail, his horse's hooves clacking on the stones.

"Damn you, Salty!" shouted Digley. "I got to go where the doctor is!"

"Where's that trail take him, Leon?" Cleve asked.

Leon shook his head. "That I do not know. I reckon he'll look for a place to turn back south. I will not chase him alone—he'd ambush me on the trail."

Cleve decided he did not have the time to pursue the confidence trickster. He needed to get to Axle Bust, for the sake of the wounded man and a pocketful of other aims. "I expect he's fearful of being hung," he remarked.

"You have shot me," growled Digley, "and you propose to take me to a doctor in a town where I am to be hung? You compound your barbarities!"

"I will see that you are not lynched," said Cleve. But he said it reluctantly. In Cleve's view, men who ran confidence games on the gullible were parasites, like ticks or mosquitoes.

They rode on, and the trail widened enough that Leon could ride up beside Cleve. "Major, how long since you left Fort Slocum?"

"I resigned my commission a few weeks after the last prisoner left," Cleve said.

"That when you come out west?"

"No, I went to Europe for a time."

"Europe!"

"Oh, it was a wonder. But if I thought I was going to forget the war there—but war is practically the mortar for the bricks in European history. The fine constructions, the museums, the food, the women—now that did take me out of myself, a while."

"And—*French* women? Is it true that they—"

"Leon," Cleve interrupted, "I am a gentleman."

"So they *do*!"

"They do. Had to go back to the States soon enough. Tried to keep busy in Ohio for almost three years. My uncle Terrence is an engineer, the sort for bridges and machinery, and hired me on as a secretary. Then he invented a portable steam pump—or so he thought. But it had a tendency to blow up and scald the unwary. Terrence is a good man, but he has a bent to . . . enthusiasms. Well, he ran through most of his money, and half of mine, and he caught the gold fever. He came out to the gold fields, and I went into fur trapping and scouting, out west. Then I went to Denver, for a rest, never intending to stay, but a friend talked me into joining the police force. I carried a badge—and on the side I did some gambling. It's curious how often those two go together . . ." He cleared his throat. "I was there for several years. Then I too caught the bug and made my way to Pike's Peak and the hills 'round Virginia City, trying my hand at prospecting—and 'games of chance.' Once again, it's curious . . ." He shrugged.

"It's surely so—those two go together as well," Leon said, amused. "Gambling and prospecting. Anyhow, I have read that it's so. But my prospecting experience is thin."

"And where did you go, after leaving Slocum?" Cleve asked.

"Texas, of course. Back to Austin. Had to rebuild the Studge Ranch, take care of Mama. Pa was sick. Two of my brothers were dead, killed in the war . . ."

"I'm sorry to hear that." He did not ask which battles took their lives. After a period as an Army scout, Cleve had been elevated to Captain, leading men into the Battles of Shiloh, Memphis, and Devil's Backbone. It was not likely he had fired a bullet that killed one of Leon's brothers, but neither was it impossible.

Leon squinted up at the sky. "Seems like I told you, back

at Slocum, the only reason I joined up was because my brothers and my best friend did—and my middle brother, poor Stanley, was killed." He rode silently for a space and then went on, "Not too long after I come back, the Texas fever killed our beeves and then Pa died—died of despair, maybe, for he had to sell the ranch. Ma went to live with her sister, and I took to building fence for folks, a time. Then I drifted west, worked in a slaughterhouse—cain't abide that job—and I did some buffalo hunting for the railroads, to feed the hammer-hands, and rode security for them too. Saved up a thousand and eighty dollars . . ." He shook his head. "I've been out here about a month, trying my hand at prospecting and finding little but skarn. There's much I do not know—that's come clear now. I owe you a debt, Major. You saved me all that money. I should split it with you—it would have been gone entirely, but for you."

"You may buy me a meal, and that's the end of it," said Cleve. "You know that fellow Mark Twain?"

"The one who told that Jumping Frog story?"

"The very same. In a book he brought out this year, he said a gold mine is but 'a hole in the ground with a liar standing next to it.'"

Leon laughed. "Today, I surely do believe it."

"But it's not always true, and I believe my uncle's claim will stand. If you want to come in on it with us, we could use the help—financially, to stake the price of timber and tools, and help with the labor too."

"A silver strike?" asked Leon.

"Why no—it is gold. There's a small vein and some more in quartz. But there's some dispute with a fellow as to the claim—and some other matters to settle with him. Perhaps I should not ask you to come in with us. There might be some risk."

Leon grinned. "I would be charmed to throw in with ya'll."

They rode onward. After a while, he cleared his throat and asked. "Say, did you ever get yourself a wife? Could be you have sons and daughters by now!"

"I have no wife, no children. I came close to marrying a couple times, but it seemed too much like settling for what had wandered my way, and my heart wasn't in it. One summer I did have a live-in lady, I do confess. But marriage did not come about. Perhaps I should have asked her. Uncle Terrence says that I'm a fool of a romantic, and should give off waiting on some fairy-tale ideal. But then Terrence never did marry. And you, Leon?"

"Why, I was married, or close to it. A Mexican senorita, name of Lupe." A certain bitterness entered his tone when he added, "I sent her money every last time I got paid. Finally got back to Texas to find she'd run south of the border with a vaquero. Her pa told me she got tired of waiting on me to come home."

"Too bad. But might be for the best, if she's so flighty as that."

"I do love me a senorita," Leon mused. "Now had I done the church marrying—could be she'd have stayed, on the priest's say-so."

Digley groaned when his horse stumbled slightly on the trail. He roundly cursed them. They ignored him.

Leon lifted his hat long enough to scratch his head. "Here now, Major, you spoke of Denver—seems to me I read something in a news sheet about an officer C.T. Trewe in a shooting affray in Denver. I thought maybe it was you."

Cleve nodded. "Two in Soapy Smith's gang. They did not wish to return the jewelry they swindled out of a merchant, whereas I did wish them to return it. The disagreement became a trifle hot."

"A trifle? You killed two men in a gunfight!"

Cleve heaved a sigh. "The shooting soured me on the

job. Two men dead at my feet. Till then I brought them in with a threat and maybe a knock on the head." He thought about it and added a caveat. "However—I'm willing enough to kill a certain Lester Wissel, if it can be done legally. But on the whole—well, I saw enough killing in the war."

They rode on, in thoughtful silence, both of them pondering the years that had rolled so inexorably by.

The downpour commenced when the three riders were just descending from the hills south of town. At first the rain dropped straight in heavy, splashing drops; and then it slanted, slapping at them in the rising wind. The trail soon became a slog for the horses.

But they were now within sight of their destination: Axle Bust, Nevada.

To the north rose two jutting hills of craggy stone, and from between their bases, after several falls, rushed Axle Bust Creek. A swaying pillar of mist, rippling with shards of rainbow, rose from the bottom-most pool of the falls. The creek widened, almost approximating a river, to the west of town, then narrowed as it cut to the southwest. After a long journey, it would find its way to the Humboldt River.

The rain-laden wind was swirling the gray-brown wreath of woodsmoke over the mining camp. Axle Bust was a jumble of buildings, shacks, and cabins in a basin below Beaver Peak, in the foothills of the Tuscarora Mountains. The gray and raw-wood yellow-brown shacks, the canvas tents and false-front buildings seemed as random as a tumble of rocks, so far as Cleve could make out, though a rutted, crooked passage that ran between enough of them might serve as the town's main street.

Axle Bust was hand-painted on the sign at the edge of the

mining camp, but local folks mostly called it Axle. Cleve's uncle had told him what little he knew of the place. It had grown up quickly after an enticing placer strike downstream, six years back, and a hard rock mine, the Golden Fleece, was chiseled into the eastern hill overlooking the town. There were said to be several assayers here, and one of them did some banking; there were a couple of liveries, a sawmill. The few shops were greatly outnumbered by saloons and impromptu whiskey tents.

As they rode closer, and the rain eased, Cleve could see the lineaments of placer sluice flumes for separating gold from sand and soil, paralleling the creek down the slopes to the north. They passed rocker boxes, used for further sifting, and an acreage studded with tree stumps. Evidently a modest forest had been cleared—the tree-trunks, sawn and shorn, had become the structures straggling with little order alongside the creek on the west side, and in rough, kinked lanes extending to the east. They rode past a sawmill gushing steam and smoke, and a corral where horses bowed their heads in the rain.

The town was still growing. As they rode up to the main street, Cleve noted almost as many tents as wooden structures. One of them was particularly large; some commercial enterprise. Around the edge of the basin, cabins were beginning to glow with lantern light, haloing in the smoke and mist. Rising from a broad ledge upslope from the tailings around a hard-rock mine—likely the Golden Fleece—was the framework of an unfinished ore mill and smelter. A partly built brick chimney jutted from its brick foundation.

Cleve had spent nigh two years prospecting, on and off, and learned of a mining town's life cycles. First would come the tents of the prospectors; then, when word spread about good placer takings, came opportunists of various stripes: miners and those who sold goods and services to the miners. Ever more placer miners flooded in, staking claims and arguing over them, to pan and sluice gold flakes, gold dust, and sometimes nuggets. When the placer gold thinned out, the first wave of prospectors might sell their claims to a second wave, hard-rock miners and combines. Exploratory shafts were dug, and when a lode was struck, a third wave of gold seekers came—agents of mining concerns, who bought up claims and promising mines.

The work of digging a shaft from an open-cut was back-breaking and dangerous. It took time and blood and sweat to exploit the gold, with just a few men working alone. But an established mining company could afford to pay miners and set up a mill. They need not invest their own blood and sweat.

To Cleve's eye, Axle Bust was in transition, shifting from a period of feverish prospecting to the systematic takeover of big Eastern Money. Such a transition could be rowdy.

This was Elko County, but they were far from the county seat, and Cleve thought it likely there was little law here apart from miners' courts—which were often as not run by the local bullies. Sometimes a "constable" was brought in by a mining concern, like as not a hired gunman with some history as a deputy. He had once heard James Butler Hickok say, "Any jackass can be a deputy and some of 'em decorate wanted posters." Wild Bill was right: Cleve had encountered deputies, in Colorado and Arizona, who'd turned out to be wanted for killings across territorial lines.

As Cleve, Leon, and their prisoner rode down into town, Cleve heard a double *crack*. He at first thought it might be lightning. But when it recurred, he realized it was gunfire. It might be a drunk shooting at the sky or at another drunk.

The sky to the west reddened, the sinking sun stretching

shadows over the basin; the smoke over the town was tinged by the sunset light, and it became the color of diluted blood.

Maybe they could locate Les Wissel this very night. But first they must rid themselves of the wounded Mr. Digley . . .

Chapter 2

Cleve and Leon watched as Dr. Phineas Hull bent over Digley. The wounded confidence man was stretched on a leather-padded table under a dangling ceiling-lantern. Digley's eyes were squeezed shut; his hands clenched. The young doctor wore a surgical apron, his rolled-up white shirtsleeves clasped with garters, a string tie loosened at his neck. Axle Bust's only physician had paper-pale skin, sharply contrasting with his utterly black hair. His neatly groomed beard, clipped exactly two inches out from his chin, was shiny black; his thick black hair carefully trimmed. He had a prominent nose and lips so red they seemed almost rouged.

"Well, sir," he said, addressing Cleve, "the ball is tolerably deep, but if you gentlemen will hold the patient, I believe I can extract it with little fear of further damage. I have dosed him with laudanum, but I'm quite out of ether and the laudanum may not be enough to calm him."

Cleve said, "I see you cleanse your hands in spirits before you set to work. I applaud you for it."

"Semmelweis, Pasteur, and Snow are in the right of it, sir. Micro-germs are the cause of infection. The miasma theory is quite exploded."

Leon took hold of Digley's knees and Cleve gripped the

wounded man's shoulders. They held him down as the doctor began to probe with a pair of sterilized needle-nosed forceps. Digley's eyes snapped open and his back arched.

"Damn you all!" he rasped, as Cleve and Leon strove to hold him down.

"Come-come, it is as nothing compared to having a probe done without opiate," murmured Dr. Hull, digging about in the wound.

Cleve, who had a battlefield bullet pried from him without the availability of an anesthetic, said, "I can testify to that, Digley."

"Ah!" With a curiously precise wriggle of his hand, Hull extracted the bullet and dropped it with a clatter in a small surgical pan. Digley relaxed back onto the table, gasping.

"Now," Hull murmured, "we will irrigate the wound, sterilize it, and begin sewing . . ."

In fifteen minutes, the work was done, and Digley—his opiate reinforced, his wound sewn shut, a bandage in place— was snoring loudly upon the table.

"It being evening," Hull said, "it is time for my own medication."

Cleve, Leon, and Hull were soon seated around Digley in the small examining room, each man holding a triple tot of reasonably palatable brandy. Hull had only two drinking glasses on hand so he used a little laboratory beaker for his snifter.

The examination room was one of two adjoining chambers Dr. Hull was renting in the Gideon Hotel, the other being his place of residence.

He took a sip of his brandy, set it on an oaken lamp table at his elbow, and began to tamp a briar pipe with tobacco from a leather sack. "You seem to have some medical training, Mr. Trewe."

"Don't you know," said Leon, leaning forward, "Major

Trewe was the provost in chief at Fort Slocum, in charge of all the prisoners and guards, and we had many a wounded man come in. He learned nigh as much as them doctors, and more'n some of them!"

Cleve shook his head. "I picked up what I could while I was there. I had read Pasteur and was convinced that germ theory was correct. Some of the doctors resented being told by me to sterilize their hands before operating. I out-ranked them, however, and made it an order."

"Before the major come there," Leon put in, "I saw many a man die from wounds that should not have been fatal. I was there three months before he took command. After he came, most of the wounded survived!"

"Leon here was a Confederate prisoner of war," Cleve said. "And he was a great help to me."

"What was your greatest difficulty at Slocum, Mr. Trewe?" asked the doctor.

"The hardest part at Slocum was food. There was rarely enough for the prisoners."

"He spent his own money getting us food," Leon said. "And he got donations from folk too!" He shook his head. "It was a wonder."

Hull looked at Cleve with renewed interest. "What brings you here? I have not seen you in town before this day."

"I've just arrived," Cleve said. "I am here protecting a claim." He drank a little brandy, while Digley gave out a roaringly vibrant snore. "I was wondering how you yourself came to be here, doctor. What school of medicine did you attend? You seem more knowledgeable than most who style themselves physicians out here."

"Harvard, it was."

"From Harvard—to Axle? Forgive me, but . . ."

Hull showed a rueful smile. "Yes, it's quite a jump. I was

in private practice in Cambridge, Massachusetts, for three years, but . . ." He exhaled a sigh along with a plume of pipe smoke. "A young woman came to me for help—a man had forced himself upon her. There was an unwelcome fetus, still in the first month. The local authorities, most of them Catholic, discovered that I helped her be rid of the rapist's embryo . . . and I was then urged to 'Go West, Young Man.' I was told the mining camps were dreadfully short of doctors, and I had a friend at this one." He turned Cleve a sharp look. "Perhaps you too are offended? Have I revealed too much?"

Cleve shook his head. "I'm not in haste to judge such a thing. If the procedure is early enough, then . . . But I don't know if I could have done it myself, even had I the training."

"I understand," said Hull. There was a prolonged, uncomfortable silence. Then he said, "You spoke of defending a claim. Perhaps you should know more of the lay of the land, here. Conroy Mining has bought most of the shares within a mile of town, and it's expanding the Golden Fleece Mine. Duncan Conroy, son of the company's magnate, has something of an estate here. The house is called, strangely enough, Conroy House." He chuckled at his own minuscule joke. "It's the only two-story house in the Axle basin. It's out of place, almost as if it were whisked entirely from some tony district in Boston. He lives there with his sister, Berenice Tucker—a widow. One look at her and I myself took a fancy—but she didn't so much as glance my way. She made excuses when I tried to call on her. Perhaps she still grieves—Lyle Tucker died almost two years ago, in a mining accident. As for Duncan, he owns so much of the town he tends to regard its residents as his serfs, and indeed many of them work for him."

"Miners whose claims led to nothing?" Cleve asked.

"Just so. Or—they wasted their meager treasures on gambling and, ah, riotous living."

"It often happens. They've burned through their grub-stake and must find work—and end up in someone else's mine, paid pennies on the dollar."

"But there's a miners' guild afoot, and rising friction between its organizers and the Conroys. Tense times in Axle. Hence, if your business conflicts with Duncan Conroy's, you will find him especially contentious, I fear."

"I have no reason to lock horns with Conroy if he accepts legal proof. Do you know a man named Wissel?"

"Whistle?"

"Ha, that's what I thought too," Leon put in.

"There is no *t* in this Wissel's name," Cleve said.

"I do not know the gentleman," said Hull.

"He's a ne'er-do-well from Virginia City and points south. He attacked my uncle Terrence over a claim—my uncle is a man of sixty-six. Wissel gave him a severe beating. Terrence is under a nurse's care now, in Elko . . . and the claim, ten miles south of here, was registered in Axle." He sipped a little brandy, then concluded, "I am in search of Les Wissel."

"A man like this Wissel?" Hull tapped a fingernail against his beaker. "Try the Tom Cat saloon. It is across from the Gideon Hotel. Meanwhile, gentlemen, it is my supper time. The hotel has a restaurant, where the food is tolerable. Would you care to join me?"

"What about Digley?" Leon asked. "I never noticed a marshal's office here . . ."

"Alas," said Hull, "the only law enforcement in Axle Bust, if law is the proper term, is the 'Mining Constable.' He works for Duncan Conroy. Russell Brewster is his name. From what you told me of the case, he would doubtless hang Mr. Digley here out of hand. There's a man named

Kinney, who travels about the county—styles himself a Justice of the Peace. I think he's but a jumped-up attorney. We also boast a vigilance committee, but they too are quick with a noose."

"Couldn't we just tar and feather ol' Digley there?" Leon asked.

"Sadly, I do not number tar and feathers amongst my supplies," said Hull, smiling.

"Let's think further on what to do with Digley," said Cleve. "As for supper, I'm hungry enough to eat boot leather."

Digley gave out another thunderous snore.

After dinner with Hull, Cleve and Leon left the horses at Kanaway's livery. Before leaving the stable, Cleve gave thought to Axle's reputation as a "rough camp." He took his gunbelt from his saddlebags and buckled it on. Leon had his old Confederate pistol.

They rented a room in the Gideon, with two single beds on copper-plated iron frames. Cleve used a kerosene lamp to carefully inspect the thin ticking for bedbugs and lice before paying over his money.

Once they'd taken the room, Cleve leaned his Winchester against the wall and they started out for the Tom Cat saloon.

"That doctor talks as lacy as a preacher on a two-hour sermon," said Leon, as they started across the muddy street. The feeble light from lanterns hanging before the hotel and the saloons reflected dull yellow from the mud-puddles. "And so did you, jawing with him."

"Oh," said Cleve as he picked his way along, "I try to speak the language, wherever I am."

"Well, when I was doing the hard work of eating that

very old steak, you two sure went on and on about that Hippocrat."

"Hippocrates. A physician of the ancients. *Damnit!*" He'd stepped into a puddle, deeper than it looked, and felt water suck in over his boot top. It was hard to see in the dim light. The rain had abated, but it had left pools in the streets, and few places to cross, though some effort had been made to shore up the streets with graveled mine tailings.

It took a full minute to finish crossing the road without another misstep, and then they were upon the wooden sidewalk, striding with boot-thunking confidence—and a little boot sloshing. They passed a line of irritable horses shifting their hooves in the mud and came to the Tom Cat saloon.

The front doors of the Tom Cat opened, spilling yellow light and noise and cigar smoke, and a man still wearing his miner's overalls came swaying out. He held his helmet with its little candle-holding light box, in one hand; the other was reaching out to stop the world from spinning.

"I do believe I over . . . indulged . . ." he said carefully.

"I believe you did," said Leon. "You think you can get home all right on your own, pard?"

"Certain . . . certain . . ." He licked his lips to make the word easier to say. "Certain . . . ly."

The miner staggered off down the walk, and they entered the Tom Cat saloon. The air was gloomy with smoke from tobacco and the leaky pot-bellied stove. Noisy yammer in the crowded room overlapped to become the curse of Babel, to Cleve's ears, since scarcely an individual phrase could be made out. The air was rank with mud and sweat and tobacco. Every table was chock-full, most with miners, some with shopkeepers dressed in suits. At the largest table in the room's center sat six men playing stud poker, all wearing their hats. They squinted at their hole cards under a dangling oil lamp.

Against the wall on the right stood a man Cleve knew from Denver, a tall gangly faro "banker" looming over a green-felt table. He wore a lime-colored suit and a brown plug hat. Mick Stazza: pugnacious when he was hung over, and well-armed anytime, but a sound source of information.

The bar was crowded too, yet Leon found a spot at the far corner and elbowed a man aside so Cleve could wedge in. "Make room for the Major!"

On the wall behind the bar was an enormous, smoke-darkened oil painting of a buxom woman lying abed, facing the viewer, legs apart, the skirt of her lingerie lifted, her privates hidden by a striped tom cat strutting boldly up the mattress to her. Her eyes and mouth were wide with surprise as she eyed the cat.

"There's that ol' tom cat," said Leon, cackling.

There was only one woman in the saloon, a blond bargirl with an abundance of sausage curls. She wore a tight, shiny scarlet dress trimmed with pink ruffles. She had extraordinarily wide hips and narrow shoulders. But the prodigious hips were more to the point, Cleve supposed.

He waved to the barrel-chested, red-maned bartender. The barman wore a red-checked shirt and stained white apron. "What'll you boys have?" he yelled, some Irish in his accent.

"Is the beer cold?" Cleve asked.

"It is by no means cold," said the bartender, still bellowing to be heard over the talk, the scraping of chairs, the banging of cups onto tables. "Sure, it's the saints' miracle if it's not steaming in this overheated shebeen!"

"Have you brandy?"

"Well now, some call it that, but I wouldn't. I recommend the hot spiced rum. The water's been boiled."

"That'll do fine. Bring me a cup of water too, if you will."

Leon ordered whiskey and a water as Cleve looked down the long, dented bar. Could any of these grimy men be Les Wissel? He had no clear description of Wissel from his dazed uncle and could make no determination.

The drinks came, and Cleve decided he'd wasted his time ordering water, as it had already been added to the liquor with a heavy hand. He glanced over at Mick Stazza's faro table, where two bearded men in shabby hats were bucking the tiger, one of them angrily shaking his head, the other wagging a finger at the cards as if to compel them to turn favorably. As he watched, both men straightened up of a sudden, their fists clenched, as Mick scooped in their money.

One of them shouted something lost in the noise, and suddenly a pocket gun was in Mick's left hand. It was a copper-plated Hopkins & Allen .32, Cleve judged. The gamblers put up their hands and backed away from the table.

Keeping the gun leveled at the gamblers, Mick jerked his head toward the door; they took the hint, and Cleve watched them push their way out. When he looked back at Mick, the gun was already tucked away as if it had never been there.

"Leon, I see an acquaintance," Cleve said. "I'm going to seek his counsel."

Crossing the room, Cleve caught a hard, assessing look from Mick, which changed to a kind of rueful, grudging welcome. His mustache drooped low; his lengthy nose drooped too, its tip curving close to his thin lips. His lank black hair grew past his collar; his long tapering fingers took up the cards on the table and shuffled them, as his green eyes appraised Cleve.

"It's early in the evening to be flashing pistols, Mick," Cleve said.

"They accused me of dishonesty," said Mick in a clipped, brittle tone, "and that I cannot allow. I must work to live, and there's nowhere to work if my reputation is slighted."

Cleve nodded, thinking that Mick's reputation, anytime, was far from sterling. His presence in Axle Bust suggested he was no longer welcome at the lucrative gaming emporiums of Denver. "Do you know, Mick, I saw ol' Salty Jones on the trail. He was trying to honey-fogle a friend of mine out of a thousand dollars."

"Why, it being Salty Jones, it would have been strange if he hadn't been doing that very thing."

Cleve smiled. "True enough. He had a big fellow named Digley with him, pretending to be a lawman. And pretending to be called Washburn. Do you know him?"

"That might be Arnold Digley. Suspected stage robber, sometimes swindler. That's the last fact I give out here for free, Cleve Trewe."

"If you can tell me where a man called Les Wissel might be found, there's a double eagle in it for you."

"I reckon you do not know him by sight?"

"Meaning Wissel is in this room?"

"He is." Mick cocked his head, looked at him, and waited.

Cleve sighed, and considered just asking each man here his name, and saving the money. But no, Wissel might hear him asking, and slip away.

"Here you are." Cleve fished the gold coin from his pocket and slapped it onto the table.

Mick gave a quick nod. "Let us pretend you're playing a hand with that, so that it doesn't look like I'm giving anyone up. And mayhap it may draw other players."

He dealt the cards, and they went through the motions of

a hand. Cleve was unsurprised when he didn't win. The coin vanishing into Mick's pocket, the gambler leaned forward as he shuffled the cards and said, "He's right behind you at the bar. The man with the brown bowler, the red-striped vest, the sash, and the mutton chops. For no further remuneration, I will also say he is known to have boxed for prizes, and to have killed a man, possibly two, with a gun."

Cleve glanced over a shoulder, and spotted the man described just fifteen feet away, laughing with the heavy-hipped bar girl. Not a truly fat man, but double-chinned. His nose looked like it'd been broken a time or two. Cleve turned back to Mick, saw that he'd been joined by a bleary-eyed man who seemed positively eager to part with his money.

Cleve didn't bother thanking Mick, whose full attention was on the roll of bills hovering over the table. He strode to Wissel, and tapped him on the shoulder. "Lester Wissel?"

Wissel turned to Cleve, looking him up and down, frowning. He was brawnier than he'd seemed from the side, and there was a pepper-pot pistol poking from his blue silk sash. "Well?" demanded Wissel. "And who are you?"

"My name is C.T. Trewe." He did not offer to shake hands. It would feel false. Cleve had a bone-deep aversion to falsity. "I am told you are the man who assaulted my uncle."

"I don't go about assaulting uncles. What's the old boy's name?"

"Terrence Trewe."

"Oh indeed, there was a drunken old fellow by that name, who came at me with a pistol! I pushed him down a hill to avoid being shot, and he got himself bruised up."

"He does not drink and he would come after no one with a pistol. He informed you that the claim was his. Nothing more."

Wissel snorted. "Whoever told you that was lying."

"It was my uncle who said it! You have offended me by drubbing him, a man too old to properly defend himself, and now you have called him a liar. I believe I have every right to ask for satisfaction."

Wissel hooted at that. "Do you hear what this scoundrel is saying, Tootsie?" he said, speaking to the bargirl. "He's lying about me and threatening me too!"

"Oh!" she said, her mouth and eyes both going round. "You should call the constable, Les!"

Cleve gave a soft snort. "Wissel, I have asked for satisfaction. Will you give it to me or not, sir?"

"You can ask for a duel and you won't get it!" Wissel said, with a porcine snort. "Where do you think you are? Georgia?"

Cleve was peripherally aware that Leon had approached them.

"If I kill you," Wissel growled, "it'll be in the manner of my choosing! I will not blaze away in a mud puddle out there!"

"It's dry enough in here," Cleve pointed out.

"You can go to hell, mister!" Wissel said, jerking the pepperpot.

But before the compact multi-barrel pistol could be brought into action, Cleve pressed the muzzle of his Colt Army revolver up under Wissel's jaw so it dimpled deeply into the double chin. He cocked the gun as he said, softly but quite clearly, "Drop that or die—you have a one-count. One . . ."

The pepperpot clunked to the floor. Cleve could hear it clearly because the place had gotten quieter, as men stared and nudged their friends to look.

"If you wish to back-shoot this man, Wissel," said Leon, scooping up the pistol, "you'll find someone's keeping watch."

"I didn't say I was going to back-shoot anybody!" Wissel protested, sputtering the words.

"I heard you say you'd fight in the manner of your choosing," said Leon. "I know full well what that means. If anyone shoots this man in the back when I am looking away, I will figure it was you. I will not ask. I will just kill you dead, mister."

Cleve was moved by this sudden steely loyalty. He said, "Would you be so good, Leon, as to pick up that man's pistol?"

"My pleasure, Major." Leon scooped up the pepperpot, and Cleve holstered his Colt.

"It is my understanding, Wissel, that after you beat my uncle, you tore up his claim papers," Cleve said.

"Another falsehood!" sputtered Wissel.

"It happens that they were also registered at the county seat. I have proof of that with me."

"That mine is even now being worked! I have the claim papers, and I have men there working it!"

"Then you'll have to turn over the ore, Lester Wissel."

"Is that so!" Wissel barked, red faced and fist-clenched. "D'ye know who my partner is? Duncan Conroy!" His voice rose as he went on. "He's got fifty-five per cent of it! Why don't you go talk it over with him! And while you're there I'll speak to Constable Brewster about your threats!"

"You're a loud man. A man telling the truth's got no need to shout it," Cleve said. "I will see Conroy, and the Justice of the Peace—anyone I need to see, first thing in the morning. Leon, I'm going to turn in."

Cleve holstered his gun, turned on his heel, and strode to the door, Leon at his side.

"Give me back my gun, you black thief!" Wissel bellowed.

"You'll find it outside in the first muck I see!" shouted Leon.

He was as good as his word, tossing the pepperpot in horse droppings as they stepped onto the sidewalk.

Leon kept glancing back at the saloon, as they crossed the road, but Wissel did not show himself.

"That was a good speech, Cleve, but from what Hull said, there's no regular justice-of-the-peace in Axle Bust. He's around sometimes, hard to say when."

Cleve was more troubled by the news that Duncan Conroy supposed himself to own a share of the stolen mine. He remembered what Doc Hull had said about the Conroys. The magnate's son was unlikely to give up his share of a claim without a good deal of arm twisting.

"Did I not hear you say something about a wariness of killing?" Leon asked, as they turned toward the hotel.

"You did."

"Did you not just challenge a man to a duel?"

"Why . . ." Cleve frowned.

"I am not judging you, Major. But if we're going to work together, I need to know how much I have to watch my back. If you go about dueling, you will surely make enemies. I will stick by you, Cleve. But I'd like to know."

Cleve found he wasn't sure himself. "I guess I've been simmering over his attack on my uncle for some time now. And the truth is, a man can desire to set aside force of arms, but out here it may not be so easy."

"You've got that right, Major. My grandpa said, 'Sometimes it takes a will not to kill.'"

Cleve was too restless to sleep, so once settled in bed he read Tennyson by lamplight. Leon sat cross-legged on his own bed, cleaning his gun, then using a toothpick to clean his teeth and—oblivious to Cleve's attempt to read—rattled off a number of colorful stories of his days riding track for the railroad. Cleve was inured to this long-winded story-telling from their time at Fort Slocum.

"Now the crew boss on the rail was a terrible big man with a terrible big temper," said Leon, "and you will tell me that my showing an interest in his girl was foolishness, but when I see a girl I cotton to, my good sense melts like an icicle in a fire. Well, he caught us together but the beating I got was almost worth it. I was laid up for a few weeks, but . . . just a few days later . . ."

At last, they blew out the lamps. They both kept their guns handy.

Cleve lay in the darkness, listening to the street: shouts, a gunshot, the clatter of a wagon, an angry slurring shout . . .

He slept poorly, waking up from time to time to wonder if he'd been a fool to come here. Axle Bust was not a fit place for a man to die. But when he set out to do something for family, he would see it done. And the gold in his uncle's mine gleamed in the dark recessions of his mind, like a thin vein of ore glimpsed in the breast of a mine shaft.

After breakfast the next morning and a pot of coffee, Cleve found a barber with a tin bathtub, where he gave himself a more refined gloss. Directly on donning his one suit, still creased from being folded up so tightly in his rucksack, he set out, Leon in tow, toward the only finished two-story house in Axle Bust.

The Conroy House was to the northwest, according to the lady who owned the Gideon. The house was set on a green piece of land not far from the creek, a little distance from town.

The sun shone as they walked up the wooden sidewalk,

and the ground was in large part dried. The sound of bullwhackers cracking whips and men hammering nails at the new mill carried over the whickering of horses. The drumming and swishing of the multiple waterfalls filled in the background.

"Mister!" called out the hostler. Black, tall, and broad shouldered, wearing a straw topper and bibbed overalls, he hurried up to Cleve and Leon on the wooden sidewalk. "One of the horses you brought in was taken this morning!"

Cleve was not surprised. "Was it the swaybacked roan with the blaze?"

"It was, sir."

"And the man who took it was big, with a waxed mustache, and a frock coat and maybe stiff with pain when he mounted?"

"That's the very fellow! He would not be refused. Claimed it was his horse."

"Far as we know it was. You have nothing to be concerned about. He's doubtless given Dr. Hull the slip and fled this burg. I did not get your name yesterday, friend?"

"Why, it's David Kanaway, sir."

"I am Cleve Trewe, Mr. Kanaway. This is Leon Studge." They shook hands all around. "How is my Ulysses and Leon's Lily?"

"Very well, sir. I have grained them this morning, and they're in the corral."

"Capital. Here's five dollars to keep my horse fed, stabled, and corralled during the day." Cleve handed over the silver coins. "Will that serve for a few days?"

"Yes Mr. Trewe, it will, and a day more."

"I may be in town for some time, so I'll come 'round to see you."

Leon paid for his mule's keep, and they continued on their way. "That Kanaway seems like a decent sort."

"You know, he was probably once a slave, Leon. Yet here he is, with his own business."

"It does my heart good. I believe it's some easier for a former slave out west."

They turned right, then left, then right again, working through the maze of cabins and tents toward the hillier north of the basin. Flowing up the valley from the south, nudged back by the enclosing hills, the breeze shifted on a whim; blowing north and east and west, sometimes bringing the pungency of the pines; sometimes the cool living scent of the creek; sometimes the reek of feces from the privies.

Most miners' wives waited back in their hometowns, but some came along. Cleve and Leon passed a frowning, care-worn woman in a long blue flannel dress sitting on a stump in front of a ramshackle cabin, darning her husband's red long johns.

They strolled by a tent where the sound of a miner's snoring cut through the town's noise, and another where two bearded minors, wearing new hats, crouched outside their tent, one smoking a pipe, watching while the other fried bacon over an open fire. Both were young men; they seemed curiously clean, and their clothes and tent seemed new. Cleve suspected they had just come out to prospect the hills, using Axle Bust as their base camp. Good chance they'd end up working in the Conroy mine.

"I heard last night that the mill will be open in just a week," said Leon. "The Conroys have crews working on it day and night. And the ore stamper will be going like billy-o before the roof's finished."

Cleve had seen stamping machines in Virginia City. They were driven by rushing water, which turned a wheel, propelling a camshaft that lifted and dropped a series of steel hammers. The hammers banged in sequence down on chunks of ore, reducing it to smeltable gravel and grit. "That a Cornish stamper they're building?" he asked.

"No, t'aint. It's the new one, the California stamping, more efficient-like."

"The mine's being worked, is it not?"

"Sure enough, and that's day and night too. I've heard they have extended it without enough beams to hold the rock, in there. They figure the rock's hard enough to hold, and Mr. Duncan Conroy wants to press on."

Cleve shook his head. "Haste in mining has been the death of many a man."

They tramped up a slight slope, then turned another corner, avoiding mud puddles and horse droppings, coming to a street of saloons and gambling tents. One two-pole tent, with four tables in it, had been sloppily hand painted with the drippy legend, "Games of Chance."

Most of the wood-building saloons were closed at this hour, but two tent-sheltered whiskey mills were opened, and a half-dozen men stood talking at what passed for a bar: boards lying over sawhorses.

"Here they can open the saloon any time night or day, it seems," said Leon, shaking his head. "Back home they wouldn't allow any such. Saloons got to toe the line."

"I'm surprised the miners' committee doesn't close them," Cleve said, as they pushed past a cluster of men watching two drunks wind-milling their fists at each other.

"Why, those are miners who are out of work, in that bar, so I don't suppose the committee will say boo to them," Leon said, wincing as one of the drunken combatants fired a pistol. The other fighter shrieked a curse and fired back . . .

Reminding himself that he was here purely on business, Cleve paced onward.

Looking down an alley between two saloons, he saw a

big red-striped tent, a red lantern hanging from a pole in front of it. Soiled doves; fallen women. He always asked himself the same thing—how had they come to be there? Had they no recourse?

They hurried past rank garbage trenches at the edge of the camp, and at last struck the embankment of Axle Bust Creek. They followed the stream north on a well-beaten path between scrubby pinon trees. Passing abandoned flumes in the creek, they skirted piles of mucky rock where placer miners had been sifting.

As they left the shacks and cabins behind, the air was cleaner, though it carried the agreeable tang of a living creek. Perhaps, Cleve thought, he might get some fishing in while he was here. Long as it was upriver from the camp, he would not have to fear cholera.

"That must be the place," said Leon, pointing, as they emerged into a mown field close to the creek. They passed through an open garden gate in a new wrought-iron fence.

The Conroy house was white, trimmed with gold paint; it was a tall two stories, with scrolled gables and silvery lightning rods atop two conical towers at either end. White lacy curtains draped the windows. "Looks to be new-built," Cleve said.

He stopped with some surprise and admiration to take in the landscaped garden within the fence, festooned with rose bushes and spring daffodils abloom. And he was beyond surprise and admiration when he saw the gardener. Cleve was struck by her alertness, her unassuming grace as she straightened up from pruning the rose bushes; removing her kidskin gloves as she turned to him.

"May I assist you gentlemen?" she asked.

She was a slender young woman in a long, simple, dark blue dress. An abundance of chestnut hair was piled on her head, just a little askew. Her delicate features contrasted with her strong chin; her skin was pale, but seemed to subtly glow with life. Her eyes . . .

Like dark brown tourmaline, he thought. Intelligence glittered from onyx pupils.

He felt something he'd never felt in the presence of a woman, before.

It was *certainty.*

Chapter 3

Cleve took off his hat, and gave her a short bow. "Ma'am . . ." His voice seemed oddly caught in his throat. He cleared it and went on, "My name is Cleveland Trewe. May I ask . . . if it's not an intrusion . . . Who I have the honor of addressing?"

She smiled, seeming amused. There was a certain mischievousness to the curve of her roseate lips. "You are addressing Berenice Conroy Tucker."

Oh Lord, Cleve thought. She is Duncan Conroy's sister . . .

Leon touched his hat. "My name's Leon Studge, ma'am! This here's a fine garden."

Cleve grimaced. He had fairly forgotten that Leon was there.

"You're very kind, Mr. Studge," she said lightly. "The garden was started last summer, before the house was built. Quite in reverse of the usual pattern. Do you garden at home?"

"Well now, I raised spuds and onions and turkey-neck squash when I was a boy. My ma had me out there hoeing every morning."

Her smile widened, showing her teeth. It lit up her face—a glorious sight.

"I admire your industry, Mr. Studge," she said. "I have not yet planted a vegetable garden. But I have it in my sights."

She looked again at Cleve, and he said, "Ma'am . . . Miss Conroy . . ."

"Yes?"

What *was* it he wanted to say to her? He had no idea.

"Did you want to see my brother?" she suggested. "Duncan?"

"I . . ."

"Why, Berenice, you've gone right to it," Leon said, grinning. "That's exactly it. The Major has some business with Mr. Duncan Conroy."

Cleve looked at Leon in dull astonishment. Had Leon really used her first name?

"The Major?" she asked. "Is Mr. Trewe in the cavalry?" Her eyebrows were raised, as she looked at Cleve. He wore no uniform.

"He was an officer of the Union Army, ma'am," said Leon, nodding far too much. "A graduate of West Point. A hero of the war, from the Union side. I can call Cleveland Trewe a hero, though I fought on the other side, for once I saw him pack up his medals to send his pa, though he don't like to show 'em. He saw to it I did not starve when I was his prisoner at Fort Slocum. We became friends, don't you see, and he just yesterday saved me from some fellas who—"

"*Leon.*" Cleve grated. "We have no need of a biographical recitation."

"But it's all very interesting, Mr. Trewe!" Berenice said, with a soft laugh of delight. Her eyes had gone from an analytical glitter to a quiet merriness.

Cleve fell once more to gazing at her. But then—he must get on with his mission, mustn't he? No point in wasting the lady's time. For there was no hope of courting such a woman. She was Duncan Conroy's sister. Did that not scotch the notion? Not even a notion, but sheer fantasy. Some madness had swept over him when he'd caught sight of her.

Take command of yourself, C.T. Trewe, he thought.

"Yes Mrs. Tucker . . ." Cleve managed. "I can . . . is there someone who could tell your brother, that . . ."

"I fear you have missed him. Just ten minutes ago he took the buggy to his office at the mine. The miners call it the 'boss shack.'"

"Then . . . I shall find my way there." Cleve could not resist reaching out to shake her hand. She gave him the formal clasp, less dainty than he'd expected. Her skin was soft in parts, but the tips of her fingers were rough from work. Perhaps sewing as well as gardening.

He looked into her eyes.

"Mr. Trewe?" she said softly.

"Yes?"

"May I have my hand back, if you please?" There was no hint of censoriousness in her voice.

"Oh!" He dropped her hand. "Forgive me, ma'am. I . . ." He felt his cheeks burning. "Good morning to you."

He turned away. Leon began, "You know, Berenice, we're staying over at the . . ."

"Leon!" he growled, turning back to tug Leon away.

Leon came reluctantly along and they hurried out the gate.

Once back on the road, Leon whispered, "You didn't have to worry about me, Major. I could see you was smitten by her. I wouldn't take her from you!"

Cleve could only sigh. "Let us head for the mine, Leon. And let us say no more about the lady."

* * *

They found "the boss shack," about ten yards from the mouth of the open cut. Over the door a neatly painted sign read,

D.R. Conroy, Mgr.
Golden Fleece Mine
Conroy Mining & Smelting Co.

Cleve hesitated at the door of the small, freestanding wooden office. How would he handle this? Fifty yards below them, the workers erecting the stamper mill set up an incessant din of hammering and the grating of saws. He glanced over at the entrance to the mine. The rectangular adit in the side of the hill extruded a small set of cart tracks. Over the wooden beams supporting the entrance, a rusting metal sign read,

Golden Fleece, Shaft 1
Tunnels 1 & 2.

A muscular man in a soiled linen shirt, his gasping mouth open wide, pushed a cart of scrap rock out of the adit. Beyond the big man pushing the iron cart, Cleve could see the wooden headframe, in the interior of the mine, supporting a pulley for the miners' elevator and the skips. Two oxen stood ruminating to one side, yoked to a wheel that drew the cable for the pulley.

"You going to *knock* on that door, today, Major?" Leon asked, eyebrows raised.

"Just wondering what it would take for a man in charge

of all this to give up a mine," Cleve said, keeping his voice low. "He must be a man who won't want to be challenged."

"Duncan Conroy's the manager of this mine, right enough—but the real owner is old man Conroy, back East. I reckon Duncan will do whatever it takes to carve something out on his own."

Cleve nodded. "I expect that's so." He took a deep breath and knocked on the door. There was no immediate answer. He rapped again, harder.

"Well?" came a brusque voice as the door opened.

"Mr. Conroy?"

"Yes . . ." Duncan Conroy's tanned brow was furrowed as he surveyed Cleve and Leon; he had a quill in his hand. Behind him was a standing desk overflowing with paperwork. He had a thin mustache, a fine pin-striped suit and vest. The jacket was draped over the chair behind him. A stocky man, Duncan Conroy was looking up at Cleve, who was a head taller. "You don't seem like a fellow looking to sign on as a miner."

"I am not seeking employment," Cleve said. "But I do have business. My name is Cleve Trewe." He watched to see if the surname was familiar to Conroy. But the man didn't react to it.

"And who is this?" Conroy asked, nodding impatiently at Leon.

"Mr. Studge here is my business partner." Cleve drew a folded paper from his inside jacket pocket. "You are, I believe, familiar with mine number one-seventy-one of this county—in Deerstalker Canyon, about six miles south and west?"

"Certainly, I am a partner in it. What is this about?"

Cleve unfolded the paper and passed it over to Duncan. "This document establishes the claim of my uncle, for mine number one-seventy-one of this county. The Trewe Mine. I am part owner in that mine and Mr. Studge here is an investor in it. I am told that a certain Mr. Wissel claims the mine, with you as investment partner. His claim is baseless, sir. It has no validity."

Conroy took the claim paper and unfolded it. He scowled at it, and then snorted. "Look at the date, here, Trewe! July seventeenth of last year! My partner's claim is dated to June tenth, of the month prior. Your uncle filed the claim after that site was already taken. The papers were made out already, whatever the County Clerk supposed."

Cleve shook his head. "Wissel was not there in June. He did not come to this area till September—that's what I was told in Elko. His papers are falsified. The Trewe Mine, number one-seventy-one, belongs to us, Mr. Conroy."

"You accuse me of claim jumping?" Conroy demanded, his cheeks flaming, his hands balled into fists at his sides.

"No sir. I suggest that your partner is the claim-jumper and that he has defrauded you. You have been deceived by Lester Wissel. What's more, the man attacked my uncle—who is no longer a young man. He was severely injured."

"Many men have a sharp disagreement with a claim jumper," Conroy said. "I assume Wissel identified your uncle as such."

"No sir. We will prove that my uncle was working that mine before anyone else." Cleve wasn't entirely sure how he would prove it, but he was determined to find a way.

He took the claim paper back from Conroy, and folded it up.

"You can trust Major Trewe, here, sir," Leon said earnestly.

Conroy raised his eyebrows. "'Major'?"

"No longer," said Cleve, thinking he must insist Leon

stop calling him Major. "When Leon and I met I was an officer in the Union Army."

"That will get you no special treatment here, I assure you," said Conroy dryly. "Judge Kinney was a Confederate sympathizer."

Cleve wasn't pleased by this revelation, but he shrugged it off. "If he is an honest justice of the peace, it will not matter."

"I can guess what happened," said Conroy, taking his quill back to the desk and sticking it in its inkwell. "Your uncle came along well after Wissel found the mine and filed his claim. Perhaps Wissel's claim-sign had been removed by someone. Your uncle filed a claim too and someone at the county assay didn't notice that it was already spoken-for. But that can be cleared up and the prior claim brought into evidence."

"Wissel's claim has been falsified," Cleve said.

"We shall just see about that," Conroy said sharply, turning him a glare. "I've invested twenty-nine hundred dollars in that mine already, and I will not give it up, though it's only a thin, puny vein that looks to peter out fairly soon. That mine is not worth your being hung by a miners' court, Trewe. I urge you to retire from the field."

"I can raise the money to return your investment," Cleve said, "if you will give up your claim."

Conroy gave his head a single decisive shake. "No sir! Now I have a fair heap of work to do. The Golden Fleece has gold waiting to be taken, from lode and from ore, and we are hard at it. We have no time for flim-flammery."

Cleve tensed at the implied insult. But he would gain nothing by calling the man out. And this was the brother of Berenice Conroy Tucker . . .

"I will find a lawyer, sir," said Cleve icily.

"Ha!" Conroy turned back to his paperwork and retrieved his quill. "A lawyer in Axle Bust? Good luck to you!"

"Come on, Leon," Cleve said.

Cleve turned away, tucking the document in his coat pocket, and they walked down the hillside, past the dusty, hammer-banging construction site for the mill.

They found the unfindable lawyer late that afternoon, on the side of a ridge three miles from Axle Bust, and in the same gorge where Trewe's mine was located.

Caleb Drask was the only attorney in Axle Bust, and he didn't like it known. He had a canvas-roofed shack in town, where he did not hang his lawyer's shingle. Drask's practice was in Elko; he was in Axle purely as a prospector. "Another poor victim of the gold fever," Dr. Hull had told them, shaking his head. "You'll find Caleb downriver, or down creek if you prefer, and west up Deerstalker Canyon . . ."

The gorge fed a turbid stream from the west; a muddy tributary to Axle Bust Creek. Swept by yesterday's rain, much of the muck was washed into the stream from the sluices up the gorge. On the south side was a substantial group of Chinese miners. One man worked alone on the north side. That was the lawyer.

"Caleb Drask?" Cleve called out, as he clambered from the thin, steep trail onto the ledge.

A man in round spectacles, dusty coveralls, a pickaxe in his hand, was up to his knees in a hole just under a steep sandstone rise. He swiveled, startled, toward Cleve.

"What's this now?" blurted the miner.

"Lordy," Leon muttered, puffing up after Cleve. "Mining is a crazy-man's work. A man goes halfway up a mountain only to start digging his way back down."

The miner climbed out of the hole. A fine red dust covered

the lenses of his spectacles and he took them off to have a
better look at Cleve and Leon. The lines of the miner's face
were marked out with dust, making him look older than he
was. He had a high forehead, streaked with dusty sweat, and
a weak chin, but there was strength in his hard blue eyes.
The man spat dust, and said, hoarsely, "Gentlemen, I have
established my claim, here." He pointed toward white-
painted posts, crookedly set up nearby. "There are my
markers. I have my papers filed in Elko. Indeed, I am a—
that is, I have some knowledge of the law . . ."

"Easy, friend," interrupted Leon. "We're not after your
claim. Are you Mr. Drask?"

"I am. What do you want from me? I am tired and thirsty
and am short on patience."

"We want something wicked all right," Leon said, smiling ruefully. "We're looking for a lawyer."

Drask winced. "I deny all, sir!"

"You deny being a lawyer?" Cleve asked.

"I am, as you can plainly see, a miner."

"A miner who is also a lawyer?" Cleve asked.

Drask tossed his pickaxe aside in disgust. "Yes, I am an
attorney. Someone has played the rat on me, I see! But I
have no interest in legal entanglements out here. My profes-
sional work—for which I have acquired significant dis-
taste—is in Elko. In Axle Bust, there are too many men who
drink and fire their guns at the same time. It's a dangerous
place to practice law. Boys, you have come to the wrong
shop. Now if you were selling brandy . . ."

Cleve persisted. "My name is Cleveland Trewe, Mr. Drask.
My uncle has a claim in this very gorge. I believe it is about
a quarter mile west of here. Have you made his acquaintance?"

"I have. You're Terrence's nephew?"

"Yes. Are you aware that Terrence was attacked, and beaten nigh to death, by one Les Wissel?"

Drask stared, aghast. "I was not. That is sour news indeed. Was it over a mining claim?"

"It was."

"Oh, but of course it was." Drask sighed, turning to look into the hole he'd dug. "I am finding not a speck of color as yet. I was sure this hillside would yield gold or silver. There was considerable gold dust found down there, on the Angry Wife, and some silver nuggets."

"That's the name of the crick there?" Leon said, squinting down at the brown stream at the bottom of the steep hill. "Angry Wife Crick?"

"Yes: that stream comes and goes in enthusiasm. The stream gave up some gold—and then would give no more. Hence the name. But the placer gold came from these hills. Now the Chinese prospectors have located small lodes. But not me, I confess. This is my fifth hole dug." He stuck his hands moodily in his pockets, and heaved another sigh. "Terrence helped me when I first came up here, prospecting. I got myself in a pickle and he helped me out. I suppose I'd best listen to your story . . ."

Just under an hour later, Cleve rode Ulysses, Leon rode his mule Lily, and Caleb Drask rode a small but sturdy paint-pony he'd christened Judge Hoof. Leon led the way up the meager trail following the bank of the thin but surging stream. They came around a bend, and looked up the rocky sides of the gorge, studded in white and yellow rock, interspersed with sage. The sun was nearing the mountainous horizon, and it glared into their eyes.

"That's it," Caleb called. They felt easy with this man,

strangely sincere and straightforward for a lawyer, and already called him Caleb.

Cleve reined in and Caleb drew up beside him, shading his eyes and pointing up to the south. He had cleaned his spectacles, and light glinted off the lenses. Up there on the slope—you see the smoke?"

Cleve had spotted it already. He could discern the mine's entrance adit about halfway up the slope; a gray twist of smoke rose close outside it, on the broad ledge. Likely a campfire. A few stunted yew trees shaded the camp.

"Is that a bridge, over there?" Leon asked, pointing up the creek.

"A few skinned logs roped together," said Caleb. "It serves as a bridge. I cannot guarantee it won't give way."

Though somewhat splashed by the rushing, turbid water of Angry Wife Crick, the bridge held up as they crossed over. The gorge wasn't so steep-walled at this end, and a trail, well-worn by miners, wound sinuously up to mine one-seventy-one. Here, a bluff blocked the sun enough to throw a shadow across the hillside as Cleve's party rode up the trail.

"Hello the mine!" Cleve called, as he rode up to within ten yards of the mine entrance.

"Who the bejeezus is that?" someone yelled. "Sneakin' right up on us."

Cleve reined in, the others drawing up behind to the right and left. With one hand, Cleve gripped the reins; with his right, he held his rifle laid across the cantle. He had no wish to point it at anyone—but he was ready to, if need be.

There were three men around the fire, two sitting on extra wooden beams that lay across the dirt; one man was standing, a double-barrel shotgun cradled in his arms. A bottle of whiskey, more than half empty, stood on the dirt between them—that would be the reason the men seemed surprised when Cleve called out. They were too drunk to watch the trail.

The man with the shotgun had a brass badge pinned to his red vest. He had a squat red face under a wide brown hat, the front of the brim folded straight upward as if it were waiting for a sign to be posted there. Clamped in his yellowed teeth was a clay pipe, no longer burning. His eyes were small, under bushy brows; his nose large and crackled from daily drinking; his red-brown beard was brushy enough to hide his mouth as he said, his voice slurred, "Now who the hell is this?" The pipe wagged in his mouth as he spoke around it.

"Told you I heard horses, Brewster," said a yellow bearded man in grimy overalls, clutching a tin cup in his hand. His pinched face was dirt-streaked, his hands blackened. He'd been working the mine.

The man with the badge and shotgun must be Constable Brewster, Cleve thought. Duncan Conroy's bully-boy.

The man on the other side of Brewster, in canvas trousers and a torn, dusty blue-flannel shirt, had long gray-streaked red hair and was missing several teeth, the gaps displayed as he gaped at the strangers. Piled behind him were pickaxes, crowbars, and shovels. "Well shit, I knowed somebody was coming, my own self."

"The hell you did, Frissmeyer," Brewster growled. He glared at Cleve. "Well—what do you men want?"

"I've come to see my uncle's mine," Cleve said. "I have a share in it. My name is Cleveland Trewe."

"That's the feller Dursk, on the pony there," said the blond man, with a Scandinavian accent, nodding toward Caleb.

"Drask," Caleb corrected him. "Caleb Drask is my name, Spiegel. There seems to be some question as to the ownership of this mine."

"If you men plan to pay us a better wage, why sure if it was up to me you could sure have the damn thing," said Spiegel.

"Shut up, Spiegel," said Brewster sharply. "Trewe, you said? Some old man by that name tried to claim the site here, but it was already taken."

"That 'old man' was the first to dig here," Cleve said. "You mind if I have a look inside?"

"Why sure, I don't care—" Spiegel began.

"I told you to shut up, Spiegel," Brewster said. With that he struck out with the butt of his shotgun, glancingly striking the back of the man's head.

"Ow, Brewster, by golly that hurt!"

"You want another? No? Then shut your yammer hole."

Brewster walked slowly around the fire, approaching Cleve. The shotgun in his hands was not yet pointed at a target. Brewster must've noticed Cleve's hand on his rifle.

"There is no question about this mine," said Brewster, coming three steps closer to Cleve and stopping. The pipe bobbed in his mouth as he went on, "You sure as hell cannot enter that mine. That's private property. You get on out of here. Wissel said someone might be coming around . . ."

"That why you're here, because Wissel told you to come?" Leon asked quietly. But his meaning was loud enough.

Brewster's glance darted at Leon. "What d'you mean by that?"

"Only that you're a company man, Brewster. You're no real lawman. You're sent here to scare us off."

Cleve nodded. "Leon's right. You haven't the authority, Brewster."

Brewster set the shotgun butt on his hip, ready to drop the muzzle if he chose to fire. Cleve's hand tightened on the Winchester . . .

But another gun was up—Leon was pointing a pistol at

Brewster. "You fire that shotgun I'll shoot you dead, brass badge!"

The pipe in Brewster's mouth bobbed again—and then he ducked the shotgun toward the ground. "You're threatening a law officer!"

"When we get a law officer here, we'll treat him gently," Caleb said. There was resignation in his voice. It was as if he had hoped to not take a side—but here he was. "There's the Elko County sheriff—he's the law. You're just a company man, like Studge there says."

"You'll find out just how much goddamn authority I have," said Brewster. "Sheriff Purslow never comes to Axle. And you're not going in that mine. Not unless you're walking on my dead body."

Cleve shrugged. "No need for all this foofaraw. Just wanted to see the layout here." He nodded at Spiegel. "I would indeed pay you better. First, I'll get the claim cleared up. We can prove this mine doesn't belong to Wissel or Conroy. It belongs to Terrence Trewe. Good day to you, gentlemen." He backed the sorrel up, and then turned to go down the trail, saying, "Leon, let us be off."

"I'm coming, soon's he puts away that shotgun," Leon said.

Cleve looked over his shoulder, and saw Brewster turn away, heading back to the mine and the bottle. "Let's go, Leon. It's all right."

"He's a back-shooter, sure enough."

"Would not surprise me. But there's too many of us. He'll wait. Come on."

Leon put his pistol back in his waistband, turned his horse, and followed Cleve and Caleb down the hillside.

"Leon," Cleve said, after they'd ridden to the trail, "I don't know if I should thank you or cuss at you."

"Because I pulled that gun?" Leon snorted. "He like to've shot you! He had a gleam in his eye I've come to know."

"It could have ended in a general gunfight," Caleb pointed out. "And me without a gun in hand but just as like to be shot."

"Shooting that Brewster might've saved us some trouble later on," Leon said, chuckling. "But if you don't want me to back your play, Major, you say the word."

"Well, I guess I shouldn't complain if a man backs me. And you were there in the Tom Cat too. You can ride with me any old time you please."

They rode along the Angry Wife, which ran enthusiastically toward Axle Bust Creek, and then came to another bridge, built in a more solid fashion, painted, and with ropes for railings. It ran to a stairway, cut in the soft rock under a mine entrance. A Chinese guard sat outside the entrance, his broad straw hat shading the paper he was writing on with a black-inked brush. He had a buffalo gun leaning against the rock wall beside him.

Two more miners were just turning onto the bridge from the trail ahead, each leading a donkey laden with supplies. Cleve took the men to be Chinese, though dressed in the usual rough working clothes of those who labored beneath the earth. One of them wore a conical straw hat like the guard, the other a dusty Miller hat.

"Johnny!" Caleb called out. The younger man in the Miller hat looked up and smiled.

"Caleb!" he replied.

"That's Johnny Wing," Caleb told Cleve. "Speaks good English. Good man too. He knew Terrence."

"Did he?" Cleve murmured, interested.

Fresh faced, with just a thin spray of beard on his narrow face, Johnny Wing waited for them to ride up.

The man beside him in the conical hat was much bigger,

with long arms and work-reddened hands. He looked at them with rampant suspicion. A wine-colored birthmark splashed his right cheek.

"Caleb," Johnny said, "how goes the diggings?"

Caleb made a *tsk*ing sound. "Let us just say the crick here has earned its name. She's angry with me for sure."

Johnny laughed. "Maybe you and I will go prospecting sometime! The Lucky Star shines bright upon us!"

"I bet it's more hard work and skill than luck," Caleb said. "And not working alone!" He sighed and rolled his eyes. "Lord my back hurts. I think I may decide that a courtroom is easier on a man than a rocky hole in the ground."

"Ha! There is wisdom! And your friends?"

"This is Cleveland Trewe and Leon Studge. We just met, but if they're unlucky they may yet be friends."

"Trewe, you say?" Johnny looked at Cleve.

"My uncle is Terrence Trewe. I understand you know him?"

"Oh, Terrence, good man! I have not seen him, oh, a month now. Maybe more."

"He was injured—beaten by a man named Wissel. He's under a doctor's care now."

"No! That's very bad. Many times, Terrence brought gifts for my men when he came from town. We shared meals, three times, and he liked our wine! I have met this Wissel. A most undesirable man."

"I don't suppose any of you folks saw the attack? It was at his mine."

"No, the one-seventy-one is around the spur there. We cannot see it from here."

"Did you meet him before this Wissel showed up?"

"I did! He was prospecting here, very soon after we came. It was in July. He said he had staked a claim."

"Wissel says he staked the same spot in June."

"Ha! We always have a guard, always, we know everyone who comes! Much later, when Wissel came! September."

"That's what I figured. Would you be willing to say so in court?"

Johnny gave him a sad smile. "We have our courts. Your courts, they do not accept us as witness. We have to have our own courts. The Chinese man cannot be trusted, so they think." He shook his head and spat toward the creek. "And the Chinese Tax—that is how your law treats us."

"Chinese Tax?"

"Oh yes. A tax on the gold and silver we find—only for Chinese. Not for the white miners. Special tax for us."

Caleb growled in his throat. "Yep. It's so, Cleve. They won't let them testify in court and they put taxes on them the white miners don't have."

"That's a travesty of justice," Cleve said.

Leon nodded. "It ain't right."

"But—you are friends of Terrence and Caleb," Johnny said, brightening. "Come and have a meal with us!"

"We'll do it one of these days," Cleve said, "if the invitation holds. Got business to attend to in Axle just now." He stuck out his hand. "Good to meet you, Johnny." They shook hands.

He offered his hand to the larger man in the conical hat. "Didn't get this gent's name."

The big man looked at Cleve's hand and frowned like a carved temple demon. He stepped back.

Cleve dropped his hand.

"This is Cho," Johnny chuckled. "Don't feel offended. He doesn't like the *gweilo*."

"Am I a *'gweilo'*?" Leon said. "Somebody forgot to tell me. Well, I hope it's not too bad an insult."

"It means men foreign to China," Caleb said. "Though there's a smell of suspicion to it."

Cleve nodded. "From what Johnny says, I can't blame Mr. Cho much. Boys, we got to be moving on. You come to town, Johnny, dinner's on me. Any friend of Terrence is a friend of mine."

Johnny gave him a sort of humorous salute. "You tell Terrence, we have medicine for him if he comes here! Good Chinese cures. Goodbye, goodbye!"

He led the weary donkey over the bridge, Cho led his own, without a backward glance.

"I'd like to try that Chinee food," Leon said. "Heard it's something new."

"Not to the Chinese," Cleve said. "Let's head back."

Nothing more was said as the three men rode to Axle Bust.

Chapter 4

"Because I am a fool, doomed to die young, I will represent the Trewe Mine in this matter," Caleb Drask morosely declared, as they waited for their dinner in the Gideon Hotel cafe. "But I cannot predict success. Conroy and his father are powerful men. The judge, when his circuit brings him back, may be averse to giving you a fair shake, Cleve."

Caleb was cleaned up, now wearing a sack suit and string tie, as they sat at a corner table under a giltwood sconce flickering with oil-light. Cleve and Caleb were sipping coffee—branch-water and whiskey in Leon's case—and they spoke in low tones.

Caleb's remarks left Cleve feeling that the deck was stacked against him in Axle Bust. He felt a tension growing in him, as night drew over the mining camp.

When Cleve thought of Duncan Conroy's arrogant dismissal at the Golden Fleece office, he found his thoughts drawn to Conroy's sister, Berenice.

Did Conroy treat her well? Did he abuse her?

Leon asked, "Say, Caleb, you speak China-talk?"

"I grew up on the San Francisco Bay, and we had an inpouring of Chinese immigrants when I was a young fellow. I did learn enough Cantonese to have a fair chinwag.

Cantonese being the very dialect spoken by these folks on Deerstalker Gorge. And they all learn some English. They are a quick-witted people. Brisk learners. Now, I met a certain Chinese girl, one Jia Li. I was fifteen and she was fourteen . . ."

"Ah ha!" Leon said. "We think we figure our own lives. But it's women . . . !"

Caleb shrugged. "There's something in that." He drank a little coffee, and then said, "My father sold goods to the men from the gold rush and did well. He found the Chinese to be good workers and reliable. He hired them to unload goods to the dock and to work in the store, so that gave me an excuse to learn the language, but Jia Li it was who bent me to the task."

"Do Chinese girls marry whites in San Francisco?" Cleve asked.

"Sometimes it's done. When we got to seventeen years old, we asked to marry. My father was willing to consider it. But hers was not." He shook his head. "In time, she married a Chinese scholar, who was a considerable businessman. He is twenty-seven years her senior."

"Those China folks at the gorge—is their mine producing?" Cleve asked.

Caleb nodded. "More and more. And it worries me—because of what happened just a hundred and ten miles northwest of here, in Idaho. Shade Tree Canyon. You hear about it?"

"I don't believe so."

"Ten Chinese murdered—seven miners, along with a woman and two children—shot dead in their camp. Two of the men had been tortured to find out where the gold was hid. They were working for a Chinese investment outfit, and they'd accumulated a good deal of gold. They were massacred by bitter, less fortunate white miners." He grimaced. "The murderers packed the gold out on mules and left the bodies in the sun."

"Were the killers tracked down?" Leon asked.

Caleb shook his head. "Locals reckon they know who the killers were, but the constabulary shrugged it off and said the Chinese were to blame for intruding into mining territory that should only go to whites."

Leon shook his head in disgust. "Any justice, that constabulary should go to jail along with the killers."

"When was this?" Cleve asked.

"A year and a half ago. And no justice was done. It's sure to happen again. There's been talk against Johnny Wing's people—I fear for my friends in Deerstalker Canyon."

This too wore on Cleve. But it also summoned up another notion, just the sprout of one. If Brewster was what passed for a constable here, and if the sheriff didn't deign to ride through, it could be that Axle Bust was in dire need of some law . . .

Cleve had sworn he'd given up lawing. Then again a man may be against caring for other people's children—but if he sees an abandoned baby on a trash heap, he'll carry that baby to his own wife.

"If those Chinese folks are your friends, they're mine too, Caleb," Cleve said. "Now here's our ham and beans, come at last. Let's hope the ham is more agreeable to being chewed than the beef was yesterday."

Leon, having overindulged at the High Nevada Saloon, was still asleep when Cleve went downstairs for a light breakfast of coffee and biscuits with sorghum.

After breakfast, Cleve headed out alone, stepping into the jangling of wagons and the futile *hush-hushing* of the waterfall. He headed for the stable to see that Ulysses was well taken care of.

He was pleased to find the sorrel brushed, watered, and grained by the diligent Kanaway, but shifting restlessly, foot to foot in the stall.

"He wants to get him a run, Mr. Trewe," Kanaway suggested, coming in with a bale of hay on one of his sizable shoulders.

"He shall have one, then, Mr. Kanaway," Cleve said. He wanted to take a look at the falls and the land north of the town. He supposed any gold easily gathered was already gone from the pools under the waterfalls, and creek below to the south. But perhaps higher up in the hills . . .

Cleve saddled Ulysses himself and rode to the creek, knowing that gold, of the mineral sort, was not what he was actually looking for. He was hoping for a glimpse of a certain someone.

He turned Ulysses north along the stream, looking up at the fragments of clouds racing by in a brisk wind, blocking and unblocking the sun so that the sunlight fell in transient beams, shifting here and there, as if in theatrical limelight directed on unknown actors.

All the world's a stage, Cleve thought, remembering The Bard. *And all the men and women merely players. They have their exits and their entrances . . .*

He wondered if he'd come to Axle Bust, a town abundant with danger, only to find his exit from the stage.

Riding past the Conroy House, Cleve told himself sternly that he must not stop by. He had no right to call upon the lady when he would likely be taking her brother to court. It might end with her receiving some harsh rebuke from Duncan.

Still, there was no harm in merely glancing into the garden.

He rode by as close as he could with propriety and was disappointed to catch no sight of Berenice Conroy.

Onward Cleve rode until he came to the lowest pool of the falls. Here the highest of the triple-stacked cataracts almost drowned out the clatter of the town. A cloud drew away from the sun, and suddenly the light shifted so rainbows appeared in the rising mist of the cascade, as if to announce an event. Cleve smiled—and the smile froze on his face, when a figure emerged from the mists, about fifty feet away.

Berenice Conroy Tucker was walking across the flat white stone that covered the nearer bank of the pool. She wore a man's brown trousers, a fisherman's galoshes, a simple gray bodice under a man's rust-red riding jacket. On her head, a bit incongruous, was a white sunbonnet. Her chestnut hair spilled out of it on the sides. Over one shoulder was slung a leather satchel.

She looked up and stopped, her eyes widening as she saw him. Her voice came faintly in the hiss and rumble of the falls. "Mr. . . ?"

Cleve raised his hat, then dismounted, and led Ulysses to within a few steps of her. "Cleveland Trewe, ma'am." He bowed a little. "Mrs. Tucker."

He straightened up to see her cheeks burning red. He was surprised to see a lady who'd been so confident now seeming out of countenance. But instantly she lifted her chin, and put on an expression of cool detachment.

"Oh, I recognize you now, Mr. Trewe. I was thinking of you as 'the Major,' really." She gave him a teasing smile. "As your man titled you."

"Leon's not my hireling, ma'am. He is a friend—and a

business associate now. He is coming in with me on a mine I hold in trust for my uncle."

"Of course, it had to be mining. You're not the sort of man to be a merchant."

"Am I not?" Cleve was a little put off by the assumption. "I'd happily be a merchant." But inwardly, he supposed she was right. If he'd wanted to be a merchant, like the "gentleman merchant farmer" his father was, he'd had only to take up Pa's offer to take over the rich and sprawling Trewe Farm. His father had done well, and turned his profits to buying up more land, and starting his own mercantile. But Cleve had been restless after the war, mayhap unsuited for peace. He was content to let his brother Rowan inherit. "Could be you're right." He noticed mud on her boots and the knees of her pants, and on her hands.

"Your eyes are straying to my clothing, Mr. Trewe. You are wondering at the contrast. When last you saw me, I was dressed as the lady of the house would for gardening."

Cleve cleared this throat. "I assume you have your reasons for your . . . your habiliment, Miss Conroy—that is, Mrs. Tucker."

"Oh, do call me Berry. Most people do, who've met me more than once."

"Then I would be honored if you'd call me Cleve."

"You have manners my parents would approve of, Cleve." There was something arch in the way she said it, that suggested she was not particularly impressed with fine manners. He was beginning to see she was an odder sort of woman than he had supposed. But that did not slow the race of his pulse when she reached up, and with delicate but muddy fingers drew a few strands of wind-blown hair from her face.

"These clothes—" She waved a hand dismissively. "I am

on my own small scientific expedition today. I must dress for my task. You would perhaps be scandalized to see me in my 'habiliment' of yesterday evening—that of a beekeeper!"

He was about to say, *Nothing you could do would scandalize me.* But then Cleve realized he could seem to be approving scandalous behavior. Instead, he managed, "You keep beehives, ma'am . . . ah—Berry?" One of his uncle's preoccupations was beekeeping. Cleve had always been fascinated by it.

"I do! They're of compelling interest to me. So many aspects of nature to see in a hive. A whole society in a box. And the honey for a beekeeper's reward, if one is patient, and doesn't mind the occasional sting. It's early in the season—the bees are just now awakening from their dormancy."

"It is an interest I share. I . . ." He wanted to ask if he might see the hives. But she was Duncan Conroy's sister. He would not be welcome on the property.

"Beekeeping interests you?" She looked surprised. "Oh! No one else has ever said so to me—except a few correspondents I've never met."

"My uncle keeps bees. My cousin is seeing to them now. I used to help Uncle Terrence harvest honey, and he showed me all about bees. The hives are a marvel!"

"Yes." She took a step back and cocked her head as if to see him better. She had a bold way of sizing him up that he found both flattering—flattering that she took the trouble— and unnerving.

But it seemed to him that her gaze was softer when she looked him in the eyes now. She cleared her throat and said, "The Egyptians are known to have kept bees thousands of years ago."

"So my uncle told me. Are you out here today to

study"—fortunately, the word came to him after a moment's searching—"entomology?"

She seemed pleased, and clasped her hands together. "Yes, entomology—among other things! I have gathered some butterfly larvae this morning. They are marvels themselves! But I was also curious about the geology of the rock under the falls. My family takes its living from mining, so I grew up with geology. But as for entomology . . . Wait!"

Berenice seemed to flutter with a sudden excitement, and whipping the leather satchel from her shoulder, she set it down, knelt beside it, and began rummaging about inside. He could see metal tools, jars, and little wooden boxes in the open satchel.

"Look here!" She held up a glass jar in which was a monarch butterfly, deceased but exquisitely preserved, with iridescent black and gold wings. The partitions of its wings reminded him of panels in stained glass.

"And here!" She opened a small wooden box and took out a slender leaf from a pile of cuttings. "This is milkweed—" Berry turned and pointed up at the cliff with the leaf. "You see that shelf, over there, covered in green plants?"

"I do."

"That too is milkweed—just the sort that the Monarch Butterfly prefers. She lays her eggs on the underside of the leaves—you see?" She turned the leaf over. "The little light-green ovals there? They are her eggs. So far as anyone can discover, the Monarch will only lay her eggs on milkweed."

"And why would that be?"

"Her larva will feed only upon milkweed! And milkweed gets most of its pollination from monarch butterflies! How, one wonders, did natural selection lay the course for such an exclusive relationship?"

He had no answer for that, and he could only think to say, "You are a proponent of natural selection?"

"Why the evidence for it is mountainous!" Berry gave a little laugh and put the leaf carefully away, beside the jar. "Mr. Darwin is quite correct. Now as I'm certain you're aware, Cleveland, the caterpillar attaches its body to a leaf and envelops itself in a chrysalid. Within the chrysalid, a sort of cocoon, a metamorphosis takes place. Have you ever studied the metamorphosis of the butterfly?"

"I have not."

"Well then . . ." She went on to explicate the stages of metamorphosis, from caterpillar into butterfly and its life-cycle thereafter, in some detail, speaking so rapidly he had to work hard to follow her. Then she seemed to catch herself and smiled sheepishly. "But there—my enthusiasm has bored you!"

He shook his head firmly. "No, Berenice. You have . . ." He wanted to say, *Only deepened my admiration of you.* But again, that would be too forward; even leeringly sentimental. "You have expressed it all quite eloquently." He glanced into the satchel again, to keep himself from staring at her. "I see you have a sketch pad."

"Oh, yes—I do some sketching, and water colors. My . . . well, my personal icon really, is Maria Sibylla Merian— you must have heard of her."

"The name seems familiar."

"She was a German woman, but living chiefly in Holland, born in the seventeenth century. She was a scientist— self-educated. I sometimes fall into self-pity, when I think how my father refused to permit me to go to college. I went to a dreary finishing school. He holds that studying the sciences is inappropriate for a lady." Moodily, she closed the satchel and stood up, slinging it over her shoulder. "But then, Maria Merian changed the course of natural history. She was also an artist and was the first to really detail metamorphosis—most scholars didn't believe metamorphosis was real, till she came along—and she painted each stage, with fine art and insight! She filled books with her studies of insects, and other creatures. In fact—she crossed the ocean, to Suriname, the coast of South America, to study flora and fauna in the jungle."

He was surprised at that. "They let her go to the jungles of Suriname?"

"You are quite right to be startled! Women were even more constrained then. And we are but a form of serf, even in our time."

She is a suffragist too, he thought. He found this a little intimidating—but he admired her for it at the same time. He knew full well it took bravery. Berenice was extraordinary for her intelligence and courage. They shone out even more than her beauty. He wanted to tell her so. But once more . . .

He merely said, "You seem to have found a way to educate yourself in the sciences."

"I read any book I can obtain on science. I've been corresponding with natural philosophers, some of them women, since I was a girl. Most scientists will write back if your question is intelligent. My late husband was an engineer—and rather a good mathematician. I learned a fair amount from him . . ." Her voice trailed off and she turned to gaze at the falls.

"I am sorry you lost him."

"It's been almost two years. He was killed in an accident. The Corazon de Oro mine in New Mexico. He'd tried to warn them the mine was unsafe. And then it took his life."

He stood there awkwardly, thinking he'd like to prolong this time with her, and not sure how to do it without blundering.

Then she said, "I . . . I'd best go back to the house. I must speak to the cook about dinner. And . . ."

She darted a glance at him—held it for a moment, then

looked away. She seemed to be waiting for something. So he took a risk. "Might I . . . escort you to your gate?"

She nodded, just once. A smile flitted across her face like a butterfly, then it was gone. "If you choose. I usually have Jonah here to keep watch over me. Duncan insists because, well—Axle Bust attracts its fair share of rogues."

"'Jonah'?"

"Jonah Bentworth. He was a town marshal once, in Kansas, and a cavalryman before that. Now he does security for Conroy Mining. He's getting old, and can't travel much, so Duncan assigned him to watch over Conroy House, and the property—which, in their minds, includes me. But Jonah has gone to look into something with Constable Brewster at another mine . . ."

Ah, he thought bitterly. Mine one-seventy-one. "Then you have no one to protect you, when you're out here alone?"

She reached into a pocket, and drew out a pearl handled, gold-inlaid derringer. "I have this. And a pair of well-sharpened shears in my bag."

He grinned. "You're armed for bear!"

"I take a rifle when I ride out, too. I'm a fair shot. But today I walked here, quite alone, so I could study the new blossoms along the way. Jonah will be looming over me soon enough. He means well, he's a good man, but he does insistently try to keep me from climbing the rocks—and I *must* climb them to get my samples."

"I'd be honored to escort you to the house, when you're ready, Berry. Shall I carry your satchel?"

"That won't be necessary. I am strong and hale."

He thought about offering her the use of his horse. She could ride and he could walk beside her. But he thought she would decline. She didn't like to be fussed over.

She did look the sorrel over. "You haven't introduced me to your friend."

"Ah! That is Ulysses. Three years old. A well-bred, good-natured fellow. Brave as they come."

"Ulysses! And he's a brave horse! A Homeric name for a Homeric horse." She patted the horse's neck, and he nuzzled her shoulder in return. "Oh, and affectionate too!"

"He is . . . very impressed by you. Ulysses—this is Berenice."

With Berenice walking beside him, Cleve led Ulysses over the flat rock, and back to the trail near Axle Bust Creek. The stream rushed along furiously, fed by heavy rains in the north. "Seems closer to a river than a creek," Cleve remarked.

"There has been some debate about that," Berry said. "Its riverine qualities diminish in dryer seasons. But it needs a good ford for crossing, even then. It's rocky—thus the name. Many an axle was broken in crossing it at the wrong place."

"I'm surprised they didn't put the mill close to the falls. They could have run it with a waterwheel."

"Why, it's too far from the mine. But tomorrow they begin a wooden aqueduct from the falls to the mill by the Golden Fleece. They'll divert some of the falling water into a sluice, slanted twenty degrees—it'll gather gravitational momentum to run a wheel turning the shaft for the stampers. They may reach thirty percent efficiency. When the water pressure reduces this summer, I predict they'll have to substitute a steam engine. I have recommended they blast out a recess for a millpond. They can store up more water power that way."

Cleve was impressed by her knowledge of engineering. Berry's busy mind was a force of nature.

They were quiet for a time, strolling by the old wooden placer-mining chutes; the horse clopping behind, the creek gurgling. Cleve thought he ought to tell her that he was likely to enter into a court tussle with her brother. But he was afraid she'd decide she had to go home alone, then—he'd have to leave her unescorted on the trail. Only—it wasn't that, not really. He felt himself in a curious state of grace, walking beside Berenice. It was a feeling he'd almost forgotten about. Something he'd experienced, now and then, before the war. But never since. He was reluctant to let it go.

"Leon said you'd distinguished yourself in the war with the rebels," she said suddenly. "What did you do after the war?"

Cleve sketched out the version he'd given to Leon, but he added, "I did some wandering too, I must confess. I rode with Bill Cody, for a time, scouting, and did my share of buffalo hunting. If hunting you can call it. I did some fur trapping, and lived for a season with the Paiute, along the Platte River . . ."

"Oh! Will you tell me about the experience with the Paiute? I wasn't permitted to spend much time around Indians—I long to understand them better."

"The truth is, the tribe doesn't go by 'Paiute.' They called themselves the Numu . . ." He told her some stories about his time with the Paiute, and added, "The Indian way of living is very different from ours, and yet they're very like us. If you think about it, most of us are in tribes. I was in a big tribe, the Union Army. I am in the tribe of white men who are raised by merchant farmers—and I am in the tribe of men who were raised with a church. The Sioux, the Paiute, the Shoshone, the Washoe—they see life differently, and their way of living is closer to our ancestors. But they love their children, just as we love ours; they love stories, and myth, as we do. They are inventive and resourceful." With that, he was disappointed to see they'd reached the gate outside the Conroy House—his walk with her was coming to an end. "I just want to say, Berry . . ."

He broke off, hearing a buggy approach. Duncan Conroy was driving toward them. "Here is your brother, I believe. I should say goodbye."

She glanced nervously toward her brother. "I meant to ask you how your business went with him."

Cleve's heart sank. "It did not go well. We're in dispute about mine one-seventy-one, and it may be that I will take him to court. I'm sorry about that, Berenice, I wish to do nothing to cause you distress. But you see, his partner, Les Wissel—"

Then the buggy drew up. Face like a thundercloud, Conroy interrupted Cleve, shouting, "You sir! You will remove yourself from this property!"

Conroy stopped the buggy and jumped out, the draft horse snorting and stamping its hooves as if somehow sharing its master's fury.

Before Cleve could respond, Conroy strode straight to them. He had the bearing of a man who was a whisker away from violence. He had no visible weapon—but then Cleve knew that Duncan Conroy could use other men as his weapons. As Uncle Terrence had found out.

"Berenice!" Conroy grated, his face red, his eyes flashing, as he stopped just out of arm's reach. "What lies has this mountebank been telling you!"

Mountebank? First it was *Flimflammer,* now it was *"mountebank."* Cleve felt his own anger rising; he felt it in his stiffening arms, his fisting hands. But for Berry's sake, he reined himself in. "I merely mentioned that you and I had a legal disagreement about a mine, Conroy," he said, working to keep his tone level.

"You're lying, Trewe!"

"Duncan!" Berry gasped. "This man is here as my guest. He walked me home. Jonah was not available. We spoke of science, and Mr. Trewe did not . . ."

"He will lie to you about that uncle of his," Conroy interrupted. "He'll tell you the man was attacked by my partner."

"And so he was!" Cleve snapped. He made himself mount up. Once in the saddle, he said, "Conroy—send one of your representatives to Elko. They can see his injuries. Speak to his physician."

"I asked Wissel about the matter! He says the man threatened him with a dragoon pistol!"

"Wissel is lying. Terrence possesses no such weapon! Had he a gun, why would he allow the man to beat him? It's absurd! My attorney is Mr. Caleb Drask. You will hear from him, sir."

Cleve looked down at Berry's horrified face, and his heart twisted within him. "I am sorry, that I . . ."

"Get off my land, sir!" Conroy shouted.

Cleve raised his hat to Berry, then nudged Ulysses into motion, keeping the horse's gait to a walk. He had no wish to gallop away as if he were afraid of Duncan Conroy.

"Berenice!" Conroy said, behind him. "I insist you go into the house!"

"You are not to speak to me that way, Duncan!"

Cleve wanted to look back at them, but decided it was best he didn't. It already was hard enough keeping himself cool-headed. He was feeling thrown, disoriented—for he had felt, for a little while, that he was right where he belonged in the world, simply walking with Berenice, talking to her. He was nervous with her, but very alive, and curiously contented.

Then, Conroy shattered that contentment. And now Cleve felt off-kilter, staggered in a way he hadn't felt since Fredericksburg, when so many men around him were slaughtered by the entrenched, massively defended Confederates.

How strange to be so shattered inside now, in this backwater Axle Bust Creek, just because an angry man had parted him from a woman he barely knew.

How had he come to be so vulnerable? Was he some moonstruck adolescent boy?

That mustn't happen again. He must hereafter keep his emotions well armored.

Cleve increased Ulysses' gait to a trot, then a canter, and left Conroy House behind.

"Ulysses," he said, when he was out of sight of the house, "let us have a good run, the two of us. I think we both need it."

With that, he spurred the horse into a gallop, and they raced south to the trail along Axle Bust Creek, Cleve's knuckles white on the reins.

Chapter 5

Berenice was reluctant to go to dinner. Venison with gravy, turnips, turnip greens, and yams—all of it steaming on the table, and Duncan, she knew, was waiting for her. She also knew he had been nursing a decanter of cognac, and she suspected he was still brooding about Cleveland Trewe's legal challenge on mine one-seventy-one.

Berry didn't want to argue with him about having taken a walk with Cleve, though she was still quite vexed with Duncan.

It was odd, she thought, how her brother swung like a pendulum between extremes. Sometimes Duncan would come quietly for advice and reassurance. Other times he was in a carping mood, and everything she said displeased him.

She made up her mind. She would not permit Duncan to play the tyrant. She must face up to him, once more.

Berenice looked in the oval mirror, straightening the cameo of her mother hanging on the azure ribbon around her neck. She adjusted the drapery of her hoop-skirt dinner dress, which she had put on to appease her brother. He wanted her to be "more the lady she should be." She despised modern fashions; the voluminous dresses were cripplingly impractical.

Tugging up the dress a little to negotiate the stairs without tripping, she descended to the ground floor and crossed the entry hall to the dining room. The new silver chandelier above the table was lit up, its glass-enclosed candles making the wineglasses and silver glitter. "Good evening, Duncan," she said, sitting across from him.

"Good evening," he muttered, the words half growled. He had a brandy snifter beside him, one hand on it, as he glumly studied the new chandelier.

"The chandelier looks fine, all ablaze," Berry said.

"Yes. But it's a great chore to get it all lit."

"A Mr. Joseph Swan of England has suggested we shall soon have electric lighting, requiring no flame, and no candles. He is developing something he calls the incandescence tube. As it transmits its power through wiring, candles may become quite outmoded—"

"Do stop that eccentric prattle of yours," he snapped. He closed his eyes as if weary. "Candles will always be a necessity."

"The word *prattle* is ill-chosen, Duncan," Berry said coldly. "You are prone to disrespect when you indulge in spirits."

"I've barely touched the cognac."

But Berry could hear the slur in his voice. Their father, a teetotaler, would not have approved. She fell to pondering the production of alcohol, and Pasteur's paper explaining that the generation of alcohol from fruits and grains was due to the living activity of yeast fungi. As a byproduct of single-cell metabolism was alcohol not a foul excretion? She knew better than to point this out to Duncan. Admittedly, she sometimes drank a little wine or a posset.

A fire had been made up in the dining room hearth—one

of three fireplaces in the house—and Jacob came in to serve them. He was a gangly, white-haired butler in a frock coat, staid and quiet, except when he used his free day to haunt the gaming tables in Axle. Recently, Duncan had been forced to go into town at an inconvenient hour to pay the butler's gambling debts and see to his release from the dirty little cell that Brewster called a jail. The fine was high, perhaps because Jacob had punched Brewster in the nose. "The old rascal shows his true colors when he's drunk and gambling," Duncan had observed. He'd paid the fine, though Brewster was his employee, because the money went to the town treasury, used mostly for graveling the roads.

As Jacob had served their family for a generation, they couldn't bring themselves to discharge the old man, but he was now on probation. He moved meekly about the room with the serving dish, a dull sadness in his eyes.

"Thank you, Jacob," she said, meeting his gaze and smiling as he served her.

She forced herself to eat a little of everything, so that the cook would not be insulted—Annette was touchy.

Duncan ate quickly and angrily, jabbing his fork at the food. Then he put his fork aside and took up the wineglass. "Berenice—do you value loyalty to family?"

Berry immediately knew what he was up to. But she was left no choice but to respond, "Of course."

"Then you will no longer discuss our business affairs with this conniving 'Major' Trewe!"

"I discussed nothing of the sort. Nor would I."

"I know what you think—that the mine in question is small, unimportant compared to the Golden Fleece. But one-seventy-one is my own—anyway, it belongs to me and my partner. The Golden Fleece belongs to Conroy Mining.

To father. I'm a Conroy—but I am of little significance to the company."

"Oh, not true!"

"But it is! The Golden Fleece was already well underway when father sent me out to build the mill. He already had Mike Canning supervising the miners. The mill was in blueprints. I need to show Father I can build something of my own. I . . ." He broke off, shuddering.

Berry noticed Duncan's eyes moistening, his hands clasping. One of his dark moods was settling on him. Then he shifted into anger and slapped his hand flat on the table. "You must swear to have nothing to do with that man! Nothing!"

She shrugged noncommittally. Perhaps she should simply declare she would avoid Cleveland Trewe. After all, she was not in search of a husband. Berry was content enough, for the most part, to turn her passion to botany and entomology and hydrology and astronomy. She sometimes went with Jonah to a hilltop a few miles away from the town's mists and smoke for an unblurred look at the stars and planets through her telescope. The old lawman liked to look at them too, though he understood none of her talk of orbital centricity and her theories regarding Saturn's rings.

Berry wished she were on that hilltop now.

"Come, speak up, Berenice," her brother prodded. "I saw how you looked at the man! And how he looked at you—though how he could tell you were even a woman in that grotesque outfit you wore . . ."

Berry frowned at her wineglass. She'd only had the merest sip and suddenly she wanted another. Had Cleve Trewe looked at her that way?

She could not pretend she wasn't drawn to him. He was intelligent and handsome and appeared to be genuinely interested in butterfly metamorphosis. In fact, he seemed sincerely interested in whatever she was saying. Berry suspected she could have spoken to Cleveland Trewe, quite happily, for hours. She might even have shown him the beehive. And her copy of Merian's *Metamorphosis Insectorum Surinamensium.* Someday, perhaps if they'd ridden to exercise their horses together, she would have let him kiss her. She might have . . .

Good Heavens! She was startled at the course of her own thoughts. Was all this seething in her brain since Cleve had come across her at the falls? The mating instinct was indeed insidious.

"Do you think," Duncan said, "that it was an accident he found you, out there? He was *looking* for you, Berenice. Probably hoping to enlist you to testify in court!"

"What!" The idea was ludicrous. She was more perceptive than most people—certainly more than her brother—with respect to character. She'd known immediately that Cleve was a gentleman and someone to be trusted. "He never broached the subject! Except when he saw you arrive— then, only to—"

"Ah ha!" Duncan slapped a hand on the table again. "Then he did bring it up!"

"Because I asked him how things went between the two of you! It was only a polite inquiry. And I would like to know, Duncan, how sure you are that this uncle of his was not attacked by Les Wissel! I have *met* Mr. Wissel! It was *he* who looked at me in a disrespectful way—not Cleveland Trewe."

"You, my sister, will learn to put family ahead of your fondness for . . . for an adventurer. I quite understand that you are lonely. It must be hard, being a widow, after having experienced connubial—"

"Duncan," she interrupted, in a warning tone she rarely used with him. "That is quite enough."

He glowered at her but held his peace.

Berry took up her napkin, dabbed her lips, and made to stand up—Jacob was there, pulling the chair out for her. She'd quite forgotten he was in the room. Deplorable, his having heard what Duncan had said. But doubtless Annette had heard it as well.

She sighed. "You have questioned my virtue, Duncan," she said. "I will not permit you to speak to me that way. I am going to my room now. I shall have a posset." She looked at his snifter. "Just *one*."

She marched off to the stairs, her dress rustling, and he called after her, "You did not swear that man off!"

"Oh!" She stopped with a hand on the banister and looked over her shoulder at him. "I scarcely know the man! You are possessed by one of your manias!"

"Furthermore, Berenice—you will cease your ministrations in the camp with Velma Haggerty! You two, who should be respectable ladies—calling on prostitutes! Acting as if they're worth saving!"

This in particular affronted Berry. "We are doing good works, and we shall continue them! Do calm yourself, Duncan!"

She lifted her dress, hurried up the stairs to a room, removed the hated hoop-skirts, and threw them angrily aside. They clattered against the wall.

The High Nevada was said to be Axle Bust's saloon of class and respectability. But it seemed little more than one cut above the Tom Cat, to Cleve's eye.

Cleve was drinking rye, alternating with beer; Leon was

drinking bourbon and branch water. They were sitting at the corner of the bar, so Cleve could keep an eye on the place. Wissel and Brewster could come in, hunting them.

The saloon had no wanton paintings of ladies and cats over the bar, it was true. Nor were there bargirls whispering and winking. The High Nevada's walls were covered in red velvet, imprinted with silvery flowers. Neatly spaced ornate sconces lifted oil lamps. The bar had shiny brass spittoons, and a brass footrail. The floor was some degree cleaner than most saloons.

On a small stage in a corner, a dapper gent serenaded them with "Ida Mae," in a pleasant tenor, to the accompaniment of a pianist and a fiddler. He made dramatic gestures as he sang to them. He wore a sweeping mustache, a three-piece suit the color of sulfur; his swept-back pomaded hair was parted in the middle.

An attractive lady with long, curly-blond locks tended bar with deft motions, adroitly evading grimy hands grabbing across the bar. She called herself Flora. Though her shoulders were bare, Flora's red-velvet dress's decolletage did not plunge outrageously. For one song, she stepped away from the bar to sing in a contralto voice alongside the man with the pomaded hair.

And yet—the place was occupied by the same sort of tired drunken miners and card sharps who frequented the Tom Cat.

Cleve spotted an exception: Doc Hull, in shirtsleeves and hatless, frowning down at his cards. The sleek man seated across from Hull wore a yellow top hat and a cream-colored suit; the very personification of a tinhorn gambler, to Cleve's eye.

Against the farther wall, on a special high seat, perched a chunk of a man in a straining red vest and plug hat. The saloon sentry was narrowly scanning the room; he held a gnarled club across his knees and a pistol stuck under his gray frock coat, its ivory butt peeping from just under his lapels. He was seated there mostly as a deterrent.

The air in the saloon was just as fuggy with cigar smoke as the Tom Cat, and the men's loud voices and peals of harsh laughter were rankling Cleve, who was still feeling torn and angry inside.

Why, Cleve asked himself, am I still so knocked into a cocked hat?

To distract himself, Cleve said, "Leon, that pistol you pulled, yesterday—that wasn't one of those we took from those scalawags. Was that what I think it was? With a brass frame on it?"

"It ain't brass, it's bronze."

"Is it, by God! Where'd you get it—from an archaeologist?"

"Now don't talk smart about my gun."

"The working parts are iron?"

"They are. It's a Spiller and Burr."

"I had them popped at me aplenty in the war. Confederate revolvers! Copy of a Whitney! Haven't seen one since."

"My cousin give me this one a few years back. It was his in the war. He said he shot some Yankees with it. I'm truly sorry if that offends."

"I bet a double eagle the Yankees he shot wasn't the Yankees he was aiming at."

Leon grunted. "Are you saying my Spiller and Burr ain't accurate?"

"The rebs never hit me with one!"

"Probably let the bore get rusty. Now it's a mite heavy, being iron. But I used it plenty since the war and it hits what I aim it at."

"Maybe if you're aiming up close and personal, nose to nose."

"Ha! You want to put it to a test, we'll have a target shoot! We can go down the crick and you can choose a twig to aim at. Best of six rounds, ten paces from the target."

Cleve nodded gravely. "We'll do it. Maybe tomorrow, unless there's some news from Caleb to summon us elsewhere."

He shot some Yankees with it . . .

"We never did talk about the war much," Cleve remarked.

"Good'n sufficient reasons for that, Cleve."

"Because we were across the fence from each other."

"That's right. And who wants to think about bad times, anyhow?"

Cleve nodded. "But I have one question. Doesn't matter what side you were on. Do you ever feel—well, that just about the time you've put the war behind you, it comes back somehow? Like you're still mad enough to fight—as a man is in a battle?"

"To keep on fighting Yankees?"

"To fight . . . anyone handy."

Leon took a pull on his whiskey and branch water. Then he nodded. "Yep. I do get that feeling. And it does feel like it's the war again. And nope, it doesn't matter who it is, long as I'm mad. But if I gave in to that feeling, odds are I'd-a been shot dead by now." He looked at Cleve. "You feeling that way?"

"I guess I am."

"Because you ran into Duncan Conroy?"

"That's some of it." He hadn't said much to Leon about Berenice. "I have learned not to act on every insult that comes along. But sometimes I think I should get into the fight just to burn it out of me. To work it off, like. Because if I don't . . ."

"You starting to feel kinda hair-trigger, Cleve?" He glanced at the Army Colt that Cleve had strapped on before coming to the High Nevada.

"It could be."

"That why you tied down the hog's leg?"

"After the run-ins with Wissel and Brewster and Conroy, I don't want to go unarmed." He reached for his drink—then drew his hand back. The hot recklessness coiled in him might be set free if he kept drinking.

"Well now, I reck' it's time to go back to the hotel and read some of that Tennamen."

"*Tennyson*. Alfred Lord. 'Half a league, half a league, half a league onward,'" Cleve recited. "'All in the valley of Death rode the six hundred. Forward the Light Brigade! Charge for the guns! he said! Into the valley of death rode the six hundred!'"

"Is that Tennyson? I thought it was about that King Arthur?"

"That's *Idylls of the King*. Tonight, it's the *Charge of the Light Brigade*."

"I had no notion that your Fred Tennyson was such a man of blood! I can see we better get you back to the hotel and ol' King Arthur."

"King Arthur was no slouch in a fight either."

"Come on, Cleve, let's push on out of here. I think you're halfway to drunk and that's close enough."

"Who the hell is that?" Cleve asked, staring at a man clad in buckskin at the door—a short, broad-backed man shoving a woman in ahead of him.

"*That* is Buckskin Jack," said Leon. There was some worry in his voice. "Frenchie Canuck trapper. He's a bully when he's drunk, which is most of the time that he's in town."

Buckskin Jack was grinning, pleased with himself; he had bristling, matted blond-red hair, deeply drooping gravy-colored mustaches, two days fuzz on his great chunk of chin. On his left hip was a long knife with a bone handle. Loose in his left hand was a buffalo rifle—Cleve judged it to be an 1866 Allin Springfield breech loader. Stuck in the trapper's belt, slanted across his gut, was an old Navy six-shooter.

The young woman stumbling ahead of him looked to be Asian. She wore a loose shift. Her feet were bare and muddy.

"This woman I buy from the Comfort!" crowed Buckskin, his voice heavy with a French-Canadian accent. "This woman no one touches but me!"

"No!" the girl shouted, trying to pull free. "He hurts me! No!"

"You know the girl, Leon?" Cleve asked softly, as Buckskin Jack grabbed the girl by her upper arm. Everyone had gone quiet—even the musicians. They all stared at Buckskin.

"I do not know her," Leon said. "Looks like one of the Chinese girls from the Comfort Tent. They keep 'em barefoot so it's harder to run off."

"That the place with the red stripes and the red lantern?" Cleve asked, getting off the barstool.

"That's the one."

The girl tried to bite the trapper's hand. Buckskin laughed—and backslapped her, sending her sprawling across the floor.

"I should have gone back to the hotel," Cleve said, with a sigh. He was watching the saloon sentry to see if he would intervene. The man was scowling getting off of his perch. "Maybe the bouncer's going to need someone to back his play."

Leon shook his head. "Look at that Arkansas Pigsticker ol' Buckskin's got there, Cleve. And them guns. Best leave it to the bouncer. The girl's as like to be hurt as helped if you take a hand."

She sat up, weeping. Blood trickled from her mouth. Dr. Hull walked over and squatted beside her, offering his hand. "Has he hurt you badly?" he asked.

Then Buckskin stepped in, jabbing his rifle butt at Hull—hitting him in the right shoulder, knocking the doctor onto his side. Hull cried out in pain.

"Well now!" Leon said, getting off his seat. "Dr. Hull is a friend of mine." Hull was standing now, looking dazed but intact.

"You! Jacques!" the big man with the club shouted. Apparently Buckskin Jack was Buckskin Jacques. "Take her outside! We don't want any trouble here!"

"And *you*!" Buckskin bellowed, pointing at the saloon sentry. "'Monsieur Happy Club'! You bring me a bottle of zuh finest brandy! I will take this table!"

He pointed to a table occupied by two muddy, goggling miners—who got up and hastily backed away from the table as Buckskin drew his Navy revolver. He leaned the rifle against the table and cocked the pistol.

"Monsieur Happy Club" was stalking toward Buckskin, raising the cudgel—and the Navy revolver roared. The saloon sentry staggered backward, gasping with pain, clutching at a blood-gushing hole in his side. He crashed against his own chair, splintering it, and slid to the floor, trying to get his gun free from his coat . . .

The girl was trying to crawl on all fours toward the door.

Buckskin cursed in French, and jerked her by the upper arm to her feet, making her squeak from pain.

"Buckskin Jack, vous avez fini ici!" someone shouted.

Then Cleve realized he'd shouted it himself. That hot, wound-up fury was coming uncoiled. His hand was on the butt of his Colt.

Buckskin swung toward him, startled by the challenge in French, the Navy pistol half raised—then he saw that Cleve was poised to draw the Colt Army.

"Qu'est-ce que tu m'as dit?"

Cleve chose to go on in English. "I said, *you're done in here!* You can go now. Without the girl."

"Who you now, eh?" Buckskin demanded.

"Just get out! We'll see to the girl!"

"Non! I have *buy* her! *J'ai payé beaucoup d'argent!"*

"We don't buy people anymore in this country! *Get out!"*

Buckskin was breathing hard, his eyes becoming hot red beads. Snaggled teeth bared—

And Cleve waited. He didn't want any confusion about self-defense. He saw the fur trapper aim at him—and he turned sideways, to make a smaller target as Buckskin fired. The Navy's shot cut past Cleve's belly, so close he could feel it tugging at his vest.

Then in one smooth motion, without thinking, his whole being in the act—Cleve drew his Colt and fired.

He aimed at Buckskin's heart—he might have hit him in the head, which would kill him surer, but then again, he might have missed.

Buckskin stumbled, raised the gun—and looked in surprise down at the red gushing wound over his heart. *"Merde!"*

Then he pitched over onto his face, his body spasming.

Cleve stared at the dead man through a harsh blue cloud

of gunsmoke. He let out a long breath, holstered his gun, then turned to look behind him. "Anybody hit back there?"

Two men behind him looked down at themselves and then shook their heads.

"Y'all saw Buckskin shoot first!" Leon called out. There was a general roar of assent.

Cleve heard a sobbing, a clattering, and turned to see the Chinese girl scrambling for the door.

Phin Hull was already rushing after her. "Wait, now, wait— let me examine you!" Hull called. "I won't let anyone hurt you!" He followed her outside, and Cleve hoped he caught up with her and kept her from running off into the wilderness.

Where else had she to go?

"You know, Cleve," Leon remarked, pointing at Jacque's pistol, "that fight was Army versus Navy."

"So it was. Army's always going to win."

"Now there I agree with you. But one time a sailor and I disagreed—this was in Houston, and he . . ."

Cleve couldn't make out the rest of what Leon was saying due to the hooting and hollering in the bar, as the men got over their shock and reacted to the gunfight. Flora was shouting for the Doctor to come back and help Daniel, who must be the wounded saloon sentry.

"I suppose the Doc should have tended to the wounded man first," Leon said, stepping up beside Cleve.

"Doc's coming back in," Cleve said, nodding toward the front door.

Doc Hull was leading the barefoot girl gently back into the saloon, her hand loosely in his. She looked exhausted and as scared as before. He took her to a chair at his own table, and gestured for her to wait. Then he grabbed his doctor's bag tucked under it and brought it to the groaning saloon sentry. "Move aside, and I'll patch him up enough we can get him to my office."

The bartender brought the Chinese girl a glass of water, and sat down with her. Most of the other men were crowding around to watch the doctor.

Cleve turned back to the bar, and found his drink. He drank the rest of it off. A couple of miners slapped him on the back as he bantered about the gunfight. The reek of gun smoke mixed with cigar smoke. Blood spread across the floor. Cleve hoped he had done right. He might've endangered the girl's life by intervening. But there was something larger to think of.

"Let's go, Leon," Cleve muttered. "There's no law in Axle, no one to take our statement. Maybe I'll send a letter to the county sheriff. Tell him what happened." Then a thought struck him. He dug in his vest pocket, and found a twenty-dollar gold piece. He held it up and shouted, "This is to pay for Buckskin Jack's burial!"

Cleve clapped the gold on the bar and hurried out of the High Nevada, Leon close behind. Their boots made hollow thumps on the wooden walk as they struck off toward the hotel.

A soft rain cooled the back of Cleve's neck. The night seemed quieter than usual. They could hear the waterfalls swishing and murmuring.

"We should get us our own place, somewheres," Leon said. "If we're going to get that mine back, we'll be here some time. There's always a miner leaving town, selling a cabin . . ."

"Yes," said Cleve. The word sounded dead in his ears. A yes with no life in it.

"Say now, Caleb said there's the question of gold already

taken out of your uncle's mine. How much is there, and how do we reclaim it?"

Cleve cleared his throat. "Cross that bridge when we come to it." He realized Leon was trying to divert his mind from the gunfight. Must be he looked awful grim.

"You know, Cleve, that Buckskin Jack—it's thought he killed a squaw woman he married. He says she run off, but it's fair-certain he killed her. You probably saved that China girl's life, Cleve."

"Saving one life by ending another . . ." He had never liked ending a man's life. But some men needed killing. And sometimes Cleve seemed called to do it.

He wished he knew who to go to, so he could tell them stop calling.

Chapter 6

A fog clung to the rutted road the next morning, as Cleve and Leon went into the hotel and knocked on Dr. Hull's door. "Phin, it's Cleve and Leon!"

Hull called out, "Come on in, gentlemen!"

Cleve opened the door to Hull's office and they found the physician administering laudanum to the wounded saloon sentry. Shirtless and much bandaged, "Monsieur Happy Club" was propped up on an elbow to drink down the dose. His legs were somewhat overlong for the low cot against the wall. Groaning, he lay back and closed his eyes. On an iron surgical stand beside the examination table was a bottle of boiled water and spirits for cleansing wounds and a steel bowl containing a bloodied scalpel.

Cleve looked around for the Chinese girl—he felt some responsibility for her, after what had happened, but he didn't see her.

"How's Daniel, there, Doc?" Leon asked.

"I have tried to remove the bullet, but it was not possible. It lodged close to the celiac trunk artery. I have administered a second dose of laudanum—a heroic dose—and once he is sufficiently at ease, I may try again."

Daniel the saloon sentry lay there with one arm extended,

mouth open, eyes shut, mumbling, slightly twitching. As Cleve watched the wounded man seemed to quiet some.

"I thought to run into you boys this morning 'round the hotel," said Hull, corking the laudanum bottle. "I had to stay there myself last night to keep the tongues from wagging. I gave Mei Ying my bed last night." He took a metal dish from a small table, adjusted his chair, and sat down.

"We had a talk with Caleb Drask early this morning. Is the lady still here?"

"She is. I brought her some breakfast, which she lit into quick, a little while ago, in my bedroom."

"How tongues will wag," Leon chuckled.

Dr. Hull snorted. "No one need suppose I would lie with a prostitute." He put the bottle on its medicine shelf. "As a physician, I know better. I have seen the ravages of the pox. God send that we may have a better way to treat it, one day."

"*Is* she poxed, Doc?" Leon asked in a hushed voice.

"For a purported soiled dove, she's mighty modest. She would not permit me to examine her closely where the examination was most needed. Hence—I do not know. Even with a close look, one cannot be sure if they're clean of syphilis." He turned to Cleve. "But that beast you put down manhandled her so badly her shoulder was dislocated. I had a time persuading her to let me set it right."

"She speaks English then?" Cleve asked.

"Very little. I had to explain with gestures."

"Caleb speaks some Chinese. He said he would come by and speak to her for you."

"That will be a great relief. She may choose to run off at any time. I have no right to stop her but I hope to find her some better place to go to . . ."

A knock on the door announced Caleb Drask.

Ushered in, Caleb shook hands with Hull, whom he knew quite well. "Phin—is she still here?"

"She is. Her name is Mei Ling. At least I think that was it. You speak her language?"

"If she's Chinese, I can manage a good deal of Cantonese and some Mandarin too."

"She's in there, finishing her meal. Go to the door and call out to her in Chinese and head on in. She's fully dressed."

Caleb crossed to the door, called something in Chinese. There was no response—he opened it, and through the open doorway they all saw Mei Ling poised halfway out the open window. She had a sling on one arm, and she was cleaner than she'd been the night before, but her feet were still bare. A chill wind blew in, fluttering the curtains as Caleb spoke gently to her in Chinese. Crouched in the window, she hesitated, turning Caleb a bewildered look. Then she spoke, and he answered, shaking his head and smiling. He dropped to his knees, spread his hands, and looked her in the eyes. Then he spoke again.

She looked past him at the others and saw Cleve. Their eyes met. He took off his hat and smiled, nodded to her.

Cleve's presence seemed to close the deal. She climbed back into the room and closed the window with one hand. After an uncertain moment, she sat on the edge of the bed and looked curiously at Caleb. She seemed small and fragile and very young.

Caleb stood up, and bowed to her, as if in gratitude. He glanced back at the doctor. "How badly hurt is she, Phin?"

"Just some swelling, a little bruising. I gave her a dose of acetylsalicylic acid."

"*What* acid did he say?" Leon asked.

Cleve nudged Leon. "It's willow bark, Leon."

"Oh sure, we used that back at Fort Slocum!"

"I expect her arm will heal in a few days," Hull said.

The girl was watching them warily. Cleve said, "Caleb—

ask her if it's true she was sold to Buckskin Jack. If he actually bought her, for keeps, like a slave of old."

Caleb spoke to her again in Chinese. She responded. The exchange took several minutes. Daniel, unconscious now, was snoring softly.

Then, Caleb turned back to the other men. His face was clouded with anger. "It's true! Mei Ling says she was stolen from her family, taken from a camp outside Virginia City. The kidnappers brought her here, and tried to force her to serve men at the Comfort Tent. She bit the madame, who beat her for it—but still Mei Ling refused. They tried to give her opium, and she wouldn't have it. They were going to start whipping her when in came this fur trapper, offering to buy her off them. I guess it must have been good money, and they thought it easier than having to break her."

Cleve nodded. He had seen countless men die to free the slaves. Yet there were those who still practiced slavery. The thought made fury coil up in him again. "It shouldn't be tolerated here or anyplace else."

"We could go to the county sheriff about it," said Leon.

"Why, every time he's in town, Sheriff Purslow's over there partaking of those girls himself!" Caleb said, snorting.

Cleve asked, "These men who kidnapped her—does she know their names?"

Caleb asked her if she knew their names. Mei Ling frowned, shook her head—then said one name. "Dev-ro-aw... Dev-row-a?"

"Devora?" Cleve asked. "Vern Devora?"

She nodded vigorously and added something in Chinese.

Caleb grunted. "She says he was the biggest man she ever saw and the hair was missing on one side of his head. Scarred on that side of his scalp. Lot of dirty black beard."

"I've heard of a Vern Devora that was robbing the

Chinese, in Colorado," Cleve mused. "He left pretty quick when word got out. Any of you boys know him?"

The others looked at one another and shook their heads. Hull said, "I would surely have noticed him. Caleb . . . I have some rather delicate medical questions to ask her. Can you translate for me?"

He described certain symptoms of syphilis, and Caleb, stammering a little, translated. Shaking her head, Mei Ling spoke English. "No. That no." She said something else in Chinese and looked shyly at the floor.

Caleb said, "She says she's a virgin. She was to bring a great price for the first time she was used, but then they chose to sell her."

Leon growled to himself and said, "Then Buckskin brought her into the High Nevada to show her off. Like as not meant to use one of the rooms upstairs."

Mei Ling spoke up again. Caleb said, "She wants to know if she can go. But I've already asked—she doesn't know where she's going. She just wants to get away from this town."

"I do not blame her for that," Cleve said.

"Does she have any notion where her folks are?" Leon asked.

Caleb turned to Mei Ling and after another lengthy conversation in Chinese, he said, "She does not know. They were from Sacramento. They were on their way to some place in Kansas. She does not know where exactly."

Yet another knock at the door to the office. Hull shook his head. "We'll be crowded out of here soon. I'll have to set up shop on the roof." He crossed to the outer door, murmuring, "I hope there hasn't been another mining accident."

Hull opened the door and seemed surprised to see two ladies waiting there. They were in casual walking dresses, and button-up shoes, kid gloves, and simple hats, minimally decorated . . .

And one of them was Berenice.

"Good morning, Doctor Hull," she said. "Might we speak to the girl in your care, if you please?"

"He shot Buckskin Jack in the High Nevada, did he?" Duncan Conroy drank a little more coffee. It seemed to ease his hangover. "Well, Brewster—then this man Trewe is a public menace. We can't have gunslingers disturbing the peace!"

Brewster shook his head doubtfully, making a grumbling sound in his throat that sounded almost like words. But Duncan couldn't make out what the words were.

They were sitting in the parlor of Conroy House, having coffee and sweet rolls. Finally, Brewster said, "These here sweet rolls are powerful good. That Annette who cooks for you—is she married?"

"She is not but you can forget about her. Now are you going to run this Cleveland Trewe out of town or aren't you?"

"Boss, Wallis, over at the High Nevada, says that Buckskin fired first and the whole place saw it that way. Flora too. Everybody who knew the man was glad to see him cut down."

"Makes no difference. Trewe can't go around executing town merchants."

"Merchants? Is that what Buckskin was?"

"He sold his furs here, did he not?"

"Maybe so. And I'd love nothing more, boss, than to run that Trewe out of town. And that man Studge with him and Lawyer Drask too. They were snooty with me out at the one-seventy-one. Studge pulled a pistol on me! But Trewe and his bunch hold that I'm not officialized to be law here. I don't think they're going to take me serious-like."

"You ran that Hank Gwynn out of town for public disturbance, you can do it with Trewe."

"Hank Gwynn is weak in the knees. He took but a nudge. This man Cleveland Trewe's not going anywhere unless maybe a posse takes him into custody."

"Can we not get a posse up?"

"For this? You can't compel a man to be a posse. They all measure him a hero. At least—he's a dangerous man."

"There! You are truly afraid of him!"

Brewster looked at Duncan with a puzzled frown, as if the thought hadn't occurred to him before. "Afraid of him? Why—only if I'm afraid of a grizzly bear. And I am. One time I saw a grizzly claw a man's face right off his headbones. Now this man Trewe—he has a reputation out of Colorado. He was some kind of law out there and shot some fellas who were trying to assassinate him. I came at him with my shotgun—and he didn't bat an eye. He's game, I'll say that. And I saw Buckskin's body. Trewe put a hole right through that Canuck's heart. One clean shot."

"Don't mince words, Brewster. You're running scared of him."

Brewster pointed a half-eaten sweet roll at Duncan. "I think the word—is prudent." He nodded, satisfied with the word. "My ma liked that word. I am *prudent*. But—how's about this!—the County Sheriff could run him out! You could tell the sheriff this Trewe is a claim jumper. Maybe he's a confidence man too. Many a one-time lawman has gone bad. When he come into town, way I heard it, he had a wounded man with him. Fella with a bullet in him, named Digley. Trewe took him right to Doc Hull, got him patched up. This Digley is a known confidence trickster. If Trewe was giving him aid and comfort, why, they must be pardners! Maybe they were together to try to steal that one-seventy-one claim from you!"

Having made this substantial speech, Brewster crammed the rest of the sweet roll into his mouth and set to champing.

Duncan absently turned his coffee cup all the way around on its delicate blue-china plate. "It's not so easy to get Sheriff Purslow all the way over to Axle Bust," he said, thinking aloud. "Unless he's looking for a night to howl where the Elko voters can't see him. But I'll get him here. The Mayor of Elko is an investor in the Golden Fleece. We will see that Purslow gets rid of this Cleveland Trewe, one way or another."

"In the meantime—I know a couple boys would be good to have on hand, with this Trewe around. If you'll pay them good."

"Gunfighters?"

Brewster shrugged his shoulders noncommittally. "Special Deputies."

"Very well. Hire them."

"They're right here in town. I'll get 'em badges right away . . ."

Three big cargo wagons arrived in Axle Bust that morning, overfull with freight covered in canvas, creaking ponderously along. Two were pulled by oxen, the third by a team of six stout horses.

Coming downstairs from the crowded doctor's suite, Cleve was struck by the din of merchants unloading the import wagons. He and Leon stood on the sidewalk, admiring the bustling activity. Dust rose behind the clattering incoming wagons. Wives in bonnets haggled with drummers. Workers unloaded wagons, talking loudly with one another as they toted boxes and barrels.

There were no real farms near Axle Bust and few artisans. A miner with a family on the edge of town had two acres where cows grazed and chickens pecked about. He was able to provide some fresh milk, and some eggs—not enough and at an exorbitant price. The town did have a gunsmith, a leather worker, two blacksmiths, and several carpenters— though most of those men were miners part time. Most goods, apart from lumber, had to be freighted in from Tuscarora or Elko.

"That fella there's the mayor of Axle," Leon said, pointing at a merchant wearing gartered shirt sleeves and a mustache that merged with his side-whiskers.

The mayor scribbled in an accounts ledger as two hired men lugged crates and barrels from the back of a wagon. A bearded bullwhacker stood beside him, rocking on his heels and tapping his whip on his hip as he awaited pay.

"And what's this mayor's name?"

"Silas Haggerty, owns Haggerty's Mercantile. Also took a bit of gold out of the Happy Day Mine. That played out, but the mercantile's the real gold mine. There was some kind of vote taken for mayor—leastways, some people got around to voting. I wasn't here then, and I don't know what mayoring he does. Precious little, be my guess."

Two riders, leading donkeys laden with miners' supplies rode close by, passing a heavy wagon pulling broken cap rock to the tailings, its oxen grunting with effort. Coming the other way was a wagon pulled by four horses, loaded high with planks fresh from the sawmill. Cleve could smell the fresh-cut wood, along with the droppings of the oxen and horses and, when the nimble wind changed, a scent of pine from the hills.

A voice, speaking at Cleve's elbow, was almost lost in the rattle of tackle and the voices of the merchants. "Good morning, Cleve," Berenice said. "Might we pass?"

Startled, he turned to see her standing beside two smaller women; one was Mae Ling, looking considerably more hopeful than she had. The other was a short, broad-waisted woman of perhaps forty; she had sausage-curled brown hair framing her round face; a pert nose, pointed chin, and snapping black eyes projected an inquisitive alertness.

Caleb Drask was waiting behind the ladies. He seemed amused by Cleve's unease. "Cleve," he said gesturing to the brown-haired woman in the bustled dress, "this is Mrs. Velma Haggerty. She and Berenice are going to purchase shoes and a few other things for Mei Ling. The girl will be staying with the Haggertys for a time."

"That is something my husband does not yet know," Mrs. Haggerty said, speaking rapidly and confidently, lifting her chin. "It will be a *fait accompli*, and he shall accept it, and we shall all do very well."

Cleve took off his hat. "Ladies." He and Leon stepped aside so there was room to pass down the sidewalk to the east. "Good morning, Mrs. Tucker," he said, nodding to Berry as she passed. After what had happened at Conroy House, he no longer felt empowered to call her by her Christian name.

She nodded back—and he saw emotion flash in her eyes, the set of her lips.

What emotion? He wasn't sure.

Cleve watched the women, trailed by Caleb, walk off down the sidewalk. He told himself to put Berenice out of his thoughts. But he kept watching her.

Then he shook his head.

I am doomed, he thought, chuckling sadly to himself.

"Caleb was supposed to be off to Elko on our business, instead of mooning over that China girl," said Leon, as they walked by the Tom Cat. They were on their way to look for vacant cabins.

"He's being a help to the ladies," Cleve said.

"He's lingering over it so's he can moon over that girl."

"I'll speak to him about going to the courthouse . . ." Cleve stopped in front of the Tom Cat, glimpsing through the saloon's only front window a crowd that seemed too large for the early hour. Everyone was raptly watching a man standing on a poker table and waving his arms.

"Now what the dickens," Leon muttered, beside him.

"Let's find out what the dickens," Cleve said.

They went inside, and stood near the door, hearing the stocky, clean-shaven man on the poker table bellowing, "They cannot suppose we will work for a pittance and a spit in the eye!" He wore a miner's coveralls, but Cleve noticed his clean, soft-looking hands.

"They not only suppose it, they know it!" cackled out a gray-bearded middle-aged man, cupping his mouth with his hand. "Hell, they throw in the spit for free!"

The others laughed. The orator scowled. "Make a mock, Sam Helsey! But the Golden Fleece could pay the miners double what they outlay now and still make a passel of money for the Conroys!"

There was a spatter of applause at that, and some murmurs of agreement.

Cleve nodded. It was true that most company miners were underpaid. Safety in the Golden Fleece worried Cleve even more. The more gold to be found in a big mine, the more greed. The more greed, the more haste in the mine's operations. The more haste, the greater the risk of dire accident. And a throng of miners crowded into those little spaces raised the spectre of disease. Consumption was common in big mines. Many a tubercular miner in Virginia City was carried out on a litter, spitting blood.

"I wonder, do the Conroys know about this meetin', Cleve?" Leon whispered.

"These men would most likely be at work now. The boss must've noticed their absence. They'll figure something's up. Who's the man standing on the table?"

"Don't know him. Don't seem like no miner to me."

"I'd be for a union if it could work, Tolliver!" called a man Cleve couldn't see on the other side of the room. But now he knew that Tolliver was the orator's name. "If a man goes on strike, there's always someone to take his place!"

"That's true—if that's the only move you make!" Tolliver thundered, smacking a fist into his open palm. "But some unions have gotten tougher and gotten their price! We might need to take up arms! There's many a deed can be done in the dead of night that will make them penny-squeezin' mine owners think!"

"You men are all about to lose your job!" Brewster hollered, coming in the front door. He had shined up his brass constable's badge, and it caught the lantern light. He stopped a couple strides into the room. Not seeing Cleve and Leon, against the wall behind him, Brewster jabbed a stubby finger toward Tolliver. "That fool up there—Thaddeus Tolliver—he's a liar! He's going to cost you all your jobs unless you leave here quick as a wink! We're missing most of our workers today thanks to this meeting, and we're not going to stand for it! Now anyone who wants to stay on at the Golden Fleece, get out and get to the mine! Anybody else is fired! That's the message I came with, and I didn't come alone! These men are Special Deputies!"

Stepping up into view to either side of Brewster came two men carrying double-barrel shotguns. One was a tall, swarthy man in a sheepskin jacket; he had a greasy black beard and a barrel chest. What caught Cleve's interest was the absence of hair on the right side of his head. Rough white and yellow scars showed where the scalp and his right eyebrow had been burned away. His right eye had an extra hood of skin, as if the burn had made his flesh run like candlewax. His eyes seemed hard as flint in their deep sockets.

Cleve stared. Could this be the man Mae Ling had described? Was it indeed Vern Devora?

The other man couldn't be more different, with his neatly cut suit, his bowler hat, his clean-shaven, sardonic expression and barbered sandy-blond hair. There was a professionalism in the way he held his shotgun; it was steady in his hands, aimed at the floor but ready to swing into action. Cleve figured him for a hired gun, the sort he'd seen working as enforcers on steamboat casinos.

"I am sure these gentlemen know a good thing from a bad one," the man with the sandy blond hair said cajolingly. His purring Richmond drawl, and that smirk—he was familiar to Cleve. "Now a good job's a fine thing, gents! And a union gets a man into deep water and gets himself run off without a coin in his poke! Ya'll are surely not such fools!"

"Why that's Clay Hortlander," Leon whispered, leaning close to Cleve. "He was at Slocum."

Cleve nodded. Lieutenant Hortlander, Confederate prisoner of war. Cleve had been forced to discipline him more than once. He had been leaner and bearded, back then. Hortlander had a pistol along with the shotgun; a small black-gripped revolver, holstered aslant over his waist for a cross-draw.

Brewster muttered to his Special Deputies, "Move aside, let them out." He and the two shotgun-wielding deputies stepped out of the way. The majority of the miners, looking fixedly anywhere but at the gunmen, began trickling past them out the door. Most went silently, hands in their pockets. Tolliver was climbing down off the table.

Watching Tolliver's face, Cleve thought he saw a crafty satisfaction there, as if things had in some mysterious fashion gone his way after all. Tolliver moved toward the back entrance, patting arms, murmuring reassurances, trading winks with some of the miners as he went.

Cleve thought maybe it'd be best if he and Leon slipped out too. But he had a gut feeling about the man with half a scalp.

About six miners remained in a small group near the bar, taking heatedly in low tones, glancing darkly from time to time at Brewster.

"Those boys there," Brewster said, talking to Hortlander as he glowered at the remaining miners, "are fellers that tried to work mines and failed. Because they didn't have the spine to do the work. No, they just give up and started crying 'O what shall I do now?' So they come to the Golden Fleece and begged for a job. We can do without 'em."

"I expect you're right at that, Constable," said Hortlander, grinning maliciously at the miners. "But the sight of those sniffling old women pretending to be working men . . ." He shook his head. "It offends me." He let a hand fall to the grip of his pistol.

The miners looked at Hortlander, looked at one another—and then went out the back door.

Brewster and his deputies burst into laughter and went to the bar to order drinks. The Special Deputies leaned the shotguns against the bar.

Cleve glanced around. The only other men remaining in the saloon were three poker players who'd scarcely looked up from their cards.

"What you think about miners' unions, Major?" Leon asked, in a whisper.

"I'll tell you," Cleve said softly. "I believe that any man who isn't getting a fair deal, he's got a right to organize and ask for better. Sometimes it works, sometimes it doesn't. I will not condemn it. But what Tolliver was talking about . . . taking up arms." Cleve had watched the Special Deputies closely as they leaned their shotguns against the bar. "'Deeds in the dead of night,' he says. I've seen that too. That'll give the bosses an excuse to bring hell down on the organizers. And I have to wonder what Tolliver is . . ."

He broke off, as Hortlander—hearing the murmur of voices—glanced around and spotted Cleve and Leon. Recognition lifted Hortlander's eyebrows. "Why that's Major Trewe! And his pet Reb, little Leon!"

"Trewe?" Brewster turned around and spotted Cleve standing against the wall with Leon. "Trewe! What do you want here? Was it you who called that meeting?"

"Not me, Brewster," Cleve said. "I suppose it was this man Tolliver. Now I have a question for this 'Special Deputy' of yours." He cocked a finger at the man who just might be Vern Devora. "You, sir. Your name Vern Devora?"

The man's mouth tightened to vanish into his beard. One hand went to a Remington .44 holstered on his left hip. Then he seemed to think better of it—and let the hand drop. "My name's Morgan!" he said, in a raspy voice. "Abraham Morgan."

"I've seen a circular on a man fitting your friend Morgan's description, Brewster," Cleve said. "Name of Vern Devora. Had to leave Cripple Creek, under suspicion of robbery and abduction." Cleve was sure now this was Devora. The way the mention of his name had almost made him draw his gun . . .

Brewster gave Devora and uneasy glance. "His name is Morgan. He's a Special Deputy. That's all you need to know."

"The Major there," Hortlander said, "always makes it a point to get in other folks' business."

Brewster said, "Trewe—you are under arrest! We got a

special room, used to be for storing whiskey. Good locks, thick walls. You're going to cool your heels in there till Sheriff Purslow can pick you up for shooting a man dead in the High Nevada."

"That was a fair fight," Leon said. "More than fair. Cleve let him get off a shot. Everyone saw it. And everyone thanked him for doing what he did."

"Makes no difference what you think, Little Leon," Hortlander said. He reached for the cross-draw gun.

"You touch that gun, I'll kill you, Hortlander," Cleve said, in a mild but clearly articulated voice.

Hortlander's hand stopped moving. Some of his arrogance left his eyes. Cleve's certainty had thrown him off.

"Brewster," Cleve said, "I'll see Sheriff Purslow, if he comes. But I won't be going anywhere with you. I'm not working for the Conroy Company—so I have no business with you."

The men at the bar, sensing violence in the air, were watching the confrontation. And Cleve was reasonably sure while they and the bartender were watching, no one would shoot him in the back.

Reasonably sure, he told himself, is not sure enough, when it comes to being shot down. But he wasn't going to back out the door.

Cleve turned and walked toward the front door, Leon beside him.

"Trewe!" Brewster called. "Come back here, damnit!"

Cleve ignored him. He took his time leaving.

It was a strangely long walk to the door and outside into the sunshine. Six steps seemed to take minutes instead of seconds.

But at last they were clear. Cleve turned left so they wouldn't have to pass in front of the window.

"Hell, I thought the ball was going to open in there, Cleve."

"That's why we left. If I have to kill Brewster and his Special Deputies, it'd look pretty bad."

Leon chuckled. "There was three of them. One of them would've probably shot you."

"That too would have been an inconvenience," Cleve said blandly. As he'd hoped, it made Leon laugh.

"It's kind of curious, first you meet me nigh here and then we run into Clay Hortlander. All of us knowing each other."

"I saw Mick Stazza too here. It's not so strange. Not so many people in the west as in the east. And there aren't so many places men with itchy feet wander to, in a time of gold and silver fever. I saw a good many I knew from Denver in Virginia City."

Leon glanced back. "They're not following us. But they could go out the back and flank us."

"I don't think they will. Brewster figures the County Sheriff's going to take care of it. He hasn't got the guts to try it himself."

"You got more confidence in Brewster's sense than I do. How about we cut to the left at the alley here, and head north, see if we can find those cabins. Then we can see if they're flankin' us."

Cleve nodded and they turned into the next alley, walked toward the falls. And saw no one coming from the saloon.

"If the Sheriff doesn't arrest you," Leon observed, "them Special Deputies will bide their time and shoot you in the back."

"You are a sad old worrywart, Leon. If the work's getting too warm for you around here, I won't blame you at all if you light out for a more peaceful burg."

Leon stopped on the sidewalk and stared at him.

Cleve came to a stop and turned to him. "I meant no offense."

"Didn't you just say I was a coward?"

"I did not! I just thought you might be smarter than me. Wise enough to get out of the gunsights of back-shooters and the like."

Leon looked at him with narrowed eyes. And then he grinned. "Nope, I'm just as much an idjit as you are. Let's go find us a snug place to bunk."

Chapter 7

For two weeks, when not prospecting with Leon, Cleve returned to the pool by the falls nearly every morning in hopes of espying Berenice there. On every visit, Cleve watched as dragonflies darted over the foaming pool; butterflies chased one another in their bright erratic courses; one morning a bald eagle sat on a rock overlooking the falls, till diving down, tugging a fish from the pool, and flapping off with it. The rainbows came and went in the rising mist. But Berenice was not to be seen.

Not till this morning. He rode up to find her wading in the pool, bent almost double to stare into the water. Her hair trailed down haphazardly from her bonnet. She was lifting her skirts high up a little above her knees, to keep the hems dry. He was not surprised to see how beautiful her legs were.

She was, however, surprised to catch him admiring them.

"Oh!" She dropped her skirts, then scowled as they went into the water.

"Didn't mean to startle you, Berry!" he called. "Just this second saw you."

"Just this second was quite long enough, it appears," she said, her voice barely audible over the rushing of the falls. She sloshed her way out of the water, her skirts trailing wetness on the stone bank, her bare feet leaving tracks. He watched raptly as she reached up to tuck her hair back more neatly into her bonnet.

"I suppose you could sit on that flat boulder over there and dry the skirts in the sun," he said, getting down off his horse.

"Wet skirts are the price of closely observing the life cycles of minnows and frogs," she said mildly, settling on the low boulder and reaching down to spread her skirts in the sun. "There is a fine profusion of tadpoles in there, some just emerging from the frog's eggs. The small fish feed voraciously on the eggs, but they are so many an abundance survive to become adult frogs." Her casual tone in speaking about such things seemed perfectly conversational, without a hint of lecturing. She could be a gardener lightly discussing the weather.

He led Ulysses over to her. It might be wiser to bid her goodbye, considering his encounter with her brother. But she didn't seem at all discomfited or worried, and he couldn't help but try prolonging the meeting. "Sometimes I think nature is wasteful, with how many creatures are born, only to die, to be fed on . . . or just returned to the soil. Evolution throws a wide loop."

"But every organism finds a use, one way or another." She glanced up at him, a bit self-consciously. Her wet feet were small and charming, and he looked quickly away. "Cleve—I'm sorry about my brother's reception of you, at the house. But be assured, he is not my master." She went on quickly, "I saw Leon the other day, at the mercantile. He tells me you two have taken a cabin up on the hillside."

"We have. Just one of those places that will do for a while. But not a long while."

He stood awkwardly beside her, with Ulysses close, the horse snuffling inquiringly at her. She smiled and stroked the soft skin above his nostrils. "Good morning, Ulysses! What a fine fellow you are. You have yet to meet my horse."

Was that an opening to ask her to go on a ride with him? He was about to hazard it, when she said, "Jonah is somewhere about. He's here for the day. Right now, he's probably watching you like a hawk, Cleve."

Cleve looked around. "I don't see him."

"He's up on those rocks, above us."

He shaded his eyes and saw the silhouette of a man, about seventy feet above, wearing a campaign hat and a coat that was too warm for the day. He had a rifle cradled in his arms.

"I'd best not make any sudden moves," Cleve said, only half-joking. He took a step back from Berry, and touched his hat to the figure on the rocks. The watchman did not respond.

"He won't shoot you unless you need shooting," she said, sounding amused.

Cleve had been considering sitting down next to her, engaging in some chat, and possibly asking if he might kiss her. She seemed very relaxed with him, even comfortable. And when they'd walked together, the last time, there had been that unspoken intimacy . . .

But glancing up again at Jonah, he decided this was not the time.

Anyway, he was getting ahead of himself, thinking about kissing her now. They'd only met twice before. Perhaps it was the sight of her bare legs that had sparked the notion; the profile of her rapt face, when she'd bent over, examining the life of the pool; the reflected light rippling across her lips.

Odd that how she quickened his pulse more than any other woman he'd met. He had been around some voluptuous, beautiful women in his time. They'd had a decided effect. But this woman, in her plain bonnet and her wet calico dress . . .

She glanced up, caught him staring at her, and he said, hastily, "I, ah, saw an eagle here, yesterday, fishing up above."

She nodded. "*Haliaeetus leucocephalus*—northern sea eagles. They migrate and stop over here. There are splendid raptors in this country—the white-tailed eagle, the red-tailed hawk. Why are you staring at me with that puzzled intensity, pray?"

"I—was I?" He had been watching her rosy lips moving as she spoke. "I'm sorry."

She smiled faintly. "It's all right. I was just curious."

"It's a bit difficult for me to . . . take my eyes off you."

"Was that meant as a sort of courtship compliment?" she asked. Still smiling. Still behaving as if she were merely curious.

"Just . . . the truth of the matter."

He glanced up at the rocky ledge above. Jonah hadn't moved.

"Won't you sit down, Cleve?" she said. "I do not own this rock. I think there's enough room on it that Jonah won't be tempted to fire a warning shot."

He grinned at that, and sat down at the other end of the boulder. Ulysses stepped closer, and nuzzled her neck. She gave a small laugh of delight and stroked under the horse's jaw.

Cleve said, "I think Ulysses is about to throw me over and ask for a job with you."

"My horse is hobbled with Jonah's, downstream in the cottonwoods. But I don't suppose we'll manage to introduce my mare to your stallion today. She's in heat. The timing would be gauche. Is Ulysses a working horse? Cattle drives and such?"

"He works hard enough carrying me. I didn't have him when I went on the only drive I ever worked—I was always on one of the little cow ponies from the remuda."

"Leon didn't include your life as a cowboy in his biography of you!"

"I didn't tell him, because he's been a real cowboy, and I was but a dilettante. Never was a cowboy but for those three months, working for Charles Goodnight, trailing the herd from Texas to Colorado."

"I have heard it's a rough job, and dangerous."

"Can be. Long days in the saddle. We had a dust storm that fair blinded me. Apaches cut out some of our beeves and shot me in the hip with an arrow when I tried to get the stock back."

"Oh! You were far from a physician on the trail!"

"It wasn't a bad wound, and I was back in the saddle in two days. Then we ran short of water. Drought year, do you see. I went on the trip thinking I might want to be a cattleman— but I abandoned the notion."

"A *sage* decision." Berry smiled at her own pun.

He chuckled. "I did my job, I'll say that for myself. I learned skills I've used many times—but soon as I got paid, why, I found I was in Denver and set myself to losing my money at a surprising rate of speed."

"So you're a gambler then?"

"No, a real gambler wins fairly often. I don't do it much anymore, but to amuse my friends. Mostly doing some prospecting with Leon, and . . . well . . ." He didn't want to bring up the subject of his legal conflict with her brother.

"Berenice!" called a gruff voice from above. "It's time! The ladies will be callin' for you!"

"The voice of God from above," Cleve said.

"Oh, he's just one of the minor pantheon," Berry said. "Or perhaps, after all, he's like his namesake, an Old Testament patriarch. He really is my good friend, however." She reached out and absentmindedly wrung out a wet pleat in her dress. I am having Mrs. Haggerty and Teresa McCarthy to lunch, so I must obey Jonah. I . . ." She hesitated. "I am glad you came, though you caused me to get my skirts into the pond, Cleveland Trewe. I'm glad you do not take Duncan too seriously."

He wasn't at all sure he shouldn't take Duncan seriously. But he smiled and offered his hand to help her rise. Berry took it, and let her hand linger in his for a moment. She met his eyes, and seemed to search his face for something. Then she dropped her hand and said, "I'd best go."

"I hope to see you again, Berry," he said, on impulse.

She smiled. "That was the right thing to say, Cleveland Trewe." She lifted her skirts just above her ankles and walked off toward the shoes she'd left by the pool.

Cleve let out a long, ragged breath. He mounted Ulysses, and rode off, whistling an old tune as he went.

Whistling a tune was something he almost never did.

Chapter 8

The drafty cabin wasn't so bad, until the rains commenced again.

"I knew we should've patched that roof," Leon said, as he picked up one of the empty nail kegs they used as rain buckets and carried it to the door to empty onto the muddy ground outside. The rain persisted, coming in sweeping surges, rattling the flimsy wooden shingles overhead.

"You knew we should patch the roof," Cleve said. "But you didn't offer to do the patching." He sat on the edge of his cot, in a dry corner of the cabin's only room, employing a slender metal brush to clean his guns. The corner was dry, but the cot was still damp. He'd had to move it here when rain started dripping onto it, in the night.

"I was going to suggest we both take a hand on that roof!" Leon declared, as he pushed the keg back in place, under one stream from the ceiling, and went to empty a keg under another stream. "But then I got into that card game with the damnable Q.T. Harte. He being a villainous sneak with cards—never giving away a thing, damn him—I naturally was bamboozled and sidetracked from practical matters." He emptied the other keg out the front door.

Q.T. Harte, who declined to give out what Q.T. stood for, lived in a small wooden house next door. He had managed a slate roof, to Cleve's considerable envy; the overlapping stones were tarred at the edges, so the roof did not leak. Harte was a sometime-miner and a sometime journalist. The main room of his house was mostly taken up by a small lever-operated printing press. He edited and published a two-sheet called the *Axle Spinner*. He had interviewed Cleve and Leon, and ignored the bare facts Cleve had given him. He published a highly dramatized tale of the gunfight with Buckskin Jack. In his version, Cleve had "emptied his six-gun into this mad rowdy of the mountainsides" and yet ". . . the mortally wounded Buckskin Jack kept coming, firing his weapon to no effect, as Cleveland Trewe stood there unblinking, till at last the crazed fur-trapper fell to his knees, issued a Gallic curse sending Trewe to Hell, and bloodily expired." Locals were skeptical of the strict veracity of this account, as Dr. Hull put it, but "they would have been disappointed with anything less."

Caleb Drask had gone to Elko, a little over a week before, so Cleve and Leon whiled away their days prospecting in the hills, in their amateur fashion, as they waited for word from the lawyer regarding mine one-seventy-one. They had found only one small stream with a little "color" in it. But their exploration had been enlivened by a close shave with a mountain lion; the next morning they'd had to hide ignominiously from a heavily armed party of Shoshone renegades. Shortly thereafter the heavy rains started, and as they headed home their horses had gotten stuck in a mudslide for more than two hours.

"I am informed by the experts at the Tom Cat," Leon said, as he sat down on a stool in the other dry corner, "that this here hard rain is unnatural in these parts." He lit his pipe and went on, "It doesn't usually rain so much out here, all at once. I expect some Shoshone medicine man put a curse on us."

"Or it was Buckskin Jack's Gallic curse," Cleve suggested, as he peered through the bore of his pistol.

"Ha! Anyhow—maybe we should've fought our way through those renegades, instead of hiding. I felt like a lily liver, crouching down like that."

"They outnumbered us so much they'd have killed us, sure."

"Maybe they weren't renegade a'tall. Maybe they were friendlies."

"Shoshone warpaint is known to me. And there were scalps on that chief's saddle, and not Indian scalps. Looked remarkably fresh. I'm about ready to believe in that Indian curse." He set the brush aside and looked through the gun barrel. "That'd fit right in with the way things have been going."

All in all, not a productive week. Cleve had spent much of his time, when he wasn't trailing and prospecting, thinking about Berry, and trying not to think about her.

Not thinking about her was tough-going, as Berenice Conroy Tucker was always out and doing, around Axle. He heard about her, and he often saw her, hurrying busily along Nugget Street. Once he'd made up his mind to cross the street and ask if he could walk with her—and their eyes met. She hesitated on the wooden sidewalk. And then Velma Haggerty and Teresa McCarthy rushed up to her, both of them talking excitedly, Velma taking her arm.

It would be clumsy to interrupt them, he decided.

Just before Caleb Drask went to Elko, he reported that Mae Ling had settled in at the Haggertys, was learning English from Berenice, and teaching Mrs. Haggerty some form of Chinese sewing.

Cleve had no opportunity to see Berenice alone. He hadn't found her at the falls since that morning. Unless he wanted to spark a more public fight with Duncan Conroy, which wouldn't please Berry, he couldn't just call on her.

Far more sociable than Cleve, and a sponge for gossip, Leon had reported that Mrs. Haggerty and Berry tried to persuade Silas Haggerty that an armed deputation should be raised to shut down the Comfort Tent, because its pimp and madame were now known to have sold a human being like selling a sheep. But Mayor Haggerty pleaded that any such deputation would be in great danger from the Comfort's "doormen." Silas Haggerty had no wish to be blamed when it got ugly.

Add to that, Cleve had spent two hundred eighty-five dollars, of the seven hundred he'd brought with him to Axle Bust, half the price of the leaky cabin. All these matters shuffled through Cleve's mind as he applied gun oil to the bore of his revolver. He was wearing his coat in the house, feeling chilly and damp—the cracks between the planks admitted drafts.

By and by the rain subsided, and as the two streams falling through the room abated to drips, Q.T. Harte appeared at the open door. Harte was a small man with long wavy brown hair, a *pince-nez* dangling from a ribbon, and a small pointed little golden-brown beard; he wore ink-blotted trousers, an ink-blotted vest over a dun calico shirt with the sleeves rolled up. His brown hat was shapeless from the rain. His fingertips were stained with printer's ink.

"Leon," Harte said, "you nearly drenched me a while ago, emptying that keg. I was walking by just below. You didn't see me?"

"Maybe I didn't, or maybe I did."

Harte fixed the little spectacles on the bridge of his nose and said, "I have a notion, Cleveland Trewe, that more details of your life would be of great interest to our readers."

He came in, avoiding the puddles, and leaned on a dry piece of wall near Cleve.

"All ten or twelve of your readers?" Cleve said, snapping the pistol's cylinder back into place.

"Paid circulation has arrived at one hundred and four, I'll have you know, and growing," Harte said sniffily. "Now, sir, Leon told me you rode with Bill Cody and Kit Carson. And Carson in particular is of great interest to this part of the country. A tragedy, his dying when he did. Is it true you and Carson fought a grizzly and a tribe of Indians?"

Leon cleared his throat.

Cleve shook his head. "Leon has been making up stories. I rode with Carson on a trip through the Sierras, escorting a team of surveyors. Nothing much happened."

"That was the problem," Leon said. "Nothing much happened. How is that going to make good newspaper reading?"

"I have no desire to be in any newspaper ever again," Cleve said. "Giving that interview was a most grievous lapse of judgment on my part. Especially as you cut out *my* account of the fight in favor of your asinine embroidery." He shook his head. "How I came to agree to talk to you about it at all . . ."

"I believe some whiskey was involved," said Leon.

They heard shouting from the road below. All three men went quiet and looked toward the door.

"The mine's flooding!" someone shouted. *"Men are trapped!"*

Cleve was up first, slapping his hat on his head, and grabbing his overcoat.

He strode out the door to the path. Pulling on his coat, he half-slid, half-ran down the wet trail leading sharply downhill toward the flume works. The mid-morning air was brisk, the sky roiling and gray. Thin, transient streams from the latest rainfall meandered down the slope, and Cleve had to jump several of them.

Down the hill other men were rushing toward the Golden Fleece from the center of town. The hissing and rumbling of the waterfalls didn't mute the frantic shouts and the clanging of the alarm bell at the mine. And was that a woman toiling up behind the men, genteelly lifting her skirts to better climb the wooden steps? The long-stepping gait, the determination in every step, the chestnut hair streaming from the back of her bonnet—that would be Berenice, without a doubt. Watching Berry—anguished at seeing her running *toward* a disaster—Cleve slipped, almost did a header down the hill, on the slick slope, and then managed to get his feet under him. He stumbled on, cursing.

He reached the steps ahead of the men coming from town, vaulted the railing, ran up the stairs to the graveled walk leading to the mine.

When Cleve strode up to the mine, a dozen men, miners who'd gotten out of the mine, were clustered at the adit arguing about what to do. The shift supervisor, Mike Canning, stood with hands thrust in his coat pocket, chewing the end of a mustache and looking at the dark entrance to the shaft. He was a compact little man with a ruffled gray-black beard and a dusty black derby hat. Cleve could hear a low watery rumbling from the mineshaft.

Cleve spotted Dr. Phineas Hull, kneeling by a bearded miner who was lying on the ground. The miner was coughing up muddy water. "Let's turn you on your side, Milt," Hull was saying as Cleve approached them.

Cleve knelt beside Hull and helped him turn Milt, asking, "How deep's the flood, Phin?"

"Way I heard it—Milt, spit it all out if you can . . . that's it—way I heard, it's up a hundred feet in the shaft. There's a cage stuck a little above that point—three men in that elevator. The cable's hung up on the rocks. Everyone seems afraid to try to go down there and unsnag it. Getting down wouldn't be easy, it's true. Milt, turn onto your back now and we'll get some fellas to take you to a more comfortable place—"

Cleve stood up, looking at the entrance to the mine. Men milled about there, disputing and waving their arms, but no one made a move toward it.

"I'll see what I can do to clear the cable," Cleve said.

"What?" Dr. Hull looked incredulously at him, eyebrows raised. "Cleve—you'll end up drowned down there! Wait—!"

But Cleve was exasperated by the indecisiveness that could be costing lives, and he was already striding toward the adit. He pressed through the crowd and walked by the men waiting for a chance to drive the oxen that would pull up the rope. Several miners at the mouth of the mine were arguing with Canning, and Cleve paused to listen. "We got to get them ox to pull that cage up now!" a wet, angry miner insisted. There was blood on his fingers where he'd had to scrabble on rock, getting out.

"With the cable snagged it'll bust and drop those men in the water! They'll drown!" Canning shouted back.

"Maybe it won't bust," the miner went on, "maybe it'll just come loose! That water's liable to rise up and drown 'em anyhow!"

"I don't know, Mapes. If Conroy had a steam powered pulley now, and the metal cables—kept saying he's going to get 'em, never does."

"How about clearing that cable, Mr. Canning?" Cleve asked.

"And what would you know about it?" Canning snapped, glaring at Cleve. Then he shrugged and growled, "The water rises in surges. Anyone goes down there is sure to get caught in it and drowned. I got a responsibility to the living—I can't throw them away saving men who can't be saved! If only Duncan had listened . . ."

"Better keep your voice down," Mapes said softly. He nodded toward Brewster and his two Special Deputies standing in a tight group to the left, in earnest discussion with Duncan Conroy.

Brewster glanced over and noticed Cleve. He frowned.

Cleve went into the mine and found a crowbar leaning against the rough stone. He snatched it up, slid it down inside his belt so the hook caught. He took up a pair of leather gloves hanging on a hook on a support timber and put them on.

Then Cleve took a lantern from a hook on a beam, and prepared to descend . . .

Breathing hard from the climb, Berenice removed her bonnet to cool off and called out to Georgiy Kovalyov, the chief mining engineer of the Golden Fleece, that he would need a wide-gauge drill and dynamite.

She stalked up to Georgiy, standing on a broad shelf of rock about a hundred feet below the adit. He was looking up with a spyglass, probably wondering if flooding had made the hillside under the mine entrance unstable.

Georgiy was a burly engineer of forty-five, in overalls and miner's helmet, the high cheekbones of his face emphasized by graying mutton chops. He had been born in Russia, had migrated with his parents at age fourteen to Wales and then Ohio, with polyglot results. Berry and Georgiy were friends, though she was aware that her knowledge of mathematics and engineering seemed freakish to him. He often said, "I have never known such a woman!" At times, the engineer looked at her in a way that made Berry concerned he might propose, and she would have to sadden him by saying no.

But it was he who said no to her, shaking his big head like an angry buffalo. "No, my charming Berry, nyet, we cannot risk dynamite. You must go home. It is not safe here. The hillside, it is bloody unstable, the ground is very soaking, the hill may yet come down in landslides! Please go!"

They both knew the hillside to be largely sandstone and limestone, but on the eastern side was a massive upthrust of "intrusion rock" forced there in some ancient seismological shift: granite and considerable quartz-bearing rock, where gold is sometimes found. And here in what became the Golden Fleece, the precious mineral was mined to a hundred and ninety-seven feet down.

Berry waved away the engineer entreaty. "You yourself said, Georgiy, that there are layers of porous rock, interleaved in the ore-bearing stone, yes? Limestone—even possibly karst tunnels!"

"Da, yes, once I found evidence of such a karst underground, but Berry—please—you must go. Your brother would never forgive me if anything happened to you in such a place. Even standing here, with me, is not safe!"

"Is my brother not the one who told you that you did not need more support beams in the mine? That you did not need extra cables or a steam engine for the pulley? That an escape shaft need not be dug?"

"Da, yes, sure, but he is the boss, dash it all, he says what supplies I have, he's my guv'nor, what am I to do?"

"I don't blame you, Georgiy. But listen—suppose you were to pick the right spot to release a good deal of water pressure below the level of the flood—on this very hillside? We are well east of the town, no one is below, and—"

"No, Berry!" He clutched at his side-whiskers in horror. "The danger! Everything could collapse!"

"*Nyet,* Georgiy. I have done all the calculations—there is enough load-bearing rock to support the mine even after a dramatic reduction of water pressure. And I have just the spot for a very precise use of dynamite. One stick. I know exactly."

"And where are these calculations, Miss Queen Victoria Engineer of the world?"

"Ah—they're . . ." She tapped her head. "I haven't had time to write them out. But I'm sure of them. And I heard Clem Buckner say there are men trapped in there! They'll drown unless you listen to me, Georgiy!"

"No, no, *nyet.*" He tilted his head and pouted to show his regret. "I am so bereft that I cannot accommodate, Miss Lady Conroy!" He shook his head with finality. "Now— you must go! I must try to find a way to . . . to . . ." He looked up about him, and sighed. "I am not sure what I can do to help them. Perhaps it is too late."

The shaft was awash with the smell of dissolved minerals. The raw stone walls of the mineshaft were moist and slick; they shivered in the blue-white light from the lantern dangling from Cleve's coat pocket. The rope was damp and sometimes slippery in his gloved hands. The air was bitingly chill. Cleve had forgotten how hibernally cold a mineshaft could be, especially one half-filled with floodwater. And the more he descended the slightly off-center cable—pressing the tips of his boots into slight indentations and rough cuts in the stone wall of the shaft—the colder it got.

The lantern swung jitteringly. If it broke, banging on his hip, burning kerosene could set his clothing afire. And the crowbar tucked in his belt was as awkwardly in his way as a sheathed saber would be.

The cable wasn't a true cable at all. It should have been

a metal-thread cable, but it was but a thick hempen rope. And there was only one. Still, it was easier for him to hold onto than wet metal would be as he eased himself down. Sometimes he had no footing on the wall and had to slowly slide his way down the rope into the echoing darkness.

Arms aching, Cleve passed a ledge, with wooden bracing for a "drift," a passage off to the side, and he knew what could happen if the water rose high enough. If he was still down here, when the water surged up, the flood would pour from the shaft into side passages, and it'd sweep him with it. A hard current would press him in the drift, filling it completely. He would have no chance, then. He'd drown.

The thought spurred him to descend faster. But his haste cost him, and he began to slide uncontrollably down. He had to clamp the thick rope hard with his knees and ankles and hands to slow his descent. He could see the rough cube of the "cage" elevator, and water glimmering around it, about fifteen yards below. If he fell into that cold water, it'd be the miners rescuing *him*—if they could.

"Someone's up there, Slim!" a man shouted, below him, voice echoing up the shaft.

"Going to try to clear the line, boys!" Cleve shouted.

"It ain't the line, it's the damned cage stuck!" a man shouted back.

Another ten yards down, of aching arms, wrists, and shoulders, and shivering in cold, and then Cleve saw what the miner meant.

It was difficult to see clearly in the indirect light from his dangling lantern, but Cleve guessed at what had happened. Somewhere below, exploratory chisels and pickaxes must have broken through into a karst-tunnel filled with groundwater; and under pressure from the copious rains, a deluge had rushed in and surged up the main shaft. It had caught the ascending miners' cage, pushing it out of alignment, jamming into the bottom of a shaft support frame. It was crookedly pressed against stone and rafters, unable to ascend. Trying to force the elevator cage up with the heaving oxen would have snapped the rope from the frame. Cleve could see there was an ore skip, under the cage: a cart filled with rock, attached to the bottom of the elevator. That weight would have dragged the miners down into the cold black water.

And then one of the men shouted, "Water's rising again! Get us outta here if you can, mister!"

Cleve saw the water seething up, its rolling, vitreous black surface, a few yards below, was like some living creature intent on devouring them. And the men trapped in the elevator—a "cage," they called it!—looked up at him in fear. He could see only bits of their faces; a frightened eye, an open mouth.

"Mister!" the man yelled, rising fear driving the word like the dark, cold floodwater shoving at the cage.

Cleve tugged the crowbar free, set his lantern on the top of the cage and edged across the slanted, slippery wood to the rough stone wall, where the cage was jammed against the timbers. He found a space to force in the crowbar and set to work trying to pry the elevator housing free. Using all his strength he managed only to rake out a piece of wood from the shaft frame. The cage was too heavy; too wedged.

"The goddamned water's coming up!" shouted someone below him.

Cleve looked, saw it swirling up to the miners' waists. "Can you open the gate?" he called.

"We tried! It's mashed all shut under that damn timber!" the man shouted back, barely audible over the rushing water, its hiss echoing in the shaft. Cleve was afraid—fearful he would have to watch these men drown at his very feet.

Cleve stepped over to the center of the cage, then skidded,

almost slipping off on the slick wood. He wobbled, and went down on one knee. He began to pry furiously with the crowbar at a top board, struggling to find purchase. He used his weight and strength to force the beveled iron end between two planks. The desperation in the miners' drawn faces seemed to charge his arms with strength. He pried harder, still harder, then pushed it as far as he could go, feeling like his shoulder joints might break—and then a board popped up at one end.

He grabbed it, yanked it up the rest of the way, tossed it aside, set about the next one.

The water was rising . . .

The men were kicking with their feet to keep above the water now, grabbing at the other cage planks to pull themselves up.

Then the next plank came up. He tossed it in the water, set the crowbar aside, took hold of the cable and reached down with his free hand to grab the nearest hand he could reach. He pulled the man as far up as he could. Both of them grunting, the miner pushing on a cross-board with a boot.

The miner scrambled through the gap onto the top of the cage and immediately set to helping Cleve pull the others up—a clumsy, slippery job. The miners were shivering, teeth clattering with cold. The crowbar was jostled into the water, to plunge out of sight.

They were all on top of the cage now—but the water continued to rise. It was churning over the remaining top boards, swirling icily up their ankles, then their calves.

"Get over there, close to the rock!" Cleve shouted, pointing. "We hold onto the boards and we push, all of us, with our feet, where it's stuck on the wall! Maybe we can work the cage free!"

The men sidled their way over to that corner, careful not

to knock into one another—a misstep, an unintended push, might send a man falling into the flooded shaft.

Gasping, grunting, they sat on the boards at the top edge of the cage; the water coming up to their chests as they gripped the remaining planks and pressed the stone wall with every ounce of strength left in their legs.

It budged a little. But stayed stuck. They cursed and tried again. "Everyone together—on three!" Cleve called. "One, two . . ."

But just as he was about to say three, what sounded like a thunderclap echoed through the shaft. The walls shivered, bits of rock rained down, the water heaved up over their chins, getting in their mouths. Cleve heard a watery roaring in his ears. The men started to get up.

"Stay down!" he yelled. "Brace and get ready to push again!"

Then the water began to whirl about them, rumbling within itself as it vortexed around the cage. Cleve struggled to hold on.

The whirlpool tugged at the cage—and Cleve yelled, "Now *push*!"

The men used their combined strength, shoved with their feet against the stone wall—as the lantern slid down into the water and hissed out. The darkness was almost complete.

Then the cage came loose, and began to swing, to spin, in the shaft—and the water receded. The faint light from above seemed to spin about them.

"Water's going down!" one of the miners shouted, amazed.

They steadied, and Cleve clambered over to the rope, pulled himself up it to stand erect, peering up toward the mouth of the shaft turning slowly above them. He could make out the tiny silhouettes of heads against the square of light. Men staring down at them.

"Lash the oxen!" he shouted hoarsely. "Pull us up! We're clear!"

There was no immediate response—too much noise from the rushing, gurgling of the receding water. He turned to the miners. "Everybody together, loud as you can—we'll yell, 'Pull it up!' One, two three—"

"Pull it up!" they yelled in chorus.

Nothing. "Again! Top of your lungs!" Cleve urged.

"Pull it uuuup!" Their voices echoed up the shaft.

They clung to the whirling, quivering cage—waiting . . .

And then the rope tightened. Taut now, it squirted water from its strands. The cable creaked . . . and began to lift them up out of the water.

Hurrying up to the adit, Berry saw Russ Brewster talking to a small crowd of miners. The mining constable had his hands raised to keep the men back from the mine. Q.T. Harte was at Brewster's elbow, scribbling with a pencil on a pad of paper. Behind him were the Special Deputies— she'd seen them in town a couple of times, two men who seemed unlikely to be any use to anyone. She'd heard the one with the burn scars on his head was called Morgan.

"What are those men doing, Leon?" Berry asked, as she and Georgiy stepped up beside Leon.

Leon seemed a little disconcerted by her sudden appearance at his side. "Why, Berry! There you are! Which men are doing what, you say?"

"Those two. That man Morgan and the other." She pointed at the two Special Deputies just inside the adit. She had seen them about town. Had heard her brother's feeble explanation of them. The Special Deputy with the half-scalp was startling enough. The other, though more groomed and not scarred, had something in his eyes that had unsettled her even more. Now they were looking down the shaft; standing by the taut rope that ran through the headframe pulley. The thick rope was steadily pulled back by the oxen tramping around the wheel, drawing the miners' cage up. The bigger of the two men—half hidden within the dimness of the mining apse—had a Bowie knife in his hand. "What is that man going to do with that knife?"

"Has he a knife?" Leon shaded his eyes to look.

Berry considered fetching her brother. But he was too far away—back at the boss's shack, now, where Georgiy was telling Duncan how they'd drained the water from the mine.

Leon suddenly burst out with, "By God—Devora does have a knife! And he's standing hellish close to that rope!"

The man with his hair half burnt away was reaching up, raising the big knife-blade toward the rope looped in the pulley, while the other fellow with the fine suit was looking nervously back toward Brewster and the preoccupied miners.

"Brewster!" Leon shouted, drawing his sidearm and rushing toward the mine. Berry hurried after him.

"What?" Brewster looked around, startled. "Morgan! What the hell are you doing?"

Morgan sheathed the knife. He turned to them, his face blank, shrugging, as Leon stalked up to him, six-gun pointed at his belly.

Then Morgan grinned. "Best not shoot me, Studge, or I'll fall plumb on your friend down there!"

"Get away from that rope!" Leon snarled.

Brewster stepped up, holding up a hand to keep Berry away. "Ma'am, please stand back." He turned to Morgan and Leon. "What's this about?"

"He was going to cut that rope!" Leon said.

"What!" Brewster seemed genuinely taken aback.

"No such a-thing," Morgan said. He walked calmly around Brewster, and headed down the hillside.

The other Special Deputy said, "Why, he was just worried the rope might get snagged in the pulley, thought he could get it loose!"

"You always were a damned liar, Hortlander," Leon growled.

"You're lucky you got the drop on me, skulkin' up that way," the Special Deputy said.

"That's enough," Brewster said. "You go down the hill, Hortlander, get Morgan and meet me by the mill office. We'll talk about this there." He turned to Leon. "Put away that gun, Studge. There's a lady here. She could get hurt."

Leon glanced at Berry—who wasn't at all sure she wanted him to holster the gun. She had been close to pulling her own small pistol.

Holstering the gun, Leon stepped out of Hortlander's way, and watched him narrowly as he trudged down the hill after Morgan.

"Brewster, Devora was going to kill all those men just to get rid of Cleve," Leon said. "He doesn't want the Major talking about him—telling people his real name. You better get rid of that son of a . . ." He glanced at Berry and fell quiet.

"I'll talk to him," Brewster said, frowning. He cleared his throat. "But his name's Morgan." He turned to Berry. "Ma'am, please, move away from the mine. It ain't safe."

Georgiy was walking up to them, smiling. "It is a great thing you have done, Berry!"

"You are the engineer, not me, Georgiy," she said, as Leon and Q.T. Harte joined her. "Now," Harte said eagerly, waving his pencil, "if I could just get a statement from you, Mrs. Tucker—"

He was interrupted by a shout from the miners. "Stop

that cable, the men are coming up and they're atop the cage! Quick before you smush 'em like bugs!"

Leon rushed to the headframe, and tugged down the brake lever to grip the rope.

They all turned to see the miners' cage creak to a halt partway up into the opening. The men clambered hastily off its top, the other miners cheering. And with them . . .

"Cleveland Trewe," Berry gasped.

Chapter 9

It was beginning to drizzle again, as Cleve emerged from the Golden Fleece mine. His arms were aching, and he badly wanted a drink. But the gray, drizzly world looked surprisingly lovely.

Then Cleve saw Berry, about thirty steps away, gazing at him in surprise, one hand over her open mouth. She quickly restored the bonnet to her unkempt hair. He tried not to stare at her, but he couldn't help himself.

One of the miners who'd come out of the cage put his arm around Cleve's shoulder and said, "This man saved our bacon down there! He got us out of that cage—we'd have been drowned, did he not come along!"

"He did very well, da!" said Georgiy. "But who saved the mine, shall I tell you blokes?" He turned and pointed at Berry. "Berenice, Mrs. Tucker—she is a woman wise in the geology and wise in the ways of the water and by Saint Georgivanch it was she who told me where to lay the dynamite! Now when you go down the hill, look down the cliff to the east, there you see water still pouring into the ravine, from the blast hole! She knew the spot and she directed me to it. It was she who lowered the water level so these men did not drown!"

"Three cheers for Berry Tucker!" Leon shouted, before Cleve could think of it.

The three cheers went eagerly up, and all miners rushed over to congratulate her. Cleve smiled and walked over to join them. She seemed a little overwhelmed by the ring of grinning men around her, but handled herself graciously, pointing to Georgiy and saying it was really his doing. "But thank you very much, gentlemen, God Bless you all. We are so very relieved you are safe!"

Cleve reached out and took her hand. "I was pretty sure we'd drown. But the water level went down, and I had no notion why. I should have known, Berenice. You saved our lives, ma'am—you and Georgiy. I thank you both."

Her hand lay in his for a moment, and he felt a subtle electricity in it. Everyone was quiet, looking back and forth between them.

Then Q.T. Harte said, "Oh *ho*!"

Cleve reluctantly drew his hand away, gave her a small bow, and hurried off down the hillside, Leon catching up to go with him.

Right then, Cleve was of two minds. Get the drink first—or a dry change of clothes? It was a dilemma.

Standing by the new office at the mill, kicking at a mound of sawdust, Clay Hortlander felt his hatred burn hot as he watched the man he thought of as Major Trewe walking down the hillside past the building site. Leon Studge, he noticed, was trailing beside Trewe, animatedly gabbling away.

"Studge," Hortlander muttered. "A traitor to the Cause."

The War Between the States had been over when Leon Studge's treason had taken place, but it didn't matter to Hortlander. During their imprisonment at Fort Slocum, he had seen Leon assisting Major Trewe, following the Union officer everywhere. The war could never be over, in Hortlander's mind, and he didn't believe that any Confederate soldier should be trotting obediently after a blue-belly. Not ever!

The surrender of Lee to Grant at Appomattox embittered Hortlander. He could not forgive it.

"There are no laws, anymore," Hortlander had told his father, one fateful day, at the end of a long drinking session. "The laws ended when Lee surrendered. I say we kill us some Yankee bankers, Papa, and take their gold!"

His father, much dismayed, promptly sent him away from the plantation, and Clay Hortlander had turned his back on his family and Virginia. He'd ridden west with his aching head and leading two of his father's stud horses. He'd taken them without permission, and sold them at the first chance. Thereupon, he headed straight for the gold-fields. He'd figured there was sure to be a way to make good money there, without the hard work of mining. To make good money—or just take it.

He'd found several opportunities to rob prospectors of their gold, around Cripple Creek Colorado, and then he'd taken up with Devora to go after the Chinese. Thinking it prudent to depart Colorado, they'd seen a Chinese family traveling east. Robbing them yielded little gold, so they tied the girl up and took her with them. It required some close watching to keep Devora from violating her—but Hortlander kept her a virgin. A young woman like that, so pretty and delicate, was worth so much more that way. That'd paid off all right when they sold her to the Comfort Tent.

Watching Trewe now, Hortlander figured Devora had the right idea at the mine, but the wrong timing. There'd be another chance to kill the arrogant Yankee; to execute Major

Cleveland Trewe. Someplace quiet and private. Maybe out in the wild country.

Hortlander glanced at Devora, who was leaning up against the new pine walls of the mill office, biting off a plug of chaw tobacco. Was it smart to ride with Devora? They agreed about the Confederacy, that was so. They both hated Yankees. And Devora was a good man in a fight. Always took the lead. A man could keep his scalp with Devora rushing at the enemy. But Devora reeked, quite literally stank, and he was not good company in the better class of saloon, where Hortlander liked to sweet-talk the ladies. He'd had some hope of getting into Flora's bloomers, back at the High Nevada, till Devora had joined him at the bar. She'd made a face at the sight and smell of Devora and kept her distance thereafter.

Still—he could leave Devora when it suited him. Maybe someday back-shoot him, on the trail, and take his poke, after they'd collected enough scratch. This Special Deputy job was paying pretty well, but judging by the look on Russ Brewster's face now, their Special Deputy posting might be over.

"Boys," Brewster said, keeping his voice low as he walked up, "Duncan's heard an earful about 'Morgan' here waving that knife around the rope. And there's others have heard his name ain't Morgan. Leon Studge has been noising it around. Something else too. That Chinee bit of stuff you sold to the Tent—she's been talking. She gave descriptions of you both to the mayor's wife. And Berenice just told her brother all about it. The boss wants you both gone. I'm to pay you off. The county sheriff's gonna be here any day now, most likely tomorrow, and he might want a word with you. Best you leave town right smart."

Devora spat chewing tobacco at the ground near enough

Brewster's feet, and the mining constable had to step quickly back. "We ain't leaving till we're paid."

"You'll get paid. Mulvaney's Assay and Fund Trust will pay you soon's you get yourselves down there to Nugget Street." He took two folded papers from his shirt pocket. "These here're the cheques. Give 'em to Ferg Mulvaney. And don't try to rob the place—Mulvaney has two plug-uglies just itching to shoot someone with them ten-gauge shotguns."

"Now why'd you *imagine* we'd even *consider* a thing like that?" Hortlander asked, as if shocked. Devora gave out one short laugh at that.

Brewster snorted. "Because I ain't no fool, that's why. But you listen to me . . ." He glanced around, then moved closer, lowering his voice even more. "You know Dean Bosewell's camp, up where the Red Hills Camp was?"

Both men shook their heads. But Hortlander had heard of an outlaw named Bosewell.

"I might have something nesting that'll hatch pretty soon. Bosewell's all set. There's big money in it. And he'll give me a cut. He needs more men to make it happen."

"What 'something' is that?" Devora rumbled.

"You talk to him. Tell them I sent you. Just take the trail south about a mile and a half, there's a cut up to the left. Take that. A quarter mile on, it's blocked with deadfall. You ride around the deadfall, head along the scratch of a trail east, along the gorge—ride careful, that gorge is steep and fair-deep. Four miles and there's three red hills kind of huggin' together. I expect you'll see the camp's smoke. There's the makings of a ghost town there. Ride in slow and call out for Dean Bosewell. Talk to him, tell him I sent you. Just remember I helped you out."

"Or you get us killed, mixing with that bunch," said Hortlander. "They might shoot us soon's we ride up."

"Not if you handle yourselves easy. Come in peaceful, hands raised. Now go on, get your money and kick heels on outta here. Don't even take time to get drunk. Buy a bottle and some eating supplies and be on your way."

With that Brewster turned on his heel and went back up the hill toward the mine.

"Who's he to say we can't have a drink and buy a woman's time?" Devora muttered.

Hortlander shook his head. "With that Chinee girl talking, we'd best ride out. May as well see Bosewell. We could always slip away from him if we don't like the plan."

"I want to shut that Cleveland Trewe up for good."

"We won't be far, if we join up with Bosewell," Hortlander said. "Trewe's time be along, by and by. Come on, let's get paid."

Nugget Street was drying, mid-morning, mists rising from it like sleepy ghosts, but it was still muddy. As Cleve and Leon strolled to the café, a heavily loaded ore wagon, pulled by four stout horses, was creaking its way slowly up the road with two men in the bed shoveling broken-up tailings off the back; rock castoffs to fill out the gravel.

Cleve had slept in, and he stretched his arms as he walked, and cricked his neck. His limbs yet ached from yesterday's ordeal in the Golden Fleece, and his abraded hands burned. The cable in the mine had burned through his gloves. His gun was ready on his hip, but he wondered how fast he'd be if he had to draw that Colt today.

They were almost to the hotel café, when they spotted Les Wissel across the street, standing by a mule in front of Mulvaney's Assay and Bank.

Wissel was unloading two sagging, weighty sacks, perhaps forty pounds each, tied across the back of a mule.

Beside him was Russ Brewster, with his Mining Constable badge shining brassily on his vest and his shotgun laid over the crook of one arm.

Brewster spotted Cleve and Leon the same instant they saw him and Wissel. He caught Cleve's eye and gave him one warning shake of the head.

"You know that's gold he's got in those bags," Leon murmured. "Gold from our mine."

"Seems likely," Cleve said.

"Makes me kind of sick, watching that," Leon went on, as Wissel slung the rope over his shoulder and carried the two bags to the assay office.

Cleve nodded. "I fully commiserate. There's nothing we can do. Not yet."

"You'd think we could get a stay from the judge to close the mine till it's decided whose claim is good."

"I don't think we've got that much pull around here," Cleve said.

Cleve toyed with the idea of going in after Wissel, making a case to Mulvaney that he should hold Wissel's deposit out, confiscate it till the matter was settled. But Duncan Conroy had a close business relationship with Ferg Mulvaney. And Conroy had the majority share in claim one-seventy-one.

And too, there was Brewster with his shotgun. He might stand in the way. Could be Brewster could call on the armed guards in Mulvaney's to back him up.

Cleve growled to himself, and said, "We'll see what Caleb says."

"If he ever gets back from Elko. Starting to think he's done forgot about us."

"Seems to me Caleb's the kind of man, once he's taken a case, he sees it through. However it comes out." Even if we're the losers, Cleve thought. "Let's go get that late breakfast or early dinner, or whatever the hell it is."

They continued on down the wooden sidewalk. Cleve could feel Brewster watching them go.

Leon was squinting at the newly graveled street. "You know, those tailings come from the Golden Fleece. Not supposed to be anything of value in rock like that. But I heard about a feller found a gold nugget in mine tailings, plain overlooked."

"Leon, you see gold in there, you can scoop it up, but watch out for the horse apples."

The rainclouds had herded on to other aerial pastures, and the stars overarching the breezy hilltop glittered with an austere brilliance.

"There!" Berry said. "Those stars are the Pleiades!"

"So that's them!" exclaimed Jonah Bentworth, pleased. The two of them were standing side by side on the stony hill, with her little brass telescope in a Y-fork stand of iron tubes. Just now they were using the unaided eye.

The man her family had set to guard Berenice had thick gray hair and white bushy eyebrows, a narrow white goatee cutting an accent at the base of his sunburned, rugged face. Jonah wore an oiled leather rain slicker, and his weather-beaten Indian fighter's cavalry hat, turned up at the sides; he held his antiquated carbine rifle cradled in his arms. Still gazing at the constellation, he intoned, "'Can you bind the chains of the Pleiades, or loose the cords of Orion?'"

"That's from the book of Job, isn't it?" she asked, adjusting the telescope.

"It is. My granddad was a great one for readings in Job, for he could not bear a whiner. He told us Job took what God dished out and so should we!"

"And there is Orion, the hunter—those three stars lined up . . ."

"That const-teration I do know. The schoolmarm told us about some of the stars, and that'n we remembered, for he was a hunter. In the spring, with stores about run out, we didn't eat if we didn't hunt, in our family. So we boys was interested in anything to do with hunters."

"We were never short of food, growing up, and I think it would have been better if we sometimes had been," Berry said, bending to look through the telescope. "We would understand the great mass of people better if we'd known real hunger. Duncan could learn something from it, certainly."

She glanced at the old man, gazing at the constellations with starlight on his face, and smiled. Jonah was so patient with her, always wanting to understand her better. He had become a second father. She looked back at the sky. "Ah— there is Jupiter, biggest of the planets. It has many moons, we're not sure how many . . ."

He looked up in awe. "It surely makes a man feel small, such things. Now imagine having more than one moon! That would make a confusion of the sky, wouldn't it? Lord!" He gave her an odd, sidelong look then. "Berenice . . . you believe in the Lord, or don't you? Your brother warned me you were a scoffer!"

"My brother? When was the last time he was in church?" She straightened up from the telescope, feeling suddenly lonely. Who was there in the world who could understand her? Only people far away, beyond her reach. Except perhaps one. "I go to church when there's a good one handy. But I suppose you'd say I'm a Deist, Jonah—like some of our first Presidents were. Meaning I don't know what exactly is there, behind it all, but some unknowable mind is at work. Nature seems to be writ in a great hand. But— sometimes I'm at odds with nature too."

"Now how could you, Berry, so schooled in nature, be at odds with it?"

She sighed. "Because I feel, somehow, nature wants me to marry again. It has its own plans for us—mating and procreation are part of its plan."

"I don't know who'd be right for you, but I'd be sorry to see you go on alone. Is there no one?"

"Maybe," she said softly, thinking of Cleve Trewe. "But he is gotten afoul of my family. And he is so much a gentleman—" She laughed softly. "Perhaps there's such a thing as being a little too much a gentleman. Shall I show you the rings of Saturn?"

The Queen of Engineers and a Bold Hercules
~ Save Desperate Miners ~
from the Dread Death of Ice-Cold Drowning

~An Eyewitness Account by Q.T. Harte~

Without a modern pump mechanism or a satisfactory elevation system, the Golden Fleece was long in dreadful danger of flooding when the unexpected spring downpours became a torrent of Noah's Ark extremity. No sage of the camps was astonished therefore when the mine flooded in the recent deluge and the peril became a terrifying certainty. One man drowned, whilst another, Milton Fensley, was taken grievously ill with water in the lungs, and three others almost drowned in the catastrophe. A fourth man was at grave hazard due to his own mad courage: Cleveland Trewe, former Major of the Union Army, one-time Colorado lawman of

note, and vanquisher of the notorious
Buckskin Jack. Trewe was informed that
the cable, if the hoist rope can be flattered
with the term, was snarled; he further
ascertained, on descending with ice-coated
hands down the treacherous rope into the
Stygian domain, that the elevator cage itself
was caught in the shaft, even as the frigid
water rose, threatening three miners with
the nightmare of drowning in a trap. Enter,
Cleveland Trewe, a White Knight of—

Wincing, Cleve slapped the two-sheet *Axle Spinner*
down on the café table and shook his head. "Harte, you have
gilded the lily and engaged in dime novel foolery. White
knight? Ice-coated hands? You could not restrain yourself
from saying 'Hercules'? I shall never live it down! I was
hoping to eat breakfast, and I don't think I'll have the stomach for it after all that tripe!"

Harte, seated across from him, beside Leon, pushed
aside the plate holding the ruins of his breakfast, and said,
"Why, I assure you it's a most commonplace manner of
newspaper reportage! The *Spinner* is positively subdued
compared to *The Virginia City Glorifier.*"

Cleve ground his teeth and shook his head in disgust.

Leon laughed. "Next they'll say you wrestled with Dan'l
Boone and a grizzly and beat 'em both."

Cleve snorted. "The grizzly was easy," he said, just to
make Leon laugh. "Daniel Boone was harder, because he
cheated." He turned to glare at Harte. "I hope this report has
reached no one else in Nevada?"

Harte shrugged. "As to that—when I printed this out
three days ago, I sent it by courier to Elko and Virginia City.
I am a man of enterprise, Cleve!"

Cleve sighed. He glanced down at the paper and his eyes were caught by a name heading a paragraph farther down the page:

> Mrs. Berenice Conroy Tucker explained that
> while she had some knowledge of mining
> prior to her husband's passing, that tragedy
> compelled her to acquire as much
> familiarity as she could of the perils of
> mining. Her husband, Grant Tucker, was
> tragically killed in New Mexico, when a
> mine drift collapsed in consequence of
> groundwater damage to the support beams.
> The widowed Mrs. Tucker was determined
> to do her utmost to protect other wives from
> becoming prematurely widowed. Feverishly
> she added to her considerable knowledge of
> the geological natural sciences through
> exhaustive study, and boldly sent papers to
> the Society of Mining Engineers,
> suggesting preventative mechanisms . . .

By God, Berenice is truly a remarkable woman, Cleve thought. Hell, a remarkable *person*.

Harte had not exaggerated about Berry. In her case, there was no need.

Cleve's throat seemed tight, his eyes stung, and to cover his emotion, he reached for his coffee cup and said, "Instead of jabbering about me, Harte, you should write an obituary for Daniel, the saloon sentry—he was a good man. Risked his life and lost it."

"I did not know he'd passed!" Harte exclaimed. He stood bolt upright. "I am off to gather facts!"

"To gather the facts and embellish them," Cleve muttered, as Harte hurried off. The journalist nearly ran over

Caleb Drask walking into the café. Cleve's lawyer had at last returned.

"Here's the prodigal son at last," Cleve said.

"How'd we fare in Elko?" Leon asked, as Caleb sat down beside Cleve.

Caleb sighed. "It's yet somewhat indeterminate."

Leon asked, "Meaning you ain't sure?"

"Precisely." Caleb took off his bowler hat and fanned himself with it. They were sitting at the window table, and it was a warm, sunny late-morning. "There are two gents at the county records office, with two points of view, it seems. There is a Mr. Alden Dix, who clearly remembers your uncle's claim. There is a Mr. Cortney Burnsville, who said he 'believes' that Les Wissel has the prior claim. The claims are both recorded in the county files, each taken by a separate clerk. I do not quite trust this Burnsville. He seemed very nervous, sweating profusely, and I thought a bribe may have been involved in his case. But I have no proof of that. Not thus far."

Cleve shook his head. "I gave you the countersigned copy that has the date right on it. It shows our claim was in advance of Wissel's!"

"Yes. But Wissel and Conroy claim the copy is falsified. But the *county*'s copy of it is ink-blurred—the date is unclear. Looked to me like it might have been muddled after the fact. Changed to benefit Conroy."

"By God that's crooked as an Englishman's teeth!" Leon growled.

"I suspect it was no calligraphic accident," Caleb said dryly, nodding. "We'll need to settle it in court before the magistrate."

"I'll be there," Cleve vowed. "Did you talk to my uncle?"

Caleb stopped fanning himself and gave Cleve a look of sympathy. "I did. He's taken a turn for the worse. The physician says he may have a thrombus, some clotting of his blood—a consequence of the beating he took."

Cleve took a deep breath. "I'll have to go see him."

"I don't think he'll be in any shape to go to court himself. But I took an affidavit from him on the whole affair, including on the assault by Wissel."

"How much we owe you for all this?" Leon asked. One of his contributions to the business was funding the lawyer, at the moment.

"You are still covered by the retainer," Caleb said, waving the matter away.

Cleve suspected they were getting a considerable markdown on the fees from Caleb. "I'm grateful for your help."

Caleb shrugged. "Vagabonds like you and Leon need assistance. A man has his Christian duty to aid the miserable wanderers of the world."

"Vagabonds!" Leon exclaimed, pretending to take offense. "Miserable wanderers!"

Cleve and Caleb laughed.

"You talk to the county sheriff about the beating, Caleb?" Cleve asked.

"I did indeed meet with Purslow. I showed him the affidavit. He seemed sympathetic. The difficulty, he says, is there's no witness to the attack on your uncle. It's his word against Terrence's."

Cleve nodded. "What's your feeling about Sheriff Purslow? Could he be in Conroy's pocket? I never heard of a mining concern that wouldn't buy influence."

"Now that's a question," Caleb allowed, signaling the waitress for coffee. "He's kind of a patchwork policeman, I reckon. He takes a lawman's cut from the bawdy houses, and he sometimes makes use of the girls himself. So I hear. I expect he's done a favor or two for the folks who keep the bank solvent. Hard to find a lawman that doesn't favor town businessmen."

Leon chuckled. "True enough."

"But . . . thank you, ma'am, black coffee is fine. Have you any pie?"

"We do," she said. "Dried-apple pie."

"That'll do for me." Apple trees were in short supply in Nevada; dried-apples had to serve. "I don't think Sheriff Purslow would go so far as to suborn claim-jumping or let a man like Wissel get away with beating an old gentleman to within an inch of his life. He's got a reputation for sand in dealing with outlaws, too, and for standing up for the Reservation Indians and the Chinese. Doesn't like a bully, you see."

"Then maybe he's all right," Leon said, nodding. "Maybe he'll take our side."

"He probably would," Caleb allowed, "if we had the proof to back us up." He sipped some coffee, cleared his throat, and said, "There's something else, Cleve. I understand that Purslow will be here in town quite soon. And he's coming here to talk to *you*. It's not about the Trewe Mine business, either."

"Well, what is it then?"

"I don't know. Just that he's coming to see you." Caleb noticed the newspaper, picked it up and scanned it. "Now what fresh madness is this?"

Leon laughed. But Cleve frowned, thinking of Uncle Terrence. A thrombus, a blood clot to the heart . . .

He determined to ride to Elko, as soon as he'd settled matters with the sheriff.

If the county sheriff didn't arrest him first . . .

* * *

Berenice came back from collecting larval specimens to find her brother half-sprawled on the settee in the drawing room. He was in a fugue of some kind, she could see that in the deadness, the despair in his eyes. She had been expecting it. He'd been glum since the flooding of the mine. And even glummer after reading about her part in the rescue. And Cleve Trewe's.

Duncan was slumped back, with his legs thrust across the carpet, a glass of brandy in one outflung hand. He was gazing up at a portrait of their father as a young merchant. Father had one hand tucked in his coat like Napoleon, his bearded chin was lifted as he posed in front of two prancing race horses. "It's funny to think Father got his first grub-stake breeding race horses," Duncan said, his voice lazy, his eyes half-closed.

She almost chided him for drinking so early in the day. But she did not wish to spark an eruption. At such times he was a brooding Vesuvius.

"You're usually at work now, Duncan," she ventured. "Are you feeling unwell?"

"I am," he said. "I do feel unwell." He glanced at her, and sat up a little straighter. "You're dressed like a range bum again, I see."

"I am outfitted for collecting specimens. It requires climbing, at times. A dress will not do." She put down her little rucksack, and came to sit by him. She reached out, took his limp right hand. It felt cold. "Duncan, will you not tell me what troubles you?"

He stared up at the ceiling. He did not push her hand away. "You have no need to hear of my troubles. Everyone blames me for the flooding of the mine. As if I were the deluge. And all the while *you* are triumphant. And so is your paramour."

"Oh! I have no paramour! No beau at all."

He sniffed. "That adventurer interfered in my operations. I would have gotten those men out."

She knew that was not so. There had been no time for any measure than the one Cleve had taken.

"My dear sister Berenice," he went on, his voice dripping with irony, "is being called the Darling of the Golden Fleece, because of a lucky placement of your little stick of dynamite."

"I did not mean to . . ." She wasn't sure how to put it. "I just did what I felt had to be done, Duncan. After what happened to my husband—"

"Father is sure to find out!" he interrupted, squeezing his eyes shut. "Canning is Father's man. He will report all to him."

"Father had his own mining calamities—including the one that made me a widow," she said. "He will understand. And you've made plans for improvements at the mine. A new pump, a steam-powered lift . . ."

"The miners' union is becoming stronger in all this, too," he said bitterly. He took a sip of his brandy. "They're sure to walk out. Their pay is late—there are two months back-pay awaiting, and this month's as well. Canning blames me for that, but the money was slow to be shipped to us. It's coming soon, they will have cash in hand, but they shall cry it is too little! Oh, oh, too little, a mere pittance!" He laughed bitterly. "This man Tolliver is stirring them up. If I could but get my hands on him . . ."

"Some companies have chosen to simply pay more, and reduce the hours at labor. A good profit would still be made and the crisis would evaporate!"

"That is not the way of Conroy Mining," he said, chuckling bitterly. "Our dear Papa gave me too little funds to make the mine safe—he will not let me use a speck of the gold we take for such concerns. He will certainly hold me a weakling, a failure, if I bow to the miners and pay them what they ask . . ."

"Perhaps Mother could talk to him," she said. "Perhaps Papa can be made to see you need to run things as you think best."

"Ha! The last time we spoke he called me a feckless bumbler!"

"Come, he didn't mean it."

"But he did!" His voice broke as he went on, " Berenice . . . why did God make me deficient, like a tree rotten at the core?"

"You are not deficient. Every man must find his way through life—it is a rough road, and we all stumble, Duncan."

He sighed and lay his head on her lap, and she stroked his hair as he wept. This was something that happened, once or twice a year, when he was plumbing his depths. Tomorrow he would once more behave as if he were the patriarch of the household; he would be back to imperiously ordering her about.

Berenice sighed and murmured to him, as she always did, that all would come well in the end.

Clay Hortlander pulled on his socks, grimacing at their rank stiffness. But there was no laundress in Red Hills. And his one change of clothing was just as dirty.

He was developing a powerful dislike for Red Hills Camp. Once an inconsequential trading post and a small community, it was now a ghost town: a few cabins, abandoned and vermin-haunted; the rickety old post building, a clutch of leaning shacks, two burned out ruins, a muddy rutted road, two stinking privies, and a well that smelled of sulfur. And the ghost town was occupied only by Bosewell and his men: five unwashed road agents. Seven counting Hortlander and Devora. First morning he'd awakened here, in a leaky, mossy, grimy old cabin, he'd had to shoot a rattlesnake that reared up from a hole in the floor. Nearly getting snakebit was not the beginning of a good day.

This morning, Devora was still asleep, flies hovering over his open mouth, on the bunk across the little cabin. Waking up to that sight wasn't much of a start, neither.

I am a town man, Hortlander told himself, and I need a real town. A place where a gentleman can get a decent meal and tolerable liquor; where he can buy his supplies, get his clothes washed, get himself bathed and barbered. Not that Devora cared for all that.

But Hortlander had been the scion of a prosperous plantation—or so he'd thought, till he'd been driven away by his own father.

He couldn't stick to this ghost-town much longer. He only stayed because of Bosewell's talk of divvying up "a stack of bars of gold so big you'll have to crane your head to see the top of it."

Wishing he had some brandy to drink before facing the camp, Hortlander strapped on his cross-draw holster, put on his hat, took his drinking cup from his saddlebag, and went blinking out into the unwelcoming sunlight. The camp was in a crotch between iron-red hills smelling of pine trees and dust—and the piercing odor of a skunk.

Hortlander rubbed his unshaven chin as he trudged over the drying mud ruts to the post building. He could at least shave himself—he had a mirror and a razor in his saddlebags. First, a cup of coffee.

His boots creaked on the warping planks of the floor as he walked into the shadowy building. He strode up to the Franklin stove in the corner, where the coffee pot was steaming. Bosewell and the other five were sitting in rickety chairs against the wall to the left of the stove. There were no other furnishings in the drafty room. Bosewell, the gang-boss, was a big, thickly mustached squint-eyed man in an out-at-elbows brown sack suit; he had narrow shoulders, a red bandanna around his fat neck instead of a tie.

Hortlander poured himself some coffee, and blew on it as he glanced at the other men. The skinny Deeke boys were smoking pipes, Perkins had a hand-rolled smoke, and Bosewell a thick stubby cigar. Their gray tobacco smoke merged near the ceiling with black smoke leaking from the stove.

Salty Jones, a confidence man, whose confidence seemed on the wane, sulked in the corner, chewing on a thumbnail. He had left his suitcoat in his cabin and was wearing white shirt sleeves with gaiters, mud-splashed pin-striped trousers, and a dusty little hat.

The fellow sitting nearest to the stove, Rollo Perkins, commenced one of his coughing fits, covering his mouth with the back of his hand. He was a pale man, clean shaven, with sunken cheeks, and watery red-rimmed eyes; he wore miner's boots and dungarees and a gray overcoat spattered with mud. Hortlander suspected Perkins of having consumption. He was said to be a crack shot with a rifle, but what good was a fine shooter who coughed when he pulled the trigger?

Bosewell frowned deeply at Perkins' hacking coughs—and slapped him resoundingly on the back, making him gasp from the impact.

"See there, you cough up that phlegm and you'll be fine, Perkins," Bosewell said, chortling. Perkins spat out the half-smoked rolled-up cigarette, and undertook a new fit of coughing.

"Need some whiskey," Perkins said. "That'll clear it up."

"Then it's just too bad you didn't bring any."

Hortlander took a couple more steps back from Perkins before drinking his coffee.

On the other side of Bosewell sat Chasly and Wynn Deeke. They had lanky dirty-blond hair, narrow heads, long necks. But it was their stilt-like legs and long arms that always made Hortlander stare. With their identical green flannel shirts—maybe the last shirts left in some trading post—they reminded Hortlander of a couple of green insects sitting on a log. They were supposed to be good at rustling, quick with pistols, and "they have damn good eyes," or so Bosewell claimed. But they seemed knot-headed as fenceposts, to Hortlander.

"This sure is a barrel of apples that gone to pickles," muttered Salty.

"What's that you say, Salty?" Bosewell asked, glancing at the con man. "You have a complaint to make?"

"My complaint is naught but boredom, Bosewell," Salty said, snuffling as he rubbed his nose with a finger. "You spoke of taking some gold off the haughty fools in Axle Bust. Let us do it and get it done, I say."

"Why, you'll hear more about it today." Bosewell took out a pocket watch and squinted at it. "Fair soon, too. Fair soon."

The two Deeke brothers turned in unison to gawk gapingly at the door as Vern Devora came in, carrying his own coffee mug. Devora was wearing only his red long johns and boots, his hat stuck crookedly on his head.

Well, in this shit hole, Hortlander thought, why not.

"I got an idea!" Devora bellowed.

"Is it about where we can get better liquor, clean clothes, and some women?" Hortlander asked, casually.

Perkins paused his coughing to laugh at that, as he wiped the back of his hand on his shirt.

"We're waiting on Tolliver," Bosewell declared, tossing

his cigar stub at a spittoon and missing. "He'll be here right quick and we got ideas to discuss with that gentleman. But while we wait you can declare your grand notion, if you want, Devora." He leaned back, hooked his thumbs in his vest, lifted his chin, and opened his eyes wide as if to say, *I'm all attention.*

Devora stumped over to the coffee, poured himself some, cursing when he burned himself in the process. He sniffed the coffee, and drank a little down. He spat at the spittoon. Then he said, "Boys—we're a bunch of damned fools."

"You can speak for your own damned self," said Bosewell complacently.

"What we should do," Devora went on, sniffing again at the tin cup, "is set aside all this nonsense about waiting for a payroll. We should raid Axle Bust, full out. There's no law there. There's one man there seems to be good with a gun— that Cleve Trewe. That man—I'll cut his throat while he's snoring in bed. I don't need to go toe to toe with him."

"In actual fact I'd like nothing more than to face down Major Cleveland Trewe," Hortlander put in.

His bravado went unremarked. The others were leaning forward a little, listening to Devora.

"You see, boys," Devora went on, "that town got its arms open like a drunk two-dollar whore. There sure is a big pile of money in Mulvaney's. There is *gold* in Mulvaney's too. Dust and nuggets! Nothing defending it but a Vigilance Committee of some drunken miners who couldn't hit their own toes with a pistol, and a couple of shotgun guards. Brewster is pards with us—he's not going to stop us."

"He's right about that," Hortlander said, his voice reverent at the thought of all those riches concentrated in a town without real lawmen. "It does sound like a fine Sunday dinner just waiting for some hungry men."

Then he noticed Thaddeus Tolliver standing in the doorway, listening.

Devora went on: "There's a room there where they store the gold from Conroy's mine before they ship it to Elko." He sipped some coffee, stared at the brew as if someone had put mule dung in his cup, and then shrugged. "Now, they got two men there, those boys with their Parker shotguns, and they hire out two more from Elko who show up to transport the gold. Those fellers are probably pretty good with the street cannons, and that transport wagon is some armored up too. Maybe we'd win through, hitting them on the trail, maybe not. But in *town*—they won't be expecting us. We slip up on those guards in Mulvaney's place, we kill 'em and we take every last thing in that mick money-lender's shop!"

"It's not bad," Bosewell allowed.

"There's a thousand ways that could go wrong," Tolliver said, coming in.

"You heard, Tolliver?" Bosewell asked, as the big man marched in, his heavy steps shaking the warped floorboards.

Tolliver took up a position near the stove, grabbed his suspenders, and said, "I heard, Dean. What Devora's suggesting's got its points. But there's a good parcel to be arranged first. First of all, I'm here to report that Sheriff Purslow has officially taken a greater interest in Axle Bust. Maybe he's going to bring him onto a posse. Neither man means us any good . . ."

"Jesus, son of a . . ." Hortlander began. His cursing followed till he ran out of breath.

"These men, Purslow and Trewe, are not to be trifled with," Tolliver said, looking about for a coffee cup. None was available.

"I wouldn't *trifle* with them," Devora said grimly. "I'll kill Trewe myself. And when I kill a man, it ain't triflin'. I make sure he feels it."

The others grinned at that. Except Salty Jones who gave a snort of derision.

Tolliver said, "Most assuredly, sir. But—there are easier ways than filling a wagon with stolen gold and ever-so-slowly towing it up hills behind stubborn cattle! Cash, gentlemen, is easier to transport. And when it comes in to Axle—when the cash is *brought in* to pay the miners—why, that cash is guarded—but not so much as the gold leaving is guarded. This is what the alienists call the 'bias of the unconscious mind.'"

The two Deeke boys looked at one another, and shrugged in bewilderment.

"Boys," Tolliver went on, "if you set a town on fire—even if you manage to cut that deputy's throat—and if you make off with the town's gold, well, you're going up hills with the town's treasure and every man with any pride's coming after you with every weapon under his hands. But if you take it in cash, in a lonely place, on its way to town for the payroll—" He spread his hands. "Then boys, you are . . . golden!"

The men hooted in delight at that. Hortlander knew that Tolliver was stirring up the miners as part of some further, unspoken plan. Maybe this was but one end of it.

"There are other possibilities," Tolliver said, musing aloud. "Devora there is not entirely mistook. But it'll have to wait." He cleared his throat. "There isn't another coffee cup to hand?"

"We bring our own," Hortlander said.

"You can use mine," said Perkins, offering it to him.

Tolliver looked at the cup, and then at Perkins. "You hold

onto that, Rollo." He cleared his throat and went on, "There is, however, a preliminary job we may undertake. For I know you boys are restless. I have learned that Haggerty is sending quite another lockbox of cash and gold to Elko by the stage. That's where his banker is. Now, as to when this happens . . ."

Chapter 10

The feral wind of Axle Bust was especially wild today, veering and gusting capriciously. Cleve and Leon and Q.T. Harte held onto their hats when a big gust came.

They were on their way to the church-raising at the western end of Nugget Street. Harte was along to report on it; Cleve, only occasionally a church-goer, had come mostly because he thought Berenice might be there; Leon was there because he didn't feel like going to the saloon alone.

The Baptist chapel was half built; its small steeple had gone up first, with its simple white-painted cross, on a knoll not far from the creek; the boards outlining the building, seeming rather barn-like to Cleve, were extended back of the steeple. The wind made a high humming sound passing through the wooden frame. A modest brass bell, said to have come from a half-sunken, abandoned steamboat, rested on a wooden pallet by the steeple, waiting to be hoisted into place.

A dozen men worked about the church, including the spindly, ginger-haired minister, Preacher Birch. His suit and jacket laid aside, the young minister was chatting merrily with two others helping him lay flat stones for the church's entry path. The rest of the men were hammering, sawing, and talking the while. There was some discussion of the proposed name of the church, The First Baptist Church of Axle Bust. Some thought the name wasn't reverent sounding enough; some thought it too wordy.

Cleve was relieved to see that Duncan Conroy was not among the volunteers. Kanaway the hostler stood at a saw-horse, sawing wood to form.

"We need three more at four and a half feet," one of the men said to him.

"Three more at four and a half it is, Joe," said Kanaway, nodding.

Four women stood together at an open-air table, preparing food and drink for the workers. The skirts of the checkered tablecloth snapped in the wind; the cloth was kept from blowing away by platters of dried mountain-goat meat, a bowl of cold beans, a large jar of pickles, potato salad, bread, and dried apple pie, alongside a stack of tin plates and silverware. There were tin cups by a stone jug of water. One of the ladies was Berry, cutting loaves of bread into slices. She wore a white dress, wrapped so tightly about her by the wind it rashly accentuated her figure. Beside her was Mrs. Haggerty, adding salt and pepper to the beans.

Next to Velma Haggerty, cutting pieces of pie, was a lady Cleve had met in passing—Teresa McCarthy, the only female prospector in the camp; red-haired, freckle-faced, full-bosomed; she had green eyes that went with her dark-green felt hat. Cleve noted Leon gazing at her intently, as they walked toward the table. Leon's mouth was a little open, like a child ogling a Christmas dessert, as it was each time they encountered Teresa.

Cleve watched Berry frowning as she untied the bonnet. She lay it aside, weighing it down with a fork, and tried to smooth her long and curly chestnut hair, which flashed out coppery highlights in the sunlight. She sighed, gave up trying to tame her locks, and went back to cutting bread. Her hair fluttered about her head as if in celebration of the secret wildness he suspected lay within her. She seemed to sense his attention and looked up at him. Her cheeks reddened, but she quickly regained her composure and smiled primly. "Mr. 'Hercules' Trewe! Are you—are you going to lend your ice-coated hands to the work of building the church?"

He sighed. "I was hoping you had paid no notice to that tomfoolery. This villain"—he waved toward Harte, who lifted his hat to her—"is to blame."

She gave a small laugh. "I thought Mr. Harte was rather charmingly chivalrous, in his description of me."

The other women were listening, trying not to show it, Cleve noticed.

Another of the ladies had her face hidden in a white bonnet—she glanced shyly up at Cleve and he saw that it was Mae Ling.

"Mae Ling!" Cleve gave her a short bow. "How well you look, ma'am."

She cleared her throat, concentrated, and then said, "I thank you very much, Mr. Major."

Leon chuckled at that. Cleve smiled.

Harte cleared his throat. "Say, Miz Haggerty, ma'am— may I interview Mae Ling? For the *Axle Spinner*?"

Mrs. Haggerty pursed her lips and shook her head. "I think not."

"We could get Caleb Drask to translate."

"Even so! You may not. She has been through quite enough without enduring the rampages of your prolixity, sir."

Leon stared at Harte. "You were going to do *what* to her?"

"I will let Cleve explain it to you, Leon," Harte said wearily, taking out his pad and pencil and walking toward the carpenters.

Cleve turned to Berry. "Leon and I do intend to lend a hand, ma'am."

"You are just in time for lunch, I notice," said Mrs. Haggerty tartly.

"We ate a late breakfast, Mrs. Haggerty. We'll just pitch right in and see if we can be of use."

"Well now," Leon said. "I could find room for some pie—and that potato salad looks good."

"Leon," Cleve growled, "let's just—" He broke off, hearing several gunshots from the center of town. They all glanced that way. "Early in the day for it."

"Probably just a drunk," Leon said.

"It seems to me that most men who are shot are killed by drunks," said Berry, shading her eyes to look toward town. "Our community needs a better grade of law enforcement."

Teresa nodded briskly at that. "You're right as can be, Berry. That constable's no darn good. The vigilante committee spends most of its time arguing. And Sheriff Purslow doesn't stop by here much."

"It seems to me I read you are a former lawman, Cleve," Berry said lightly. "Do you feel we're doing well without a town sheriff?"

Cleve shook his head. "No, ma'am, I do not."

"I believe I gave you permission to call me Berry," she said, vigorously cutting a loaf of bread.

"Berry, then. Thank you." Cleve was warmed inside of a sudden. She apparently did not believe the standing conflict between him and Duncan Conroy precluded their friendship. "Berry—Axle Bust surely needs a lawman. Almost as much as Leon here needs to watch his manners. But there seems to be no plan to elect or appoint anyone. It's not something I could put myself forward for—I just got here."

"Hell, Cleve," Teresa said, snorting, "we all *just got here*. It's a mining camp! People come and go like . . ."

A gust of wind tore at her hat and blew off its feather. Leon sprinted after the bright blue feather, changing directions when the wind whisked it this way and that. Cleve couldn't help laughing. At last, the feather stuck in a wild rose shrub. Leon caught it up and returned to the table with the feather in one hand and the other one behind him. "I think you lost this ma'am," he said, ceremoniously handing the feather to her.

She laughed and blushed and took it—and the wild rose, just blossomed, that he'd plucked from the shrub.

He said, "I thought you might like . . . that is, you ought to have . . ."

But then his hat blew off.

Teresa instantly caught it in midair—and ceremoniously handed it back to him.

They all laughed at that, and she said, "I haven't got any flowers for you, cowboy, but you have earned some potato salad, right enough."

Weary from seven hours of sawing boards, hammering, and lifting up frames, their lips chapped from the wind, Cleve and Leon settled into their corner of the bar at the High Nevada saloon. They ordered from the saloon's cook—fried chicken and dried-vegetable stew—and drank deeply from large schooners of beer, before Leon asked, "You believe in signs from God, Cleve?"

"I suspect coincidence explains the seeming appearance of divine signs," Cleve said. He wasn't listening closely. His mind was wandering to his uncle. For all he knew, Terrence could already be dead.

"Well, how is what happened today not a sign from God?"

"Exactly what mystical event happened today?"

"Why of course it was when the feather blew off her hat and I brought it to her and my hat blew off and she gave it to me."

"More like a sign of two Texans acting like spring colts, seems to me," Cleve said.

"Are you speaking disrespect of Miss McCarthy?"

"Not for a moment! Phin Hull told me that when there was typhoid in the camp, she spent months nursing sick miners and running through her grubstake to do it. She seems to have found some little stream somewhere in the hills, with a good deal of color, since. Maybe that's her reward."

"A sainted woman don't need a reward."

"Maybe she is sainted too. She put up with you talking her ear off every time you took a break."

"Oh, we were jawin' 'bout Texas. I'm South Texas and she was North. Her family was Irish."

"Now that's a surprise."

"Don't be such a mean old bull."

"Leon, my best friend in the Army was Irish. Tiernan Doyle. Never was a better man than Tiernan. Deserved every medal they had. But one of your Confederate sharp-shooters, perched in a tree, shot him down before we could give him the medals . . ." Cleve had to take a pull on his beer, to clear his throat. "Saved my life and never mentioned it. Was a scholar too. Knew all the great poets of English and Gaelic."

"Cleve, I'm sorry he was taken. Hell, I'm sorry the war had to happen at all."

Desirous of changing the subject, Cleve said, "You surely were slick, giving Teresa that wild rose, Leon. You are like a chivalrous bard of yore."

Leon chuckled. "That's just what they say about me in Texas!"

Cleve laughed. "I'll bet they do."

Their food came. It was cold and greasy but went down well enough. They'd pushed the plates away when Leon said, "If the sheriff does arrest you, I'll go and see your uncle. Bring your greetings and bring you a report of him."

"I'd be obliged."

"Cleveland Trewe!" came a stern, gristly voice behind them.

Cleve put his hand on his Colt as he turned to see a tall, rangy man with whitening brown mustaches, and gray-brown hair falling to his shoulders in the manner of the Plains scouts. His hat was a dark blue Stetson, red with dust. His face was almost gaunt, his gray eyes deep-set. He wore a duster, and on his dark blue vest was a silver star imprinted with *Sheriff, Elko County*. His long-fingered right hand rested confidently on the ivory butt of his blue-metal six-gun. The holster was tied down with a leather thong.

"Mister," the lawman said, his voice pitched warningly low, "you'd better drop your hand from that pistol."

Cleve nodded and did as he was told. "I'm guessing you're Sheriff Purslow."

"I am."

"I didn't know who you were when you called my name out. Am I under arrest?"

"What should I arrest you for?"

"I thought maybe—shooting Buckskin Jack. Brewster was making noises about its not being regular."

"You just saved me the trouble of shooting Jack myself,

sometime, is all." Purslow dropped his hand from his gun. "I regret there was no reward posted for the scoundrel. Phin Hull wrote to me, said he saw it all and you were in the right. Phin's a man I trust. Now I don't know about this one . . ." He nodded toward Leon, pretending to look at him askance. "Is he trouble?"

Leon grinned and said, "Only when I can get away with it, Sheriff."

"Leon's my business partner," Cleve said. "I can't seem to shake him."

They laughed and shook hands all around. "Say, I know a story about Buckskin Jack," said the sheriff, his hard eyes suddenly merry. "He was in Red Hills Station, back when that was operatin', and he run out of money. He'd already sold everything he'd trapped, and so that night Buckskin went around the town and caught every house cat living there! He killed 'em, skinned 'em, and tried to sell them back to folks the next day, said they were Mountain Beaver. Well pretty soon, people recognized their cats' markings, and he had to ride out fast! Right here in Axle, one time, he shot a man in the leg, for calling him Kitty-Trapper Jack."

Leon hooted at that story and Cleve was sure he'd repeat it widely. It might even be true.

"You had your supper, Sheriff?" Cleve asked. "So far, the fried chicken hasn't given us the bellyaches."

"I guess I'll hazard it, then. Let's have us a drink first." He took off his coat and hat, laid them on a stool, and said, "Then, once I've ate, I do have a question for you."

Partway through the sheriff's meal, the singer in the sulfur-hued suit mounted the stage, doffed a top hat to his accompanists, placed the hat on his breast, gazed up at the ceiling as if at the stars—and started singing in a high warble, to imitate some sad ingenue.

Purslow gritted his teeth. "Times like this here I wish I wasn't a sheriff. I'd like to chase him out of here to stop that caterwauling!"

The singer continued warbling. Sheriff Purslow stood up, took careful aim with a chicken bone, and bounced it off the singer's forehead.

"Someone's shot me!" the singer yelped, ducking behind the accompanists.

The saloon erupted into laughter and hooting. Flora put her hands on her hips and scowled at the sheriff. "Henry, I don't believe I'll serve you another drink tonight!"

"Sorry, Flora," he said, chuckling. He put on his hat and coat and tossed a gold piece on the bar. "Boys, let's go to a real saloon."

Ten minutes later they were in the Tom Cat, nestling into a corner table.

There were about thirty drinkers in the saloon, including a couple of itinerant speelers acting as if they didn't know how to play poker, along with Mick Stazza at his faro bank, looking deeply bored as he slapped cards in front of a bleary miner. Mick nodded to Cleve, eyed the sheriff pensively, then made his face go blank as he concentrated on dealing.

Purslow bought two full bottles of Old Overholt, and he ceremoniously arranged three double-shot glasses on the table. Cleve noticed the sheriff kept the duster buttoned, now, covering up his badge. "You can buy your own beer," Purslow said, pouring them each a double shot of the amber whiskey.

"Well, Sheriff, here's to strikin' silver, finding gold behind it, and spending it all on pretty girls," Leon said. They drank to that—no man in a mining camp would dare otherwise. Leon went on, "And speaking of that, I thought

I had struck it once—anyhow I thought I'd bought a gold mine . . ."

He proceeded to relate the sordid tale of Salty and Digley, seeming to relish it, even chortling over his own gullibility.

"So that's what it was," said Purslow. He pointed at Cleve. "I got a letter from Brewster claiming you were in with those confidence men! Something about you taking Digley to a doctor."

That almost made Cleve take another shot of whiskey, just to cool his anger at Brewster. "You didn't fall for that, did you?"

"Was many a time I had to shoot a lawbreaker and then tote him to a doctor myself. Then too, you have a good reputation out of Denver. As for Brewster, he's pretty low in my books. You may conclude I didn't believe it. Have another drink."

He poured, and with a sinking feeling Cleve took up the shot glass. He greatly disliked hangovers. He didn't like drinking contests at all, but he knew he was in for one. A man like Purslow, who set out to get drunk, would judge a man by how he could hold his liquor. And Cleve knew that he'd be a fool not to get on the right side of the county sheriff.

He drank his whiskey, shuddered, and tried to sit up a little straighter.

"Where's this Digley now?" Purslow asked.

"Don't know. He left town. There was no one here to turn him over to. Brewster's not the law."

"No, he most surely is not. You got yourself a job, here in town, Cleveland Trewe? Rummy knocker, maybe? Replace poor ol' Daniel?"

Cleve grinned at the old expression for a saloon guard. "Nope. I'm doing some prospecting. I plan to make mine one-seventy-one my job. I understand you heard what happened to my uncle?"

"I did. And I don't trust Les Wissel. But I've got no proof—it's your uncle's word against his. The injuries— well, Wissel's lawyer says your uncle was drunk and waved a pistol at him. Claims Les knocked the pistol away and the old man stumbled and fell down a hill."

Cleve snorted, "I hope to prove that Wissel's a damn liar, Sheriff."

"So I understand," Purslow said equably. "You got a job?"

"Not as such."

"You need work, and this town needs law. I am empowered to offer you the job of Deputy Sheriff in Elko County. You'd be stationed right here—stationed, that's how we used to talk in the Army. You was a Major . . . I was Captain with the Second Dragoons. Cavalry man. Got shot off my horse twice. Then I was fool enough to stay in the Army for the Indian fighting. But . . . now we're off-trail here. You want the job, it's eighty dollars a month. More than many a deputy gets."

"Why that ain't enough for a man of the Major's caliber," Leon said, bridling.

"You surely are his partner!" Purslow chuckled. "Oh, well, there's his slice for serving subpoenas, warrants, and all such. That's where a deputy makes most of his money. And Trewe—I don't care if you make the whorehouses pay you something. Hell, I do it." He poured another round. "You can have the job, I expect—Mayor Haggerty wants you in it. It was his idea. What do you say?"

Cleve was still turning it over in his mind. He had been set on never lawing again. He didn't want to spend his days dragging drunks to the hoosegow. There wasn't even a real hoosegow to drag them to. He didn't want to serve court-ordered evictions, either. But Axle Bust was always on the edge of chaos. Someone had to enforce the laws. As for whorehouses—Berry had called for someone to close the Comfort Tent. To help women like Mae Ling.

For Berry—for Berenice Conroy Tucker, a woman he scarcely knew . . .

"I'll take the job, on one condition, Sheriff. If you'll let me *do* it."

Purslow leaned sharply back. "What the devil do you mean, let you do it?"

"You know about Mae Ling?"

"That the Chinese girl Buckskin was dragging around? Bought her from the Comfort Tent?"

"That's her."

"I read something about it in the newspaper. How's she figure in?"

"They sold her like a slave, Sheriff. I don't have the authority, unless you deputize me, to do anything about it. She's free now, but the town shouldn't permit such barbarity."

"You fixing to take them to court for slavery?"

"I figure they'd collect witnesses saying she went with Buckskin of her own free will. Some of the other girls there—they'll say whatever they're told, so they're not beaten. And a jury, like as not, will take the attitude that since she's Chinese, they don't believe her."

"Could be," said the sheriff. A hardness had come into his face.

"Instead, I'd just close them down. Escort them out of town. They're violating county ordinances. Now I know—those ordinances are customarily overlooked. Long as the girls are working of their own accord, I have no problem with a bawdy house where the women are treated fair. I was good friends with a lovely lady who ran one in Denver. But these people have shamed this town. They beat those women."

"And Mae Ling was kidnapped and sold to the Comfort Tent in the first place," Leon said. "And we know who done it."

"Who'd that be?" asked Purslow, knitting his shaggy brows.

"The two Special Deputies Brewster hired on," Leon said. "Ain't no doubt. One of them goes by Morgan but he's a wanted man—what's his name? This whiskey's pushed it right out of my noggin."

"Vern Devora," Cleve said.

"I know that name," Purslow muttered. He poured another drink, then noticed that Cleve hadn't drunk his own yet. "You going to drink that or run home to your mama?"

Cleve sighed, then smiled, raised the glass to the sheriff, and took down another double-shot. "Devora"—he had to stop and let out a gasp as the liquor hit him—"is wanted in Colorado."

"That was it." Purslow drank his whiskey down as if he were drinking cool water on a hot day. "I saw the circular." He had a little trouble now saying the word circular without lisping. "It was these deputies kidnapped that Chinese girl, you say . . ."

"They did. Brewster denied Morgan was Devora. Refused to take Mae Ling's word for it."

"They're not any kind of real deputies," Leon said, dutifully picking up his shot glass. He drank the whiskey in a gulp, blinked several times, and swayed a little in his chair.

"They've left town too," Cleve said. "Left when the story about Mae Ling got out."

"You wanting to close down Billi June's tent . . ." Purslow said, grumbling the words. He shook his head. "I don't like it."

"You let me do it, and I'll do my damnedest for you. I'll chase runaway pigs if you want me to. I'll chase badmen into Hell."

"Is that so? Now, I've got a condition for *you*." The sheriff leaned close and looked Cleve in the eye. "If I hire you—you will *not* use your authority"—he was speaking carefully, trying to keep from slurring the words—"on Les Wissel. Not unless you got him hogtied and branded by the law! You got to have proof! Goes for anything to do with that mine!"

Cleve gave him a long, silent look in return. "You calculate I'm the kind of man would use the law that way?"

"If I did, I wouldn't offer you the job a'tall. But a man's feelings can get the better of him. Suppose your uncle dies? Shit, if it was me, I'd want to call Wissel out and shoot him dead on the street. But you got to swear to me you won't do it."

Cleve said, "I swear it on Old Glory, I will never use my gun, or my authority, without having proof to back it up. That includes Les Wissel."

"Good! Now . . ." The sheriff broke off to stare past Cleve. There was a ruckus of some kind at the bar. "Trewe— look over yonder."

Cleve turned to see two miners facing off near the bar, one with a knife in his hand, the other clutching a broken bottle. Both men wore overalls and were plainly in their cups. The miner with the broken bottle was skinny, beardless though long-haired—couldn't have been more than nineteen years old. The one waving the knife was grizzled, tanned like old leather, with a face ringed in beard.

"What you gonna do about *that*, deputy-candidate-Trewe?" the sheriff asked.

Cleve stood up, his head spinning for a moment. He steadied himself on the back of his chair, gathered his wits, and slipped into his old lawman role like pulling on a well-worn leather glove.

He walked almost steadily over to the two miners, their weapons flashing in the lantern light as they slashed at one another—neither one connecting so far. Cleve drew his gun but kept it pointed at the floor.

The old miner was snarling, "You know you done it, and I know it too!"

"Drop the cutting implements, gents!" Cleve said sharply.

The older miner spun to him, and Cleve used the gun barrel on the miner's knife-hand, hitting it hard. The knife flew away to stop with a clank on the iron base of a stool, as the miner clutched his injured hand to his belly.

"Damnit, I need that hand to work!"

Suddenly there was a swishing gleam of broken glass and Cleve had to step aside to avoid being gutted by the broken bottle wielded by the younger miner. The boy's face was contorted like a hungry, snapping coyote. The knife slashed into Cleve's shirt, just above the belt line. He could feel cold bottle-glass sliding over his skin, harmless but chilling.

Reflexively, Cleve brought the gun barrel down on the boy's head. The young miner grunted and fell flat on his face, out cold.

Cleve took a deep breath. Mick Stazza, sauntering up, laughed dryly. "Why, Trewe, old Simon there wouldn't have hurt you. That boy, Scrap they call him, is the dangerous one. He's been stealing from the miners' tents and got called on it. And Simon here only pulled his knife when the boy there smashed that bottle."

Cleve nodded. "I didn't see it clear, that's for damned sure." He reached a hand out to Simon. "Mind if I look at your hand, Simon?"

Simon grudgingly let him take his hand and look it over.

"Not too bad," Cleve decided.

"I don't think it's broken," the old man allowed, "but it's gonna hurt for a day or two."

"Sorry, old-timer, I should've come at it so's you could see me clear. You say this boy was stealing?"

"He was! I saw him!"

"The County Sheriff's here. He'll take him into custody. Can I buy you a drink?"

Simon paused, tilted his head back, narrowing his eyes as if deciding a matter of national importance. Then he said, "I reckon so."

They were up against the bar, as the sheriff ambled over, chuckling. Seeing Purslow, Mick hurried back to his faro.

"For having a brick in your hat, you did okay, Trewe," Purslow declared.

"Oh, I'm not that drunk, Sheriff. But I did hit the wrong man, first thing. Seems that kid started it and he's a known thief. They call him Scrap."

"We'll stick Scrap there in Brewster's lockup, for tonight, and make our determination tomorrow or mebbe next week. Now—I accept your terms for taking the job—*if* you accept my terms too. How's about it?"

Cleve put out his hand. "I can stand it if you can, Sheriff."

Purslow grinned and they shook on it. "Now, if a man works with me, he can call me Henry if he wants. I don't allow it for just anybody."

"Henry, then. Call me Cleve."

"We'll make you County Deputy tomorrow, in Elko. Has to be done there at the town hall, with a witness. Kinda fancy."

"That fits with my plans anyhow, I'm going there to see my uncle."

"That's what I figured. Now—are you man enough to have another drink?"

Cleve groaned inwardly. But he gave a solemn nod. "Henry, when you fall to snoring in your chair, I'll carry you over to the hotel."

Purslow barked out a derisive laugh. "Is that so? We'll see who carries who! Now let's get this boy over to what passes for a jail here. I got the keys when I came in today."

"You must've got here when I wasn't looking."

"Oh, I figured to take the new stage on its maiden journey from Elko early this mornin.' Save me the saddle sores."

"What new stage line?"

"Where you been! The Mulvaney Mail Coach! First stagecoach line in Axle Bust. Goes as far as Virginia City. The mayor met it this morning, and there was some crowd too. There was hip-hoorays and handshakes and speech-making and all that twiddle twaddle."

"We were asleep then. Our place is some distance up the hill."

"You just be in front of Mulvaney's Assay for that stage to Elko tomorrow mornin'. Let's get to dragging this young fool—and then we'll get to drinking."

They got it done, leaving a note for Brewster on the door of the store room, and then the sheriff led them doggedly back to the Tom Cat.

After the first four double-shots, Cleve sometimes raised the glass as if drinking but didn't take any down, so he was only about half as drunk as the sheriff. But it was sufficient.

He knew he'd feel it in the morning. He felt bad about pretending to drink as much as Purslow, but somebody had to stay closer to sober, in case things went catawampus. As it stood, he was drunk enough for the room to spin if he moved too quick.

Somewhere about 2:00 A.M., the bartender persuaded the last of the drunks, along with Cleve, Leon, and the sheriff, to take their whirling heads to the street. Henry Purslow, Cleve observed, could at present walk up to three steps on a perfectly consecutive course, but the fourth one invariably veered for points unknown. Leon and Cleve perforce walked on either side, keeping Purslow on track for the hotel. Muttering about the Kiowas, and sometimes letting out a sob over a Kiowa woman who was "a better wife than any white woman born," the county sheriff eventually made it to his room in the Gideon. He fell facedown across the bed, snoring before the mattress springs stopped squeaking.

They tugged his boots off, delicately removed his gun belt, and decided that was the extent of their responsibility.

Cleve and Leon headed wearily toward the cabin. "Ain't public drunkenness a crime?" Leon asked, as they climbed the steps to their musty little domicile.

"Most places," Cleve said. "And most places that particular law is ignored by the public and the police."

"You'd think a sheriff would have a little more sense, that's all I'm sayin'," Leon muttered. Inside, they minimally undressed, in the faint light from the coal oil lamp. Cleve stretched out on his bunk.

"Leastways, we got the roof fixed," Leon muttered, flopping onto his bunk.

"After it stopped raining," Cleve murmured. Then he was asleep.

* * *

Sunrise can be a cruel time for some.

Down on the plains, it had been dawning for close on an hour. Here, the sun was just breasting the foothills when Cleve's eyes popped open.

"Oh, hell," he muttered, as the sun coming through the one window struck his headache like a hammer to an anvil. "Son of a . . ."

He was now all too fully awake—and the stage was leaving an hour after dawn in the morning. He was supposed to be on it, with Purslow, when it left.

Leon was still snoring away as Cleve got up. Just standing made his stomach lurch. He lit the lantern, went to the wash basin, splashed his face, looking at himself in the piece of mirror on the little shelf over the bureau. His eyes looked hollow in the uneven light.

Cleve washed himself as well as he could, shaved, and dressed in the mostly-clean spare clothes hanging over the back of a chair. He strapped on his gun, put on his hat, drank a mug of water mixed with willow-bark powder, and went to roust the sheriff.

As Cleve set out, the rising sun seemed to throb angrily in his head. He traipsed down to Nugget Street, waving to a couple of prospectors leading their mules out into the hills. Experienced older men getting the edge on the late risers.

When Cleve got to the hotel, he spotted the stagecoach, the driver yoking the team in front of Mulvaney's Assay. It was trimmed in red and gold, the colors still bright with newness. *Mulvaney's Mail Coach* shone in ornate glossy-red letters across the doors. To Cleve it looked more like a circus wagon than a stage.

"Howdy," he said to the driver: a lean young man with greased-back hair, a scruffy brown mustache, dungarees, and a patched overcoat; he had rounded shoulders and he gawped at Cleve as he walked up. But all the while his hands were expertly working with the tackle and harness.

"I'm Cleveland Trewe, going with the sheriff this morning back to Elko. You the driver?"

"I am. Folks usually call me Turtle." He finished the yoking, then squinted at Cleve as if to see him better. Was the stage driver near-sighted? "You bought your place on the stage? I got to leave soon."

"He don't have to pay for it, Turtle," said Sheriff Purslow, surprising Cleve as he strolled up, a carpet bag in hand. Cleve had figured on having to drag Henry Purslow from his bed. "County'll pay for it," Purslow added, tossing his bag on the roof of the coach. "I'll put in for it when we get to Elko." The sheriff's red-rimmed eyes drooped. His hands shook a little. He seemed to sway a mite—still badly hungover.

Turtle nodded. "Okay, Sheriff, if you say so. Horses are grained and harnessed. When you want to go?"

"Let's go right this damn minute."

"What about young Scrap? We left him in Brewster's lockup. Maybe we should take him with us. Jail him up in Elko."

Purslow spat at the ground and rubbed his head. "No, I don't want to trouble with him now. I left word he's to be fed and given water and a waste bucket. Let him cool his heels for a couple days, teach him a lesson. He's durn young— hell, you could just put him on the first freight wagon out of town. Give him a dollar and tell him not to come back. We'll reimburse the dollar."

"Reckon he'll be okay in Brewster's care?"

"Sure, Brewster knows better than to fool with my prisoner. Now let's go—I need me some sleep," Purslow growled, climbing painfully into the coach.

Cleve shook his head. Did Henry Purslow really think he was going to sleep, hungover, in a jolting stagecoach?

But in five minutes, as they were bumping along up into the hills, the sheriff was perched on a bolster in a corner of the coach, long legs stretched out diagonally, arms crossed over his chest; head drooping, hat slipping off, mouth slack—sawing logs. His stretched-out legs—knees locked, feet jammed against the farther corner—kept him stable, so he wobbled and bounced less than Cleve did. It was Cleve's surmise that the sheriff had evolved this sleeping strategy over long experience with stagecoaches.

Cleve sighed, stretched his legs under Purslow's, and settled in as best he might.

Almost two hours passed, the throb in Cleve's head in counterpoint with the squeak of the stage's undercarriage. He tried to think of something pleasant. All he could think of was Berenice. But when he saw her face—crystal clear in his mind—Duncan Conroy loomed up behind her . . .

Cleve tried thinking about his trip to Paris. A pretty, aristocratic French lady in a barouche passing him on the boulevard. Was her name Berenice? He dozed.

Gunshots.

His eyes snapped open, and the world spun. The brake shoes squealed, and the stage lurched so that he was thrown against Purslow's legs.

"What the Burnin' Hell is this commotion!" Purslow shouted, coming awake on the floor.

Tugging out his gun and getting his feet under him, Cleve shouted, "Do not stop this stage, Turtle!"

"They's shootin' at me, damnit!" Turtle yelled back, his voice almost lost in the clatter and another gunshot.

Chapter 11

Turtle kept the team pounding hard down the dusty road despite the shouted demands of the outlaws to halt. Guns boomed; bullets whined by.

Cleve lifted the leather dust-curtain partway from the window and saw a rider with a smoking pistol: a thin man wearing a flour sack with ragged holes cut for his cold eyes. The outlaw's mask was like something from a folktale to scare children, Cleve thought, as he snapped off a shot of his own.

Cleve's first one missed. The outlaw fired back at him—and a bullet hole cut through the door, letting a dusty ray of light into the shadowy interior.

Cleve let his hand and eyes track the rider, then fired again—and a thunderously-loud shot came from behind him, exactly as the outlaw was pitching over from Cleve's bullet. The rider fell off his horse, his limp body dragged from one stirrup.

The sound of the close gunshot just back of Cleve was making his ears ring, as he turned, saw through blue smoke the sheriff with gun in hand, squinting, crouched on the floor. "I got him, didn't I? Did he go down?"

"Yep, you got him, Henry," Cleve said, though he knew it was his own shot that had taken the outlaw down. "You nearly blew my head off too." He knelt on the rocking floor, peered out the window, saw three more riders, faces in flour sacks, the big one shouting at the driver—Cleve fired another shot, heard Purslow firing out the other window.

The big rider clutched at his side; Cleve had hit him but not solidly. The wounded outlaw veered his big dun quarter horse off into the underbrush, and the other riders followed—Cleve counted three more—as he sent two shots after them, the second aimed at a man turning in the saddle to fire back at him.

Cleve thought he hit the last one, but he wasn't sure, and then he lost sight of them when the stage careened around a curve.

"Hold on now, Turtle!" the sheriff called, "brake 'er!"

Cleve glanced at Purslow, surprised. Was it wise to pull over here? The owlhoots might well be close by.

But the brake shoes screamed, and the stage lurched, slowing, slowing—stopping. A cloud of dust caught up with them, making them cough, as they climbed out, guns at ready.

Coughing, Cleve looked around, wiping dust from his eyes—he saw no horses and no one hiding in the trees. But that meant very little.

Dust sticking to sweat on his face, Turtle climbed down, wiping his blood from the side of his head and scowling. "Goldarn it."

"You hit bad?" Cleve asked, looking him over.

"Just a graze. I'm lucky to be above snakes. They was blazing away so I laid out flat on the top there and kept the reins, keep 'em from a good shot."

"Good thinkin'," the sheriff said. "You've got sand, Turtle. You did good."

Turtle seemed startled by the compliments—as if he wasn't used to them.

Cleve looked at the driver's perch of the stagecoach. It was chewed up with bullet holes. Turtle had been lucky.

"Mulvaney's not going to be happy about his brand-new stagecoach all shot up."

"Oh, 'round here, Cleve," Purslow said, his eyes studying the underbrush, "that's how we christen a new coach!"

Turtle went to the anxious, champing, lathered team, gentling the horses down.

"What'd we rein up here for, Henry?" Cleve asked. "Kind of exposed, aren't we?"

"I wanta look at that son of a bitch I shot down," Purslow said, trudging off back down the road. "Turtle, hold on here! Have a rest in the shade."

"What, by myself!" Turtle replied, goggling over at them with dismay.

"You'll be fine! Get your shotgun, Turtle, take some cover and wait there!"

Cleve shook his head. But he followed Purslow down the hill. Both of them scanned the brush as they went, pistols drawn and ready.

About a hundred and fifty yards back down the trail, they found the dead man in a stand of pinyons and juniper, still dangling from the saddle of his mustang paint; the horse was neighing, eyes wildly rolling, its bridle caught in the underbrush. Purslow bent over and unhooked the dead man's foot from the stirrup—the bloody ends of the outlaw's broken ankle were sticking out through the skin and a torn boot. The instant the dead man came loose the horse reared, sun-fished, and tore loose from the tangle. It galloped off into the underbrush, tossing its head.

"Well, hell," Purslow said phlegmatically. "There goes his horse." Then he pulled off the outlaw's mask.

Cleve glanced down, saw a gaunt face he didn't recognize. "You know him?"

"I sure as shit do. That's Rollo Perkins. A lunger, wanted in Virginia City for robbing a mercantile. Almost caught him once. Guess I got him this time."

"Guess you did. You got any notion who the others were?"

"Might be Bosewell and his boys. Might be anybody."

"I think I hit one, on the way out. Looked like he was tipping off his horse."

"Well then, Cleve, let's have a little look-see."

Hungover but game, the sheriff led the way up the slope toward the tree line. Twice Purslow stopped, to hunker down and listen; Cleve did the same. No sound from the woods but distant crows cawing.

"There's your man," Purslow said softly.

Creeping through some juniper, they came on a man shot through the side. Looked like the shot had cut upward, through the rib cage, emerging just below the heart.

There was something familiar about the dead man's clothing. That poorly matched suit.

Cleve crept up to the corpse, which was already beset by flies, and pulled the flour sack off the man's head.

"So that's where you went," Cleve said, recognizing him.

"You know him?"

"That's Salty Jones. Confidence trickster. One of those who tried to swindle Leon." He glanced at the woods. It was still silent. With two men shot dead, the law at hand, the bandits had made for the willows.

"We going to carry these bodies up to the stage, Sheriff?"

"Hell no! I'll send some boys to find what's left of 'em. Come on." Purslow straightened up, scanned the brush. Listened. Then he said, "I calculate they're gone."

"Glad you're sure of that, Henry."

"Can't you feel it?"

Could he? Cleve peered at the woods, and thought, *Maybe so*.

"Come on. These flies are showing an interest in me."

They went back to the road, and Purslow said, "I'm gonna piss me out some bad water, and we'll get back to the stage." He stepped to the side, and urinated on the bole of a tree that gave him cover in case anyone was up in the woods. Cleve kept an eye on the underbrush.

Still no sight nor sound of the outlaws. Not even a startled bird.

They walked back down to the stagecoach, and persuaded Turtle to drive them on to Elko, despite the slight head wound.

Wedged onto a bolster, five minutes later, Cleve was amazed to see the sheriff already asleep, again stretched out from one side of the coach to the other.

Cleve resolved that next time he was in this coach with Henry Purslow he would ride aloft with Turtle.

About six thirty in the evening, Berenice, Velma Haggarty, and Teresa McCarthy were standing with Constable Brewster in front of the padlocked door of the storage outbuilding. It had been a hot day, and the heat lingered muggily. All three ladies having long dresses, they kept handkerchiefs in hand to dab away sweat. Next to the door was a bucket of water with a wooden ladle, and Berenice was tempted to make use of it.

"I do think you may regret going in there, ma'am," Brewster said. "Why the smell alone . . ."

Berenice looked at her companions in feigned puzzlement. "Are you ladies afraid of a foul smell?"

"Living in Axle Bust?" Teresa gave a short, mocking

laugh. "If I was, I'd never go downwind of the shacks on Dogleg Street."

Velma chuckled at that. "Indeed! Mr. Brewster—we insist on visiting the prisoner. We are on the committee tasked to bring about a new jail. My husband is the mayor, and as such he has the right to permit visitation to the incarcerated."

"We ain't got but one incarcerated, it's that boy Scrap, and he never bathes, and he's got what he needs. There's a bucket in there for his, ah, *elimination*, and we feed him some. Furthermore, he's a thieving scamp who's on the wrong side of the vigilante committee here, and they don't want anyone rootin' about in their tents and cabins . . ."

"Russell!" Mrs. Haggerty snapped.

Brewster jumped a little. "Ma'am?"

"You will open the door or I'll get my husband and several other stout men who know what's right."

Berenice smiled at that, thinking that Velma was as tough as Brewster, in her way.

"Furthermore, I've done my share of nursing," Teresa said. "I don't care about the smell. I'll empty his bucket. I've seen and smelled worse."

"What you got there, Miz Tucker?" Brewster nodded at the small brown-paper package in Berry's hands.

"It is bread, cheese, watercress, dried beef, and two apples."

"Oh, why, we feed him once in the morning. We give him water twice a day too."

"Once in the morning will not do," Berenice insisted. "We will not have prisoners here subject to malnutrition and scurvy."

"He's only been in there since last night—ain't long enough for scurvy."

"Mr. Brewster—open the door!"

Grumbling—the only words Berenice could make out was *"town women!"*—he unlocked the big rusty padlock, pulled it from the hasp, and drew the door back.

The odor was considerable. Vomit, feces, and a long-unbathed male.

"Oh!" said a thin voice from within. "Can I go'n out now, Cons'ble?"

"No, you cain't! You'll be sorry when we do bring you out too! Now these ladies have brought you a little something . . . Ma'am don't go in there!"

But Teresa was already bustling into the little room. She quickly emerged, carrying a bucket out by its handle, one hand over her mouth and nose, striding determinedly toward the ditch behind the building.

"These ladies come here seein' me?" the boy asked, in amazement. He was hunkered down in the beam of daylight from the open door, about ten feet back. A pale face gazed up at them in amazement with one large dark eye, the other puffed mostly shut from some blow. "I didn't steal from no ladies." There was a wheeze in his voice, and he coughed.

"That cough sounds bad," Teresa observed.

"Why, he's had that cough since I knowed him," Brewster said. "Ain't you, Scrap?"

The boy did not respond. He just gazed at them with that large dark eye, his mouth a little open.

Berry took a deep breath and went in.

"That's close enough, ma'am!" Brewster called. "Your brother will have my hide if he makes a grab at you!"

Berry squatted across from him and placed the package on the floor. "It's a little food."

"Food!" He looked nervously up at Brewster.

"Well, go on, take it boy!" Brewster growled.

Scrap snatched up the package.

"Here!" Velma wasn't ready to come in, but she handed

in a ladle of water. Berenice took it and gave it to the boy, who drank thirstily.

"Surely your name's not Scrap?" Berenice asked gently.

The boy coughed and handed back the empty ladle. "I don't like to say. My pa and uncle was on posters."

"Perhaps you could tell me your first name?"

"Oh, that's enough of this!" Brewster shouted. "I think I see your brother's rig coming, ma'am! He'll have my job if he sees I let you in!"

"I'm sure we'll find some way to plead your case, Scrap," Berry said. "We can get you moved to Elko. It'll be better there."

"Yes, ma'am," the boy said. His lips were trembling.

Berenice didn't want a fight with her brother. Not here and now. She stood up and went out, as Teresa was coming back. "Gertie had some dirty laundry water. We used that to clean this out best we could," she said, handing the emptied bucket to Brewster.

He only grunted, threw the bucket inside, and pulled the door shut. He locked it, scowling, took the ladle from Berry, and stalked away.

She looked up and down the road but did not see her brother anywhere about.

It was near midnight when they got to Elko. Too late to disturb his uncle. Exhausted, Cleve stretched out in a spare bed in an unlocked jailcell, and on that narrow, lumpy cot he slept better than he had in years.

On waking, he shaved, changed his shirt, combed his hair, drank some coffee in the jail office, and went straight to the city hall to get sworn in by the mayor. The sheriff pinned the silver badge of the county deputy on Cleve's vest.

Having been congratulated with vigorous handshakes, and gently evading Henry Purslow's hints of a mid-morning whiskey celebration, Cleve went to the Elko Inn where his uncle was said to be convalescing . . .

Dying was more the case, it seemed to Cleve, as he sat in a straight-back wooden chair by his uncle's bedside.

Terrence, lying abed in a nightshirt, looked much older than his years. His hair had been closely barbered, blond streaked with gray; now it was long and white; his cheeks had been round and rosy; now they were pallid and sunken and half-hidden by a straggly white beard—he had always been clean shaven. His eyes had been bright, merry blue; now they were rheumy, red-rimmed, sunken. His hands trembled on the bed clothes.

This is all Les Wissel's doing, Cleve thought, grinding his teeth.

Terrence squinted confusedly at Cleve, blinking. Then he said, "Cleveland? You have come!"

"I have. I only just found out that you were in such straits. Your letter gave me to understand you were recovering."

"Oh, I . . . that is . . . I'm sure I shall . . ." Terrence said vaguely, worrying his sheets with gnarled fingers.

"I've been pursuing our interests on the one-seventy-one . . ."

"On the . . . ?"

"The Trewe Mine, Uncle!" Cleve reached out and clasped Terrence's clammy hands. "My lawyer—I believe he called on you—he's looking for the proof we need. As for the man who attacked you, he would not fight. Tell me this—have you a Dragoon pistol?"

"A Dragoon? A pistol?" He blinked and rubbed his shaky hand over his face. "I have no pistol. I never took to them."

"That was what I thought. Never saw you with one."

"A rifle. I have a Springfield. I tend to leave it in the scabbard. Had no cause to use it. Wish I'd brought it along that day."

"They're saying you pulled a gun on Wissel. A Dragoon pistol."

Terrence gave him a creaky, whispery laugh. "I'd shoot off my foot with such a weapon."

Cleve drew his coat back so that Terrence could see the badge. "I've been appointed Deputy Sheriff of this county, Terrence. Now, the law says I cannot just arrest Wissel, us having no witnesses. But I'll see to him one way or another."

A clarity came into Terrence's eyes then. "Boy . . . Cleveland . . . do not get yourself shot over me. You find yourself a good woman and a home and live peaceful."

Cleve gave him a rueful smile. "Not sure living peaceful is in the cards for lawing in Axle Bust, Uncle Terrence. But I'll take no foolish chances. Leave it all to me. You must rest and rebuild your strength. Who's your doctor?"

"I can't . . ." He rubbed his face again. "Can't seem to remember his name. Ahab something. The lady who turns the bed, she runs the place. She knows. I haven't seen him but once."

"Once! I'll see you get a better physician." Cleve squeezed his uncle's hand, and stood up. "Is there anything I can bring you?"

"Oh, Madge downstairs, she sees I get some soup in me. She and her handyman, young fellow named Joel, they lift me onto a chair and change the sheets and empty the pot and all. Joel, he gives me a little brandy when I ask. So you see . . ." Something faded in his eyes, then. "Cleveland . . ." He closed his eyes. "I should have made that pump work . . ."

Cleve patted his shoulder. "You get yourself a nap, Terrence. I'll be back."

Feeling swept along by his anger, Cleve strode from the room; his boots banged on the stair. He startled the landlady with his vehemence as he asked the name and whereabouts of the doctor.

Leon stopped at the end of the path, and stopped for a long look at Teresa McCarthy.

Bent over to pan gold, she had the pant legs of her overalls rolled up to her calves, away from the splashing stream wending down the gorge. Her skin seemed ivory pale, with the faintest touch of rosy pink; her dangling hair, not lately washed, was the hue of a strawberry that wasn't quite ripened. The creek water purled lovingly around her legs.

Leon thought Teresa looked beautiful. "Morning," he said.

She straightened up, startled, spilling water from her pan. "Why Leon, what brings you to my stake?" She looked less than pleased.

"Why, I thought—well I need to learn about how gold prospecting works, now I'm a partner in a mine, and I thought, you being an expert, and doing well with it . . ." He cleared his throat. "I brought some biscuits and bacon." He lifted the greasy package up for her to see.

She stared—then she laughed, and he thought she was pleased after all. "A lady doesn't like to be seen at a disadvantage," she said, "but, *Madre de Dios*, I could use a respite."

He came up to the stream bank. "*Madre de Dios*, you said! Did you have a Mexican minder looking after you when you were a little one?"

"I did."

"Well, so did I! And from time to say I say *Madre de Dios* too . . ."

She grinned, poked about in her panning tin for a moment, and then dumped it out. "Come on, then!" she called out. She waded out of the stream and sat on a fallen log, in the shade of a cottonwood. He decided that the log was big enough he could sit next to her without being too forward. He sat down and began unpacking the food.

"Now to pay for this food," she said, swiping her hair back with one hand, "I am to tell you how to pan for gold? It's not much of a mystery. I will bet four bits you already know how to do it."

"Well—sure. But what I don't know is how to find the place worth the trouble to pan it. You found this here place that yielded and some others."

"Want to know who told me how?"

"Who?"

"Just guess." She cocked her head and looked at him like a schoolteacher waiting to see if you knew your sums.

"Berry, was it?"

"It was! It's the news of the world, to know half what she knows."

"Cleve has a high regard for her."

"I bet he does too."

He cleared his throat, and handed two biscuits and three rashers of bacon on a greasy piece of calico. "Careful you don't get that cookin' grease on your clothes now."

"Nobody could tell the difference, with this dirty old thing. Did Cleve ever confide in you what he thinks of Berry?"

"Who? Oh—Cleve? Well. I don't know. He is not a man of many words, most times."

"Berry has noticed that."

"How do you mean?"

"I don't mean anything, Leon. Thank you for the biscuits and bacon. I had naught but a little porridge for breakfast, and I was famished. *Madre de Dios*, it is a miracle!"

He nodded and said, "Yes ma'am. *Madre de Dios*."

"You going to just watch me eat, Leon Studge?"

"You don't want me to?"

"What lady would? Bad enough you see me out here dressed like this."

"I never saw a prettier miner, if you'll forgive me for saying so."

"Never saw a prettier miner? That isn't saying much, Leon Studge. But I might forgive it if you have a biscuit too."

"Then I'll have a biscuit."

They ate their biscuits and looked at each other, and Leon had never been happier.

Cleve found Ahab Sutch, "former ship's doctor," sitting at a poker game in the Rampant Ram Saloon, on one of Elko's backstreets. It wasn't much more than a large shed with four tables. A couple of planks laid wall to wall constituted a bar. The place smelled of brimming spittoons and piss.

"Ahab Sutch!" Cleve called out, coming in. He remembered, at the last moment, to take his badge off. This could not be an official action.

A stocky man with dirty-white shirt sleeves, a blue vest, and a dented bowler hat glared over his shoulder at Cleve. He had a spreading red beard, a large drink-reddened nose, and small drink-reddened eyes. "The doctor is out!" he said, turning back to the game.

Cleve walked over to him, and ignored the two other men

staring up from across the table. He took Sutch by the collar and dragged him to his feet.

"I've got winnings on that table!" Sutch cried, flailing, as his hat and his whiskey glass fell to the floor.

"Boys," Cleve declared, "the doctor has bet it all and lost!"

Holding Sutch by the back of his trousers and his collar, Cleve bum-rushed him to the bat-winged door—only one wing remained—and pitched him onto the street.

Cleve stalked out to stand over him. "Get up, Sutch!"

Sutch cursed, got to his knees, and struggled awkwardly to his feet. He snarled and reached into a pocket—then froze as the muzzle of Cleve's gun pressed his forehead. "Take your hand away from whatever's in that pocket."

"I was reaching for money," Sutch said, raising his hands. "You'd be a creditor, I expect." His voice trembled. His eyes were crossed to look at the gun muzzle.

"I am the nephew of Terrence Trewe. You claimed to be his doctor. But you have done nothing for him. He's dying in that bed, and you saw him but once."

"He got his skull cracked!" Sutch protested. "Once a skull's cracked, why, like as not a man's brains are spoilt! They get all jiggled and bruised! Nothing I could do about it!"

"You never thought to try. There are things that can be done. I was in the war and spent a power of time with doctors when I ran a prisoner camp."

"I was a Navy surgeon and I cut off many a limb! I'm a good sawbones, by God, but what am I supposed to do for a man with a crack on his noggin? Cut off his head?"

"You took his money, you should have done something for him. Now—you will lead the way to the best doctor in town. I'm going to holster this gun, but by God I'll shoot you if you try to thwart me. Who else can doctor in Elko?"

"Well—there's Merrick. Some says he's good."

"Lead on!"

Dr. Merrick, a black-bearded man with a shining gold watch-chain, was having his Spanish boots shined at the Gentleman's Parlor. Cleve saw to it that Ahab Sutch paid the physician in advance for a quick visit to Terrence—which required every bill and coin in Sutch's pocket. Merrick seemed puzzled but shrugged and took the money. Then Cleve sent Sutch stumbling away in search of a drink.

Cleve explained himself, and Merrick was sympathetic. "Take me to your uncle, and I shall examine him," said the physician. They walked to the Elko Inn, Cleve trying to make polite conversation. But his mind was on Les Wissel, and what the claim-jumper had done to Uncle Terrence.

Merrick took his time examining Terrence. He asked pertinent questions; he palpated Terrence's chest, checked his reflexes, examined his eyes.

Half an hour later, Cleve shook hands with Merrick outside the Elko Inn and watched him walk away. The prognosis offered by the physician was not encouraging. Cleve thought he'd go and sit with his uncle for a while. That's when a horse clattered up to him, with Henry Purslow in its saddle.

"Where's your badge, Cleve?"

"Got it here." Cleve fastened it back on.

"Best keep it on 'cept when you're in long johns. You never know. Right now, I've raised us a small posse. Short notice—only six men countin' us. But we got to see if we can pick up the trail of those road agents. I got a couple of loose-mouthed fellas on the shady side of the street, says it was Bosewell, but they don't know where he's hiding out."

"My horse is in Axle Bust," Cleve said.

"We'll issue a mount for you. Right up the street to the left, tell Bob Heaps at the stable I said so. Meet me at the courthouse. We ride out in twenty minutes."

"They're going to hang that boy," declared Velma Haggerty, the moment Nan Yang ushered her into the sitting room.

Berenice rose to meet her. "You must sit down, have some tea, and explain yourself, Velma. I have no notion . . ." She turned a smile to her housekeeper. "If you could bring us tea, Nan, I'm sure we'd both be grateful."

The plump Chinese housekeeper gave the faintest bow and hurried off, as the ladies sat across from one another, a small pink-marble table between them. Berry was still digesting the news. "Someone is to be *hanged*, you said? You don't mean Scrap?"

"I do!" Velma set a small pearl-trimmed handbag on the table and began to peel off her white gloves.

Berry felt sick thinking of the pale, gaunt face looking at them with awe and a glimmer of hope in the malodorous storeroom cell. "He's but a teenager. Scarcely eighteen. A starveling youth, stealing from tents just to eat—and they've decided he must hang for it?"

"Just so. I have heard more than once of miners' courts hanging thieves, without recourse to law. But it has not happened here. I know a whipping was given out to one man, but after punishment they let him leave the camp."

"Is it the vigilance committee?" Berry asked.

"It is. Russell Brewster is all for it too! Tolliver and Brewster have the miners stirred up—the drunken ones anyhow. They have a miners' court slated for after supper. And they purpose to murder the orphaned boy soon—perhaps tomorrow night."

"Sunday? They have a strange sense of timing. What's Tolliver up to?"

"If he can push them to hang someone, it gives him power over the miners. Who knows what he'd do with that power?"

"What can we do, Velma?"

"I was thinking you could speak to Duncan—he employs most of those men."

"I will try. But—" She sighed. "Duncan will probably not intervene. He'll like as not avow he has enough problems with the miners as it is."

Nan brought in the porcelain tea service; finger sandwiches, honey cakes, and Chinese tea from San Francisco. "I'll pour, Nan."

"Yes." Nan cleared her throat, lingering, plainly wanting to speak.

Berry glanced up at her. "Yes, Nan?"

"May I ask Mrs. Haggerty—how is Mae Ling?"

"You certainly may!" Velma said, smiling. "She's very well. Learning English apace. Teaching me what she can. She has become my assistant. That lawyer, Caleb Drask— he seems to have taken a great interest in her! I can hardly pry him from the house!"

Nan and Berry laughed. Then Nan clasped her hands over her apron and said, in a small voice, "Perhaps to consider my sister, Li Na. Perhaps someone . . ."

"Oh!" Berry understood what was on Nan's mind. "May I tell Mrs. Haggerty where Li Na is?"

Nan nodded. "I thought . . . we must."

"Well then. Velma, Nan's sister is in the Comfort Tent. She was on her way to Virginia City and ran out of food and money and they recruited her. But she didn't know what it would be like. They won't let her leave. Your Silas is the mayor, Velma. Can he do something?"

Velma shook her head sadly. "I have asked Silas to close the place—but always, he tells the same story. He hasn't the authority! It is true that his post is mostly ceremonial. If the town were to take steps to officialize . . ."

Berry took Nan's hand and squeezed it. "We'll see what we can do to help Li."

"Thank you, ma'am." With that, Nan bustled away.

"Caleb Drask is an attorney, Velma. Perhaps he can represent Nan's sister. He could go to the circuit judge for her."

"If we can pry Caleb away from Mae Ling."

"He thinks himself the white knight coming to Mae's rescue?" Berry suggested as she poured the tea.

"It may be. But . . . she asks often about Mr. Trewe."

Berry felt Velma watching her closely. She pretended to be interested only in her tea. "Nan makes the tea in the Chinese fashion, and it might seem watered down—but one quickly realizes it's simply more subtle. Do try some, Velma."

"Mr. Trewe, the Major," Nan put in. "He helped Mae Ling. He could help Scrap and Li Na."

Berry shrugged, as if indifferent to Cleve Trewe. "But . . . he is not in town. Some errand has taken him to Elko. Perhaps to see his uncle. I don't know when he'll be back. And—volunteer the man for a chore like that. Duncan prefers I do not speak to Cleveland Trewe at all."

"Oh? Why is that?"

"Really, Velma," Berry murmured. "I do not wish to discuss every little . . . ah . . . point of friction with my brother."

Velma raised her eyebrows. "I am too inquisitive? You think I might gossip it about?"

Berry was quite sure that Velma was given to gossip. But she said, "No, it's just . . . a family matter. Anyway—you and I certainly have quite enough dropped in our laps. We have Nan's sister to think about and we must intercede in this hanging. Scrap is but a boy! We mustn't allow him to be hung! It's as if the Deity has decided we are the law in this lawless town!"

"Two women?" Velma gave a soft, sad laugh. "There are charitable efforts we can make. But—to stop a lynching? Berry—you are a Conroy—perhaps these men will listen to you, Berry."

"It seems hardly likely. They're threatening to walk out on the mine. They're defying my brother. They would not listen to me. But we shall think of something. We cede responsibility to the men far too often, Velma. We need not follow them about like idiotic little lambs. Women must speak out—and indeed, take action for what is right! We must find a way to help—decisively. More tea?"

"We shouldn'ta give up on that stage," Devora said. He was standing by the stove, which was unlit that afternoon, in the warm weather. His coffee cup had whiskey in it now—Bosewell had dug into his private supply and brought it out to conciliate the men over the stage robbery fiasco. They were all there, all but Devora seated against the wall. All except Perkins. Those two—being shot dead and all.

"We had to get out of there," Bosewell said mildly, pouring a little more bourbon into his cup. "There were two men we didn't expect in that coach, both of them a-blazing away. And one was Henry Purslow. That other could shoot too. One of them killed Perkins and somebody cut a groove in my side. It's no great inconvenience, this time—little more than a graze. But if we had failed to kill the sheriff, and he got away, why he'd have half the county out looking for us."

"He will anyhow," Hortlander observed, looking sadly into his empty cup. "We shoulda shot one of those stage horses. That would've brought 'em up short all right."

"Those horses are worth money," Bosewell said. "I had it in mind to sell 'em."

"Sure be a shame to kill a good horse, they're val'able," said Wynn Deeke.

"That's right," his brother Chasly agreed, nodding over and over. "Made some good money selling folks' horses."

Hortlander snorted, and shook his head, but said nothing.

"All the gold in that box and we let it get away," Devora said. "I figure you didn't want to shoot them horses, Bosewell, because you saw the sheriff and that other in there. So you rid out. You didn't want the fight!"

"You saying I yellowed on the job?" Bosewell snarled, closing an eye and looking at him buzzard-like with the other. "I lived this long because I listen to my gut. Felt like it might be a setup. I thought there could be a power of other riders coming up behind them, just waiting to catch us. Like as not there was nothing in that box at all!"

"Oh hell, I could just about smell that gold," Hortlander said bitterly. "You panicked, is all it was."

Bosewell's hand snaked inside his vest and came out with a two-shot that he pressed against Hortlander's head. "You go on and say that again. Say it loud so everyone can hear it. A man's last words should be noted by all present."

Devora dropped his hand to his gun. "Leave him be, boss." It didn't profit Devora to have his partner killed. Not yet.

Bosewell slowly moved the hideaway gun away from Hortlander's head. Devora's hand tightened on the butt of his gun. Then Bosewell fired the little gun at the ceiling. The sudden bang made everyone jump a little and Bosewell grinned. "Just so you know who's boss. I got another bullet in this one and six more in reach too." He dropped the derringer to his knee, held it casually under his hand, and watched the smoke rise from the small muzzle. "I'll have no more disrespect. We are going to make our move soon. And it shan't be just one move, boys. It's two. First it's the payroll cash—then it's the gold."

Chapter 12

It was coming onto sundown when Sheriff Purslow finally called a halt to the search. The six tired men in the posse, including Turtle and Cleve, had been following the trail most of the day. They were downstream on Axle Bust, miles from town on the east bank of the creek between steep, forested hills. The creek widened here, becoming marshy in places, and cattails grew in thick bunches. It was humid by the stream; the dimming sunlight was tinted green, filtered through the trees. Water midges hummed thickly around them. Dragonflies darted at the midges and a speckled brown trout jumped in the sun-dappled water. Mosquitoes were beginning to hum up from the reeds.

Cleve dismounted and knelt on the hardened mud to peer at the shallows. Was that a hoofprint in the sand under the water or wasn't it? He decided it was. It was turned toward downstream.

"They cut into the creek, headed downstream, looks like," he said. "We could follow them."

Purslow grunted and wiped sweat from his face with a bandanna. "Mebbe."

"Be foolishness to follow here, Deputy Trewe," said Turtle. "Going to be dark soon. It's a ravine downstream from here."

Purslow nodded. "That creek runs right straight through that ravine. If we ride down the creek they can sit in the brush on that hillside and cut us to chunks. It'll be too dark to spot 'em."

The other men were in agreement. A weary bartender, a bank clerk running for mayor and wanting to say he'd ridden with a posse, and the owner of the Gold Sweepings Mine— all were vociferously in favor of giving up and going home. The bartender said anyhow he had to go to work.

"We'll locate them in our own good time," Purslow said. "Next time they make themselves known we'll track them down."

Cleve mounted up, and the four posse-men rode past the sheriff, up the game trail toward the road. Cleve just sat his horse, and looked at a quivering dragonfly perching on a cattail. It glittered in the sparse light, making him think of jewelry on a lady's hat. What would Berenice have to tell him about dragonflies? What could she tell him about the hawk he could hear calling to its mate high overhead?

She'd have something to say, he knew that. He ached to hear her say it. To walk with her by the creek, just the two of them, and listen to her natural-philosopher talk, Berenice made the world seem almost rational. He longed to see the reflected light from the creek rippling on her skin . . . Her lips . . .

"Cleve!" Purslow called. "You coming or staying put?" He was partway up the hill, sitting on his horse. "You thinking of going fishing?"

"Yep," Cleve said. "That's what I was thinking about. But I believe I'll head to Axle Bust, and start work."

"You can catch the stage Monday morning. I want to go over some county ordinances with you, come breakfast time—and we got to sit down with the city attorney, talk about the State laws."

"I'm going to be in Elko for two more days?"

"You'll survive it. You can't just take a job like this without getting the word from on high, boy."

Cleve shrugged, and started up the trail, wondering if he'd ever again walk somewhere peaceful, just him and Berenice Conroy Tucker.

Torches waved and shed black smoke. Berenice looked with cold dread at the crowd of armed and drunken men as she and Velma got out of the runabout along the creek trail.

"How many men here?" Velma muttered, peering through the dimness to see. There was some torchlight, some moonlight. At night the white spillway of the falls caught shine from the town lanterns, and gave it back in a faint eerie blue glow. Whatever awfulness went on belong in the town, Berry thought, the waterfall kept crashing down, the creek kept bubbling by, marking time and uncaring.

The men crowded were around the cottonwood near Axle Bust Creek; some shouting, some discoursing, a few laughing.

"Close to sixty-five men," Berenice said, at last answering Velma's question. "Far from all the men in town. But enough."

She wished Cleve were there.

"Where is my husband now?" Velma said, mostly to herself as she turned her head this way and that, peering about. "Silas should be here, trying to dissuade these men. Shouldn't he?"

Berry had no answer for that. "We must try to get closer, push through to the front—if we are to speak sense to them, we must have their attention. And it might delay them."

"Is that a noose already hanging from the limb of that tree?"

"I think so. It's hard to see but . . . Look, here is Teresa!"

She was riding up to them on a donkey. "Velma! Berry!"

Teresa McCarthy climbed down and took Velma's hands. "We must try to stop them, Velma! Is Silas here?"

Velma chewed her lower lip. "I don't know. I went to the house and he was not home. I am not certain where he is, Teresa. He may be arguing with Fennig and the other merchants about this—trying to get their support in stopping it."

"Let us push through and see what we can do," Berry said. "Surely the men won't hurt us. They know I'm Duncan's sister and you're Silas's wife. They all respect Teresa."

"I don't know," Velma said.

Indecision was unusual for Velma, Berry thought. Here, even the intrepid Velma Haggerty was unsure what to do.

"Where is Preacher Birch?" Berry asked.

"He was arguing with the vigilantes, and then old Goss came and pushed in front of him and said this was no time for bleating lambs. The men laughed and they took the boy up . . ."

"But there's been no trial!"

"By their lights, there has. Some men appeared before the vigilante committee and said they'd caught him stealing. They said he'd had a whipping and he'd been warned, but kept at it."

"That doesn't make a hanging right!" Berry asserted.

"Oh, why isn't Silas here?" Velma said, looking around, stamping a foot.

Berenice put her hand on Velma's arm. "I say again, it's come to us to do this! Let us push through and demand . . ."

A mingle of moans and cheers came up from the crowd, then, smothering her suggestion. Something was happening, out of their sight behind the crowd.

"Oh no," said Teresa, stepping to one side to see. "Oh! Oh no . . ."

Leon and Q.T. Harte were waiting for Cleve when he got out of the stagecoach at three in the afternoon.

"Morning, Deputy Trewe!" Harte called cheerily, as Cleve took his bag from the coach. "I put out a special sheet yesterday, when I got word we were to have some law here. Ah, and there is the badge! That being the case, it's your job to tell the members of the press about the villainous attack on this stagecoach. I see the bullet-holes in Mulvaney's brand-new coach—we heard an hour ago from Elko . . ."

"It's not my job to do any damn thing of the sort," Cleve interrupted irritably. He wanted no more to do with stage-coaches for a while, nor newspapers. He wanted a glass of beer and some lunch. "You can ask Turtle about it. He was wounded."

"Major, there's something you got to see," Leon said in a low voice. "There's been a hanging."

Cleve stared at him. "A hanging!"

The cheeriness vanished from Harte's face. "It's true. A disgraceful affair."

"The miners' court do it?" Cleve asked.

Leon nodded. "Miners pretending to be a court. It was that boy Scrap. They broke him out of that storeroom he was locked in . . ."

Cleve closed his eyes. He had himself delivered Scrap to that cell. "Goddamnit. Where's his body?"

"Still hanging! They declared he had to be up for three days as a message to thieves! They've got guards on him! About a quarter mile from here, near the creek."

"No one tried to stop it?"

"Oh, we tried!" Harte said. "But it was us against twenty

armed men! I've written it up and I'm working up the nerve to print it!"

Cleve frowned. "Why should you need nerve to print the news? Someone threaten you?"

"There were dark hints, yes indeed," Harte said, glancing around. "When you see the men at the hanging tree, guarding it with shotguns even now, you'll understand my, ah, judiciousness as to a publication date."

"There's something else," Leon said. "On the way to meet you, I heard Mrs. Haggerty and Berry Tucker went up there to try to get the miners to cut the boy down and bury him. Preacher's there too."

Cleve's mouth dropped open. "Berenice!" He took a long breath. "I'll get my horse!"

Cleve, Leon, and Harte galloped up to the tall cottonwood that had been used as a hanging tree near Axle Bust Creek. They had to rein in abruptly, Ulysses arching his back in the sudden stop, as two men with shotguns stepped into their way. They both wore red shirts and miners' overalls, the unofficial uniform of the vigilantes. Cleve knew them. Their cabin was a short climb of the hill from his.

Cleve raised his eyes to Scrap's body, dangling from a cottonwood limb. Someone had used an old horse feedbag to cover his head. To cover the full horror of their crime too, Cleve thought.

The boy's body was swiveling in the wind; it would turn one way, seem to linger for a second, then suddenly turn back the other way. Then it would start over again. As if the corpse were trying to express something with the motion. This way, and that, over and over. The only death knell was the creaking of the rope. Cleve remembered the deserter they'd hung from the train trestle, in that hot August of '84. The soldier's corpse had expressed itself differently than Scrap's, he thought. It swung like a slowing pendulum.

About twenty paces from the body, Berenice, Velma Haggerty, Teresa, and Preacher Birch stood in a small group in the shade of a willow tree, all of them looking toward Cleve. All but Berry had hope dawning on their faces. But Berry had a hand over her mouth and Cleve saw fear in her eyes. And he knew the fear was for him.

Cleve looked back at the shotgun-toting guards from the "vigilance committee."

"Rafe Goss and grandson Curtis," Cleve said equably, as if they were meeting as acquaintances on the street.

The short, bowlegged one was Goss, a surly, aggressive old-timer with yellowing blue eyes and a tobacco-stained beard. One of his cheeks bulged with a chaw. The taller, younger one was Goss's grandson Curtis, with greased-back rust-brown hair, a fox-face, and a goatee. Twenty-two years old and looking to prove something.

"You have business here?" said the older Goss, in his guttural voice.

Cleve ignored him. He turned a glare at the younger Goss. "Curtis—did you enjoy watching that boy strangling on a rope?"

Curtis swallowed. He looked away. "I . . . well . . . he was a thief."

"You didn't answer the question."

"And you didn't answer mine," rumbled Goss. "This execution place is under watch by the vigilance company, till sunset tomorrow. What do you want here?"

"I saw in that broadsheet, he's a county deputy now, Grandad," Curtis said. "He's got the badge there."

"I seen the badge. But he's too late to have any kind of say-so here!"

"You had no authority to hold court on that kid," Cleve said. "No authority to find him guilty. No authority to hang him."

"Constable Brewster was there," Goss said. He spat tobacco juice at the ground. "He didn't try to stop it!"

"He told you go ahead and hang him?"

Goss shrugged. "Not as such. But we've established a miners' court here since this camp was set up!"

"You ever hang a man before?"

Goss glared at him. "No. And we're sorry we didn't. Too much crime here."

"I believe the word was around town," said Harte, "that we had a new County Deputy coming."

"Tolliver said it weren't true," Curtis blurted. "He said it was a lie spread by the Conroys! So's we wouldn't go on strike and such!"

"Tolliver is up to no damn good," Leon muttered.

"Doesn't matter if the law was in town or not," Cleve said. "State law forbids non-judicial hangings."

"Why, no one abides by that!" Goss said, snorting. "It's ignored in many a camp and no one says a damned word."

"We're saying it here and now," Leon said.

"Who did the hanging?" Cleve demanded. "Who was the executioner?"

"As to that, Cleve," Leon put in, "I meant to tell you. It was Les Wissel did the job. He set the rope and he slapped the boy's horse. I got there too late to do anything about it— but I saw it done."

"Wissel!" Cleve exclaimed.

Leon cleared his throat. "I thought you had enough to work on without hearing that first out of the box."

Cleve nodded. Wissel's involvement was a dilemma. If

he arrested Wissel for the hanging, it might look like he'd used the law for personal business.

One thing at a time, he told himself. But he sure couldn't let Wissel get away with a lynching. "Cut the boy down and do it now, Goss."

"Sunset tomorrow!" Goss said, clutching his shotgun and leaning forward like a fighting rooster. "The body can then be buried. But not till then!"

Cleve shook his head. "You got a knife on you, Leon?"

"I do!" He took the knife from its belt sheath.

"Hand it here."

Leon frowned but handed the knife to Cleve.

"I'm going to cut him down myself right now. I'll see he has a decent burial. Then I'll decide who is to be arrested."

With that, Cleve nudged his horse in a walk toward the hanging tree.

"You are not going to cut him down!" Goss roared.

"Drop that gun or I'll blow off your head!" Leon snarled.

"Cleve!" Berry cried out.

Cleve reined in and turned in the saddle to see that Goss was facing him, had his shotgun against his shoulder. A twitch of Goss's trigger finger would blow Cleve off his horse.

Leon had stepped up behind Goss and had a gun pointed at the back of the miner's neck. "I said drop it!"

A curious feeling came over Cleve then. He was going to do something he knew the others might not immediately understand. And the curious feeling came from the realization that he might well die today as a result.

"Leon," Cleve said mildly. "I thank you for covering me—as you always do. God bless you for it. But you're not sworn in as a deputy. And . . . I'm asking you to put that gun down. If this man wants to kill me, he'll do it in front of all these people. And we'll see where the law stands in Axle."

Leon's eyes widened. "Cleve—no!"

Cleve winked at him. "Yes! Holster that gun. Please, Leon."

Leon gaped at him. Then, very slowly, he holstered the gun.

Cleve looked at Goss. "Now you make up your mind what you're going to do."

Berry called, "Cleve—wait!"

But he couldn't change course now. Cleve turned toward the hanging tree, and trotted Ulysses across the open ground. Feeling the shotgun aimed between his shoulder blades.

"Granddad!" Curtis hissed. "Don't you do it!"

Cleve rode on, knife in his right hand, reins in his left. He rode up to the place where the rope of the noose was tied to the tree. From there it angled up to an outstretched branch. This close, he could smell the dead body.

Ulysses shied some, as he got close to the boy's corpse.

"Easy, Ulysses." Cleve turned the horse sideways to the bole of the tree. He was still in range of old Goss's shotgun.

He reached to the rope just above the noose, began sawing with the knife.

Then, in his mind, he saw once more that other young man. Horatio Taylor, the deserter. Legally hung, according to military law, but it had never felt like justice, to Cleve. Taylor had been in three battles. He was only nineteen. Couldn't take the fear and the horror anymore. As an officer Cleve had accompanied the deputation of execution. Taylor's feet made running motions as he strangled, as if even then he was trying to get traction to escape. And then he went limp, and the slow pendulum began to swing . . .

Now, the falls at Axle Bust shushed and softly rumbled—and the rope holding Scrap's body parted. The corpse fell, now just a haphazard collection of flesh and bones in a man's clothing.

Scrap. What was his real name? Not likely.

"They've gone, Cleve," said Leon softly, riding up.

"Who?"

"Goss and Curtis. They've started back to town."

Cleve climbed got down from the saddle. He looked at the fallen body, the noose still around its neck, and said, "Let's get the rope and hood off . . ."

He turned to see Berry, walking up, with the preacher and Velma Haggerty, trailed by Teresa. "I prayed they would not shoot you," Birch said.

"Seems your prayers were answered, sir," Cleve said, his own voice toneless in his ears. "I appreciate you putting in a good word for me."

"Cleveland Trewe . . ." Berenice said. There was a tremble in her voice. "I heard you tell Leon not to stop that man. *Why?* What rashness was that?"

He nodded toward Goss and his grandson, walking across the sward toward town. "They must recognize the law. They all must accept that I represent the law. That doesn't mean they can't fault me, or dispute me. But they must respect the law. Or all is lost."

Berry made a slight nod. She looked at the boy's body, and then turned away, and started back toward Conroy house. Velma and Teresa followed her. Preacher Birch remained.

"What will you do with the corpus?" Harte asked, walking up, pencil and pad in his hand. Cleve looked at the pad and pencil—Harte cleared his throat, and then pocketed them.

Cleve said, "Let us put the body across my horse. I believe Dr. Hull does duty as an undertaker?"

"He's the closest we've got to one," said Harte. "We've got extra coffins left over from the typhoid. A couple went unused."

"We'll take the body to Hull, see what he can do about preparing him for a coffin. Fetch out one of those coffins, and bury him in the town cemetery. If we can find out Scrap's real name, we'll put up a stone for him."

Preacher Birch said solemnly, "That seems fair. Let us get to it. We will round up some fellows to help us with the spadework, at the cemetery. And I'll read from the Book."

Cleve walked to the body, and set about loosening the noose.

Chapter 13

Cleve and Leon left Preacher Birch, Q.T. Harte, Dr. Hull, and Kanaway at the graveyard. As they walked down off cemetery hill, Harte called after them, "Deputy! You going to arrest those men?"

Cleve glanced back and saw Harte had his pad and paper back in his hand.

Cleve called out, "They lynched a man, contrary to the laws of the County of Elko and the State of Nevada. You write that down, Harte."

"Where we going to look first, Cleve?" Leon asked.

"I saw Tolliver, twice, going into a room at the Gideon . . ."

At the hotel, the clerk, at first reticent, was finally convinced by Cleve's badge to reveal that Tolliver had indeed been staying there for some time. "But gentlemen, Thaddeus Tolliver checked out of the hotel an hour ago."

Cleve wasn't surprised. Word had spread that a County Deputy was now in residence. Tolliver had discreetly ridden out.

"Supposed to be a miner," Leon said sourly, as they left the Gideon. "What miner lives in a hotel?"

Cleve shook his head. "He seems some sort of shill to me, Leon."

"You figure Wissel's out at the one-seventy-one?"

"I saw that Swedish miner of his on Dogleg the other day, and I asked if Wissel worked the mine himself. He said Wissel's never there except to pick up gold—and to check the miners' pockets, and saddlebags."

Leon chuckled. "All the same, I bet those boys tucked away some of that gold when Wissel wasn't looking."

"We'll try the saloons first."

Asking in the Tom Cat, the High Nevada, and a tent saloon, they encountered conflicting stories on where Les Wissel might be.

"Might be at the Comfort Tent," said Tootsie, the chunky sausage-curled bargirl, standing outside the tent saloon with her arm around a drunken, freckle-faced young miner.

The young miner, uninterested in Cleve's errand, had a broad grin in his sparse red beard, as he waved a sagging rawhide poke of gold dust. "Look at that fat poke! An' I got me forty double eagles for the rest of it!" he crowed. "And that ain't all there is!"

"You've got the nose for gold, Titus!" Tootsie said, kissing him sloppily on the cheek. She had a proprietorial air about the fellow, Cleve noted.

Cleve was concerned the young prospector could rashly lose his poke, his gold coins, or possibly his bachelorhood, all in a night. But a bargirl had to make her way in the world too, he reflected.

"The Comfort Tent, Tootsie?" Cleve said. "Wissel goes there regularly?"

"I expect he's got him a discount by now, Deputy," she said, laughing.

Cleve looked at the young miner. "Titus, is it?"

"That's me!" Titus said, reaching for a grimy cup of moonshine. "Top man in the camp!"

Cleve said, "Boy—you keep waving that poke around and talking up your gold, you're liable to get a knock in the noggin, before long, and wake up with empty pockets."

Leon chuckled at that. "Right enough, Titus."

"Oh, well—" The boy darted his eyes around, blinking.

"Might be just as well you don't shout it out like that, hon," Tootsie whispered, wrinkling her nose and nodding.

"Were you there when that boy Scrap was hung, Titus?" Cleve asked.

"What?" The young miner swilled a little whiskey, rocked in place for a moment when it hit him, and gasped out, "I seen it happen, sir, I did."

"You on the Vigilance Committee?"

"Me? No, sir!"

"That boy Scrap—did you ever hear his real name?"

Titus shook his head. "No, he . . . Just wouldn't tell nobody."

"His first name was Ronald," Tootsie said.

"How do you know that?" Titus asked, looking at her askance.

"Why—we had a drink, private like, one time, and he told me."

"Ronald . . ." Cleve sighed. "Better than nothing for a grave marker."

Leon said, "Supposing we put on there with his Christian name, 'Hung for too little, too young.' Might be a sort of warning for people to think hard before proposing a man hang."

Cleve nodded. "We'll do it. Titus—you know the men who voted to hang him?"

Titus opened his mouth to speak—and suddenly closed it. He wiped his mouth and looked at the ground. "No, Deputy, I don't know 'em."

Leon shook his head in disgust. "I wonder if they're all going to lie to us about that."

"Like as not," Cleve said. "No man desires it known he suborned murder—or stood by those who did the deed." He found himself wondering if Scrap—*Ronald*—was stretched out in a coffin as yet. No time to find out. "Leon—I propose we pay a visit to the Comfort Tent."

Cleve was standing with Leon outside the red-striped Comfort Tent, right next to the red-tinted lantern hanging from its pole, talking to Reggie the "doorman."

The bouncer wore a grubby tweed suit that was a size too small for him, and casually twirled an ax-handle in his fingers as if it were a twig. A hulking Cornish miner, he'd came to America at the behest of the Conroy Company, was fired for willfully breaking another miner's arm, and took a job as a whorehouse bouncer instead. All this had been confided to Cleve by Leon, who knew Reggie from drinking bouts at the Tom Cat. "Kind of a jolly old feller, but once Reggie gets full-on drunk, I sure can't understand a darn word he says."

He was clear enough this afternoon. "It's nuffin' personal, Deputy," said Reggie, "but I just can't let you in without the lady there's say-so, right?" He pointed across the road at Billi June.

The Comfort Tent's madame had just arrived, her buggy drawing up in front of the small but tidy house Billi June had built for her own use. Cleve knew her on sight, Harte having pointed her out. A well-dressed, florid-faced man was seated in the rig beside her.

He recognized Billi June's curled glossy brown hair and almond-shaped brown eyes; her eyebrows plucked and her painfully precise makeup. She wore an elegant promenade gown of blue velvet, her matching hat tricked out with a small peacock feather. A blue and red silk purse hung from a gold-threaded cord around her left wrist.

The florid, black-haired man was wearing a tailored gray silk suit, and a flat-top derby. He looked about fifty. His air of ownership, and his costly clothes, suggested he was something more than a mere escort. Affecting haughty unconcern, Billi June waited as her dapper escort came around to hand her out onto the road. She was noted for her "fancy airs," as Leon put it.

But she seemed to Cleve that she was a younger woman than she at first appeared. Now, looking at her hands, her skin, he suspected she was twenty years younger than his first impression. He'd thought Billi June a handsome woman past fifty. But the lines around her mouth weren't from age; they seemed formed from a flinty core of ruthlessness. He had seen the Billi Junes of the world before. A hardening, a deep, secret bitterness sapped away the hopeful vibrancy, the trustingness of youth, in some women—even while they were young. He had known elderly women who seemed, in some way, more youthful than this woman in her thirties.

"Mum," said Reggie, as Billi June walked up. "The Deputy Sheriff here wants to go in the tent and look for some bloke. I told him he'd have to ask you."

Leon reflexively took off his hat to her. Cleve merely touched the brim of his hat.

"Oh, the new Deputy, I just heard a few minutes ago!" she said, smiling at Cleve, as if she were really pleased.

"I was empowered by the county of Elko and the state of Nevada to enforce the laws here," he said. "We're here for Les Wissel. You can let us look for the man we're seeking—

or you can have him brought out to the street, if it's done quickly."

His eyelashes fluttered and she cocked her head as if puzzled. "Deputy . . . you are Cleveland *Trewe*, I believe?"

"Yes ma'am."

"I read about you in that scurrilous yellow-sheet published by Mr. Harte. He was kinder to you than he has been to me. But I do take it that you are to be congratulated for saving lives."

She beamed at him then—the hardness was still there, but Billi June was giving a polished performance. He suspected she'd been on the stage somewhere. Maybe New Orleans. Now he saw how Henry Purslow, a lonely man and weary man, could find comfort in this woman's "Comfort Tent." Doubtless with Billi June herself. The sheriff saw only this side of her.

"Deputy," she purred, "you must know that discretion is fundamental, here. We cannot just drag our gentlemen out of the . . . boudoir. It would be shockingly bad for business."

"Ma'am—your 'gentlemen' walk in and out the front door, in full view," Cleve said, asking himself why he was indulging her this far. Perhaps it was an instinct for town politics that every lawman needs. "If Les Wissel is there, he must be produced. The man is wanted for carrying out an illegal execution. I have just seen to the burial of the young fellow who was hung. Les Wissel set the noose and he slapped the horse. It may not be recognized by some here as murder—but it is a most serious crime."

"Sir—!" It was Billi June's escort who spoke now. He had a raspy voice, but there was most definitely a New Orleans accent in it. "You had not taken your appointed place, here, when the hanging took place. Indeed, you have not yet formally announced yourself to the people of this settlement."

Cleve said, "The law has been the same all this time. The vigilante court is not recognized by the law. Now I can't arrest every man involved. But I can find the two men at the heart of this killing. Thaddeus Tolliver and Lester Wissel."

"Sir, you will have to go to Elko and get the papers necessary to search our premises," the man rasped.

"You have never had any kind of legal standing here," Cleve said. "Your business is but tolerated. I need no papers. Who are you, mister? I will have your real name, not some whoremonger's alias."

The man grew even more florid. His right hand twitched by his side; a twitch that Cleve knew meant a man was considering drawing a gun.

"His name is Desmond Farr," said Billi June in her most genteel tone.

"I heard the name in Dallas, once," Cleve said. "There was a killing attached to it."

"Cleve," Leon put in, "suppose during all this fuss Les Wissel is on his way out the back? Last week, I was out behind the Tom Cat, heading for the privy—I saw women being taken out the back of the tent to those sheds they have there. Wissel could get out the same way."

"Could be," Cleve said. "But we didn't make a lot of ruckus asking for him. We'll look through the tent."

"Reggie . . ." Billi June gave the guard a significant look.

Reggie scratched his head with the ax handle. "Ma'am— I don't think it would end well for me if I cracked a deputy's nut. It would end with me running from a posse. Best let him in."

"I cannot allow it!" Farr said.

"What kind of a Comfort Tent has lawmen rooting

through it?" Billi June said. "You know, we can compensate you, Deputy, for the inconvenience of having to look elsewhere. . ."

"Just let go of that idea, Billi June," Cleve said. He didn't hold it against her; the proprietors of brothels paying off lawmen was so commonplace it was scarcely considered bribery. "Leon, about your friend Reggie here—you still have that Confederate bronze with you?"

"The Confederate . . . ? Oh!" Leon drew his old Confederate pistol and pointed it at Reggie's face. "No one can ask you to keep that drunk-clouter in your hand any longer, Reggie!"

Reggie gave a relieved shrug, dropped the ax handle, and put up his hands.

"Back away from the entrance there," Leon said. "In fact—why don't you head over to the Tom Cat and have a drink. Maybe I'll join you later."

"Believe I will, at that," said Reggie. He backed up and then strode hastily down the street.

Cleve watched Reggie to make sure he was going—and then a flicker at the corner of his eye told him Desmond Farr was making a move toward his gun. But before Farr could get a good grip on his hideaway pistol, Cleve had his Colt clear of the leather and pointed.

"Disadvantage of a hideaway gun, Farr," Cleve said. "Slower to draw."

Farr seemed to brace himself—probably thinking of slapping Cleve's gun aside and yanking his own.

"Desmond, you idiot—" Billi June hissed, clapping her hand over his wrist. "He'll shoot you dead if you try it."

"The lady shows some wisdom," Cleve said. "Raise your hands—'Desmond, you idiot.'"

Farr's jaw clenched but he slowly raised his hands.

"Now turn around."

"Do as he says, Desmond," Billi June muttered.

Farr turned, and Cleve reached out, fished the pistol free of Farr's pocket. Keeping his eye on Farr and Billi June, Cleve said, "Leon—you are not deputized. I can't ask you to go any farther with this. There's likely other men in there with guns."

"You going to insult me again, Cleve?" Leon asked, indignantly. "You ain't going in there without me."

"Then on your own head be it."

"Oh, I know that right well."

Cleve looked Billi June in the eyes. "Ma'am, you and your whoremonger can stroll into the tent, taking your time, and we'll be coming right behind you. You will give us a tour."

They walked in through a pool of red light thrown off by the door lantern, and Cleve said, "Hold on a moment." He wanted to take his bearings.

Standing just inside the Comfort Tent, he looked around. It was like twilight inside, as the roof was coated with tar to more easily shed rain. The Comfort Tent was not quite as voluminous as a circus tent, but it was the biggest bordello tent Cleve had ever seen: a good many frontier mining camps erected tents of two and three poles for shops, warehouses, storage for buffalo hides, saloons, and institutions of ill repute. This one had five vertical poles; canvas, draped over rickety wood-pole frames divided the tent into "boudoirs" and passages. The floor was a deck of planks.

Ahead, on Cleve's right, the canvas walls screened lamp-shed shadows moving like sluggish ghosts, cast from a chamber on the other side. Could that be Les Wissel, with one of the girls? The passage stretched fifteen strides to a cornering, where stood a potbelly stove for winter, and the little pine platform for musicians. He could see another shadow, there, stretching across the planks from around the corner. It was the slanting shadow of a man with a long gun in his hands. Likely a shotgun.

"I heard you was going to raise a nice two-story building, for your business, this year, Miss Billi," Leon said, sounding like a man chatting with a local merchant. So he was, in a way. But it was a strange circumstance for it.

"Yes, we have those plans on paper," Billi June said, adopting her purr again. "You shall both be invited in for free drinks."

"The devil they will," Farr said.

"Desmond—hush!" she whispered.

"You going to keep those guns pointed at us?" Farr asked.

"We'll keep them handy," Cleve said. "I did not choose to search Billi June but I reckon she has at least a der-ringer."

"I would be a fool in this rough camp to go without one," she said.

"Let's move on," Cleve said. "Sing out to your man with the shotgun back there. Tell him to save his life and toss that street cannon out where I can see it."

"Harry!" Billi June called out. "Deputy here says toss that shotgun out. Careful doing that, mind, I don't want to catch some buckshot."

"Yes ma'am!" The guard tossed the shotgun out so it faced away from them.

"Come on out, hands up!" Cleve called. He had his gun at ready now. "You make a move for a pistol I'll cut you down!"

The shotgun guard walked around the corner of the canvas partition, hands up. Harry wore a short-crowned top hat, and a wrinkly blue suit just as too-big for him as

Reggie's was too small. A thick black mustache crossed his face.

"How many others guards are there?" Cleve asked.

"None," said Harry. "Only fella that works here besides me, at this hour, ain't a guard. That's Digley."

"Digley!" blurted Cleve and Leon at once.

"He came in to hide, and we got in some trouble together back in St. Louis," Harry said. "So I asked Billi to give him a job. Emptying chamber pots and spittoons and serving liquor and suchlike. And o' course keeping an eye on the girls. Mebbe ol' Digley is keeping too close an eye on 'em."

"Digley?" Farr said, snorting. "You mean The Complainer?"

"Yessir," Harry went on. "He had a bullet wound, and he whined about it some, and having to stay in here, but one time me and him slipped out and, boy howdy . . ."

"Shut up, Harry," Farr said wearily.

"Is Digley armed?" Leon asked.

"Not that I know of," Harry said.

"Where's Les Wissel, Harry?" Cleve demanded.

"He was here a minute ago, but he heard the shoutin' to me, drop your gun and all, so he run off out the back."

"Son of a bitch!" Leon muttered.

"Leon, you know Wissel's horse?" Cleve asked.

"Yep. When he's in town, he keeps that stallion at Kanaway's."

"I'm going to inspect these rooms, in case this man's lying. If you're willing, Leon, you might catch Wissel at the stable. If he's riding out, don't try to stop him. Stay out of his sight if you can. If you can get saddled up fast enough, follow him. I want to get some idea where he's going. But stay back and *don't leave the main trail*. If he rides off it—

you just come on back. I don't wish to see you bush-whacked."

"I can do that, Cleve—but that leaves you to keep an eye on two men and Billi June all on your lonesome. Three men with Digley."

"I'll manage. You better make tracks."

Leon nodded, holstered his gun, and hurried out the front entrance.

"Harry," Leon said, "where's Digley?"

Harry spat at the floor. "Truth is . . ."

"Damn you, sir," snarled Desmond, "you've been told never to spit on the floor in here."

Harry cleared his throat. "Sorry boss. Digley—I think he might be sportin' with one of those girls. He pulls 'em out of the back cabins when you ain't here."

"And who gave him permission to do that!" Billi June demanded.

"Wasn't me, ma'am. I heard one of them girls squalling and crying, like he was not takin' no for an answer, and I asked m'self . . ."

"Shut up, Harry!" Farr grated again.

"You got a pistol on you, Harry?" Cleve asked.

"Nope."

"Show me."

"No pistol, Sheriff." Harry opened his coat to show he was now unarmed.

"I'm the county deputy, not the sheriff," Cleve said. "Now get over here, close to your employers, and we'll take that tour."

"Henry is not going to put up with all this nonsense," Billi June said coldly.

Using Purslow's given name was a message. The sheriff was an intimate of hers. "I've already settled that with the sheriff. You won't be building that bordello house in Axle, Billi June. And you will cooperate or I'll chain you and that pet snake of yours there"—he nodded toward Desmond Farr—"in that storeroom they kept Scrap in. Now go on ahead of me and stay close. I'm going to discover for myself who's here."

"Trewe," said Farr, "when you said 'pet snake,' you saw to it that you would not live out the week."

"I said walk on ahead of me," Cleve said. "Now lead on."

Desmond Farr gave him a venomous look and led on.

As he waited outside the stable, hidden behind a stack of hay bales, Leon Studge was of two minds. Having been punished by his own impulsiveness more than once, he'd learned to question himself some. He held a certainty, however, when it came to Teresa McCarthy—his mind had been returning to her since seeing her at the hanging site of the boy Scrap. She had been there to demand a burial, and to bear witness. Wasn't there a saint named Teresa once?

He had one hand on the grip of the holstered Confederate pistol, his gaze fixed on the open double doors of the stable, but as he waited, his mind kept drifting to Teresa. It revisited the conversation he'd had with her at the first service of the completed church the previous Sunday.

Leon had spruced himself up for the church that Sunday. Shaving, putting on clean clothes and a string tie. He'd only gone to the chapel in hopes of seeing Teresa there, maybe walking her back to her cabin. But sitting on the half-finished log-hewn bench, and listening to the sermon, Leon found that the smiling Preacher Birch's enthusiasm fired the imagination.

"Now folks," the preacher had said, "to build a town fit to glorify God, we know it must grow two by two—as couples marry. A marriage often means children, and folks build a community with care out of love for their children. And I will tell you now, that there is a marriage being discussed, by certain persons"—Birch glanced at Caleb, seated two benches closer than Leon—"and I feel that we'll have the marriage liturgy here fairly soon."

There was a smattering of applause at that from those unused to the quiet imposed in a chapel.

"Right away, in Genesis," Preacher Birch went on, "the Bible tells us of the profundity and power of marriage: '*Therefore a man shall leave his father and his mother and hold fast to his wife, and they shall become one flesh.*'"

This verse struck Leon deeply—and he couldn't help but look at Teresa.

He found she was looking back at him and blushing.

After the sermon wore itself out, Leon was moved when the choir—Berenice, Velma, Teresa, and Mr. Kanaway, who had a fine baritone singing voice—sang "Rock of Ages." Those who knew the words sang along.

Leon managed the parts he knew: *"Rock of Ages, cleft for me; let me hide myself in Thee . . ."*

Leon was smiling when he left the church and found Teresa standing to one side of the murmuring congregation, taking her time tying on her light-pink bonnet. She was dressed in a snowy-white cotton dress ruffled at the hem, a pink sash, and white pearl-button shoes. It seemed rather like a wedding dress to Leon.

He had just put his hat on again, but he took it off for her. "Teresa . . . You . . . You are . . ." He wanted to tell her how pretty she looked but he didn't want to seem like he was ogling her. "That's a fine . . . a fine pink bonnet."

She covered her mouth for some reason, and her eyes twinkled. "Why thank you, Leon. It was a stirring sermon, was it not?"

"Yes. I confess to not attending church meetings much as I should . . . but young Birch, he was much more interesting than Father Lopez back home."

Teresa pretended to adjust a glove as she asked, "What did you think of that quote from Genesis?"

Now he was in a quandary. Was it best to say he liked the verse, or had she found some fault with it? The use of the word *flesh* had seemed bold. But then again, it was the Bible—could the Bible be too bold?

He felt called, of a sudden, to be honest with her. "I felt it was a fine saying, Teresa, and it spoke to me." He felt a curious, agreeable burning in his heart, as he said it to her. So he repeated, "A fine saying."

She blushed again—and pursed her lips. "Sure, and I do agree. Well now. I have to go to tea with Berenice. Please excuse me."

She walked quickly over to Berenice, and he looked after her in a kind of awe. In asking him about the verse, had she been hinting something?

Now, reliving the moment in memory, it seemed to him that she had indeed.

A clopping of hooves brought Leon back to the present, as Les Wissel came riding his tall dun stallion out of the stable. He seemed in a hurry, spurring out that fast. He never looked back.

Leon ran into the stable and put a bridle on his mule. "Kanaway! I'm taking Lily!"

"Yes, Mr. Studge?" Kanaway was brushing down a dappled gray.

Leon slung the saddle onto the mule. "That Wissel there—he say where he was going?"

"He did not, Mr. Studge. But I will tell you that Mr. Trewe asked me to carve a double X on that stallion's horseshoes, and I done it for him."

Leon buckled the cinch, made two more quick adjustments, mounted, and cantered out. For the first time he regretted not having a faster steed. But peering at the road he could see the tracks of Wissel's horse clearly printed. He could see the *X*s in the dust.

He hadn't known that Cleve had asked Kanaway to mark those horseshoes. He grinned, thinking of it. The Major was wily.

He caught up with Wissel enough to catch a glimpse of him turning onto the road south, toward Elko.

Was he going to the one-seventy-one mine? Likely. But Leon stayed on the trail just to be sure . . .

A complexity of smells swept over Cleve, the instant he'd gone around that corner in the Comfort Tent. The waft carried cheap perfume, rosewater sprayed from some aerosol bottle, but the rosewater did not disguise the smell of carnality and sweat. There was liquor and tobacco in the mix too.

To either side were two rows of curtained off chambers totaling ten. Three of them were glowing softly from the lanterns inside. Only two of them showed the shadows of occupants.

From the one on the left came the sound of a man snoring. "Hold there, folks," Cleve said.

Keeping one eye on Farr, Cleve reached over, and pulled the canvas flap back. The snoring man was a half-naked miner, lying facedown on a bed, his pants and an empty whiskey bottle lay beside him on the floor. Beyond the bed an oil lamp glowed on a small, splintery table.

The miner had a remarkably hairy rump. Cleve let the flap drop.

"We'll move to the next one," Cleve said.

The next lit-up "boudoir" was on Cleve's right. Someone giggled inside. It was not a woman's giggle.

Cleve waved the barrel of his colt at the flap on his right. "Draw that flap back, Harry. We'll have a look inside."

Inside was a working girl and an old miner, seated companionably on a bunk just big enough for two. They were both glazedly drunk. She was barefoot, and her breasts were exposed; her customer was fully dressed, even to his hat.

"Simon!" Cleve said. He couldn't keep from grinning. It was the prospector he'd disarmed in the Tom Cat.

The woman at his side had long, stringy brown hair draped over her bony shoulders, and her left eye seemed to be sealed shut, and a little sunken in. She'd lost an eye at some point. Her lipstick and rouge were smeared. She was hugging a half empty bottle of unlabeled brown liquor, cradling it in her arms like a baby. He guessed she was a little past forty years old.

"Ain't you got nothin' to do but spile every fun I got, Cleve Trewe?" Simon said, rubbing his bruised wrist. He reached over toward the girl and without taking her eyes off Cleve she put the bottle in the old miner's hand. He took a long drink.

"That's a handsomeish man," she said, looking Cleve up and down. "You want a poke, Deputy? Simon says he's too tired. And he already done paid."

"He's going to have to pay for his own, Twilla!" Simon protested.

"Not today, ma'am," Cleve said. "But thank you." A twitch in his peripheral vision made him turn the Colt toward Desmond Farr. "You thinking of slipping off somewhere, Mr. Farr?"

Farr stared back at him with burning eyes. "Sir—if you have completed this vulgar intrusion, I strongly urge you to finish your business and depart. Do not come back. Were you a wise man, you would leave this valley entirely."

"I'm going to be finished with your tent soon as I can,"

Cleve said. "But you're done with it too. You and Billi June have till tomorrow noon take down the tent, break camp, and take your stock and yourselves out of Axle Bust. Or I'll arrest all three of you and anyone with you. You will not go to Elko. You will leave this county entirely."

"What!" Billi June said. She laughed dryly. "Why there's several dozen gentlemen in this town that would never let that happen. I bring a lot of joy to a lot of lonely men. They won't abide it!"

"Mae Ling has friends too, Billi June," Cleve said. "And today you will find the stout-hearted men you hope for will melt away like icicles in an oven."

"Trewe!" Farr barked. "We are not going anywhere! You've had your way—but if you trouble us further, I'll shoot you down!"

Billi June glanced at Farr—but said nothing.

Cleve said, "Noon tomorrow. And you will not be taking any of your girls with you—not unless they convince us they want to go. Now—do not move. One twitch and I'll shoot you, Farr."

He looked at Twilla. "You want to go with Billi June?"

Twilla looked at Simon. "I . . ." She shrugged. "Don't know where else."

Simon scowled at her. "I told you more'n once, you could come out of here with me."

"Billi June wouldn't let me go nowhere." She pulled up her blouse to cover her bosom. "And anyhow she owes me thirty dollars, at least!"

Cleve cleared his throat. "You can both go right now. Wait—hold on."

He looked back at Billi June. "Give her the thirty dollars. In fact—make it forty."

Billi June opened her mouth to protest. Then she sighed,

shook her head, and opened the little purse. She pulled out a roll of paper money, dropped the bag on its strap to dangle from her wrist, and counted out forty dollars. She handed it to Cleve.

Keeping his eyes on Billi June and the two men, he held the money out to Twilla with his left hand. She got up and took it and, whispered, "Come on if you're coming, Simon, you silly old goat."

They hustled out behind Cleve, taking the bottle with them.

"Now," he said, "That room over on my left, with the light—open it up."

But the flap opened on its own—and a man came rushing out, gun in hand. "I got 'im, Desmond!" the man shouted, teeth bared.

It was Digley, drunk and wildly firing a derringer at Cleve. A bullet cut by—and Cleve fired twice, both bullets catching Digley close to the heart, spinning him around. The swindler took one step and fell on his face.

Behind him, a frightened Chinese girl cringed in the corner of the little canvas cell, clutching a blanket to herself.

"Hell, I guess ol' Digley left them back cabins and brought him a girl up here," Harry said, apologetically.

Gunsmoke drifted through lamplight—and Cleve saw Farr looking at the small gun in the dead man's hand.

"Make a move for that gun, why don't you, Farr," Cleve said, looking at the terrified, naked, bruised girl in the little canvas room. "I'd like that."

Farr turned away from Digley's body. "That's my damned derringer he stole."

Cleve looked at the Chinese girl. "Do you speak English?"

She frowned and closed her eyes, turning her head away.

"That's okay," he said. She probably didn't comprehend him, but he hoped she understood him from his tone of voice. "I'll take you out of here. It'll be all right."

"Have you any more indignities to heap upon us—Deputy?" Farr demanded.

Cleve snorted. "I should jail the three of you. I believe you guilty of kidnap. Proving it might be chancy. And this morning I promised Henry Purslow I'd give Billi June a chance to leave town if I could. She may as well take you men with her—because you sure as hell aren't staying here. Let's have a look at those sheds in back."

An hour later, Cleve was standing on Nugget Street, alongside six shoeless women wrapped in blankets. Five of them were Chinese, looking around at the disconcerted wagon drivers and the staring miners, in fear and confusion. One of the shoeless women was a mixed-race woman. She'd given her name as Paulita Little Bear. She was the only one who spoke English. The only other thing she said to him was, "Sure took you long enough to get us out of there, you *cabron* sons of bitches."

To that, Cleve had replied, "Yes ma'am."

Cleve contemplated the Gilead Hotel, which was directly across the street. He expected outrage, should he insist on billeting the women there.

But they're whores, even if they didn't want to be! But we don't even let Chinese stay here!

Still, in a way—those complaints were good reasons to insist.

"Was it you, firing that gun, Trewe?" Brewster demanded, as he strode scowling up to Cleve and his bevy of rescues.

"It was," Trewe said, barely glancing at him. "I had to

kill Digley. He shot at me." He turned to look narrowly at Brewster. "Did you know he was hiding out in that Comfort Tent?"

"Me? I have no truck with that place!"

"He's a liar," said Paulita casually. "I had him in there three times. Tu Leng had him there too. You fellers have any smokes? I smoke a pipe but they took it away."

"You can believe that slut if you want," Brewster said. "But all whores are liars."

Something flickered through Paulita's face. Then she kicked Brewster in the groin. He bent over, hissing between clenched teeth.

She said, "That's for that whuppin' you gave me last time."

Cleve, though tired and feeling burdened, could not help but laugh.

Brewster straightened up—pulling his sixer as he came. All in one quick motion, Cleve drew his Army Colt and cracked him over the head with the gun butt while forcing Brewster's gun-hand up with his left hand. Brewster's bullet cut the sky.

Brewster went to his knees, clutching his head. Cleve twisted the gun from him. "Promiscuous shooting is now illegal on the streets of Axle Bust," Cleve said. "I am confiscating this pistol."

He reached down and snatched the constable's badge from Brewster's vest. He handed the copper badge to Paulita. "Here's a souvenir. You can pin that blanket closed with it."

She gave a cackling laugh at that and did as he'd suggested.

The Chinese girls were staring at Brewster—then at Cleve. Then they understood, at last, whose side he was on. Crying and smiling at once, they all began to talk to him, without a word of English.

"Brewster, get up and go find Conroy. Tell him we no longer recognize the authority of a mining constable here. I have that from the county seat. You can be a hired hand for Conroy, but you no longer have the privilege of carrying a gun on these streets and if you trouble these women, I'll let them kick you as long as they want."

"You're going to pay for that," Brewster said, through gritted teeth. "All of it." He got up and walked off, his knees almost knocking together.

"Walks kind of funny now, don't he," Paulita said.

"He does," Cleve said, nodding.

"It's been a busy day for you," said a familiar female voice at Cleve's elbow.

His heart was thumping as he turned to Berenice. Gunplay and threats had not made his heart thump this way. "Berry . . ." He was vaguely aware that Velma and Teresa were with her. But he could not take his eyes off Berenice Conroy Tucker.

She was smiling at him from within her bonnet. "I was looking for you, to ask if you could do something about the release of these very women. And here you are with them!"

"I . . . I was looking for Wissel at the Comfort Tent, and . . . and, happens that once I was there . . . I thought, well, seeing as . . ."

"He sometimes seems to lose the power of speech around you, Berry," Teresa observed. "Cleve—where's your shadow gone?"

"My—?" He blinked. "You mean Leon?" Worry about Leon had been nagging at the back of his mind. "He's on an errand for the town." Cleve didn't want to have to explain his full suspicions about Les Wissel, not just now. "Maybe you ladies can advise me—I've just been pondering the

Gideon there, calculating the likes of their taking in these ladies. The county would pay for it, I expect, but . . . could be I would have to lean on the owner some."

"No need to make enemies of the merchants, Deputy Trewe," Velma put in. "I have a simpler solution. I've got the use of two cabins, at least for a while. Silas had them put up, finished a few days ago. He intends them for hired men, and we've furnished the cabins with bunks, and stoves, but he'll just have to put up some camp tents for those men, for now. We'll let the ladies have a use of the cabins."

"Those the cabins on the hillside there?" Cleve asked, nodding up at one of the low, sun-washed hillocks over-looking the town, just under the new water chute from the falls. Two identical cabins stood there; unstained and solidly built. They seemed to bask in the sun while they were waiting.

Paulita shaded her eyes to look up at the cabins. "If we got to be sold somewhere, they look more comfortable than them shit-holes they had us in."

Cleve turned hastily to her. "Hold on now! That's just temporary housing till we can figure out where you girls need to go. We'll send you in a stage to home, or find you work here—I mean, regular work. No one's going to sell you, that's all done."

She looked at him a long skeptical moment. "First I thought maybe you was a good man. Then I thought, hearing about those cabins, you was like them others. Now, if you're not lying to us, then I guess you're okay." She frowned. "But that Billi June promised things too. She promised me to be paid and treated right. She barely even fed me and they beat me when I kicked a fuss."

"He is not lying, miss," Berenice said gently. "May I know your name?"

"Aren't you fancy," Paulita said, looking at Berenice with

suspicion. "Paulita Little Bear, it is. Now I has a question for you—do we got to stand around here wrapped in these blankets, with all these people staring?"

"Not at all!" Berenice said. "We'll soon . . . Oh! Here comes Nan! She can talk to her sister and explain. I do hope her sister is here with you . . ."

Berry's Chinese housekeeper ran up to them then, calling out, "Li Na!"

Breathing hard, Nan rushed to one of the Chinese girls. They threw their arms around each other, Nan sobbing, "Li Na!"

Watching them, Cleve and Berry smiled. Even Paulita Little Bear smiled.

Then Cleve heard a rumbling in the sky. He looked to the south, where dark clouds rose in a shape like an anvil.

"Cumulonimbus clouds," Berry said, following his gaze. "Looks like a thunderstorm coming."

What with rocky ground and the marks of freight-wagon wheels, Leon lost the tracks of Wissel's horse, and was almost ready to turn back. But he kept on, and picked up the trail again a quarter-mile south. Another quarter mile, and the tracks suddenly turned from the main road. They now led east, up the very side-trail Salty Jones had taken when he'd galloped away. Cleve had told Leon that Salty was dead—killed with the outlaws. Was this trail related to a hole-in-the-wall used by the gang?

There were other tracks here too, besides those marked with the double X. Shod horses, quite a few of them.

Leon heard a long peal of thunder, then, and on the freshening wind he caught the brooding airs of a storm coming. He peered through a break in the trees and saw high, dark clouds swarming just a mile or two south. "Thunderstorm, coming, Lily. Another reason to go back to town." He could almost hear Cleve's voice telling him not to follow Wissel off the main road.

But Leon decided to follow Wissel a little farther. Might give him a clue where the fugitive was headed.

The trail led Leon up a hillside, to a place where a fallen, lightning-blasted fir tree blocked the way. On a very narrow trail the hoofprints wended around the tree and south, tracing the edge of a steep, scrappily wooded ravine. There was a thin stream at the bottom of the ravine—it wasn't Axle Bust Creek, which ran to the west.

The sky rumbled. Leon decided to keep going. He might get a glimpse of Wissel's hideout. He trotted Lily onward, following the thin trail beside the precipice. The track was nearly overgrown with ferns, but here and there they'd been crushed under a hoof. The marked hoofprints were still visible from time to time.

The sky rumbled again. Leon glanced up and saw the thunderstorm's anvil. The air was damp, and it carried that peculiar burnt scent that prefigured lightning.

There came a crunching sound; the snapping of twigs. He peered into the tree line to his right, saw something big and brown shouldering through the brush. Lily scented the animal and lifted her head, ears standing erect to listen. "Yep, there's a big old bear, in there, girl," he murmured. "Headin' off away from us, thank the Lord. We don't need to fool with a bear. We got enough worries."

Leon kept on, till the trail seemed to end at a gap where the cliff had collapsed into the gorge. A doomed pine tree leaned there, stretching bare roots across the gap. He rode closer, and could see the tracks turned west, away from the canyon, through a narrow passage between the tree and an outcropping of sandstone. Didn't look like there was room to even sit on a mount through there. A man would have to climb down from the saddle and lead his horse through. And it'd be touchy even then. Good place to turn back now.

But as the wind rose, whipping the treetops, and a distant thunderbolt struck, Leon dismounted and led Lily through the narrow passage. He stayed on Wissel's trail.

The sky rumbled. Hortlander thought they were in for a thunderstorm. He hoped the food was ready before the storm arrived.

Bosewell's men were gathered around the cookfire. It crackled and hissed just off the road, by the broken-down saloon. The boarded-up saloon's only customers now were woodrats, and possibly a snake or two. Devora had torn boards off the windows to start the fire under the rusty grill. Now he was leaning near the fire, squinting from the smoke, using a stick to stir an iron pot of stew, the pot as rusty as the grill.

The men were surprised when Devora made his first pot of stew for them, a few days ago, and did a good job of it too. For a makeshift stew of squirrel, wild yams, salt and wild onion, with flour-and-grease dumplings, it wasn't bad.

Sitting on a log by the fire, their tin plates waiting in their laps, were Chasly and Wynn Deeke. "Where'd you learn to cook like that, Vern?" Wynn asked.

"My daddy had a trading post, for a time," Devora said. He sniffed at the stew and nodded to himself. "He cooked for folks, two bits a meal. Don't know where he learned it. But he taught me some. We used to give 'em possum and say it were chicken."

"What become of him?" Chasly asked.

Chasly was always asking about their families, Hortlander had noticed, and the questions were always unwelcome.

"When he was drunk," Vern said, "he used to whip me with an old, busted ox tether. Day come when he whupped me one too many times, being as I was near growed."

Chasly grinned. "You take that strap and whupped him with it?"

"No . . ." He sipped a little stew broth from a wooden spoon. "I took his shotgun and I blew him near in half. He wasn't dead, after, but I just let him lay there, a-whimperin', and I loaded up everything he had in that cabin. I knew where he hid the money too. Then I got his whiskey, sat on a stump, and waited till the buzzards come. He started squawking when they set to on him. Too weak to stop them."

Hortlander's stomach lurched. He had not heard the story in so much detail before.

Bosewell ambled up, Tolliver at his side. "Gentlemen," Bosewell said, "the payroll cash is going to Axle Bust tomorrow, very early. We can catch it on the road, and that'll be a good start. You can thank Tolliver here for this—he's the one prodded the miners, so that Conroy to get teh payroll cash to coming quick . . ."

"Might want to get our share, after we done that, and light out," Wynn observed.

"You will be missing out on the real strike, if you do," Bosewell chided him. "There are two more objectives that will pay off splendidly before I quit this vicinity!"

"This information on the payroll come from you, Tolliver?" Hortlander asked.

"No, it came from a man close to Conroy—our good

friend Constable Brewster. He's in for a cut. I doubt he'll be Constable much longer."

"Why's that?" Chasly asked.

Tolliver stuck his thumbs in the suspenders over his substantial belly, and a look of amused speculation spread over his round face. "Because Cleve Trewe is now deputy, and they say he laughed at Brewster's badge."

"Trewe was on that stagecoach," Wynn said. "Him and Purslow. They done killed two of us already."

Hortlander suspected Wynn was still thinking of taking a powder after getting his share of the payroll robbery. Maybe he had the right instinct, at that. But Hortlander wanted more than a thin cut of a payroll job. He wanted something that would set him up. Clay Hortlander planned to go to Jamaica, and buy himself a sugarcane plantation. He would buy a legion of slaves and build a house twice the size of his father's. Then he would invite his father to visit him and have the old man thrown off the property soon after he arrived.

"Somewhere along the line we'll take care of Deputy Trewe," said Tolliver. "Bosewell's right, you'd do well to stick with . . ."

He broke off, swiveling toward the road, where a horseman was pounding across the weedy ground toward them. It was Les Wissel, looking pale and troubled. He reined in, the stallion skidding, and grimaced as he climbed down. "Nearly rode off a damn cliff," he said. "Anybody got whiskey?"

"You are pleased to make yourself at home, Wissel," said Hortlander. "I never heard you were riding with us." He looked inquiringly at Bosewell.

"He isn't," Bosewell said. "But he and I robbed a mining wagon, three years back, out east of Sweetwater. I guess that gets him stew and a drink. What you got for us in return, Les?"

"I'm more curious as to why he is riding up here in a lather," Tolliver said, scowling at Wissel. "The law after you?"

"In Axle they are," Wissel admitted, coming over to the fire. "But I got clean away. Trewe is after me for something that was *your* idea, Thaddeus!" He dusted off his trousers and stretched. "My back hurts."

"What—he's after you for hanging that fool Scrap?" Tolliver demanded.

"That's it," Wissel said. "I was hiding out at the Comfort Tent, and they came in looking for me."

"Indeed! Farr allowed that?"

"They got the drop on Farr—Trewe and that Studge."

Hortlander growled to himself. Leon Studge, the traitor.

"The hanging was to unite the miners," Tolliver said. "So's they'd feel strong—demand that payroll from Conroy, force him to get the moiney and put it on the trail."

"You take the long way around, seems to me," said Hortlander.

"Oh, we're just about there," said Bosewell.

"Say, don't you have a man watching the backtrail?" Tolliver asked. "How'd Les here ride in here without us knowing?"

"I meant to put one of the Deekes on that," admitted Bosewell, looking nervously at the trail from the north.

"I do have something in mind," Wissel said, coming close enough to inspect the stew. "Those Chinee over at Deerstalker Canyon. I've been watching them. I haven't seen them take any gold out for a while, but they've been busy, and you can see on their faces they're finding the goods. Now I think they're hiding it in a drift tunnel, till they're ready to freight it out."

"That is most interesting," said Bosewell. "We shall keep it in mind. Let us eat, and I will ponder the matter."

The stewpot was duly dragged off the grate, and a cup was shared as a ladle. They hastily ate their stew, as the wind rose, the smell of imminent lightning grew, and Bosewell muttered asides to Tolliver.

Lightning lit the horizon, the thunder pealed, the treetops seemed to shake their heads in trepidation as the air grew sickly warm and thick.

If ever there was a bad omen, Hortlander thought, this storm is it.

They'd finished their food, and no one wanted to admit there was any whiskey left to share, so Bosewell said, "As for Wissel and his notion—let us keep it in our vest pockets. But it just might be the answer."

"Who the blazes is that?" Wynn Deeke said, standing up and pointing at a rear corner of the saloon.

Hortlander stood up and looked, one hand going to his gun. "I don't see anything."

"He was there!" Wynn said.

"If Wynn says it, he saw it," Chasly said, standing up and drawing his gun.

"An Indian, was it?" Les asked, his eyes wide. "Indians—they make me nervous."

"Spread out and look 'round the saloon," Bosewell ordered.

Then a motion caught from the corner of an eye made Hortlander spin on his heel.

A man he was pretty sure he knew was running along the tree line close to where the trail came into Red Hills. "I see him! Leon Studge!" He drew and fired, shouting, "Cut him down!"

Chapter 14

Wood spat from a pine trunk beside Leon's head, and two more bullets cracked past his neck as he sprinted along the edge of the trail. He felt a stinging at the bottom of his right ear and ignored it as he dodged to the left, into the brush, the rough branches scratching his arms and face as he shoved through, ducking down as much as he could. He smelled pine and juniper resin and blood, and he felt the wetness on the wind lashing the back of his neck. Shadow drew over him as the clouds teemed overhead. Lightning struck somewhere in the trees to his left, flashing the shadow away for an instant.

Panting, Leon emerged into the little clearing where he'd left Lily, her reins tied to a small tree. The mule was contorting her whole body, digging in her hooves, her eyes wild with terror as bullets slashed by and lightning flared.

He pulled her by the bridle, so he could get some slack in the rawhide loop he'd used to hold her. Getting it untied, he whispered, "Easy Lil ol' girl, easy, I'm here and we're gettin' gone fast as we can!"

Something cracked nearby. A gunshot?

They'll be on me in a moment or two, he thought.

Then the mule was loose and almost dragged him off his feet as she backed away, trying to run. He jumped forward, grabbed the saddle's pommel, swung up onto Lily's back and was almost pitched off as she charged down the trail to the north before he could get his boots in the stirrups.

Leon held fiercely onto the saddle horn, clamping her heaving ribs with his boots. She was in a furious gallop now, and his heart was galloping too; both he and the mule were panting. A bullet hissed by and Leon ducked his head into Lily's mane. Following the curve of the precipice, the trail snaked a sharp left up ahead. He was going to have to slow her to get around that curve . . .

"Lily my girl!" he called. "Ease up now!" He tried reining her in, but she didn't respond. Lightning or bullets, she usually kept calm, but facing both was too much to ask of her. She galloped single-mindedly toward the hairpin turn.

Maybe they could make it around the bend without her skidding over. Lightning flashed, briefly washing all the color from the trees and brush, and thunder rolled by—and then they were at the curve, the mule turning to follow it . . .

Lily screamed when a bullet hit her, and she sunfished in agony. Leon grabbed the saddle horn with both hands but then they were off the trail, falling through space. He jerked his feet from the stirrups and pushed away. She struck the rocks just below him, shrieking, and he fell onto her, was bounced off, all the air knocked out of him. Gasping, Leon flailed—and then he was plummeting on his back into cold water. The water closed over him—and he hit the bottom of the shallow stream. The impact made him suck for air but water came instead, and in a panic he wrenched about, rolled over, found he could rise to his knees, a little above the water. He coughed water, tried to take a breath—coughed out some more. The world seemed to spin.

The next breath made it to his lungs, just as he heard the voices from the trail up above. He couldn't hear quite what

they were saying. But an echo came to him that might be,
". . . see his mule down there!"

Thunder rumbled.

Still gagging, trying to keep from being heard, Leon
crept on all fours up onto the clay bank. He ached, but it
didn't feel like he had broken limbs, though his pain shot
through him from his ribs.

There was Lily, sprawled on her side over a spur of rock,
about fifteen feet above him, legs projecting toward the
creek. One of them twitched a little, but there was no breath
moving her chest, and he knew she was dead. The mule's
blood was splashing and slithering down the rocks toward
him, and her body was draped over the stone spur in a
drooping way that told Leon her back had broken.

Grief and anger surged through him, and, in a state of
mind that wasn't quite sane, he snickered softly at himself
for it. He'd been raised to treat animals like stock, nothing
more. You weren't to get fond of them. He could hear his
pappy saying, "You might have to eat that mule, sometime,
things get bad enough, boy."

Still, Leon's heart ached, because Lily had been his con-
stant companion for seven years, and she had certainly
seemed fond of him.

Should have listened to Cleve. He'd followed Wissel too
far. Lily had trusted him, and today he'd led her into the
black pit of death.

He climbed up a little more, till he was pretty sure he was
hidden under the bulk of her body. The mule's blood ran
past him, and over his hands and knees. He felt for his
pistol—it was gone. Lost in the fall. Most likely in the water
somewhere. And most likely busted.

He'd not brought a rifle along. He was unarmed but for
a knife.

"There's blood in that stream down there." The voices came from somewhere above. Clearer now.

"You see his body?"

Thunder smothered the reply.

"We'll have to go further down the trail, see what we can see, but I think he's dead . . ." *Thunder.* ". . . a long fall. Broke his damn neck . . ."

Leon looked down the gorge, saw a place where the brush and reeds were thick along the banks. Closer by, a shelf of muddy rock hung over the bank. Maybe it would hide him.

Limbs aching, he got up to a crouch and slipped quietly along the base of the slope till he was under the overhang. He huddled there for a time.

The storm, in its last phase, let loose with rain. That and the threat of more lightning might keep Hortlander and the others from coming after him. They might convince themselves he was dead.

But it was a long way back to town, and every movement, right now, shot pain through Leon.

Aching from bone-deep bruises, shivering from being soaked, Leon huddled under the overhang, waiting, knowing a thunderstorm rain didn't last long.

He had to move on, soon as he could. He had to get back to town and warn Cleve.

Berenice was standing at a newly built table in the cabin, unpacking clothing from a wicker chest. The storm had spent some of its fury by the time it rolled on to Axle Bust, but listening to the lightning's hiss and bang, as it tossed off its remaining thunderbolts, she feared it might strike a building in town and kindle a general fire.

The newbuilt bunkhouse smelled of fresh-cut wood and

plaster. The dresses and under-garments she was arranging had been donated by the wives of Axle Bust and Mayor Haggerty's store, for the women of the Comfort Tent. Dr. Hull was sitting across from Berry, in a new, wicker-seated chair examining Tu Leng. Teresa stood beside him, patiently assisting. Caleb was hunkered nearby, translating Hull's questions.

The other women had been examined and treated as well as Hull could. Two of the women had signs of venereal disease; Hull would treat them—also as well as he could. Li Na, Nan's sister, was in Nan's room at Conroy House— Duncan did not know she was there. Since Li Na had been kidnapped recently, she might not have been poxed. Dr. Hull would examine her last.

Paulita was in the other cabin with the rest of the girls; the Chinese girls talking in Cantonese, and Paulita napping.

Paulita had been recruited, not kidnapped, but held against her will once there. With customers, she'd used a sponge she carried; the sponge absorbed the customer's ejaculants, and if taken out and carefully washed soon enough after, the chance of venereal disease or pregnancy was much reduced.

Thinking of the men who'd so merrily exploited these women, Berry pondered the sexuality of the human male. Many a man could be tender with his wife, could be caring and chivalrous—surely Cleve Trewe would be chivalrous. But men could also be condescending, presumptuous, and even brutally authoritarian toward women. For them, women were for pleasure or breeding purposes. And many a man could be violent with women. It seemed to Berry that some men lost some of their native intelligence when their sexuality was aroused. They became temporarily obtuse; morally and intellectually stupid.

She knew women who were perfectly happy being

spinsters. She had thought she might well go the rest of her life without marrying again, and be reasonably content. She and Grant Tucker had conceived only one child, a girl lost to stillbirth. The hurt of it was still with her. Why risk another grief? Why not choose the life of a cheerful, respectable, independent widow? Such a life offered peace and dignity. Till recently, she had made up her mind to it.

But Cleveland Trewe had thrown her half-formed plans into confusion.

He was the only man she'd ever met who not only attracted her, but who seemed to understand her. He respected her fascination with the sciences, even shared them. He was a kind man, but also a man of courage and decision who instinctively protected the weak and the innocent. Such a man was rare and precious.

She had caught herself imagining Cleve proposing they elope, to elude her brother. Perhaps that was sheer vanity on her part, and it seemed almost like a schoolgirl fantasy, when she considered it now. Cleve had to think of his uncle's mining claim, and now he was the only law in Axle Bust. He had no time to come and sweep her off her feet.

Best she put him out of her mind.

"Oh, I see Cleve is on his way here," Teresa said, looking out the open front door.

Berenice gave out a soft gasp. Lightning cracked, thunder pealed, and Cleve Trewe was coming to the cabin.

Thunder rolled like the sound of the first boulder in an avalanche.

Cleve walked up the graveled path to the cabins, wanting to know how the Comfort Tent women were doing. He was wondering too, what had become of Leon. He wanted to go and look for him, but if Leon had followed Wissel off-trail, he might be anywhere.

Told him not to do that, Cleve thought. But Leon was not a deputy; was his business partner, not an underling.

Cleve saw Jonah Bentworth standing out front of the door of the easternmost cabin, smoking a pipe and watching the thunderstorm. The old trooper's faded-blue cavalry winter coat was missing most of its brass buttons; his dark blue Cavalry campaign hat was tilted back on his head. An old carbine rifle was leaning against the wall beside him.

Cleve and Jonah had met briefly at the High Nevada, six weeks back, and they'd shaken hands. Jonah was an old man, but his leathery grasp was strong. They'd talked of the rain and whether the trails were clear. Cleve had quelled the temptation to ask about Berry.

"Deputy Trewe," the old man said in his deep voice as Cleve walked up now. They shook hands. Jonah nodded toward the sky. "Storm looks like it's all but blown out."

They both turned, as men will, to ponder the clouds. Cleve grunted agreement. "Threw one more lightning bolt just to let us know it could, and now it's breaking up."

"Heard you had some trouble with them whoremongers. Had to shoot one."

"Word darts around this camp like a tree swallow, don't it?"

"It does," Jonah said, chuckling.

"I've got to ask you, were you there when they hanged that boy?"

Jonah's nostrils flared, and his eyes narrowed. "Conroy had me out watching that little mine at Angry Wife for him. A miserable bore of a job it was, but when I heard Berry was there at the hanging—that she had to see all that, with those roughnecks shouting for a lynching, some of them firing their guns at the sky—by God I was angrier'n a bull with his nuts caught in a fence! I told Conroy I was done guarding that mine. He could fire me if he wanted."

"And did he?"

"He kept me to watch over Berry. Cut my pay some, but I don't give a good goddamn." He cocked an eye and a gnarled finger at Cleve. "Let me tell you, Deputy—I'd have done anything I could to stop those drunken idiots! You know, most of the miners weren't even there, way I heard it. It was just that Goss and that Tolliver and the men that follow 'em."

Cleve nodded. "Meant to ask you about the campaign topper." He pointed at the old cavalry hat. "Indian wars style?"

"It is. I was a quartermaster for you boys with the big appetites, in the Civil War, trying to keep you in food. I tried for a transfer to fight the rebs, but they said I was too old. Said I could keep the peace with Colonel Sibley up in the Dakotas."

"That peace didn't last long."

"No, it did not. We got into a war with the Sioux pretty quick. I was breveted captain. I hear you was breveted up in the war with the rebs."

"Twice. The rebels had sharpshooters killing our officers. That a Spencer carbine, there?" Cleve asked.

"It is."

"How old is that gun?"

"Now if you're saying an old gun's no good—"

"Oh, I've got an old Army Colt here."

"I got a newer Colt, the '72 model, right here under my coat. Say, I had a lieutenant under me in the Indian campaigns—fella you might know, Cleve. He gave you that badge."

"Not Henry Purslow!"

"Purslow it was. It was him that got me this job! He writ to me, you see. I was a county sheriff in East Texas for a time and my old bones couldn't take those long rides anymore. So I quit, thinking I'd sit in a rocker on some widow's porch maybe. I was a little too long in the tooth to take the job you got. But he knew Conroy was looking for a man could handle himself, to watch over his place—and his sister."

"Now just between you and me and the fencepost, Jonah, what do you think of Sheriff Purslow? Will he stand by a man?"

"Why, sometimes he throws a wide loop, but he's a man to ride the river with. Saved me from a scalping and carried me on his back across a battlefield, caught an arrow doing it and kept going—hell, he's my friend. He steps in a gopher hole now and then, but he gets right in the end."

"That's good enough for me. I haven't known him long. I'm not sure how he's going to take something I've got to do now. I've got to arrest Les Wissel. There's a personal matter between me and Wissel—it won't look good when I do it."

"I heard about that claim jumping bastard." Jonah leaned against the wall, raised one of his feet enough to tap out his corncob pipe on the wooden heel of his boot, while squinting up at the sky. "Henry will do what's right, you can be sure of it. Here comes the rain! Won't last long, if I'm any judge. But you best come on in, them ladies be happy to see you. 'Specially one I know."

The gang was gathered in their usual corner by the cold stove, the Deeke brothers playing head's-up poker, using an unoccupied chair seat for a card table, the others standing around holding their coffee cups. Tolliver had finally broken out the whiskey and they were sipping it, Hortlander mixing his with cold coffee. The rain was still pattering down outside.

"I say we ride out of here now, Bosewell," Hortlander

said. "Even if Leon Studge is dead, how do we know he wasn't sent up here to spy on us? If he was, they know we're here."

Bosewell spat at the floor of the abandoned trading post. "That's balderdash. The law would be here right now, if they knew where we were! They'd have opened the ball and you'd probably be on the floor ducking rifle balls."

"We didn't see Studge's body, that's sure enough true," said Wynn Deeke, slapping a pair of aces on the chair between him and his brother. "Just his dead mule!"

"Studge is most likely dead, down in that gorge," said Tolliver.

"And if we leave Red Hills," Bosewell said, "where do we go? This place offers shelter, and it can be defended. There are only two trails in, and we can guard them. I say we stick here—but not much longer."

"When it stops raining," Hortlander said, "maybe you and me go see if his body's down there, Vern."

Devora said, "I ain't climbing down them rocks. He's dead anyhow."

Hortlander shook his head. He badly wanted to know for sure.

"Got ourselves in a kind of pickle here, ain't we?" Chasly said, dealing another hand.

"How's that?" Bosewell growled.

"Don't know if we should stick or ride out. Got no good place to ride to."

Bosewell snorted and poured himself a little more whiskey from the nearly empty bottle. "How I got myself mixed up with you whining, sniveling ne'er-do-wells I don't know."

"I pondered on that myself," said Hortlander.

"Pondered on what?" Bosewell demanded, glaring.

"You and Tolliver seem kind of like gents who'd be

strutting with the town men, on the city council or such. How long you been on the dodge, Bosewell?"

"Hmph!" Bosewell drank a dram and said, "Of course not! Nor were you if I'm any judge. I was the financial officer for one of the best universities in the east, that much I'll tell you."

"Which one?" Tolliver asked.

"Never you mind! But they accused me of misusing funds, and, ah, I felt it was wise to move on."

"Hand caught in the till, was it?" Tolliver chuckled.

Bosewell scowled but didn't deny it. "Now, I was always skilled with a rifle and a shotgun, had many a hunting trophy. So I took my guns and headed west with all speed. They were looking for me, but . . ." He laughed bitterly. "I found that the farther west you go, the less they look for you. And pretty soon they give up." He sipped a little whiskey and went on, "I also found I wasn't suited for most of the work about. Farm work, ranch work, hard-rock mining. Why, it is below a man like me! I applied to clerk at the banks out here but they wouldn't have me—they demanded proof of my tutelage, references and such, and I was unwilling to provide it. So I set myself to take their money another way."

"I was impressed by that robbery in Carson City, I must say," Tolliver admitted, nodding. "You got away with a fine big sack of money."

"Surprising how money doesn't last, though, isn't it?" Hortlander said, knowing his own proclivities. "It's like candy in the hands of a hungry boy."

"Money don't give me a stomachache like candy," Chasly observed. "I got you beat with three queens, Wynn."

"Sounds like the rain's 'bout done," said Devora, glancing at the ceiling. Very little was leaking through now. "Thunder's done too."

The door opened, hands went to guns—but then they relaxed. It was only Russ Brewster.

"Brewster!" Hortlander said archly. "You here in your capacity as a constable?"

Everyone but Brewster had a laugh at that.

Brewster walked in, anger in his gait, and said, "That son of a bitch Cleve Trewe disarmed me and took my badge and I will see him dead."

"Why, you came to the right store!" said Hortlander. "Say—did you see Leon Studge on the road, coming in?"

Brewster shook his head. "Not hide nor hair of him."

"You see there, Clay?" Tolliver said. "He's dead. Or he'd have been somewhere on the road."

"That's right," said Bosewell, nodding.

"So you say. But he could have slipped on down that gorge."

"He couldn't survive that fall."

"It's not that far down." At that moment, Hortlander made up his mind. "I'm going to go look for that damned traitor's body. I need to know he's dead. None of ya'll coming with me? You should be—we need to know he didn't get word back to Trewe."

Wynn dealt another hand. No one spoke up.

"So be it," Hortlander said, stalking toward the door.

"And suppose you're delayed," Tolliver called after him. "You'll miss out on your share. You're not there for the job, you get not a penny."

Hortlander turned back at the door. "Tomorrow we hit the payroll? Hell, I'll be back tonight, sometime. Might find him quick. Or I might have to trail him. But I'll be here."

"Just the same, Hortlander," Bosewell said, "don't bother coming back here, if you're too late for that job!"

"I heard you first time you said it," Hortlander muttered, clapping on his hat and heading out.

Whether Leon Studge was dead or alive, Hortlander silently vowed, he would be found.

Closing the door behind him, he heard Brewster say, "Well, is anyone going to give me some of that whiskey or ain't they? After all I been through . . ."

"I will consult with my friends at the Chinese mine," said Caleb. "How they will feel about these women I don't know. But maybe they'll help them."

"We'll find them work at the store in the meantime," Mrs. Haggerty said. "If I can get a certain someone to agree on that . . ."

Sunset, and they were standing in front of the cabins— Cleve, Berry, Teresa, Jonah, and Velma Haggerty. The women from the Comfort Tent were inside, looking through the clothing and shoes that had been brought for them.

The town below them was glowing in the sunset light like a cluster of rubies. Golden lantern light winked between the crimson facets of rooftops. The mist from the falls somehow united the whole into a single gemlike image. Fragments of storm clouds were racing along overhead, red as embers. Cleve heard a pop from the wilder end of Axle Bust, probably a gun. He walked over to the top of the slope, listening and watching. There was no recurrence, not yet. Two or three times a night some celebrant fired their gun at a rodent or at a fence post or at the moon. He looked over at the falls, and the sunset-glow rippling like a flame in the falling water, an illusion making the light seemed to ripple up as the waters tumbled down.

"Sometimes, it really is astonishingly lovely here, isn't it?" Berry said, walking up beside him.

He turned a smile at her, "You do have a way of sneaking up on a man."

"Oh, I *am* sorry, Mr. Trewe!" she said, her eyebrows raised.

His smile became a grin. "You can sneak up on me anytime you like, Berenice."

"I was in hopes you might walk me down to my rig. It's at the bottom of the hill. I've really got to go home and look in on Nan and her sister, and see that everyone's fed."

"It'd be my privilege," he said.

He thought, *If she just wanted someone to walk her, Jonah was handy*.

Jonah did stride up then, carrying the carbine. He'd been keeping an eye on the two of them. "You going on down the hill, Berry?"

"Yes, it's been a full day. That boy's body—thank God Cleve got him down and buried. Then the tending to the Comfort Tent girls. My brother will be sending a hunting party for me if I don't go home."

"He surely will. I'll go on ahead. Getting dark down there." Jonah walked stiffly but with purpose down the path.

"Sometimes Jonah likes to go on ahead of me," Berry said softly. "Says he's scouting the terrain to see if it's safe. He's as conscientious as he can be. And so very patient. He climbs some small mountains to accompany me, and it must be hard for him at his age. Never complains."

"He's a good man."

She took Cleve's arm, her hand in the crook of his elbow—as if it was the most natural thing in the world—and they started down the path. The setting sun was half melted in a notch on the western horizon. On the north of the basin, deep shadows pooled like crude oil under the hills. The path took a turn to the west, along a thick stand of sumac, chokecherry, and dwarf maple. The air was scented with tree resins and the rich smell of soil after rain. Up ahead it was quite dark, and Jonah had vanished in the shadow, somewhere around the next bend in the path.

"Oh look!" She tugged softly on his arm and they stopped to gaze out at the sky framed between two shadowy trees. To the southwest, a star glowed, faintly greenish, seeming to quiver with energy, as heat from the cooling earth rose to make it shimmy.

"What star is that?" he asked.

"It's actually a planet. It's *Venus,* Cleve. How she dances! What better omen?"

He turned to look at her. The muted evening light giving Berry a roseate glow as she gazed at Venus. Compliments came to his mind, remarks about Venus, the goddess of love, but he wisely decided to voice none of them. All he said, very softly, was, "You figure it's an omen?"

Berry turned and met his eyes. She seemed puzzled. Her voice was almost a whisper, "You don't think so?"

Cleve looked into her eyes. There was nothing to do, then, but put his arms around her and kiss her.

Her lips were just as soft and warm as he thought they'd be. The feel of her lips, the way they moved with his, communicated more than mere passion.

Yearning. A long wait coming to an end.

Deeply moved, he reached up and stroked her hair, drew her a little closer . . .

Berry broke off the kiss, panting a little, but stayed in his arms, her cheek against his.

"You . . . you need a shave," she said softly in his ear. She kissed his cheek.

"Yes, I do," he said.

"I don't mind it," she whispered. "At this moment, I've lost all good sense, and I feel not a bit ladylike. It is quite appalling."

"Yes, it is. Let us have some more of it." He kissed her again, and she moaned softly.

It was he who broke the kiss off this time. Berry's body

was warm and yielding against his—the feeling was almost overwhelming.

It was only a first kiss, he told himself. You're a gentleman. Step back for now.

"Berenice, I . . ." Cleve swallowed hard. "I'd best take you to your buggy. Jonah will come looking for you . . . And I've got to look for Leon. I'm worried about him. But . . . can I see you tomorrow? Maybe we could meet at the falls for a ride, around noon. We can ride along the creek."

Berry's lips were parted, her breath coming rapidly. The shadows had deepened, but in a streak of light coming through the trees he could see her eyes, glistening with life and a little tearful. Her voice was husky when she said, "Yes I'd . . . I'd like that . . ."

"I dislike to meet in secret. But seeing how Duncan feels . . ."

"I don't need his permission, Cleve. But yes. For now. Let's meet at the falls."

She put her hand on his arm again, and they walked down the path a little farther.

Then came two muzzle-flashes below, one answering the other, the gunshots echoing up from the inky shadows near the bottom of the hill.

"Cleve!" Berry's hand tightened hard on his arm. "It's Jonah!"

"Go back up to the cabin," he said. He pulled away, at the same time drawing his Colt.

He hurried down the path, turned a switchback, and saw another muzzle-flash; heard a charge of shot hiss by his left shoulder. Still moving, he returned fire, and someone in the brush gave out a yelp of pain—and then Cleve ducked to his right, into the uncertain cover of a copse of pinyon pines and junipers. And almost immediately, just off the path, he heard a man groaning. There was just enough indirect light to see that it was Jonah, lying on his back. His old carbine and faded-blue campaign hat were lying beside him.

For a sickening moment, Cleve was afraid he'd accidentally shot Jonah in the dark. But no. The man he'd shot was nowhere near this spot. He heard running footsteps from the path.

"Jonah!" It was Berry.

"Get back up the hill, Berry!" Cleve yelled. "They're still out there!"

But she ignored him. She hastened to Jonah, knelt, and took his hand.

Jonah rasped, "Berry . . . girl, go up the hill like the man says . . . I'll be . . ." He let loose a bubbling cough. "I . . . calculate I hit one. There's another in them trees."

Then a spinning light arced like a comet through the air, and a lantern smashed onto the ground between them and the thicket. The oil burst a bushel-sized fireball of yellow and blue, illuminating Berry and Jonah with a ghastly sulfur colored light. A man was staggering toward them, flame light limning the barrel of a shotgun. Cleve could tell from the silhouette it was Harry, from the Comfort Tent.

Cleve fired from the hip, twice, and Harry staggered, spasmodically firing the shotgun into the ground. Then he fell, and the shotgun clattered.

A decoy, Cleve thought. He stepped out in front of Berry—between her and the place the lantern had come from.

"No!" Berry shouted.

A gun fired from somewhere behind him. He turned to see Berry, kneeling, with carbine in her hands, smoke from the muzzle showing in the firelight. "He's there!" she cried, her voice breaking. She pointed with the gun. "He was going to shoot you!"

Cleve looked where she was pointing and saw a man stumbling off through the trees. Desmond Farr. "Looks like you hit him."

She put the carbine down and took Jonah's hand. The old man's white hair was fanned out around him, his mouth trickling blood. He peered up at her, whispered, "If I could have a daughter . . ."

"I wish you had been my father," Berry said, her shoulders shaking.

Jonah clasped her hand—and then a ghostly final breath whispered out, and he was gone.

Cleve went to her, hunkered down and put an arm around her shoulders. "I'm sorry." It wasn't enough, but it's all he could manage, then.

Berry said nothing for a long moment. The fire around the broken lantern was dying on the damp ground, spitting and hissing. Then she said, "Cleve—I think that was Billi June's partner I shot. What was he trying to *do*?"

"Planning to kill me, I expect. Shot Jonah to lure me down here. Kill me and anyone who stood between him and those girls. He did not want to be run out of town."

She reached out and closed the dead man's eyes.

Cleve said, "You know Jonah got off a shot, and wounded that shotgun guard from the Tent. If a man had to die, at his age—I figure he'd be glad to go this way. Protecting you."

He could hear Caleb's and Dr. Hull's voices, up the hill. "They're coming down to us, they'll look after you." He stood up.

"Don't go, Cleve. He'll ambush you!"

"I'll be careful. You saved my life, Berry. I'm not going to throw that away."

Cleve brushed her cheek lightly with his hand. Then he started after Farr.

* * *

The storm had passed but it was already dark down in the gorge.

Leon was walking unsteadily along the stream bank; each step hurt like the dickens, sending shockwaves into his chest. Every few steps he stumbled on the slick, uneven surface, having to work hard just to keep from falling over.

He was making his way downstream, and the way the brook was bending here, turning to the west, it occurred to him that this was likely the creek that Teresa was working. Wouldn't it be something if he found her there, come morning. He could almost see her, now, looking up with those green eyes, and smiling at him.

He swayed, and the world seemed to shift on its axis. "Busted axle," he muttered, chuckling. "Whole world got a busted axle."

His head was throbbing strangely. Must've hurt himself worse in that fall with his Lily than he'd supposed.

A trickle of water from the recent shower was coming off the roots hanging over a granite outcropping. He paused and let it wash over his face. The cold water brought him back to his senses enough to realize he was still in a bad fix. "Oh Lord, I need to get to town. Cleve's got to know."

"I have you now, traitor," said a familiar voice, just above him.

Leon stepped back and looked up to see Clay Hortlander, standing on the ledge above him, six-gun in hand. Hortlander's booted feet were less than a yard over Leon's head.

He heard Hortlander's gun cocking.

Leon grabbed Hortlander's ankles and pulled hard.

"You son of a—" Hortlander shouted, firing wildly. A

bullet sang into the brook as Hortlander fell, sliding on his rump past Leon.

The outlaw gave out an "Oof!" as he struck the stream's bank in a sitting position, his legs splashing partway into the water.

Leon turned and crouched—and then the world spun around him. He fell to his knees, as Hortlander turned to him, hissing out a curse, and brought the gun up. But Leon grabbed at his gun hand, his reflexes finding it though the whirling world didn't want him to, and he wrenched it with all his strength. Twisting the gun broke the bone of Hortlander's trigger-finger and he screamed in pain. The gun fired, the bullet ricocheting off a boulder. The outlaw hooked a smashing punch at Leon, catching him hard on the side of the head.

The blow sent dark reverberations through him, and he almost went along with them into the blackness. But he struggled to stay conscious, and with a final jerk tore the gun free and cracked its steel butt down on Hortlander's forehead. Cursing, Hortlander raised his fist to batter at Leon again. Leon brought the gun down harder—and Hortlander fell back, shaking, trying to get up.

Leon crept closer and raised the gun again. "This one is for Lily." He brought it down with all his strength, crushing Clay Hortlander's skull.

Then, gasping for air, Leon felt the strength going out of his arms. He let go of the gun, and managed to sit up. He stood. He turned . . .

And fell, out cold before he hit the ground.

Colt Army in hand, Cleve reached the southern edge of the thicket and paused, crouching under a spruce. There was lantern light from town, streaking the open slope between him and the nearest shacks and tents. He spotted a trace of Farr: a glistening trail of blood. Almost like the track of a slug, he thought. He peered at the spaces between the shacks, trying to see if Farr was lying in wait for him. Cleve couldn't see him.

He slipped out of the thicket and ran across the open ground, to the widest opening between a saloon tent and a half-fallen soddy, scanning for Farr. He paused at the back corner of the soddy, leaning out to look.

Once more the only trace was another track of blood. Seemed to Cleve the track was angling toward the Comfort Tent.

He ran on, startling two men and a woman at a cooking fire in front of a shack, and prompting a small yellow mutt to yap at him and snap at his heels.

Cleve hurried around a corner, keeping the anger over the murder of Jonah Bentworth coiled down inside him. If he let fury control him, he'd be more likely to blunder into a trap.

A wagon trundled out of the way, and about fifty feet ahead he saw Desmond Farr crossing the road, walking doggedly toward Billi June. She was putting a carpet bag into the buggy in front of her house. She had her hat and blue velvet jacket on, and every appearance of a worried woman about to leave town.

"You will not leave me, Billi June!" Farr shouted, his voice hoarse. He had a pistol in his right hand; his left was clamping his side, where blood had darkened his coat.

"Leave me alone!" she said.

Cleve hesitated. Farr had stopped right in his way. If he shot at Farr, Billi June might be hit. He was innately reluctant to shoot a woman, no matter who she was.

"You will not take the money and you will not go!" Farr cried, two strides from her. "I am not through here! I will *not* be driven off—nor will I let you ride out on me!"

"Farr!" Cleve called. "Get away from her and drop your gun!"

But Farr was fixated on Billi June and would not look away from her.

"You can tell the law all about it, on your own, Desmond!" She said, her face hardened into taut lines, her voice almost the caw of a crow. She raised the buggy whip.

Farr shot her through the neck.

"Oh Lord in heaven," Cleve murmured, as she fell forward, clutching at her throat. The startled horse shied, and lunged off, pulling the buggy. Farr aimed again at her, his hand shaky.

"Farr!" Cleve bellowed, loud as he could, striding close. "Turn and face me!"

Farr swayed, then turned toward Cleve. He leveled the gun at Cleve who had his own weapon poised to fire.

Then Farr dropped the gun and looked down at the blood coursing from his wound.

He raised his hand, stared at the blood—and went limp, falling on his side.

The buggy's horse was rearing, its way blocked by the freight wagon.

Cleve walked down the street to the buggy, past buggy-wheel tracks smearing Billi June's blood. He found her slumped over the splashboard, twitching in death, a little blood still oozing from her neck.

Chapter 15

Teresa was there, just as Leon had seen her in his imagination.

The Angel of the Mining Camp, in her overalls and white blouse and dirty bare feet, was sitting by her placer claim, cross-legged in the morning sun. She was holding something small and golden and glittery up, between her thumb and forefinger, to look at it in the light. It seemed to trade light and color with her red-gold hair. Leon's head wasn't whirling so much now, but the scene before him rocked slowly back and forth like a cradle.

He was about forty paces downstream from her, able to stand only because he had one hand stretched to an outcropping of sandstone, close to the little brook.

"Teresa!" he called.

She lifted her head, but seemed unsure what she'd heard. Maybe because his voice was only a croak.

"Teresa McCarthy!" he called, loud as he could, his voice breaking.

She turned and spotted him. "Leon?"

Teresa put the little gold nugget back in the tin pan, and hurried toward him, her eyes growing rounder, her face more concerned with each step. "Leon! What's happened to you!"

He didn't answer at first. A stab of pain was lancing through his head. He closed his eyes and ground his teeth till the pain ebbed some.

"You holding up the hillside with your arm there?" Teresa asked gently, as she came close.

"It's holding me up! Some fellas shot at me, Teresa. They killed Lily. We went over the cliff. Been creeping along all the night . . ."

She came and took his other arm and eased it over her shoulders so she could take some of his weight.

"You look in a state," Teresa said. "How much of that blood is yours?"

"Mostly it's Lily's and Hortlander's."

"Who's Hortlander?"

"An outlaw is who he is. *Madre de Dios!* I need a spot to lay down."

"Lean on me, and let's go, you can stretch out in the back of my wagon." They started out, him wobbly and she stepping firm. "I'm taking you into town lickety-split. You need Doc Hull."

"If he don't kill me, mebbe he'll cure me. And God bless you, Teresa."

"Just you keep walking, one foot after the other. The wagon's under the aspens right over here."

Riding Ulysses toward the waterfall, an hour before noon, Cleve felt a deep tiredness. After a mostly sleepless night, he had ridden out at dawn to look for Leon. Had not found him.

The tracks, Leon's and Wissel's, had been washed away in the storm. The day was sunny, but Cleve was under a cloud of gloom. He'd had to kill two men the day before.

Men no one would miss. But he didn't want the reputation of a gunman.

He rued the decision to let Desmond Farr go free, after searching the Comfort Tent. He should have taken him and Billi June to Elko. Let them stand trial. But he'd promised Henry Purslow differently. So he'd warned them, and taken the girls out of the Tent.

Leon, sent off to follow Wissel, had not come back.

Then Farr, hunting Cleve, killed Jonah Bentworth, beloved protector of Berenice. Had driven Berry to shoot the killer in revenge. And Farr had killed Billi June and died himself of blood loss. There was yet blood in the street.

Four bodies lay in the old barn, by the corral, that they were using as a morgue. Cleve's actions had triggered those deaths. And maybe if he'd taken another course with Farr, from the start, Jonah Bentworth would not now be lying in his coffin, on a bier in the parlor of the Conroy House.

Cleve thought about the way people looked at him, as he rode through town this morning, with doubt and questions in their eyes. And one of those people was Preacher Birch.

It wasn't that he felt sad for Billi June, Farr, or Digley. It was just the feeling of bringing the chaos of violence to a place—even in a just cause—where the better element yearned for peace. It was not a good feeling.

He'd failed to catch Les Wissel or Tolliver too. Failed to prove, as yet, that a man could not be lynched with impunity in Axle Bust. What would Henry Purslow think of the job he was doing?

Piss poor, likely.

But his spirits lifted as he rode up to that big flat rock at the pool under the falls. The rainbows were gathered in expectation of Berry's arrival. A few monarch butterflies flapped over the rock jasmine blossoming from the clefts near the top of the falls. It was noon.

Soon it was a quarter past noon. Then it was half past. Berry did not come.

He shouldn't have expected her, he thought.

They'd made plans to meet. There had been a tacit understanding. Saying almost nothing, she had opened her heart to him.

Then came two gunshots. A dying man; a shattered, burning lantern. Death and more gunfire.

Of course, Berenice wasn't here. She wouldn't be coming, he told himself. The moment they shared had been tainted.

Gunfire and blood, within minutes of their kiss. How could any woman of sense give herself to a man who was going to carry her into his personal war?

The falls roared in agreement.

Ulysses was drinking from the waterfall's pool, unconcerned and content enough. Cleve decided he'd best use this time to go out and look once more for Leon.

He turned Ulysses from the falls and rode out into the sunshine.

Then he saw her, riding along the creek, upstream toward the falls. Berry was on a dappled gray Arabian mare, seeming confident in her command of the big steed. She wore a black riding bodice, a long, divided skirt, and a wide brimmed black hat trailing a black scarf. Mourning colors.

He cantered to her, and they both reined in, side by side—but he was facing south and she was facing north. Each pointed their own way, he thought.

"Berry," he said, taking off his hat. The Arabian snuffled at his horse's mouth. Ulysses eyed her and cocked his ears. "I thought you had decided not to come. I figured—well, I understood."

"I was delayed—Velma called at the house. She said they were looking for you."

"Who?"

"Dr. Hull, in particular. Leon turned up at Teresa's claim, and he's in sorry shape. He had a fall, maybe cracked some ribs, and he got in a fight with someone. Velma says the outlaws shot his mule."

"And Leon—is he wounded?"

"She didn't say."

"He's at Hull's office?"

"You'd better go over and see, Cleve!"

"I will." He was relieved and worried at once. And when he looked into Berry's eyes, he felt both hope and sorrow. "I shouldn't have let Farr go, Berry. I should have arrested him at the Comfort Tent. Jonah would still be alive."

"You delivered those women out of the hands of Billi June and Farr—my grandmother liked to say it hurts to have a bad tooth pulled and it hurts to have a good baby born. Everything that's needful has a cost."

"Will I see you again, Berry?"

"I . . . have had a letter from my mother. I . . . Cleve, we haven't time to talk about it now. It seems Leon has news you must hear."

He nodded. "I'm going. That's a beautiful Arabian."

"Her name is Miss Susan B. Anthony. But you may call her Suzie."

"I hope to see you riding Suzie again. The two of you make a fine pair."

He clapped his hat on his head and rode off, going to a gallop when he was clear.

* * *

All the Golden Fleece miners not on shift had gathered outside the Tom Cat saloon, sandwiches in one hand and schooners of beer in another. Cleve slowed to a trot to get past the crowd.

"He said the money'd be here this evening," said one of the miners, before taking a long pull at the brew.

"He'd better be," said another. "Or there'll be hell to pay. It's been three months with a piddlin' fraction of our pay!"

Cleve rode on to Hull's office and was soon pounding the door.

Teresa McCarthy answered. "No need to break the doctor's door, Cleve," she said, stepping out of his way.

Bare chested, Leon was lying in a cot, head propped on two pillows. He had long white bandages around his chest. They didn't hide the extensive bruising on his belly.

Hull straightened up from applying salve. "Come and see one of the wonders of the world," the doctor said. "Biggest bruise ever seen. By me anyway. It runs from his groin to his collarbone. Part of it is covered up now, but I may yet write a paper on it."

"You hear that, Cleve," Leon said, his voice weak. "I'm a wonder of the world."

"The world has long wondered at you," Cleve said, pulling up a chair to sit by him. "No bullet holes?"

"No," said Hull, "but I fear there may be internal bleeding. His urine is pink."

"Don't tell nobody," Leon said. "Pink."

"Cleve," Teresa put in, coming over to gaze worriedly at Leon. "Leon followed Wissel to the Red Hills."

"The Red Hills?" Cleve shook his head. "I don't know the place."

"Nobody's lived there for years," said Teresa. "It's an abandoned trading post. Times past it was a little settlement.

Some prospectors know it, and sleep there of an evening, if they're out in bad weather."

"Then I'll look there for Wissel," Cleve said.

"Hold your britches now," Leon said. He pointed at Cleve and tried to lift up on his elbow—and then lay back with a groan.

"Lay still, sir!" Hull said, in a doctor's voice of authority.

Leon's voice wasn't much above a whisper as he said, "I saw Bosewell's bunch there. I heard 'em talk of attacking Axle Bust for its gold. And Wissel suggested going after the Chinese at Deerstalker Canyon. Those Chinese miners keep some gold there."

Cleve felt a chill go through him. "We'll have to get word to Purslow. When does all this happen?"

"Couldn't tell. I was listening from a piece off the road. Then one of those boys saw me and they all started in shooting. Hortlander and Devora was with 'em. And Tolliver!"

"Can't say I'm surprised they're part of it. How many men with Bosewell?"

"Well now, if Wissel's there, that's six men—leaving out Clay Hortlander." Leon gave Cleve a sickly grin. "He came all alone to find me, make sure I was dead. Caught me down the gulch, near shot me. But I got his gun and"—he glanced at Teresa—"I kilt him."

"All busted up like this, you did that?" Cleve shook his head in amazement. "Leon, you should have my job."

"I don't want another fight like that one. Anyhow, not likely to live long enough to be a lawman—the doc here has me in a bed where a fella died not so long ago."

"Surely you're not a superstitious man, Leon?" Hull asked, as he poured out a dram of laudanum.

"Ain't saying I am but ain't saying I'm not."

"Probably impossible to find a physician's bed where someone hasn't died," Hull pointed out.

"What's that tell ya'll about physicians!" Leon returned.

"Could be we should have a town meeting about the outlaws," Teresa said. "Seeing as they plan to attack the town. But with only six of them coming . . ."

Cleve turned to Teresa. "A town meeting is a good idea. People listen to you, Teresa. Lot of people here owe you. Maybe you and Mayor Haggerty and Mrs. Haggerty can get it set up."

"I'll do my darnedest," Teresa said.

"Soon as possible! Tell people to meet outside the church." He shook his head at Leon. "If you weren't so busted up, I'd punch you in the snoot for chasing Wissel that far. Nearly getting yourself killed!"

"Hell, it's best I did it! Least you can be ready!"

"I was coming around to that." He patted Leon's arm. "Doc has a dram of medicine for you. Drink every drop and get some rest."

"Wish we had a telegraph here."

"I'll send a rider to Elko, if I can find a volunteer."

"Slim Opie—he's one of the miners you saved. I think he'd ride to hell and back for you. He's got a good fast horse too."

"I'll find him."

Cleve stood up, as Hull bent to give Leon his laudanum. When the doctor finished, Cleve caught his eye and nodded toward the door. Hull met him there.

"Phin," Cleve said, his voice low. "How's his chances? Internal bleeding—that's not a good sign."

"Doesn't seem like heavy bleeding. I think he'll pull through. He's a stubborn young rascal and that helps."

"Stubborn he is, at that."

* * *

Teresa went to the church, where there was already a meeting of the church committee—and Cleve went to the Tom Cat Saloon.

He went through the open doors into the smoky, muggy room, and pushed over to Mick Stazza who was just setting up his faro bank. "Mick."

Stazza glanced up from stacking his chips. "Cleve. Deputy Trewe now, I hear."

"It is. I heard you were a fair shot and no shrinking violet. So you'll forgive me for asking if you'd be interested in joining a posse."

Stazza, still stacking chips in their bank-box, emitted a creaking noise that Cleve at last realized was his way of laughing. He'd never heard Stazza laugh before. "Deputy, you do have a sense of humor. Me join a posse!"

"This is your town too, long as you're here. Bosewell gang's planning to roust it and loot it. If they come in here, they'll rob you."

"Bosewell, eh?" He straightened up. "Dean Bosewell?"

"You know him?"

"Oh yes, indeed," said Stazza, laughing bitterly. He straightened up and leaned close. "Knew him in Denver. Played poker with him at a private game. He lost more than he had to me. Said I could pick the rest up the next morning at his hotel. I got to the hotel in time to see him getting on a buckboard with some owlhoot." He slapped the faro table and his face contorted with an old fury. "I shouted at them to stop. Bosewell turned around and shot my horse out from under me!"

"Thereupon he absquatulated?"

"He did! Off the buckboard goes! I cracked a leg when my mare fell on me! Hobbling around for half a year!"

"Does sound like you owe him one."

Stazza picked up a chip, thoughtfully flipped it in one hand from finger to finger. "Suppose I was to help you get him—if my luck is running good, kill him my ownself. Can I get my money back from whatever he's carrying? He always had a money belt."

"Unless I know it's stolen money, I'll pretend not to see you take it."

"Then I'm with you! When do we ride?"

"When was the last time you went to church?"

Another creaking laugh. "You are a paragon of comic wit today, sir!"

Cleve chuckled. "You don't have to go in. We're having a meeting outside the church and soon. We'll explain everything there. Maybe we'll wait for him here—maybe not. But you'll get a crack at him."

Two miners came over to Cleve, hats in hand. He recognized them both from that day down in the shaft of the Golden Fleece.

"Deputy Trewe," said the short, slim one, about thirty. He had a pointy red-brown beard, a red plaid shirt, wide blue eyes and a lot of teeth when he smiled. "I never got the chance to properly thank you for busting us out of that cage in the mine!"

"Same goes for me!" said the older miner, with a gap-toothed grin.

"Just happened to be there," Cleve said. "And it's Mrs. Berenice Tucker you should thank." He looked at the slender miner. "Say, you wouldn't be Slim Opie would you?"

"I am at that."

"You were just recommended to me. Now if you wanted to help me out, there is something you can do. I have written up a letter for Sheriff Purslow in Elko. It's a good long ride, but I understand you're a horseman with a fine steed. We have a state of urgency, boys . . ." Quickly he told them about the danger of attack by the Bosewell gang. "I need to tell the sheriff the gang's likely in Red Hills. Would you take the letter to him in Elko?"

Slim nodded vigorously. "I'll do 'er, Deputy, and proud!"

Cleve took the envelope from his coat and handed it over. "Here's the letter for Henry Purslow. Do you know Angry Wife Creek?"

"Sure, prospected there some, but all the placer pickings were stripped away already."

"You know the Chinese miners there?"

"I do—Johnny Wing is a friend of mine. Talks United States, like. Nice young man. Helped me out when my horse went lame one time."

"I've met Johnny. Stop over there, on the way to Elko, tell 'em from me there may be an attack on their holdings. We don't know when, but it'll be soon, if it happens. Bosewell and Les Wissel are behind it. Tell them to be prepared."

"I'll tell 'em!"

"I understand you're to be paid today?"

"Miners for Conroy are—the payroll's coming in today."

Another potential target for Bosewell, Cleve thought.

"Does worry me not to be here when they're counting out my money," Slim admitted, thoughtfully scratching in his beard.

"I'll see you get paid when you get back," Cleve said. "If I have to squeeze it out of Conroy with my two hands."

"*If* he gets back you mean," said the older miner, frowning. "Those road agents might waylay him."

"If they come across him, they won't know what he's about," said Cleve. "But I won't pretend there's no danger in it."

"Oh, I'm bound to do it," Slim declared. "I'll ride out soon's I get to my pony."

With that he turned and strode rapidly from the saloon.

Cleve looked around, saw ten men in the saloon, others just outside, all caught up in their beer drinking, their gossip, their high talk.

It would be a chore to get them to the church for the town meeting. He sighed, and then reached out and slammed his fist down three times on the bar. "Gentlemen!" he shouted. Voices quieted—heads turned his way, and faces looked in at the door. "As Deputy, and emissary of Mayor Haggerty and the county, I am calling you to an emergency meeting! Let every man with his manhood intact attend!"

It was getting toward four when they held the meeting. Under a lowering sun that speared its light at their eyes, the crowd had to turn down the brim of their hats, tilt their bonnets, and shade their eyes with their hands. About two hundred and twenty town-folk were gathered around the little porch of the church entrance where Mayor Haggerty stood, grasping his lapels, giving his spiel. A few sat on their horses at the back of the crowd, bemused. Teresa McCarthy was there, standing with Velma and Cleve and Preacher Birch to one side of the porch.

Cleve scanned the crowd and decided it was a pretty strong turnout: miners and shopkeepers, bartenders and blacksmiths, and wood-dusty workers from the sawmill. Some fourteen women were there in their long print dresses and bonnets. The assay boss and banker, Ferg Mulvaney, a heavily freckled man in gold-tinted spectacles, stood just in front of the mayor. He listened with frowning skepticism, his arms crossed over his exquisitely tailored frock coat, his ginger hair tucked under his silk top hat.

". . . and so in this hour of need our community must come together . . . Deputy Trewe has offered some advice to those men with firearms, who wish to stand guard at the places we have determined . . ."

Cleve's gaze kept returning to Berenice, who was sitting on her Arabian, still in her riding togs, at the outer edge of the crowd, listening to the mayor and looking grave.

He ached to go to her, to take her hand and ask what was in the letter from her mother. But he had to put it out of his mind.

". . . and so men will be posted at the end of each street, and in front of Mulvaney's, and now," Haggerty intoned, "the Deputy will call for volunteers . . ."

That's when Duncan Conroy's horse-and-buggy trotted rapidly up—startlingly quick, so he had to pull hard on the reins to get the brown quarter-horse to stop before it could trample someone in the crowd. Beside Conroy was a man with blood on his handlebar mustache and spattered down his shirt. His left arm was up in a sling and his face was white with pain.

Conroy stepped out of the rig and called out, "I wish you all to know that the payroll cash for the Golden Fleece mine was sent on its way here, leaving Elko at four this morning! You are not to think we didn't send it! We sent it early in hopes of evading any road agents—but the wagon was attacked, three men lie dead on the road, and . . ." He turned to the bloodied man beside him. "Tell them, Finch! Tell them what happened to the payroll!"

"The bandits have taken the money," said the wounded man. "Nine thousand dollars!"

Chapter 16

Cleve Trewe and Duncan Conroy stood on opposite sides of a four-poster hotel bed.

"I scarcely got away with m'life, Deputy," said Hiram Finch, his voice weak. The payroll guard was lying on his back, now stripped of his shirt, in room twelve of the Gideon Hotel. He had a bandage on his left lower abdomen. Dr. Hull was sitting close by in a wicker-seat chair, taking the shotgun guard's pulse and looking very solemn. "They come out of the woods on both sides, and they cut the others down," Finch went on. "Wounded me in m'side and m'shoulder here. M'horse went wild and carried me off with him and I let him go where he pleased, I do confess. There was seven men firing at me and I could do no more. Jamie got off a shot, and Herbert got one off too. But I don't think they hit 'em. I was the last alive . . ."

"Seven men," Cleve said. "You sure it was seven and not six?"

"I am."

"Did you know them, Finch?" Conroy asked.

"They had those flour-sack masks. But I heard one of 'em say to shoot me, 'fore I got out of range. And I thought I knew that voice. I spent many a poker game hearing it."

"Well who *was* it, man!"

"I scarce like to say, not seeing his face. Maybe I was wrong about who it was."

"Out with it!"

Hull glared at Conroy. "You have done enough, Duncan—do not shout at the man! I told you not to bring this man out in your rig. You should have left him on my operating table!"

"He had to tell people in person—they'll riot, if they think I wasn't going to pay them!" Conroy muttered, looking away.

"Could I have some water, Doctor?" Finch asked.

"Certainly," Hull muttered. He took the pitcher from the bed table, poured water into a cup, and lifted Finch's head with one hand, helping him drink it with the other.

"You!" Conroy said suddenly, turning toward Cleve. "What will you do to recover the money?"

"We'll go over them and the money," Cleve said.

"Could be," Hull said, laying his patient back. "They have ridden out of the state with it already."

Cleve shook his head. "No, from what Leon heard, they're planning several jobs. Nine thousand dollars will not seem like a great take for seven men."

"I don't understand how they knew where the wagon would be, this morning," Conroy said. He began to pace, hands in his pockets. "We were quite secretive about sending them out before dawn. We even refused to say what day it would be, the very morning of it!"

"Someone knew," Cleve said. "Hiram—will you do me the favor of trusting me, and tell me whose voice you heard?"

Finch glanced at Conroy, then looked back at Cleve. He said, "I think it was Russ Brewster."

Cleve nodded. "That's what I figured. He was your security man, Conroy. He'd have known when the payroll was on the move."

Conroy stopped pacing and turned to stare at Cleve. "Russ? No!"

Cleve said, "It's likely he's been in with them for a long time. They think they killed Leon—so they might still be at Red Hills."

With that, he turned and went to the door.

"Wait. What are you going to do?" Conroy demanded.

Cleve opened the door and said, "I'm going to raise a posse. I've got one man already. You want to come along, Conroy?"

Conroy licked his lips. "I've got to stay here—the town's got to be protected."

"Sometimes the best defense is attack," Cleve said.

Figuring Conroy wasn't fit for a posse anyhow, Cleve went to the door, closed it quietly behind him, and headed down to the street.

Cleve stepped out of the third saloon he'd tried—and came upon two men bracing Kanaway, the stableman, at the door. Cleve noted Kanaway had an old dragoon pistol stuck in his belt.

"You can go 'round back, buy some liquor and take it home, boy, but you can't drink it in there with us," said the tall, fair-haired man with the carefully sculpted beard and white-straw hat. Cleve knew him as a gambler from Texas, name of Jude Chilman. He had a reputation as a gunman—but he'd declined to ride in the posse. Now, with one hand on a holstered six-shooter, he blocked Kanaway from the bar.

The other man was a stout, squinting man chewing a

toothpick. He nodded. "It's like he said, Kanaway. Cain't go in there, the likes of you."

"Mr. Kanaway!" Cleve said. He stepped between the two white men. He reached out and shook Kanaway's hand. "What brings you here?"

"I am not here for a drink," Kanaway said, looking askance at Chilman. "I heard you might be here, Deputy—and you needed men to ride down the bandits."

Cleve nodded. "I'm looking for experienced men. Was hoping to find some veterans of the late war, but no one will admit to being one, except Arne Baker."

"I was such a veteran, Mr. Trewe. I was a sergeant with the 54th Massachusetts Infantry. Under Colonel Shaw."

"Were you indeed!" Cleve said. He had heard good things of the black soldiers of the 54th. "A storied regiment. Abe Lincoln let it be known that the 54th was critical to defeating the traitors against the United States."

Kanaway gave a slight bow. "I do not disagree with Mr. Lincoln."

"What's this you say?" Chilman sputtered. "'Traitors against the United States'?"

Cleve turned to Chilman with a look of feigned puzzlement. "Why yes. Confederate soldiers were challenging the sovereignty of the United States. How can that not be treason, sir?"

"The Confederacy simply rebelled against tyranny!"

"Is defending the rights of man, tyrannical?" Cleve demanded. "But I can admire the bravery of the men we fought in the war. Which regiment of the Army of the Confederacy did you serve with?"

Chilman growled in his throat and made a dismissive gesture. "I . . . was in a militia, for a time. I was not in the Army of the Confederacy, ah, as such."

"So, you were too frightened to join the fray then—as you are afraid to defend this town, today?"

Chilman's nostrils flared. His eyes narrowed. His shoulders stiffened. "Sir—I demand you retract that slander!"

"I retract nothing," Cleve said mildly. "Do you wish satisfaction?" He moved his coat out of the way of his gun. "Let us step into the street."

Chilman's companion cleared his throat. "Best not, Jude. Come along, I'll buy you a drink. Let's spill whiskey, not blood."

"If—if you insist," said Chilman, relieved. He let his friend tow him into the saloon.

Kanaway was laughing—though it was silent laughter. Then he turned to Cleve. "I knew you, sir, when you came to the stable. I almost spoke of it. You were pointed out to us, in the war. You were a Captain then. A man of glory, they said."

Cleve shrugged. "Some of us managed to do our duty." He considered Kanaway and then said, "You know, I saw the 54th on the road, after the Battle of Grimball's Landing. Your regiment was said to have done a fine job there—and I noticed your men's discipline in the march. You kept an admirable line."

"Thank you, sir," said Kanaway, visibly pleased. "We passed each other in the road, then?"

"It seems we did. I need a man like you who understands military strategy, today. Will you ride with me?"

"Honored, Major Trewe."

"Good! Well, here's Arne."

A Virginian, Arne Baker was an overly energetic, stocky man, wearing a gold-colored vest under a blue frock coat. He had a big head and a yellow beard shaped like a duck's tail. He was always working on a project. Sometimes Arne was a miner, sometimes he was a shopkeeper, sometimes he dealt in furs or mining tools. He had sold his little tool shop recently and was at loose ends. He'd fought for the Confederacy, but as he was a decent sort, Trewe wanted him along for his military experience. Arne's gaze was always darting around as he talked. "I got my shotgun, and I got my mustang saddled. I can go anytime ya'll want, and by gum, Deputy Trewe, I'm your man. We won't have any rascals trying to take our gold, no sir, and as I see it, this here's a battle we can agree on, and we will face them together and see them done dirty!"

"Very good, Arne," Trewe said, reaching for patience. "Saddle up and meet me in front of the Gideon."

"By gum, I'll do 'er, Deputy!" He stuck out his tongue in an odd delight, did a gleeful dance step, and then hurried away, almost running.

Curtis Goss was walking up, Henry rifle in hand, his hat tugged low, so that he was looking from under the brim at Cleve. He seemed nervous, as if worried he'd be sent away. "Deputy Trewe," he said. "Could I have a word?"

"Why Curtis Goss. Any hangings planned for today?" But Cleve felt sorry for the remark, seeing the resultant misery in Goss's face.

"I didn't ever feel right about that hanging, sir," Curtis said. "But my grandad, he's all the family I got. That Tolliver was pushing him to get the vigilantes into it, and after all the liquor, they kinda lost their sense. Now, I want to be of better use, so I come to join the posse. I was a shotgun guard for a summer, and I done rode in two posses out of Carson City, and I volunteered in a fire department in Tonopah. Near got cooked too. I could ride in this posse."

"You're young to have done all that."

"They were short on willing men. I stepped up is all."

Maybe I've misjudged this boy, thought Cleve. "Can you hit what you're pointing at with that Henry?"

"Most times, sir."

"All right. Saddle up. We're going right quick."

The posse found the bodies where the bandits had left them, on the main road to town. Buzzards were circling overhead, preparing for a feast.

Cleve sat on his horse and contemplated the corpses of the payroll guards. Flies were still there, crawling across the staring eyes of three dead men.

"Murdering scum, them who done this," Curtis muttered.

"It is a terrible shame," Kanaway said.

A dead horse lay bloating at the edge of the road. On the other side was a small freight wagon with two crates on it. The crates had been half pried open to expose the machine parts within: nothing of interest to bandits.

There had been two guards on horseback, two in the wagon. The metal box containing the payroll money had been pried open, looted, tossed aside. They'd taken the wagon's horses, the horses of two of the dead men, and the dead horse's saddle too.

"Well, Trewe?" Stazza asked. "I hope you have a notion where we go from here?"

"I do," Cleve said. He was studying the ground. There was enough light to see the tracks. Including some with double Xs in them.

Cleve fervently hoped the bandits weren't already on their way to Axle. He'd arranged for miners and shop-keepers to watch for them, to stand picket over the entrances to the town. But they weren't likely men who were used to fighting desperate gunmen. Suppose they quailed? Suppose they ran?

Riding to Red Hills was a gamble, and Cleve knew it. He was gambling that the outlaws had returned to their hideout—that they hadn't already taken some side trail to Axle Bust.

Cleve wished Leon was here. But Leon was too busted up to ride.

He turned to look at the other men, sitting on their horses about the dead, looking at him for guidance: Kanaway, Mick Stazza, Arne Baker, Curtis Goss. Their eyes seemed hollow in the fading light.

"What we do now, Mr. Trewe?" Arne asked, shifting about in his saddle. "Should we ride on, or ride back or mebbe we should, that is, I'm thinking by gum, that mebbe we oughta . . ."

"We ride for Red Hills," Cleve interrupted. "No time for anything else."

"And where's the Red Hills?" Curtis asked.

"Let's hope Leon told me right. Three miles south there's a trail goes east, then south again." He dismounted. "Let's move these men off the road, at least. Cover the ones we can. There's some tarp there, in the wagon. Then we ride out."

Silently, they dragged the bodies to the side and arranged them as best they could.

Still silent, the posse mounted up. Cleve spurred Ulysses— just a light tap with the spurs was all that was needed—and he was galloping down the road. The rest of the posse were soon with him. They headed south, Cleve scanning the brush beside the road in case the outlaws had set a trap. He slowed the posse, from time to time, to give the horses a chance to get their wind back.

Three miles. A little more . . .

Cleve slowed, seeing the side-trail Salty Jones had taken. He signaled to the others and they turned east, up the thin trail climbing the hillside. There was the deadfall; they made their way around it, in single file, and went on in a canter, when they could, along the edge of the gulch. Soon they were forced to slow their pace; the precipice to their left felt like it was waiting for a chance to swallow them up.

They came to the out-jutting tree Leon had mentioned, blocking the trail. They had to get down and lead their horses through the narrow detour past the outcropping.

Cleve looked around, saw that the sun was setting on the pine-covered hills to the west, darkness seeping into the trees and deepening the shadows. He raised a hand, and the posse gathered around him. The horses snorted and looked around uneasily, their ears cocked.

Cleve kept his voice low. "Way I heard it, from this point it's about a half mile up to the break into Red Hills. We're going up quiet as we can. Then I'll separate you into two parties . . ."

He told them the rest of his plan. Arne and Curtis thought Cleve had taken leave of his senses.

Mick Stazza only gave a dry laugh and shook his head.

They were gathered under a lantern hung over the dusty bar of the ghost town's saloon. Standing like a bartender in front of the oval frame of the shattered mirror, Bosewell apportioned the cash from the payroll. There were no liquor bottles behind the bar, except one containing a spider web, but Bosewell had brought out his own last bottle of whiskey to celebrate their success, and it sat at his elbow, half empty. "Now, there you are, the money's divided," Bosewell said, rubbing his hands together. "But that's only the beginning, boys."

"Better be," growled Devora. Nine thousand seemed to him it wasn't much of a payoff, divided between the seven of them. The risks were still high. And Bosewell had taken his time in sharing it out. The boss had spent the first two hours back here drinking and raking over the way Axle Bust was set up. Asking a lot of questions about the place. Bosewell had only been there once.

Russ Brewster was re-counting his share with rapt deliberation, slapping the bills down on the rickety bar next to the rat droppings; Thaddeus Tolliver was counting his out in a calm, judicious way, smiling broadly. Les Wissel tucked his share into a saddlebag, seeming pleased. The two Deeke boys, not good with their sums, were puzzling over their shares.

"Seems right to me, Wynn," Chasly said.

"I don't know. Them piles there look bigger'n ours."

"They're all the same," Bosewell snapped. "Ignorant corn shuckers."

"Not sure we needed to kill all those men," said Brewster. "We had our masks on."

"They'd have come after us," said Tolliver.

Vern Devora's mind kept circling back to Hortlander. Not that he missed him. He couldn't remember ever missing anybody, and Clay Hortlander always seemed to be a step behind Devora in a fight. Sometimes Devora thought Clay Hortlander was using him as a shield. But Hortlander always showed up for a job. And he was a good planner. What had become of him?

Caught by the law? Killed?

"Sooner we get out of here, the better," Devora said, watching a rat wriggling across the floor.

"We're just dandy," Tolliver said, tucking his money in a saddle bag. "They don't know we're here."

"Can't be sure of that, seems to me," said Wynn Deeke.

"We're departing quick as a wink," Bosewell announced, chuckling. Tonight we're going to loot Axle Bust ten ways from Sunday! Let us return our saddlebags to our mounts, and ride."

"I thought we was going to sell the wagon horses and that saddle and all," Chasly said. "We going to leave 'em here?"

"We'll come back for them, if it's convenient. Now then . . ."

Bosewell broke off, looking toward the front of the old, boarded up saloon. A horse's hooves thudded and clopped on the dirt road outside. Someone was riding in fast.

"Maybe it's Hortlander," Devora muttered. He stepped to the window where they'd pulled the boards off. He glimpsed a rider leaning forward, galloping from the north, pistol in one hand. A flash from the rider's gun—and the remaining window pane exploded inward a few inches from Devora's face.

Stumbling back, feeling splinters of glass cutting the left side of his already scarred face, Devora drew his pistol and shouted, "They're on us!"

Two more bullets struck the covered front windows, slamming holes through the nailed-over boards.

Devora rushed back to the smashed window and fired sloppily at the rider—Cleveland Trewe, half in shadow half in bloody sunset light, passing at a gallop. A deputy's silver star gleamed redly on the lapel of his long coat. Trewe was turned in his saddle, firing again and again with a Colt. Bullets splintered the window frame.

Devora roared and fired again, but Trewe had ridden well past and into deep shadow.

Cleve's head felt strangely cold as he reined in at the end of the road, turning Ulysses to a thicket of rabbitbrush and chokecherry. He couldn't see the saloon from here, so they couldn't see him either. Dismounting behind a screen of underbrush, hands slightly shaking, he touched his head, half expecting blood, though he felt no pain.

His hat was gone. So that's what it was. He remembered a tug at it and the sound of a shot from the closed saloon.

Cleve took hold of the sorrel's dangling reins. "Ulysses, all these years under fire, first time my hat was shot off," he murmured. Making sure his horse was sheltered by a stand of trees, he tied the reins to a shrub. Ulysses was snorting, withers quivering.

"It's all right, we're safe now, and you did fine." Patting the horse's neck, Cleve peered between the trees toward the cluster of buildings that was Red Hill but he couldn't see much from here.

He stepped into a thin ray of sunset light slanting through the branches so he could see to reload his Colt. Gunfights at sunset, twice in a row, Cleve thought, as he reloaded. Would Leon call that an omen?

He holstered the pistol, then pulled the Winchester from its saddle scabbard, levered a round in the chamber, and went to find a shooting position.

His hands were steady now. He felt his mind lock into the job he had to do, much like his hand sliding precisely in place on the stock of the rifle, his finger in the trigger guard.

By now, he figured Kanaway, Stazza, Arne Baker, and the Goss lad should have moved into the ghost town afoot. He'd given them cover, drawing the attention of the outlaws by coming into town pistol blazing, Ulysses' hooves pounding.

Cleve sidled up between two chokecherry boles at the edge of the thicket, and made out the dim shapes of shacks and privies, the tumbledown cabins, the old post building, and the saloon. The weather-beaten structures were limned on their western sides by fading red-orange sundown glow. They threw long angular shadows to the east. He could see a group of horses in an old corral behind the post building. Two others were staked behind the abandoned saloon.

About ninety feet away, the boarded-over saloon was set out from the other structures, close to the weed-grown road and long-vanished customers. The saloon's side door was open—and a man was framed there, looking for a target. And becoming one.

Cleve smiled grimly. He was pretty sure from the silhouette it was Vern Devora.

Remembering the dead men on the road, Cleve made up his mind Devora simply needed killing.

Cleve dropped to a rifleman's kneeling position, tucked the rifle butt into his shoulder, and aimed. Just as he was squeezing the trigger, he heard a muffled, angry shout from inside the building. Devora turned sideways to the door frame as the Winchester fired.

The bullet must have cut close because Devora jumped back a little and slipped out of sight in the old saloon.

"Damnit," Cleve muttered, chambering another round.

Then another shot came from back of the post building—sounded like a Henry rifle, firing toward the saloon. That would be Curtis Goss. Cleve had told the posse to come at the enemy from two directions—Kanaway was with Curtis, Arne Baker with Stazza—and Cleve had warned them about the risk of shooting the wrong man in those conditions. He hoped Curtis wasn't firing at Stazza.

But Stazza, Cleve figured, would keep his head down and bide his time for a shot at Bosewell.

Someone fired back from inside the saloon; there was the booming return fire of Kanaway's big dragoon pistol, the muzzle flash briefly lighting the ground between the two buildings.

Were they all in that saloon? He wasn't sure. Someone could have slipped out while he was getting Ulysses settled.

Two more shots from another direction—they were coming from the old cabin on the farther side of the saloon, which he'd assigned to Baker and Stazza.

Cleve cupped his mouth with a hand and yelled, loud as he could, "You have men all 'round you, Bosewell! You men have one chance to surrender and face trial!"

The only answer was a muzzle flash from inside the saloon; the *zing* of a bullet winging over Cleve's head. He dropped into a prone firing position.

The glow of the hanging lantern caught Cleve's eye. He laid the front gunsight on the lantern's glass kerosene tank under the wick, and carefully squeezed the trigger. The rifle bucked—the lantern exploded. Burning kerosene burst out like a battlefield shell. A man screamed, and flames licked up the dried-out inner walls of the saloon. Shouts of consternation, and an outlaw came running out with his back on fire, a lean young man in a green shirt, a gun in one hand and saddlebag drooping from the other. Yelling with pain and fear he fired frantically toward the back of the post building.

Two men ran out behind the burning outlaw and sprinted to their horses behind the cabin. Each of them had a saddlebag over his shoulder. Cleve fired at them but the spreading fire and smoke made the targets a blur, and he was pretty sure he missed.

Another man ran out of the saloon, firing wildly and running to his fellow. "Wynn!" he shouted. He dropped his own saddlebag, turned to fire toward the post building.

Kanaway's dragoon pistol boomed and the outlaw afire spun and fell, mercifully shot through. The Henry rifle banged and the other outlaw, firing toward Kanaway, caught a bullet in the chest, staggered back and fell.

Cleve squinted toward the back of the saloon, saw two of the outlaws astride horses—he wasn't sure who they were.

That hat—was it Les Wissel? He fired, again the smoke got in his way, and then they were galloping back toward the north entrance to Red Hills. He took a last shot, and one of the men seemed to jerk in his saddle, but stayed on the horse and rode from sight. More gunfire cracked beyond the saloon.

Cleve got up, tossed his rifle aside, drew his pistol, and ducked to the right, behind a short screen of trees. He paused between trees to look over the terrain. Flames snapped and fluttered, red and blue from the old whiskey bar's roof. He saw no outlaws, excepting the dead lying on the turf between him and the burning saloon. The front of the place was boarded over. No other way out. Devora was still inside, maybe Bosewell . . .

Colt cocked and ready, Cleve took a deep breath and started toward the burning saloon, keeping to the east, out of the line of fire from the saloon's side door.

Mick Stazza appeared by the west-side corner of the cabin, just as a big man in a suit came coughing out of the saloon's side door, carrying a saddlebag. The description fit Bosewell.

"Bosewell, I have you now!" Stazza crowed, stalking toward the gang boss.

"You!" Bosewell cried, turning a pistol toward the smaller man.

Stazza fired his hideaway gun from just six feet away, pulling the trigger over and over. Bosewell shrieked and stumbled back, then fell beside the cabin, convulsively squeezing a trigger, firing at the sky before twitching in death.

A shot boomed from the saloon, and Stazza spun, a bullet splashing blood from his head. He fell facedown as Vern Devora stepped out, his pistol smoking, one hand holding a bandanna over his mouth. He had a saddlebag over his shoulder. He was outlined in flames as he fired at the post building.

Ten strides from Devora, Cleve fired from the hip—thought he'd carved some skin from Devora's left shoulder, but no solid hit.

Kanaway and Curtis Goss returned fire and the bullets missed Devora, riddling the rickety wall just beside him. Each bullet-hole lit up with flame.

"Devora!" Cleve yelled, striding toward the outlaw. "Drop your weapon! Hands up!"

Devora swiveled toward him, raised the gun, and snarled, "The buzzards'll have you!"

Cleve fired, letting his instinct and experience do the aiming, pulling the trigger four times because Devora was a big man and there was no time for precise shooting.

Devora jolted with each bullet's impact but stayed on his feet as he backed up to the fiery building. The saddlebag slipped from his shoulder.

The flames roared, consuming the saloon behind him. Devora's disfigured face was contorted into something inhuman with rage, fear, and hatred as he fired at Cleve.

Feeling a bullet graze his left hip, Cleve stopped, turned sideways to Devora, aimed and fired, all in under a second. The shot went through Devora's forehead.

Still Vern Devora didn't fall. He stumbled back . . . and back . . .

And fell into the burning saloon.

Cleve came a little closer to the saloon, figuring there might be another man inside. And a figure with a bandanna over his face jumped over Devora's body, wheezing from smoke, raising a pistol.

But Arne Baker was stepping around the corner of the saloon, firing his own shotgun at the outlaw—his awkwardly-angled blast tearing the outlaw's bandanna and part of his face away, but leaving him alive.

There was enough of his face left to identify him as Russ Brewster. He was bringing a six-gun to point right at Cleve. Centering his Colt on Brewster, Cleve squeezed the trigger—but the bullet misfired. No discharge. And that was the last bullet in his gun.

Arne was frantically trying to reload his shotgun.

What was left of Brewster's face managed a hideous grin as he aimed at Cleve—and then Cleve stepped in close and kicked out hard, into Brewster's solar plexus.

And Brewster's gun was knocked off center, his gun firing haphazardly as he staggered and fell back into the burning saloon—as the roof collapsed on him.

Brewster's screams took Cleve back to the war. A man screaming as a cannonball cut him in half.

Cleve turned away from the burning saloon—and the war.

"Well shit," Arne said. "I thought I had him. Lord, you think you can't miss with a shotgun but it can be done, I can testify to it. I got him some but, by gum, I'll tell ya, I . . ."

The saloon hissed and crackled with flame, and the back wall collapsed with a *whoof* and a crunch. Sparks and flame gushed out. Cleve and Arne Baker backed hastily away.

The saloon burned on. It was the only sound as Cleve looked around at the dead men.

Two of the gang, he reflected, had got away. He reckoned them for Tolliver and Wissel. They would not try Axle Bust alone. They would either ride out of the territory—or they'd go for the Chinese mine.

Cleve's job was far from done.

Chapter 17

"I have not decided," Berenice said firmly.

"Berenice," Duncan said, "Mother is quite clear. You must go home."

He pushed his dinner plate away, and leaned toward Berry. The wavering light from the chandeliers made his grim expression shift till it appeared akin to lunacy.

She leaned forward herself—made a point of it—and met his eyes. "I will make up my own mind on the matter, Duncan."

He sighed, sat back—and tried a different tack. "You know, it's not just that Mother's afraid for her health, and she feels she must see you to stay above ground, my dear. There's also the matter of Julius Fitzgerald."

"What of Julius?" Long before she'd met her late husband, Berry had consented to marry the young geologist Julius Fitzgerald, but her father would not suffer her to marry an Irishman. "Scarcely one cut above a colored man or a Jew!" her father sneered. She wanted to elope, but a lawyer working for her father had shamed Julius into leaving town. Perhaps she had not deeply loved him—but he was a scientist, a man she could talk to. He was willing to consider giving women the vote.

"Apparently, Berenice, Julius never married. He still pines

for you—and he's a much more successful man now. You have a great deal in common. Mother wishes you to see him. She would like grandchildren. I haven't time for romance. It is you who must undertake this family responsibility. Certainly, you cannot undertake it with an adventurer—a man with a hair-trigger gun and an income below that of a tinker."

She felt her cheeks burning. "To whom do you refer?" she asked, though she well knew.

"I have heard from certain sources that your fascination with this gambling, gunfighting, saloon habitue Cleveland Trewe continues unabated. In fact, he was seen kissing you, not long before Jonah was killed. And you kissed him back."

"And who told you this?"

"No matter. Do you know how this adventurer got the job of deputy? He got drunk with Henry Purslow! Purslow, in his cups, gave him the job and was too beleaguered by a morning head to take it back the next day."

Berry's hands tightened into fists. She was surprised at how angry she felt. "I have seen Deputy Trewe at work. I saw him brave a shotgun blast to cut that poor boy's body down from the hanging rope. He it was who saw Scrap had a good burial. He liberated the women of the Comfort Tent—most of them there under duress."

Her brother snorted. "So they say!" He chuckled coldly. "You know, if Trewe had left matters alone, our old friend Jonah would still be alive!"

Her fingernails were now digging into her palms. "Jonah's death was not Cleve's fault—Jonah was murdered by the kidnapper and woman beater, that vile creature Farr."

"Still and all . . ."

Everyone assumed that Cleve had killed Farr, and not her. But she had killed him; he'd bled to death from her rifle shot. Harte's *Axle Spinner* reported that Cleve would not confirm the shooter of the procurer. "It was dark," Cleve told Harte. "A number of bullets were fired. Who can be sure?" But Harte strongly implied Cleve had killed Farr in vengeance for the death of Jonah. She was grateful for Harte's assumption and Cleve's ambiguity. Cleve was protecting her, she knew. He understood she would have no wish to be thought of as a new Belle Starr.

The killing itself made her feel strange. It was quite disturbing to feel so little regret in ending a man's life.

Once, visiting her great aunt's farm, Berry had been offered the chance to slaughter a rabbit for dinner. She could not do it and felt foolish for her tender-heartedness, for she had eaten rabbit.

But in Axle Bust she had not hesitated to shoot Desmond Farr. The world was truly healthier without Farr in it.

"'Not Cleve's fault,' you said," Duncan remarked dryly. "I see, Berenice, you now refer to the deputy as 'Cleve'!"

"Everyone calls him that." Berry wanted this conversation to be over, and quickly. "I will *consider* traveling to Boston—though it is nearly the full width of the continent away, and seeing to Mama."

"And Julius? Father has relented and would like you to let him court you once more."

"Because he has become wealthy?"

"And because no one wishes you to be a spinster."

"I—am a *widow*," she said, between grinding teeth. Berry collected herself and stood up. She turned brusquely away.

"Berenice!"

She spoke to him over her shoulder. "I told you, I would consider it, Duncan, that will have to do for now."

She hurried to the stairs, thinking that, after all, it would be pleasing to see Julius again. They had much to talk about. But Cleve Trewe . . .

Cleve had kissed her, it was true, and she had felt it like a warm summer breeze coming on an icy morning. She'd felt herself relax into that kiss. It had felt so inevitable, so right.

She knew herself to be all too human. Like all human beings, she was disposed to passions. A woman, she told herself, should think of more than passion in a mate. And of all the labels her brother had flung upon Cleve, there was one that seemed to fit. Adventurer.

But then, she thought, *Am I not, at heart, an adventurer too?*

"Too bad about Stazza," said Arne Baker. "I lost money to him and mebbe he was plenty crooked, but he cut Bosewell down, cut the head off that gang, by gum, and I'll say I knew him and he was okay, for there's many a man who wouldn'ta stood toe to toe with . . ."

Cleve ignored the rest, as he watched Goss and Kanaway tie Stazza's body onto over the gambler's nervous horse. The saloon was still afire, though it had burned down to its foundations. Smoke drifted past, melting into the thickening darkness.

The other dead men were laid out on the floor of the post building. The bodies of Devora and Brewster were naught but charred skeletons amid the smoking coals of the saloon. When the wind shifted, a stomach-turning smell of burnt man-flesh wafted out to them.

"We have enough stock back there to put those other dead on," Kanaway said. "We can string the horses together, get the bodies back to town. Unless you want to bury them here, Major."

"Best you take them back to town," Cleve said. "Along

with the wagon horses. There will be an inquest. Dr. Hull will want to examine them and write it up."

"You ain't coming with us?" Curtis asked.

"No, I've got to ride over to Deerstalker Canyon. Could be that Tolliver and Wissel are headed there. Maybe I can catch them on the way."

"I'd better go with you."

Cleve clapped young Goss on the shoulder. "I appreciate that! But we'll need you to take the dead back to town. That'll include the dead shotgun guards. You may have to drape two men over some of the horses."

They all turned toward the road then, hearing approaching hooves clopping. Cleve's hand went to his gun—reloaded now—and then dropped away from it. The rider, visible in the light from the burning saloon, was Henry Purslow.

Purslow raised a hand in greeting. "Howdy, boys."

He rode up to them and climbed stiffly down off his horse. He did a couple of half squats, grimacing. "Every long ride gets harder than the last one. I've been in the saddle since I got that note of yours, Cleve." He nodded toward the burning saloon. "Somebody get drunk and burn the place down?"

Cleve said, "I shot their lantern, hoping to set a fire and smoke them out."

"It sure worked, by gum!" Arne Baker said. "You should've seen it, Sheriff! *Boom,* like a bomb burst, and one of 'em come out on fire . . ."

"Let the Deputy tell it," the sheriff interrupted.

"Devora's body's in there," Cleve said. "Mick Stazza got killed. Devora I shot dead. And Brewster's dead too. He about shot me when my gun misfired. But I managed him. Their bodies burned up in there."

"Brewster, you say! But then—I am not surprised he was in with 'em. Stazza was with the outlaws?"

"Nope—he volunteered for the posse."

"Wouldn't have thought of him for a posse."

"He had a grudge against Bosewell. The other road agents are laid out in the post."

"They're all dead?"

"There's two more, got away. I think we winged one. Might be Tolliver. The other's Les Wissel."

"Wissel? Is that a fact, now?"

"Yep. We marked his horseshoes."

"You trying to tell me there's nothing personal in you marking those shoes?"

"Just trying to keep track of him."

"And the payroll money?"

"Mostly here. Had it divided in their saddlebags. What we have is piled up in the post building. But the two that got away took their shares. I'll have Kanaway take what we got so far to Conroy."

"Why Kanaway?" Arne Baker asked, frowning.

"Because he was a hero of the Union, that's why," Cleve said, enjoying it. "I trust him."

"By gum, are you saying . . ."

"Let's see the dead skunks, Cleve," the sheriff interrupted.

They walked over to the post building, and Cleve opened the door. He had left a lantern aglow on the old stove. The bodies lay awkwardly, side by side.

"So that's Bosewell! And those would be the Deeke brothers. Good to see 'em dead. Say—where's that payroll?"

Cleve pointed at the pile of saddlebags. "Most of the payroll's there. And there's a money belt I pulled from Bosewell. Was it me, I'd use some of Bosewell's money to bury Stazza and put up a good stone for him. The rest I expect can be claimed by the county."

"I was sorry to hear Billi June was killed." Purslow shook his head sadly. "What happened to her money? Your note said she was running from town with the bawdyhouse cash."

"Mayor Haggerty intends to put it into the town treasury, some of it to be used to build a proper jail and maybe an office for a Town Marshal. Velma Haggerty wants a piece of it to go to the benefit of the Comfort Tent women. Seeing as most of them were compelled into the job."

"I'll bet Velma gets her way too. So Les Wissel hooked up with the gang! That's kind of handy for you, ain't it?" He gave Cleve a sideways look.

"I have no plan to kill him unless he forces me to. We catch him, I'll give him every chance to face trial. Conroy, anyway, owns most of the Trewe mine."

"Sure. But Wissel beat your uncle an inch from dead."

"I'd like to pay him out for it. But I gave you my word on that, Henry."

Purslow nodded. "I believe you. Any whiskey on hand?"

"Sorry. Not a drop."

"Shame to bring out a posse without a little something. But you done a good job. I figured to come to your rescue—get to find you've managed to get the place half burned down and you've laid most the outlaws out like scalps hanging on a Comanche saddle! You are a wonder, Cleve."

"The posse did most of the work. And two of the bunch got away. I was just about to ride out after them."

Purslow sighed. "And now I've got to mount up and ride with you. Hellfire! Well, it happens I've just remembered a small bottle in my saddlebags. Let's share it around and then you and me, we'll trail on."

* * *

It was a long ride. In the first stretch, Cleve and Sheriff Purslow rode so close along the gorge that bits of rock loosened by their horse's hooves rattled down the cliffside. They reached the main trail and the site of the robbery where the dead shotgun guards lay by the roadside near a dead horse. The buzzards had been at them, but the scavengers had quit at sundown, gone to roost after dark.

"You couldn't have hidden them from the goddamn vultures?" Purslow asked.

"There wasn't time. The boys will take up the bodies soon."

Henry Purslow shook his head sadly, looking over the melancholic scene in the moonlight. "Let's shove."

They rode on to the Chinese camp by Angry Wife Creek. By the time they got there, they were both saddle sore.

Cleve and Sheriff Purslow found Johnny Wing sitting on the ground by a dead man's body, at a small campfire near the Chinese mine. The body was that of Johnny's big cousin Cho.

Beyond this sad tableau, silken tents of various colors were erected, glowing with the lights of lanterns within them. Several Chinese sat by another campfire, where grouses roasted on a spit.

"That a bullet hole in this Chinaman's chest, feller?" Purslow asked gruffly, as they approached.

"The sheriff has come!" Johnny said, snorting. "Come too late to help! But you would never have helped us. Yes—that 'Chinaman,' that is my cousin—he is shot."

"Did Les Wissel do this?" Cleve asked.

"The man with him did it—I don't know that other man. But . . ." He pointed down the slope toward the entrance of the mine. "He is in there, with Wissel."

"They're in the mine—*now?*"

"Yes."

Cleve and Purslow looked at each other. "Can I borrow a lantern, Johnny?" Cleve asked.

Carrying the lantern in his left hand, his gun in his right, Cleve descended the carven steps to the opening of the mine, Purslow close behind.

Keeping to one side, Cleve set the lantern down by the mine entrance. No sound came from the mine. Purslow, gun in hand, stepped to the other side, then leaned over, risked a look down the passage.

"Can't see anybody," Purslow whispered. Cleve leaned over and looked. Down the passage he could see a faint light from a drift on the left. He picked up the lantern and started down the passage.

"Hold it, damnit," Purslow whispered. "Wait for me!"

Cleve stopped, listening. There was only a faint sound of the soft wind coming in through the doorway behind him. Purslow slipped up behind him and Cleve eased down the passage, stopping just before the opening to the drift. They listened. Still no sound.

Barely breathing, Cleve leaned forward a little and looked down the side cut. About sixty feet in was a lantern, almost burned out, half covered in rocks. Just beyond it was a heap of big rocks and two heavy fallen support beams. A man's booted foot was sticking out from under the rocks, and blood was pooled around it. The pile of rock and stone rose about waist high.

"Holy hell," Cleve muttered, stepping into the passage. "Look at this, Henry."

The sheriff stepped up beside him. "The Devil's Red Ass!" Purslow gasped.

They walked about thirty feet into the drift to the pile of rocks and rafters, and there they could see Les Wissel's face, his eyes staring sightlessly at the rock wall. His head had been crushed by a jagged piece of gray stone. A man lay close to him, his face hidden. Cleve holstered his gun, sidled in, bent, and carefully lifted a bloodied rock free enough to see the half-flattened face of Tolliver.

Cleve let the stone fall back, and raised his lantern to look past the rockpile. Ten paces beyond it was an open packing trunk, and in the trunk glittered gold and quartz. "You see that, Henry?"

"I see it. You think that was bait?"

"That notion did occur to me."

Cleve shined the light on the rock overhead. Part of the ceiling had been chipped away, making a considerable hollow space. It looked to him that rock had been piled up, somewhat loose in that hollow—there were broken pieces of lathe mixed with the fallen stone. To one side hung a rope, and several oddly shaped pieces of wood.

"Look at this, Henry. They had it set up with a trigger. That rope was running along those spikes there, up where it was dark. Someone goes down the passage to steal the gold. So Johnny, or one of the other men here . . ."

"They pull the rope and all that come down on the bastards!" Purslow chortled appreciatively. Then he frowned. "But then—it's murder."

"If we want to see it that way," Cleve said, shrugging. "They can argue that the ceiling was just poorly made here, and it came down on these men when they disturbed it."

"Why, no one would believe them—even if they was white and not Chinee."

"Unless of course we were to report these men were killed in a cave-in. We don't have to put that rope in the write-up, nor the trap. You saw what Wissel and the Bosewell bunch did to those shotgun guards."

Purslow nodded. "That is true. They murdered that

Chinese feller too. Can't say these sons of bitches didn't deserve having rocks dropped on their heads. Still . . . there is the law."

"If they go to court, I have to stand by Johnny Wing, Henry."

"Well. I don't feel like arguing. Too damn tired. I say the hell with it. Damned mines are dangerous. Everyone knows that."

They returned to the hillside, and climbed up to where Johnny was sitting by the body of his cousin. "We see the men who killed your cousin are dead, Johnny," Cleve said.

"Yes. Cave-in. So sad."

"That is how we will write it up," Purslow said. "But we know better. We will trouble you to dig those boys out, tomorrow, and take their remains on those donkeys there, to Axle Bust. You can report the accident."

Johnny nodded. "After funeral for Cho tomorrow, we will do that."

"Where's the money they were carrying?"

Johnny grinned. "I was going to tell you!"

"You sure?"

"Almost sure! It's in my tent. You take it—and their horses. They're tied up by the creek."

Purslow tugged at one of his mustache ends thoughtfully. "Now . . . you fellas haven't got any whiskey here, have you?"

Johnny gave him a rueful smile. "We have *baijiu*. Plenty strong. Tomorrow we have a funeral for Cho. Tonight, we drink to him, and we feast. You stay to drink to him, to feast—to rest here?"

"I ain't riding another rod or furlong tonight, if I can avoid it," Henry said. "And I'm hungry as a bear."

They spent the night at the Chinese camp. Cleve had some experience of Chinese food, finding it salty but delicious; Purslow hadn't encountered Asian dishes, but seemed to delight in them. Cleve was careful not to drink much *baijiu*. Purslow was so tired from his long rides, he drank just enough with his food to get him drunk before he fell asleep.

Exhausted, Cleve fell asleep on his bedroll right away. But somewhere a little past two in the morning he woke beside the smoking coals of the campfire. He was not sufficiently rested, but an insistent inner prod kept him awake. He kept thinking about Berry. Berenice Conroy Tucker. He had spent but little time with her—but he had known right away.

When he was a little boy, he was a bit afraid of his father's enormous horses—but the first time he was in a saddle, he felt at home. When Cleve graduated from West Point, he'd felt uncertain about his ability to lead men into battle. Who was he to tell a man to charge enemy lines bristling with muskets and bayonets? But when he'd taken command of a squadron for the first time, he'd known he was suited for it. When Cleve first came to the west, he'd felt at home in its wild, wide-open spaces; when he'd ridden as a scout on the plains, it had felt right and natural, like he'd belonged there.

And when he met Berenice, he'd known instantly. He belonged with her. She was like the rivers he loved to ride beside, the mountain passes he'd loved to cross, the gloriously endless waves of breezy grass on the plains. He belonged to her, and she to him.

He'd felt that way—and then told himself he was a damn, infatuated fool besot with love-at-first-sight. He had laughed at such men in the past.

But despite their short acquaintance, Cleve felt—bitterly—she would always be a part of him, even if she chose another man. Even if she was denied him. He'd never be shed of her. He'd never be able to forget her.

When he was with Berry, all the chaos and madness of the world fell into perspective. She was a living island of peace in a world of mad gunmen and lunatic injustice.

The memory of her in his arms was so vivid he could still feel her. And he felt her absence like a deep ache inside him.

Cleve knew, in that moment, that he had to try to fill that void. He must at least try to make her his wife.

He might not be worthy of her. But he had to try.

There were two living men standing by the dead one, in the small Elko boarding house room, that morning.

Caleb Drask stood somberly by as Dr. Merrick drew the sheet over Terrence Trewe's face.

"It appears he died in his sleep," Merrick said. "Probably from an advance of the thrombus. There are worse ways to depart this veil of tears."

"True enough," said Caleb. But he felt gloomy, thinking how Cleve Trewe was going to take this. He knew Cleve's fondness for his uncle. "Doctor—in the morning I've got to take a deposition from a clerk name of Cortney Burnsville. You know him, sir?"

"I do not think I do."

"He has some association with the man who beat your patient here—the very man who killed him. I want the truth from Burnsville. If you could be at the courthouse, 'round about eleven, in Judge Kinney's chambers, we could perhaps convince Burnsville to be of help in ascertaining the true ownership of Terrence Trewe's claim . . ."

It took some convincing, and much explanation, but Merrick agreed to be there.

Just before eleven the next morning, Caleb found Burnsville hesitating on the steps of the courthouse.

A man of near sixty, in a rumpled brown wool morning suit, Cortney Burnsville looked like he'd had even less sleep than Caleb. He had the look of a frightened animal in his rheumy eyes. He tugged at his small pointed white beard, likely contemplating making his excuses and leaving the courthouse. "See here, lawyer Drask," Burnsville said, his gaze sweeping the street as if looking for some handy transportation. "I do not think today is a fitting day for this deposition. I am not feeling at all well. I propose we . . ."

"We will not delay the matter," Caleb interrupted sharply. "Judge Kinney is expecting you. He will not take to your wasting his time." He took a firm hold of Burnsville's arm. "Let us go in, sir."

Burnsville grimaced but suffered himself to be towed into the building.

Judge Kinney wore thick spectacles, a gray frock coat and trousers, a black string tie, and a beard that was as impressively black and bushy as Burnsville's was pinched and white. "Do sit down, gentlemen," the judge said, in his Georgia accent, as they came into the little room he used as chambers. A circuit judge, here he made do with a wooden table, two chairs, and candles when he was in town. He dipped his quill into an inkwell and scratched the time and the subject onto foolscap as they sat, Burnsville looking deeply unhappy.

Caleb was intrigued by Burnsville's nervousness. If only the doctor would arrive and speak up . . .

Les Wissel was supposed to be here today too, to declare his side of it. But he was nowhere to be seen.

"Your honor," said Caleb, "I believe you are familiar with the case of Trewe Versus Wissel?"

"Broadly, yes," Kinney said.

"Our contention, Your Honor, is that the official record was altered in order to support a claim made by this baggy-trousered confidence man, Wissel. Now—I have an affidavit here from Alden Dix, another claim clerk for the county—he says he remembers Mr. Trewe registering the claim before Wissel did."

"But I take it Mr. Burnsville remembers it differently, and he was the primary witness," Kinney observed. "The available documentation . . ."

The door opened then, and the doctor came briskly in, his face scarlet as if he'd been hurrying a good distance. "Sorry, Your Honor, Mr. Drask," he said breathlessly. "I had an unexpected patient this morning."

"Your honor," Caleb said, "this is Dr. Merrick."

"We have met," said the judge, nodding to Merrick.

"This morning," Caleb went on, "he declared Terrence Trewe dead."

Kinney raised his dramatically full eyebrows. "Indeed, sir! So, the claimant is dead! You failed to mention this, Attorney Drask!"

"Yes sir, I was coming to it. But as to claimants—Terrence Trewe's partners are his nephew, Deputy Cleve Trewe . . ."

"The man's a deputy?" said Burnsville, startled.

"He is, yes, Mr. Burnsville," Caleb said. "A deputy for this county. And the other partner, your honor, is Leon Studge. They are now the claimants in this matter. Now, Dr. Merrick, will you please inform the judge as to the cause of Terrence Trewe's death?"

"After a full examination," said Merrick gravely, setting his bag down and crossing his arms, "I came to the conclusion that the man was not injured in a fall. He was beaten deliberately and badly. His own recollections, as he gave them to me, and all the marks on his body, make it quite clear. He did not die immediately—but in essence, he was beaten to death."

"What!" Burnsville said, licking his lips. "Beaten to . . . ?"

"Oh yes, Burnsville," said Caleb, looking the man in the eyes. "And the man who did it was seen to pass you a considerable sum of money in the High Tone Saloon."

A bartender, sufficiently greased with cash, had been agreeably indiscreet, in talking to Caleb, who had learned that the place was Burnsville's favorite watering hole.

Burnsville rubbed sweaty hands on his trouser legs. "I—well . . . that man owed me money! A matter of . . . that is, it was a gambling debt!"

The judge was scribbling away. "And can you provide evidence of that debt, Mr. Burnsville? Perhaps witnesses to the game?"

"Ah—not as . . . as such . . . but . . ."

"Burnsville," said Caleb coldly. "Do not dig your hole any deeper. All lies will come to light! Now, it was after this money was passed that Wissel obtained the claim certification—those of us who have seen the records can point to the place where the date on the document was altered. And you were the clerk that day!"

"I . . ." Burnsville closed his eyes, his lips trembling. "I believe I should have an attorney of my own."

"Yes, you will need one, if you continue with this prevarication," Caleb said. "Of course—representation can come dear. I cannot speak for the judge but I might just propose that, perhaps, if you will tell us the truth, there is no reason that the court absolutely must recommend you be taken into custody for your part in all this. Once you have signed a document resolving the facts of this matter . . ."

"You are buttering your bread rather thickly, lawyer Drask," said the judge, now giving Caleb the arched brows.

"Yes, Your Honor. Still—in the interest of justice, and the

truth coming to light—would you be willing to overlook this man's part in the matter, if he were to be candid with the court?"

"Why—we certainly want him to be candid with us," the judge said, playing along. "In light of the doctor's opinion, and Mr. Dix's affidavit, in order to see justice done in these grave matters, we can make accommodations if Mr. Burnsville speaks frankly." Kinney took off his glasses and squinted at Burnsville. "Well, sir?"

Burnsville buried his face in his hands. "It was that damned Silver Clouds investment!"

"To what do you refer?" Caleb asked.

"I sank all I had in it—a chance to get rich on silver, they said! But the Silver Clouds mine was worthless. I lost everything! Wissel learned of this and he made me an offer. He knew of a mine that was very promising and he paid me something if I could alter the . . . Yes! I altered the document. God forgive me!"

Chapter 18

Wearing her black equestrian outfit, Berry was just settling into her saddle for a morning ride when her brother hurried toward her waving the letter. It was the very letter she'd shown him that morning at breakfast. Mother's latest letter had ended in asking her to share the correspondence with her brother, and Berry had done so—but reluctantly. She'd taken two days to do it.

"Berenice!" Duncan raised his hands to signal a halt. His manner was most peremptory.

Berry tried to pretend she hadn't seen him, and turned Suzie to ride out—

"I need a word with you about Mother's letter," said Duncan, as he stepped in front of the horse. He grabbed hold of the bridle and went on, "Julius is traveling all the way to Virginia City, just to see you—the least you can do is travel there and hear him out!"

"I haven't laid eyes on Julius in years," she said, frowning, annoyed that he'd stopped her from riding out as if she were the suspect in a crime. "Father was so adamant I should never marry him and now . . . I esteem Julius, but I don't wish to be offered up to him as breeding stock."

"That's most unfair. It's nothing like that."

They were in front of the new barn, on a beautiful day, with the sun warming one side of her face and a breeze carrying mist from the falls cooling the other side. Nature's radiance and its sweet freshness were on offer, and she longed to go freely into the countryside and make observations and enjoy the perfumes of late summer. She was trying to forget about men entirely for the day.

"Even if Father has truly changed his mind, he would never completely accept Julius. He'll still think, 'Oh, the coarse Irishman!' and probably never be seen with him in public."

"And I told you, Berenice, that Papa has decided that Fitzgerald has proven himself, and his, ah, antecedents can be forgiven."

"He shouldn't have to be forgiven, unless he's done something wrong. A man should not have to be forgiven for his family's homeland."

"I agree," Duncan conceded. "And I always liked Julius. But you are stalling. Are you going to see Julius or not? We owe him this at least. And it would soothe Mother so. She's not well."

She let out a long, weary breath. "Very well. I will see him. Not immediately, but I will."

"You really should go back to Boston as well—if an understanding is reached between you and Julius, when you see him in Virginia City, you can travel together for Boston. You could even get married first in Virginia City. Father might prefer a private wedding in this instance."

She stared at him, agog at his brazenness. "You go too far!"

"I just want to see you happy and settled."

"I am inclined to never marry again. I have told you that!"

"I don't believe it, Berenice. You're just being stubborn."

"You merely want me out of Axle! And why? Because

my activities embarrass you? Because they interfere, at times, in your every little whim?"

He looked away. "It's Cleve Trewe, isn't it? The reason you're reluctant to go."

"That's none of your business."

"But shouldn't he know about this, if he's so set on you?" Duncan held the letter up. "Perhaps Trewe should read this!"

"No, I . . ." Then she broke off. It would be best if he knew about Julius. It seemed fair. "Perhaps. I don't know . . ."

"When are you going to Virginia City?"

"I will inform you when I've made up my mind about that. Now . . ." She nudged her horse into backing sharply up, so that Duncan was almost pulled off his feet. He was forced to let go.

"Really, Berenice!"

She turned her mount and said, "Come on, Suzie!" and they cantered off toward Axle Bust Creek.

Duncan shouted after her, "Julius is only staying in Virginia City five days!"

She reined in, and without turning said, "What did you say?"

"I said he will only be in Virginia City five days. It will take you at least four to get there. Maybe five. Our family owes him something, Berenice. At least you can see him."

Her shoulders sagged. Then she said, "I will go to see Julius on one condition."

"What is it?"

"That you do the right thing. After the lynching, the betrayal of men like Tolliver and Brewster, it's time for you to do something for this town."

Conroy raised his eyebrows and cocked his head to one side. "What would that be?"

"You will raise the miners' pay. You will give them each one more day a week without work. You will accede to their demands this time. Then they will not need to strike. And we'll have some peace. The mine will still be profitable. Do it, today—and I will leave on the first coach in the morning."

He stared at her. "I . . ." He shook his head.

"It would solve so many problems for you. Let Papa rail if he must. If the mine is profitable—and it will be—Papa's complaint will be but the growl of a lion before it goes to sleep."

He sighed. "Very well. I'll do it. I'm to give them their back pay this afternoon—I will announce it then."

"Then I shall take the coach to Elko, and another to Virginia City. I will leave in the morning."

With that, she rode away, Suzie almost galloping.

Early evening, and Cleve sat on a chair beside Leon, dealing poker cards facedown onto the bed.

Stretched out on his bunk in their cabin, Leon took up the cards, and held them over his eyes. "Not enough light to see these damn cards, Major."

"Tilt 'em a little toward the window."

"You'll see my cards if I do that."

"I won't look, you have my solemn promise."

"Was it Harte I was playing with, *he* would look at them cards, the sharper. I'll take two." He tossed two cards in the deadwood and Cleve handed him two others.

Cleve's own hand included three kings, likely a winning hand. He had an impulse to let Leon win, as he was still convalescing. But then again, that was no way for a man to play poker. "I'll bet a half million catawumps, Leon." They were playing with imaginary money, each having six million "catawumps."

"I'll see your half million and raise it a million and a half catawumps."

"Will you now! I call! Show 'em!"

Cleve showed his three kings, along with a jack and an ace. Leon showed his cards. He had a Jack high straight. Leon won.

Cleve shook his head sadly. "Millions of catawumps gone. Wherever will I recover that?"

There was a knock at the door. "It's me, boys!" Caleb's voice.

"Come on in!" Leon yelled.

Caleb banged the door open, so it banged on the wall, and came in. "You mind if I light that lantern there?"

"Go ahead," said Cleve. As Caleb lit the lantern on the table, Cleve added, "You have the look of a man with a parcel of news."

"I have some sad news, and some cheering news, gentlemen," Caleb said. He pulled a chair up at the table and took a deep breath. "The good news is, Burnsville has confessed to changing the date on the mining deed. The mine is now yours, free and clear, by order of Judge Kinney! I have just notified Duncan Conroy and he has accepted the ruling."

"Lord, that's like a spring breeze!" Leon exclaimed.

"And?" Cleve asked, guessing what the bad news was. He could see it in Caleb's expression.

"Your uncle Terrence has passed on to his reward, Cleve. Merrick said it was likely the thrombus."

Cleve closed his eyes. "Seems Les Wissel's won after all."

Leon got up on his elbows, wincing a little at the pain of his cracked ribs. "Cleve—I sure am sorry you lost Terrence. I wish I'd known him. Sounded to me like he was a fine man."

Cleve nodded. He had a sinking feeling inside. He should have done more to keep Terrence safe. To see him well.

Caleb reached into his coat pocket, pulled out a folded copy of the latest *Axle Spinner*. He held it up. "Harte says

Wissel is dead. Killed when a mine caved in, as he was trying another robbery. Is that true?"

"He is dead," Cleve said. "Tolliver with him. That whole gang is deceased. Including Russ Brewster."

"Brewster was in with them?" Caleb shook his head. "Should have been plain, but I did not see it!"

"Appears he's the one told them exactly when and where to intercept the payroll," Leon said.

"Now," Caleb went on, "I arranged for Dr. Merrick to give his opinion to the judge—Merrick was convinced that Terrence had been beaten. And that the beating was ultimately the cause of his death. This made a mighty impression on Burnsville and he spouted the whole truth—his being bribed, and changing the records. Said it right in front of the judge. So there's a measure of justice in that."

"And both the men that carried out Scrap's hanging are dead," Leon pointed out.

Cleve was not cheered up by the fact of two more deaths. He wanted to leave this stuffy cabin, go into the open air. Maybe ride over to see Berenice. He needed to think about something other than Terrence's death. He wanted to know what she'd meant about a letter from her mother. He hadn't heard from her since the day after the shooting. But he'd been away from town some.

A woman called to them from the open door. "Cleve, Caleb—you're in my way." It was Teresa. "I'm here to see to Leon." She held up a calico-covered basket. "Food and medicine. I shall administer it myself."

Leon smiled. "Cleve's just heard—"

"Leon," Cleve interrupted, standing up. "I'll write you a note of promise for those catawumps."

"What's this?" Caleb said. "Catawumps?"

"Never you mind," Leon said. "Cleve's poker debts are his own!"

"I'll leave you in the gentle hands of the prettiest nurse I ever saw," Cleve said. "You can tell her all about the mine. We've got plans to make, come tomorrow. Caleb—let's go and have a drink to Terrence."

"Why, you may not have to buy the drinks," Caleb said. "The Golden Fleece miners are so thrilled with getting their back pay, they'll buy for you. That was the mood just now when I, ah, looked in on the saloon."

"Pleased to hear it. After we join them for a drink or two, I need to ride out, and see a lady."

And I will not let Duncan Conroy keep me from seeing her, Cleve thought.

Late afternoon on the Conroy property, Cleve was standing beside Ulysses, one hand on the reins.

"Have you come to gloat, Deputy Trewe?" asked Duncan Conroy, emerging from the barn. He was brushing grain dust from his hands.

Perhaps he was washing his hands of the whole business, Cleve thought.

"You have the one-seventy-one mine, Trewe," Conroy went on. "Your lawyer brought a letter from the judge. I proposed to him that you can take fifty percent of the gold we've taken out of it already, in value, after the work to refine it, of about nine thousand dollars."

"He mentioned that to me. I'll have to see the assay records."

"I'll inform Mulvaney. He will show them to you. Now you can undertake to continue mining soon as you want. The vein is mined out, but there's ore in there if you pack it out and process it. If you want more, then we'll be back in court."

Cleve shook his head. "I will have to consult Leon, but I'm pretty sure we'll take it. There's been enough trouble over the mine."

"Then the matter is settled. There's no reason for you to linger here."

"I've come to see Berenice. There was something she wanted to tell me. Something about a letter. It's between me and her, Conroy."

"Berenice is not at home. But . . . I have the letter right here. I was going to bring it to you, in fact."

Conroy took an envelope from a shirt pocket and handed it to Cleve. "You have our permission to read it. Mother misspells the town's name, but she is in the right in every other respect."

The handwriting, the envelope, and the return address—it certainly looked authentic. A lady's hand. The cancellation on the stamp read Boston.

Cleve was tempted to hand it back unopened. But he had so little news of Berenice.

"This letter is to Berry. Does she know you read it?"

"Yes. She gave it to me to read."

"But . . . would she approve of you showing it to me?"

"I mentioned I should show this to you. And she said, 'Perhaps you should.'"

He took the letter from the slitted envelope, opened it. Written in an ornate hand on fine paper, it read,

My Darling Child,
    I am feeling somewhat improved today but Dr. Pantreaux says my health is yet fragile. There is something you can do for me. We have received two quite moving letters from Julius Fitzgerald, and today he telegraphed us from Chicago. Julius is about to take train and coach

*to Virginia City, and as you are also in Nevada,
he begs to speak to you in person. His business
will keep him in Virginia City, but he hopes you
will do him the immense kindness, as he expressed it, of traveling to see him. I too implore
you to see him. Axelle Bust is too rough a camp
for you. We have received disturbing reports of
late, and we feel you would be better at home.
Julius tells me he plans to move to Boston.
Surely you perceive the hand of providence in
this? Father has quite changed his mind about
Julius, and we are agreed he will make a fine
match for you. You nearly eloped with Julius
once, and he has revealed to me that he has
never ceased to love you. Will you not take a
coach to see him?*

There was more, but Cleve already felt intrusive. "I
shouldn't have read that. Not unless Berenice asked me to
herself." He replaced the letter in the envelope and handed
it back.

"Deputy Trewe," said Conroy, in a gentle, beseeching
tone Cleve had never heard from him, "you seem like a
decent man, all in all. Will you not step aside for the sake of
her happiness? I know you are deeply attached to her. I can
appreciate that. My sister is a striking lady of high intelligence and great kindness. But if you do not stand in the way,
she will return to Boston with Julius, and she will be safer
there. Do you know a stray round from some promiscuous
shooters struck this very barn the other day? There!" He
pointed. "You can see the bullet hole! She is not even safe
on Conroy property. Not long ago she was on the outskirts
of a drunken mob, trying to stop them! She could have been

badly beaten, even killed. It is you who keeps her here, where she is not safe, Deputy Trewe. You are sworn to protect us—protect Berenice by letting her go."

Cleve was astonished by this speech, and he felt bruised and stunned as if he'd been in a fistfight and lost. But perhaps, he thought, it's more like a chess game. And he had been checkmated.

He had hoped to propose to Berry today. With the mine, he would have a little money coming in. She wouldn't have to live on a deputy's salary. But . . .

"Did she indeed plan to elope with this man?" he asked.

"They planned it—but she was persuaded against it. Julius went off to a job in Colorado. Then Berenice met Tucker. She has another chance at happiness now, Trewe."

"If she comes to me on her own, Conroy," Cleve said slowly, weighing every word, "I will not turn her away. But . . . if she does not, I will assume she's chosen Mr. Fitzgerald and Boston."

Conroy hesitated. Then he smiled. "Fair enough. But you should know—that she plans to take a coach for Virginia City tomorrow."

Cleve's heart sank. He mounted Ulysses and said, "Good evening, Mr. Conroy." Cleve mounted, turned Ulysses away, and rode almost blindly toward Axle Bust.

He needed to make his rounds of the saloons, the streets. Do his job.

Anything to take his mind off Berenice Conroy Tucker.

Ten days, Cleve thought, as he and Leon strolled down Nugget Street toward Kanaway's stable, on a breeze-swept morning. A breath of coming autumn spiced the air.

She was ten days gone.

Cleve's dour quietness gave Leon the clue. "She's sent no word?" Leon asked.

Cleve shook his head. "None."

"I admit that ain't heartening," Leon said. "Maybe you should go after her."

"I took a job here. I am county deputy. Every night, seems like I have to be on hand to stop a killing. Anyway— I promised I'd wait for her to come to me."

But now he was beginning to regret making that promise to Duncan Conroy.

Cleve felt a little silly talking to Leon about Berry, like some mooncalf. But it was no use pretending he had not lost his heart to her. Teresa knew it, Velma Haggerty knew it, Caleb knew it, and Leon knew it. Probably half the town knew it. Harte knew it too and it had taken some dark hints from Cleve to keep it out of the *Axle Spinner*.

"Sure you're good to ride, Leon?" Cleve asked. As they walked along, Cleve thought he saw Leon grimace from time to time. "You look like you're still feeling those cracked ribs."

"Bah!" Leon said. "I always heal fast. If I get the occasional twinge, it's no business of yours. Anyways, I can't stick to that cabin a day longer."

They came to the corner lot where the foundations and some of the frame of the new jail had been erected. Three laborers were hunched over, laying another row of stone blocks. Cleve was gladdened by the sight. It represented something closer to civilization than the hole where Scrap had been locked up.

Cleve, Dr. Hull, and Harte had spoken to the mayor, and the chiefest merchants, and persuaded them to incorporate as a town. Velma Haggerty had used her own weighty influence on her husband. Even Duncan Conroy had approved the idea. And the next day Cleve persuaded them to fund a small jailhouse, with a separate room for the town lawman's office. Remembering the disfigured bodies of the payroll guards, they hadn't needed much persuading.

Arriving at the stable, Leon looked around skeptically. "Well, what horse am I hiring today? He's only got a couple of tired nags for hire. I could buy my own but finding the right one, that'll take some time. Axle's got precious little trade in horses."

Cleve and Kanaway had a secret they'd kept from Leon. "Well now, Leon, here comes Mr. Kanaway, leading a fine stallion, already saddled! Half Arab, he is, by the look of him. Spirited too. Look at him toss his head!"

"What will he charge to hire out such horseflesh?" Leon asked, frowning. "Handsome animal like that." The horse was glossy black with a white blaze.

Kanaway led the horse to Leon and cleared his throat. "Mr. Studge, some of us figured as how you got yourself banged up impressive-like, from chasing Les Wissel . . . and what with you killing that Hortlander single-handed . . . and seeing as how you brought us the news that brought those outlaws down—why, we put our money together, and this horse, which is yet unnamed, belongs to you! Oh, and we threw in the saddle."

Leon's eyes glistened. Then the former Confederate soldier threw his arms around the broad-shouldered black man in the stable, and sobbed words of gratitude. Kanaway looked embarrassed but pleased.

"Lot of folks contributed for that stallion," Cleve said, slapping Leon on the back. "Including Teresa McCarthy."

Leon turned to Cleve and shook his hand. "I thank you all, before God I do!" Leon said, wiping his eyes. "Look at me—my granny always said I was a shameless crybaby."

Then he went to the horse and patted the stallion's neck,

murmuring to him. He stepped back and looked the horse over thoughtfully and said, "Now, as to his name . . ."

Please don't say Robert E. Lee, Cleve thought.

". . . it is Danny. That is the name of my brother—who fell at Chickamauga. This fine fellow is to be a Danny too."

Cleve saddled Ulysses himself, and in a few minutes they were on the road toward Deerstalker Gorge.

"What with my share of that money from Conroy, I was ready to buy my own horse," Leon said. "But by heaven this is a better horse than I'd have sprung for. He's a beauty!"

Cleve and Leon rode up to find two Chinese miners, in overalls and straw hats, shotguns in their hands, seated on a log in front of Terrence Trewe's mine one-seventy-one. Cleve was relieved they were still there.

"You know, I offered to pay these fellows for guarding the mine for us," Cleve said, "but Johnny wouldn't hear of it."

"I expect he figures they owe you. You could have been a stickler for the law."

"Leon, I'm just grateful they took care of those murdering scoundrels. They saved us a peck of trouble."

They dismounted, and the Chinese guards, grinning, stood up and shook their hands. "Thank you, gentlemen," Cleve said.

"No trouble," the taller one said.

"None? You boys tired of sitting here?"

"Nothing to make tired," said the man.

"Yep, a fair holiday from busting ass in that mine of theirs," Leon said.

Cleve shrugged. "Like as not, you and I will be busting our asses in this one, Leon. Conroy hired the men working here onto the Golden Fleece. I've been asking around town and there's pretty much nobody who'd rather work for us than the Golden Fleece, which is handy to town and pays more now that they raised wages."

"Well hell," Leon said disgustedly, as he tied his horse's reins to the small yew beside the campfire circle. "I thought my days of leisure had come at last."

"Let's have a look inside."

Cleve waved to the guards, and went to the adit of the mine. He found a lantern just inside, lit it with a wooden match, and led the way in. The passage slanted gradually downward, smelling moistly of minerals and stale sweat. Sixty steps inside, they came to a vertical shaft, over which hung a block and tackle attached to a stout oaken crossbeam. Cold air rose from below, making them shiver.

"Go easy here," Cleve murmured. "No guard rails." At the edge of the precipice was a heavy wooden ladder, held in place with rusting clamps. "Looks like they go a fair piece down to do the pick work, raise up an ore bucket with the pulley. Didn't seem like they had animals to pull it up. Must be the men did it."

"We just got to find men to work here, Cleve. But hell, let's go down and have a look."

"You're in no shape to climb a ladder, Leon."

"Not the kind of thing that makes it hurt. I'll be fine."

"Come on, then. It'll be tricky with the lantern, but if you want to follow me down and take it slow . . ."

It was laborious and unnerving, climbing down the shaft, and they'd worked up a sweat by the time they got to the first ledge. There, they found another ladder descending to another level . . .

At last they reached the bottom. The air was close, and it had a subtle underlying reek that worried Cleve. But when he raised the lantern, he could see flecks of gold glittering down the cut. A small pick-hammer was lying on the stone floor nearby. Cleve picked it up, and went into the cut to see what he could find.

It was almost two hours before they emerged from the mine, grateful for the open air and the sun. The Chinese guards had gone back to their own mine, Cleve saw.

He and Leon found a little shade under a young yew tree. They sat on a pile of lumber, both of them grimacing from aching muscles, and Leon summed it all up. "Whew!"

"Yep. I didn't see a sign of a lode," Cleve said. "Just like Conroy said. But there's the quartz ore . . . Some of it looked pretty good."

He took a chunk of the ore from his pocket and held it up to the light. Tiny threads and flecks of gold gleamed in the quartz. Leon took out his own sample, which was much the same.

"Refining takes a passel of money and a lot of work," Leon noted.

"Maybe Teresa will have some suggestions."

"She dug up some pockets, and made out all right," Leon said. "But she ain't a hard rock miner. Placer's her specialty." He glanced at Cleve nervously. "Say, Major, I didn't want to bring it up, with the troubles you got with the Conroys. And Berry. But . . . I expect you should know . . ."

"You and Teresa are getting married," Cleve said, nodding.

"We haven't told a soul! How'd you know?"

"Nothing could be more obvious. She's made up her mind and you're like a rabbit caught in a trap."

"Ha!" Leon scoffed. "Let me tell you, if I choose to go my own way, by God I'll . . . That is, I am likely to . . . well . . ."

"The ring is practically on your finger," Cleve asserted, smiling. "I can see her measuring you up for a wedding suit when she looks at you. And you're a lucky man! You couldn't ask better than Teresa."

"I calculate you're right," Leon said, sighing. "My liberty is at an end. Between this mine and a wife, I'll have not a free moment!" He cleared his throat. "Truth is, when I think of this mine—I don't know. Maybe it'll pay off in time. But it'll take some investment. I've got only three thousand dollars."

"We could work it ourselves," Cleve said innocently. He had already made up his mind that wasn't going to happen. "But for one thing, the air down there gets sour fast. And I thought I smelt something like methyl. Didn't seem like a whole lot of it but it makes me nervous. There've been mine explosions when that gas is ignited."

"Still, those fellas worked down there a long time, they come out all right. We could figure a way to get some more air down there."

"I'm not too keen on taking a chance with it. Anyway, it's such a long trip up and down, and I've got a job to do, one that suits me more."

"You thinking of selling out?"

"I am if you are. I could sell my share of the mine to you—or we can both sell it and split anything the sale brings."

"Cleve, you've cheered me up considerable! Let's go back to town and celebrate us selling this ol' hole in the ground!"

"We haven't sold it yet."

"In my heart and soul, it's sold. I'm counting the money already!"

The day had gone from breezy to downright windy, Cleve noted, riding up the hill to the Golden Fleece. And the mists from the waterfall, across the basin, were blowing about, like a flaxen haired woman tossing her hair.

He found Duncan Conroy coming out of the boss shack.

"Afternoon," Cleve said, riding up.

Conroy was holding his jacket, draped over one shoulder. He looked tired; there were blue circles under his eyes, and his back appeared a trifle hunched. No doubt he'd been working, but as an Army officer Cleve had learned to judge a man's state, and he felt sure Duncan Conroy was sunk in melancholy. Bitten by the black dog.

"What do you want, Trewe?" Conroy asked wearily. "She isn't back yet, if that's what you're wondering."

"I know that. I dropped by the house." Cleve took off his hat, as the wind threatened to blow it away.

"Haven't you taken enough from me, without trespassing too?"

"I did not trespass, I paid a call." Cleve rested his crossed wrists on the saddle horn. "I have come with a business proposition."

Conroy snorted, shook his head, and started to walk away.

"I propose to give back what I took from you!" Cleve called out.

Conroy turned back to him—frowning, but with hope in his eyes. "Meaning what?"

"I am willing to sell you the mine at a good price. You will be full owner. It'll be your own mine, no one else's. I saw no lode gold but . . ." He tugged the sample from his trouser pocket. "Here. There's quite a pocket of that, and there looks to be more." He tossed it to Conroy, who caught the rock and held it up to the light.

"Not bad," Conroy allowed. "I haven't been down there in a good while. I suspected Wissel was misleading me. Telling me there was less gold than there was."

"That would be Les Wissel—up, down, and sideways."

"You and your partner both making the offer?"

"We are."

"I see. Indeed. I'll have to outlay considerably paying for extracting the metal from ore like this, Trewe. Costly. Can't afford to . . ."

"Twenty thousand dollars."

"What! That's far too much! It's a gamble, this mine. It's a risk! I can do nine thousand."

Cleve shook his head. "Eighteen."

"Fifteen is the best I can do! Take it or ride back to that splintery little cabin of yours!"

Cleve smiled. He'd been willing to take twelve. "Fifteen it is. But when we sign the papers, it must say—and it must be posted—that it is the Terrence Trewe Mine."

Conroy grunted. He looked at the sample again. Then he shrugged. "Fair enough."

Cleve dismounted and extended his hand. Conroy took a deep breath.

They shook on it.

Seventeen days.

Seventeen days and nights since she'd gotten on the coach, and Cleve was having trouble keeping his temper with men like the one who faced him in the Tom Cat Saloon.

"You been busting heads ever since you pinned on that cheap little star," said the burly card sharp. "You ain't going to buffalo me." Jug Joiner was standing behind what had been Mick Stazza's faro table. Jug had greasy black hair, grown past the collar of his white, puffy-sleeved shirt; a round face, small blue eyes, a black bar-mustache and stubble that was in danger of becoming a beard. His left hand was on the faro shoe, and the other was out of sight under the table. Somewhere under there, Cleve knew, was a gun.

"Jug," Cleve said, modulating his voice somewhere between friendliness and warning, "I have had some complaints. Now, between times, when you're not dealing faro, you're dealing three-card-monte. As you know and I know, that's all about sleight of hand. It's a skill you're not supposed to employ when you're dealing faro. And after the fifth report of your cheating the players, I have come to tell you that we have an ordinance about such things."

"You know who bought this saloon a fortnight ago?" Jug asked, with a leer that showed more gums than teeth.

"I do. It was your cousin, Ferg Mulvaney. I'm sure he doesn't want you to drive out the customers by switching cards on 'em."

"I deal from the shoe! The deck goes right in there, in one order, the cards come out here—"

"Except the ones you're palming, Jug. You get drunk— and then you don't do it fast enough to fool the suckers. Now—all you have to do is stop cheating. You can drink and you can make your cut off the winnings. The house always comes out ahead, Jug."

"Them players is liars! They lose and they get het up and they falsify on me!"

"Jug—I saw you do it myself. And you've been threatening those who complained. You told Potts that you would kill him if he spoke of it again. If you don't quit it, I might have to run you out of town, and I don't care if your cousin is President Grant. I don't want the enmity of Mr. Mulvaney. But I do have my job. Now—bring your right hand up real slow, where I can see it. And be sure there's no pistol in it. Then we're going over to the new jail, just for tonight, so you can cool down." Cleve put his hand on the butt of his pistol. Usually, that was enough. His reputation in town was something of an advantage.

"You going to draw on me?" Jug roared.

Cleve didn't like the way this was going. "I'm just telling you to put your right hand on the table. Don't show a gun, Jug. Don't do it."

"I'm not going to any jail!"

"We got a new bed in there. Clean sheets today. It's just overnight and you won't even have to pay a fine! Come along, Jug."

Jug looked away like he was thinking about it. He said, "Whatever you say, Deputy."

But Cleve saw Jug's nostrils flaring. His right arm tensing.

Jug brought up the pistol and got a shot off—but not before Cleve, acting on pure reflex, pulled his Colt and shot him through the heart. Jug's round sang past Cleve, and a man shouted in pain.

Oh hell, Cleve thought. Oh no.

Jug sank down, his eyes glazing. His gun clattered to the floor behind the faro table.

Cleve turned, and said, "Who was shot?"

A miner he didn't know, sitting at a card table—a heavy-set man still in filthy mining overalls—was gritting his teeth and clutching his left upper arm. Blood was running down and dripping on his lap.

Relieved the man wasn't mortally wounded, but angry at himself for letting him get shot, Cleve said, "Let's get this man to the doctor. I will pay the cost."

The miner's friends helped him up and supported him out the door. Cleve followed, saying, "Everyone else stay here, we'll need your statement on what happened!"

He hurried after the miner and his friends. On the way to Hull's office, he learned that the miner's name was Lloyd Weckel and he was twenty-two years old.

As Cleve sat by the examination table, watching Phin Hull at work, splinting the miner's bandaged arm, Ferg Mulvaney and Silas Haggerty came in. Mulvaney was deeply scowling; Haggerty looking embarrassed and worried.

"*You*, Deputy!" Mulvaney barked, stalking up to him. "I have written a letter asking Sheriff Purslow to remove you from this job!"

"Does Henry jump when you snap your fingers, Ferg?" Cleve asked.

"You see fit to be facetious, when you've just killed my cousin?"

Cleve shook his head sadly. "I'm sorry, Mr. Mulvaney." He meant it. He should have been more respectful, seeing Mulvaney was a relative of the dead man. "I'm a bit on the touchy side. I nearly got my own self shot, and this man was hit by your cousin's bullet. Kind of disgusted with myself for not clearing the room before bracing Jug."

"So you admit you braced him! You went there for a fight!"

"I did not. But I have to stand ready. Jug was known to be violent—he was compelled to leave Elko for beating a man with a pool cue. Right there in your saloon he's threatened to kill some of his accusers. He was cheating players, and he was breaking the law. I have to show some authority, or a man like that will not submit."

"And you should have left it alone! You could have come to me!"

"I did come to you about it, this afternoon."

"I meant before you decide to brace him with your hand on the gun, damn you!"

"Might have been better, Cleve," Haggerty said more gently, "to be more . . . more judicious. Wait for Jug to quit for the night then talk to him . . . with some help maybe."

"Maybe so," Cleve said. "You sign that letter to Purslow too, Mr. Mayor?"

Haggerty met his eyes. "I did not. But I was in Abilene the week Wild Bill shot his own deputy. It was an accident. Hickok didn't mean it. But he was on edge. And so are you, Cleve. I want you to take a few days, go fishing maybe. I was hoping to ask you to become Town Marshal. But if you continue like this—I don't think so. I'll have to talk to Henry Purslow and we'll see."

"Town Marshal," Cleve said, making up his mind on the spot, "is a job I do not want. Nor will I keep this one. I will not be crowded by a man who allowed his cousin to cheat in his saloon."

"What!" Mulvaney bellowed, red-faced.

"I will not be punished for enforcing the law," Cleve said evenly. "I will resign as County Sheriff's deputy, assigned to Axle, the instant you find someone else to watch the town."

"Now don't act in haste, Cleve," Haggerty said. "We're grateful for all you've done. People here appreciate it. But you've got to come at things easier, sometimes."

"If I hadn't shot him, he'd have killed me," Cleve said. He took all the money in his pocket—sixty dollars—and pressed it into Weckel's hand. "You come to me if you need anything, Lloyd."

"Cleve . . ." Haggerty began.

"Silas," Cleve interrupted. "I'll keep the badge for forty-eight hours, give you time to appoint a town marshal. That'll save Henry Purslow some trouble, he won't have to assign someone to Axle. Good night, gentlemen."

Mulvaney spat at the floor. "Good riddance you mean!"

Cleve ignored him and walked out, clumping rapidly down the stairs.

A weight was off his shoulders. He hadn't wanted to stay

in this town, with Berry off marrying some geologist. He didn't know for certain that's what she was doing. But she'd been gone a long time. She'd been in Virginia City Elko with the paramour of her youth. Her family's hands were heavy upon her. She might even come to Axle Bust to be married.

Hell, she might well be married already. Right now, she could be on a train, in a sleeping car. Right now, she might be—

He punched a post that held up a little overhang above the wooden sidewalk—and knocked it out of kilter. His knuckles aching, he pushed the post back into place and shook his head at himself.

Maybe Haggerty was right. Maybe he was too much on edge. It was best that he was gone, and soon.

Chapter 19

Another twelve days. Making *twenty-nine days* since Berenice took that coach.

Long enough for Cleve to attend two weddings. First there was Caleb Drask and Mae Ling's wedding, attended by Johnny Wing, all the Chinese miners, Cleve, Leon, Teresa, Velma Haggerty, Phin Hull, Nan, and—scandalizing some onlookers who saw him walk in—Kanaway.

Then came Leon's wedding to Teresa. Cleve kept his smile propped up.

But he gave the happy couple a thousand dollars and the best new cabin built in town, a three-room affair which he and Hull paid for. Leon had tried to privately pay them for it but they would not have it.

Cleve had something to tell Leon, soon, and he had another gift for his friend to soften the blow.

The day Leon was appointed Town Marshal, Cleve bought him the latest Colt .45 revolver. A nickel-plated Top Break, seven-inch barrel. Engraved with Leon's name.

"This fine piece of hardware should be yours, Cleve," Leon said, swallowing hard, as they sat in a corner of the High Nevada. Leon admired the gun shining on the table between them. He tapped the Town Marshal's badge on his vest. "And this job should be yours too."

Cleve shook his head. "Ferg Mulvaney's a powerful man in Axle. I'm tired of butting heads with the local knobs. The fact is . . . I'm leaving Axle Bust. You're my good friend . . . I never had a better one. I have a number of valued friends here. But I cannot bear to stay. Berry is not coming back and I do not wish to see her brother, her house . . . or the falls."

"So this is a goodbye gift, is it?"

"I suppose."

"Cleve, you know, I heard that a stage carrying the mail was robbed, and all the mail lost in the desert outside Virginia City, long about two weeks ago."

"I heard that too."

"Like as not her letter was in that bag!"

Cleve shrugged. "A letter giving me the air. Telling me about her betrothal to this Julius . . ."

"You don't know that!"

"She'd have come back by now, if she wasn't going off with Julius Fitzgerald. And she's better off with him. More likely a steadier man. Less likely to make her a widow a second time, than I would be. Hell, Berry and me . . . we had no clear understanding."

"Some things don't need saying," Leon said.

"Maybe. I don't know. But I'm riding out tomorrow morning."

"Tomorrow!"

Cleve nodded ruefully. "I expect I'll see you 'round the mountain sometime. Tomorrow Ulysses and me are going up the north trail, 'round about where we saw that war party. The renegades have all gone back to the Lahontan Valley. It'll be a peaceful ride. I'll cut west, first chance, and head for California. Haven't seen much in California—just the Sierras, and some desert. It's a big state. Lot to see there."

"It is . . ." Leon took up his whiskey glass, and drained it. "It is a big state, sure enough. You going to take all your money—what is it now, ten thousand dollars? That's a lot to take on the trail."

"That's what I was doing in Elko, yesterday. I arranged to send six thousand of it to a bank in San Francisco. Western Union."

Leon raised his eyebrows. "They send money through those wires now? How's that work?"

"You just ask at their office sometime. They been doing it for a few years now, Leon."

"You are dead set on leaving town? I can't talk you out of it?"

"I am . . . and you can't."

"So be it, and damn you, Cleveland Trewe." He jabbed a finger at Cleve and looked him in the eyes. "But you ain't shed of me yet!"

"You have to stay here, Leon. You have a wife, a job, and a lot of money invested all over town."

"Cleve, I have my Granny Millicent's second sight. I get a feeling and it's always right. Unless I'm gambling— but that's because it ain't right to use it gambling. She told me that."

"Is that so? What'd the feeling tell you?"

"That you ain't shed of me! I'll see you again, after you light out, before it's all said and done. And here's the second thing . . . Teresa is afflicted . . ." He glanced around and lowered his voice. ". . . with the *wanderlust*. That's how she ended up here. That's how she was in half the mining camps in Nevada and Colorado and Arizona!"

"I've heard the men protect her, because she nurses

them if they need it. I hope none of those men shoots you for marrying her."

Leon snorted. "You think that's funny, but I've had some dirty looks sent my way!"

He toyed with his empty glass. "She says she's getting the feeling she wants to move on, maybe next year or the year after. It'd be sooner if we hadn't married, and I hadn't gotten this job . . . or if you hadn't gotten me this job."

"Who told you?"

"Velma. You talked Silas into it. Don't deny it."

"He wouldn't have given you the job if you weren't the man for it. The way you handled those drunk teamsters yesterday—better than I could have done it. You just kept talking till they about fell asleep. Worked out fine!"

Leon grinned. "I'll use this here gun if I have to. Rather not, if I can avoid it."

"That's wise, Leon."

"You know, Teresa didn't want me to take up mar-shalling."

"Understandable."

"She said I had made a good deal of money on the mining deal, and I could invest it around town, and make a living without having to spend half my time dragging drunks to the lockup."

"Sensible."

"But you see—I don't reckon I did anything to earn that money! What did I do to help with the mine?"

"You financed Caleb, who got us the claim back."

"I did *not a lick* of real work! I feel I owe something to this town."

Someone was shouting on the street for the Marshal. "You hear that?" Cleve said. "You're wanted."

Curtis Goss, Leon's deputy, came into the saloon. "Couple

of fellas swearing they'll kill one another. And their friends are lining up behind them. You want me to handle it, Marshal?"

"No, we'll do it together."

"You need me to back you?" Cleve asked.

Leon gave him a quirked smile. "If I did, would you stay in town?"

"Nope."

"Then I don't need it."

He stood up, holstered the shining Colt, and said, "I'd best go see what the fuss is. Have breakfast with me before you leave?"

"If you don't mind getting up early."

"Just this time."

They shook hands, and Cleve watched the Town Marshal of Axle Bust walk out the door of the High Nevada.

There was mist on the ground, and the first autumn leaves crunched under Ulysses' hooves, as Cleve rode up the steep trail toward the top of the second bluff. Once past the crown of that bluff he'd no longer be able to see Axle Bust.

He was thinking about this morning in the café. He'd heard a merchant, one Sol Fennig, talking at another table. "There he is and he's leaving town, after filling in a whole acre of the cemetery. He was hardly deputy any time at all. At least Wild Bill lasted something close to a year in Abilene. But this one—out in a month or two."

Leon had looked like he was going to confront the man, but Cleve had stopped him. "Let it be, Leon. Let's us have some pie."

He thought about stopping, now, and looking back,

down into the basin—at the town of Axle Bust, one last
time.

But he associated the town too strongly with Berenice.

He kept riding.

Laughable, that's me, he thought. Falling for that woman
with so little time between us.

God bless her, he thought. He was not a particularly re-
ligious man, but he said a quick silent prayer. *Let her be
happy, Lord. Let her be the person you meant her to be.*

They reached the top of the trail, and here Cleve reined in.

Before him, to the north, was a rugged maze of canyons
and pine-fletched ridges where the Tuscarora Mountains
met the Jarbridge range. Beaver Peak was on his left. There
were a few peaks high enough, in the distance, for a little
snow. He would cut west in a few miles, following the trail
around the Base of Beaver Peak, and from there he'd head
northwest till he found the trail to Northern California.
He could get there faster going south and west, along the
Humboldt, maybe even take the Central Pacific railway, if
Ulysses could bear it—but he'd encounter a good many
people that way.

The way he'd chosen led through arid country, more gray
and brown at this time of year than it was green. There were
few men in that country, for the prospectors hadn't found
much up this way. That suited Cleve. He knew he'd miss
Leon. Teresa too. But the wilderness was a tonic to him. It
always had been. It was what he needed now.

The landscape, rippling with the shadows of passing
clouds, seemed about as empty as his heart. The wind
soughed. A hawk cried out to its mate somewhere. He'd
passed through the area before but had no deep knowledge
of it. He had a working knowledge of where water was to
be found, how to avoid war parties of the Bannock tribe;

where to find game, where to find a trail that would take him west to California. But most of the region was a mystery to him.

"We'd best get on, Ulysses," he said. The horse lifted his head, and perked up his ears. "We'll need to find water. I believe I can see a gleam, through that notch, that just might be . . ."

Then Ulysses snorted and tossed his head a little, as if listening. Cleve heard it too now. Hooves, clopping up the backtrail.

He nudged the horse to the right, into the copse of pines and underbrush. Screened from the trail here, he drew his rifle from its scabbard. Probably just a prospector. Could be Shoshone renegades. Could be some back-shooting scapegrace who learned he'd ridden out carrying a few thousand dollars.

Cleve saw the head, the bridle of a big dappled gray Arabian horse toiling up the steep trail; and then its frowning rider, Berenice Conroy Tucker.

He wondered if he was dreaming.

But it truly was Berry. She was wearing her black equestrian outfit. Behind her saddle was a leather satchel; on it, tied on rather awkwardly, was a bedroll and a carpet bag, a couple of pots, and a burlap sack. A rifle was in a scabbard in front of her right knee.

She squinted, as she rode out into the opening at the top of the bluff. Her horse was sweating, its chest heaving—she'd been pushing the mare hard.

Putting his rifle back in its scabbard, Cleve watched in silent amazement as she reined in just past him on the trail, about thirty paces away. She sighed, gazing down into the wilderness. One could see for miles from there. Clearly, there was no one down there.

"Well then, Suzie," she said. "It seems we've a great deal farther to go. Let us resume."

"Best not ride out ahead of me, Berenice!" Cleve called, nudging Ulysses from cover.

She put her hand over her gasping mouth and turned in her saddle. "Cleve!"

He rode back onto the trail and up beside her.

There she was. In arm's reach, gazing at him, her mouth open, laughing a little. "Cleve, you rogue! What do you mean lying in wait for me in that way like a highwayman!"

"We heard your horse. Thought it prudent to step off the trail and see who was coming. Thought you were the highwayman. Never did I think it might be Berenice Tucker."

"No? You run off out of Axle without leaving me word! You quit your job, and you tell Leon you're leaving and not coming back! What am I to do?"

"If you wanted me found, you might have sent someone after me, or brought someone to protect you—"

She pursed her lips and narrowed her eyes. "I do not need protection on the trail, Cleve Trewe!"

"We all do, out there. Would have been smarter if I'd traveled with some other men. But I didn't want the company. I didn't think you were coming back and I had no work in town, anymore, as you may have heard."

"I heard! You insulted Mulvaney and walked out on your job—but you could have stayed with your friends in Axle anyhow! Leaving Leon and . . . everyone. You have money, you could have started a . . . I don't know, a gun shop or . . ."

"I couldn't bear Axle any longer. Your brother showed me the letter. You went to see a man you just about eloped with. You were gone a month. Duncan convinced me you weren't coming back. That you would marry this man."

"So you went sulking off into the mountains, did you? Cleveland Trewe—I certainly *did* write you a letter. An extensive one! It is believed to be lying out in the weather somewhere between Axle and Elko, along with a large bag of lost mail."

Cleve swallowed. His eyes stung strangely. "What did you say in the letter, Berenice?" he asked softly.

"It explained that there was a telegraph in Elko waiting for me when I got there. Julius was delayed, called to a job. I waited nine days in Elko, and at last he came. He spent much of his time complaining of the train and stage service, of the Indians who'd had to be traded with on the way before the stage could pass. Julius thought that an outrage. He seemed to *assume* I was going to marry him. In fact, I found I scarcely knew the man. We spent some time together over the course of a week, but we had little to say to each other. It wouldn't have mattered if he'd been a paragon of charm and virtue. I did not wish to marry him, and I said so in my letter, Cleve. I was in Elko only out of a sense of obligation to my mother and father . . . and to Julius. Just to settle the matter, and to pacify Duncan. I gave Julius his walking papers!"

"Did you!" Cleve felt as if he'd had an invisible vulture gripping his shoulders with its talons, all the time she'd been gone—and now it had released him and flown away.

"Then I received a telegram from my mother, saying she was on her way to see me! She had been in fragile health, but suddenly she was planning a trip across the country to me! I waited—and then I realized she was only trying to delay me. Father, it turned out, was already on his way to see me. But I don't wish to see *him*. I was ready to come back to Axle. And there were more delays—reports of Shoshone war bands, and the stage never seemed to want to leave. I was hoping for a letter from you too."

"I didn't know if I should write you if you were planning to be wed to this Julius. And I never got your letter . . ."

"I know, Cleve. I . . ." She sighed. "You were . . . you were not unreasonable, supposing I'd given you over. We had so little time alone together. But . . . I arrived in town just after you set out. Leon told me where you were going."

"Duncan let you set out on your own like this?"

"He didn't know I was back. He is out at the Trewe mine—the one you so kindly sold him. You could have sold it for more to someone else. But you sold it to him, as a gift to my family. Was it a way to say goodbye, Cleve?"

He nodded. "You haven't spent much time with me. It's a curiosity how well you know me."

She spoke softly, her eyes glistening, looking deeply into his. "Oh, I've felt as if I've always known you. Cleve, are you *determined* to leave Axle Bust?"

"I am. I do not want to go back. But"—Cleve took a deep breath—"if you want me to go back there . . . if you will have me in your life . . . I will do it. I will go back with you."

Berry shook her head firmly. "I wouldn't want you to do what wasn't natural and right for you. But I will say, Cleveland Trewe, in spite of your having ridden out without me after a mere twenty-nine-day absence . . ."

"That's not fair, Berry."

"Tish-tosh! You should have waited longer! Leon says you are headed for California." She lifted her chin. "Coincidentally—so am I."

"Oh? *Coincidentally* you're going to California?"

"Yes! Why not? In time I will send a letter to my family, reassuring them as to my whereabouts. Leon wanted to ride

up here with me, but I refused his help. And I have begged
Leon and Teresa not to tell anyone where I have gone. They
have sworn to it! If you don't wish to have me along . . ."
She shrugged. "Fine! You can go back or take another road.
I will continue, north and then west, alone." She peered
down the slope to the north. ". . . and, ah, somewhere . . ."

Cleve couldn't help laughing a little.

Berry pretended outrage. "How dare you laugh at me sir!"

"Sorry, ma'am." He put on a solemn look.

She straightened up and flashed a smile at him. Her eyes
were suddenly bright and merry. "I am something of a fugitive now! I have no wish to consult with my father, and I
will not live with my brother even a day longer. I shall miss
Velma and Teresa and Leon and Nan and Caleb and Mae
Ling. I shall worry about the Comfort Tent girls—though
Nan is to marry Johnny Wing, so Velma says. But I am not
going back, Cleve. I wish the freedom to be the woman I
know I should be! I wish to travel and study the world and
write about what I see. To make observations, to carry out
experiments, to feel what it's like to make a life for myself.
And for . . . for us."

Cleve was stunned. He did not know what to say.

But he felt like he had just won the first hand of a lucky
streak. A man should not turn his back on a lucky streak.
He cleared his throat. "Well then, Berenice Tucker. I am
going on to California, and you are going on to California.
It seems to me we had better ride together. You have your
rifle, I have mine. We can mutually protect one another."

She cocked a head and gave him a look of suspicion.
"Are you making fun of me again?"

"Not at all! I know you can fire a rifle with effect. I do
have a little more knowledge of the country than you do.
The trail will take us through the town of Tuscarora, where

we can rest a night and resupply. Then we'll have a hard road. We'll follow the Little Humboldt part of the way, but we'll need to cross desert too. Some ranches out there, a little silver mining, Indians who may or may not be friendly. Wild beasts. Not much else. Precious little water, but there's a place in Paradise Valley with a well and a trading post. From there, if you agree, we would go west through the Jackson Mountains, into Washoe County. Thence to California . . ."

She clasped her hands and took a deep breath. "So much to see! It sounds splendid!"

Cleve shook his head. "You'd best think twice! The ride will be wearisome; the ground will be hard to sleep on."

"But all that's just what I need to get used to!"

"There are rattlesnakes and possibly scorpions. And grizzlies!"

"Oh, I long to study all of them!"

"Endless rides, after Tuscarora. Aching backs. Saddle soreness beyond any you've known. Dangerous folk along the way—some men out there cannot be trusted. Especially with a beautiful woman along."

"You're bringing a beautiful woman too?" Berry asked, pretending not to know who he meant. "Who is this interloper?"

"You know exactly who I mean. If you come along, I'll not be leaving you alone. Even when you answer the call of nature I'll have to be nearby, with my back turned, but not far away. Oh, and we will not be able to wash much—won't be able to launder our clothing for some time. We'll be filthy before we get to real civilization."

"I look forward to the novelty of such an experience!"

"You may get tired of the smell of me, and my moodiness,

and the sameness of the food, for it'll be a long trip. It'll be hot in the day and cold at night—"

"Cleve!"

"What?"

"All that sounds desperately intriguing! But—regarding the cold nights, will we not have a fire?"

"Depends on what kindle we can find."

"Then some nights we might have to nestle together for warmth, no?"

"Oh, certainly."

"That's scandalous, I must say! I look forward to that too. Can't we get started now?"

"You are really sure, Berenice? You will endure all this?"

"Have I not said so? Now I have a question for you."

"Yes?"

"Are you going to kiss me or aren't you?"

He answered her by leaning over. She met him halfway. They kissed, on horseback, for several minutes.

Then, her cheeks aflame, her eyes bright, she straightened up and said, "Let us begin this adventure, Cleve! I can wait no longer!"

With that, she spurred Suzie and cantered down the hill.

Cleve stared after her.

Then he grinned and said, "Ulysses, let us not allow the ladies to ride on without us."

He rode after Berry, down into the wilderness, into the wide-open country on the way to California.

Look for ***Gunmetal Mountain***,
the next book in the Cleve Trewe western series,
coming in Summer 2023!

Visit us online at
KensingtonBooks.com
to read more from your favorite authors,
see books by series, view reading group guides, and more.

Visit us online for sneak peeks, exclusive giveaways,
special discounts, author content, and engaging
discussions with your fellow readers.

Betweenthechapters.net

Sign up for our newsletters and be the first to get exciting news
and announcements about your favorite authors!
Kensingtonbooks.com/newsletter